PRAISE FOR HIGHLAND SPY

"The first of Martin's Mercenary Maidens will intrigue readers seeking a story filled with a large cast of characters, plenty of adventure and heated love scenes. Martin showcases her talent for storytelling as this fast-paced tale moves from one adventure to another at lightning speed. . . . readers longing for a good old-fashioned adventure with empowered women will find much to enjoy."

—RT Book Reviews

"Appealing. . . a solid thread of teamwork and family, provided by the strong supporting cast of Ariana's fellow spies underlies the romance between Ariana and Connor, creating a community that will surely thrive as the series continues."

—Publishers Weekly

PRAISE FOR THE HIGHLANDER SERIES

"Readers will greatly admire Martin's ability to capture their attention with the combined allure of romance and the swift-moving elements of suspense."

—Publishers Weekly on *Possession of a Highlander*

"Martin's Highlander series is filled with interesting characters and is an enjoyable read."

—RT Book Reviews

"[*Deception of a Highlander*] is the first book by Madeline Martin and after blasting through this story, I have very high expectations of her career."

—Kilts and Swords

"*Deception of a Highlander* is enchanting, adventurous and down-right breathtaking!"

—Literary Junkie Extraordinaire

"An awesome story by a new author and one I looked forward to reading again. A must read!"

—My Book Addiction Reviews on *Deception of a Highlander*

HIGHLAND
Spy

MERCENARY MAIDENS - BOOK ONE

MADELINE
MARTIN

DIVERSIONBOOKS

Also by Madeline Martin

The Highlander Series
Deception of a Highlander
Possession of a Highlander
Enchantment of a Highlander

Diversion Books
A Division of Diversion Publishing Corp.
443 Park Avenue South, Suite 1008
New York, New York 10016
www.DiversionBooks.com

For more information, email info@diversionbooks.com

First Diversion Books edition January 2017
Print ISBN: 978-1-68230-295-8
eBook ISBN: 978-1-68230-294-1

To Lorrie—Thank you for loving these characters as much as I do and for being such an amazing part of this entire series.

I'm so lucky to have you in my life.

Chapter One

LONDON
FEBRUARY 1605

Connor Grant would need a new woman in his ranks.

He stood against the back wall of the enormous room and stared out into the ostentatious mass of noblemen. King James had knowingly laid the perfect trap.

Candles glittered against sconces to set a low, concealing light over the room, wine flowed with abandon, and crowds pressed into the card tables like suckling pups to a bitch. All of London nobility had been invited, from the highest of dukes down to the basest of poor country cousins.

They'd come in droves, moving about the room in a collection of colored silks and deafening revelry.

Connor glanced down to his naked finger, where once there had sat a golden signet ring, and immediately cut his gaze back to the room before him.

He would not think about why he was forced to be here—only what his task entailed.

"Have you found her yet?" asked a voice.

He turned toward the woman beside him, whose hair was somewhere between blonde and brown, and whose dark eyes twinkled with excitement. A small freckle dotted the ivory skin beside her red lips.

"Dinna worry, Delilah, I havena found her yet," he answered quietly. "Ye have time to still enjoy yerself."

And by enjoy herself, he didn't mean just feeling bonny in her new gown. He meant harvesting conversation to filter through later.

He nodded toward the lavish party. "Go on, but dinna lose sight of me. When I motion for ye, we leave immediately, aye?"

Delilah gave him a nod and sauntered forward—into the controlled chaos of wealth and entitlement. Into the crush of people who had pushed her into his care.

She looked fragile among them, naive almost. Easily underestimated.

He knew better.

None of his women were fragile—not anymore.

The perfect spies.

James preferred them to be Englishwomen. He assumed they were more malleable than their Scottish counterparts and that men of all nationalities appreciated a beautiful woman without prejudice.

James often made assumptions.

Connor worked around them.

He shoved himself from the wall and made his way through the room for yet another look. His trews were too damn tight, but they called less attention than his kilt would have.

He hated having to look for a new girl, a new spy to add to his band of fallen women. Yes, it was an opportunity to spare her before her ruin could be known, but a deep part of him hurt for the women in his employ and what they'd all endured.

At least the king had not summoned him privately. Deplorable though his current task might have been, it was far more palatable than the more delicate assignments he had been receiving from the king over the last three years. Assignments he thankfully did not receive often.

His gaze skimmed a crowd of English nobility who stood near a card table, sifting through the mundane for the extraordinary.

And then he saw her.

A lovely lass with black hair sat at the furthest card table with a stack of coins in front of her. Someone across the table said something, and her mouth widened in a laugh that lost itself in the hum of chatter.

There was something about the way she carried herself—her spine was almost too straight and her gaze slid in a manner he assumed she thought covert.

She glanced at the cards in her hand and, quick as sin, slipped something from her wide sleeves before fanning the stack in front of her.

Never once did she slouch to mask her movements, nor even attempt to duck. No, in full view of the table and with speed a veteran pickpocket would envy, she cheated.

She spread her cards on the table with a victorious smile and rose slightly from her seat to rake in her stolen coin.

Connor found Delilah's face in a sea of many, met her gaze, and looked pointedly toward the table.

He'd found their new girl.

• • •

Ariana Fitzroy had been too greedy.

She gave a charming smile to the men at the table and pulled a pile of coins toward herself. They clinked against one another, the merry tinkling rising above the din of laughter and conversation.

How she'd come to love the sound of her winnings.

Tonight though, she'd taken it a mite too far.

She'd gone beyond what she needed for the merchant's bills, the servants' pay, and the rent on her meager lodgings.

The coins were cool against the warmth of her palm.

Winning always gave her such a heady rush, a wash of heat spreading from her cheeks to her chest and all the way down to her satin-slippered toes.

A discomfiting sensation settled on Ariana, one of which she'd always been especially wary.

The weight of being watched.

A woman with dark blonde hair had joined the table and

regarded her with a quiet curiosity. Her red lips lifted into a smile, and Ariana noted she had a slight freckle beside her generous mouth.

Ariana looked down at the cards being dealt out before them, severing the connection.

The last thing she needed was one of the girls at court trying to make friends with her.

Not here.

Not like this.

Perhaps a year prior, when she'd had not a care in the world, when all her possessions were paid for with unseen coin.

She piled the cards against one another in an indiscernible stack, enabling her to see the faces with discretion while masking the number of cards displayed.

The hand was not in her favor. But then, was it ever?

Ariana glanced up at the blonde again and found the other woman's gaze had settled somewhere across the room.

Perfect.

Ariana tucked her hands lower against the table as if she were deep in concentration. And truly, she was.

In deep concentration of feeling the sharp edge of the card in her sleeve and sliding it out before anyone noticed.

Her heart pounded in her chest and her breath came faster—it always did when she cheated at cards.

Cheated.

How she despised the word.

How she despised the necessity of it.

Yet she loved winning, the knowledge that for one more day or week or month, she could afford to live.

A warning nipped at the back of her mind. She'd been at the table too long and had won too much.

She risked discovery.

A man settled at the table beside her before the final round of the game could conclude.

"Good evening to ye, lass." His congenial tone was laced with a heavy Scots accent.

She turned toward him and met his warm hazel eyes.

"Good evening to you as well, sir." She'd never spoken to a Scotsman before, nor actually seen one up close.

There was a wildness in the way his brown hair fell to his shoulders, and in how he'd failed to scrape the whiskers from his face, leaving the hard lines of his jaw shadowed and dark.

"Have you had much luck tonight?" she asked.

His gaze slipped to the neat stacks of coins in front of her. "No' as much as ye, my lady."

She let her own stare trail across her piles of winnings. Shame sizzled against her cheeks.

She had definitely been too greedy.

Perhaps she would do well to lose several hands for good measure.

"I have been quite lucky tonight," she said in as humble a tone as she could muster. The lie sat bitter on her tongue.

Was this how far she'd sunk?

From an earl's daughter to a lying, cheating pauper with naught but a good name and several silk dresses from the previous year's stock.

The man's gaze settled once more on her face and he stared at her in the way men stare at a woman when they are interested.

She knew the look well and had felt its weight touch her face often.

"Perhaps I'm lucky tonight myself," he said.

The silky undertone in his voice crept up her back like the skilled swipe of a musician's fingers strumming a harp.

"What do you mean?" Of course she knew what he meant, but the glint of flirtation in his eye begged her to prompt him for the compliment.

A golden dollop of honey dribbled to lure the bee.

And she buzzed ever closer.

He pulled his freshly dealt cards toward him. "Perhaps I'm lucky tonight because I've met ye."

His fingers were long and graceful, but too masculinely blunted to ever be considered feminine. Capable hands.

She picked up her own cards. "Well, we haven't met, have we?"

There was an engaging smile hovering at his lips, one she found all too attractive. "Then allow me to introduce myself. I'm Connor Grant."

She repeated the name in her mind.

Connor Grant.

It was smooth.

Appealing.

"How very nice to meet you." She slid him a coy look over the top of her cards. "I'm Ariana Fitzroy."

"Fitzroy. Are ye a princess, then?"

The gentle laugh she gave came out hollow. She couldn't be further from a princess. Her slippers were hopelessly scuffed and her dress had grown too large. She'd spent far too many nights choosing to sleep early rather than eat dinner in an effort to preserve her precious funds.

Sleeping, after all, was far more comfortable than being hungry.

"I think you're behind on your history," she admonished in a teasing tone. "The Fitzroys have long been off the throne."

She accepted several more cards, but found none were what she needed. Still, she added precious coins to the center pile. Again, to keep up appearances.

"And are you a laird?" she asked.

It was meant to be a playful jest, much like his quip about her being a princess.

But the light faded from his eyes. He crinkled them in a mock smile, as if he had realized the shift in his mood and was trying to compensate.

Unsuccessfully.

"I will be," he said. His jaw flexed with a determination she understood too well.

"I think I'd like to hear about that."

"I think here is no' the place." He winked.

"Then perhaps we might get to see one another again." The bold statement left her lips in a flash and set her heart pounding in her chest.

A simple, girlish hope flitted in her stomach.

Perhaps Scottish men were not like Englishmen.

Perhaps they didn't care about dowries, or lack thereof.

And perhaps she might sprout wings and fly up into the gilded ceiling.

Was she now adding husband hunter to her list of tarnishing sins?

Could she fall any lower?

"I think I'll be seeing more of ye soon," he answered.

Her heart squeezed with an eagerness she had not felt in too long. The idea of seeing him again was not unpleasant.

Everyone laid their cards on the table. She added her own miserable hand to the collection.

While seeing Connor again would not be unpleasant, losing most certainly was.

Ariana tried not to stare at the portion of her former winnings being pulled toward the blonde woman, and focused on dulling the pang of disappointment.

"It must be hard to lose when ye've won so much," Connor said.

Before she could reply, he leaned toward her. The light scent of leather and a foreign, sensual spice teased her. "I've been watching ye."

His warm breath stirred the wispy hair at the base of her neck. A shiver tickled her spine.

"Do ye regret no' having pulled the card from yer sleeve on this round?"

All the giddy hope and all the silly, girlish excitement crashed into the pit of her stomach.

Her breath came harder, faster. She was a cheat and a liar.

And he knew.

Chapter Two

Connor had deeply surprised Lady Ariana. He could tell by the way her pupils shrank to mere dots of ink amidst the clear blue sea of her irises.

Her posture straightened, her gaze darted in a discreet yet frenzied sprint around the room, and he knew her mind was processing the risk of running versus the risk of staying.

But he knew Ariana would not run. He knew she would stay.

Her nails were perfectly groomed, as was her hair in its simple twist, and though the hem of her sleeve had begun to unravel, she wore the overlarge gown like a queen's mantle.

He could tell Ariana cared what others thought of her. She would not slink from the room like a skittish cat.

"Would ye join me for some wine, Lady Ariana?" he offered. It was no escape from what he had to do, but it was at least something to soothe her stiff discomfort for the time being. He stood and extended his hand in a courtly fashion to offer his assistance.

Her fingers, long and delicate and hot, settled against his palm.

"Please." She breathed the word out on a soft exhale and gracefully rose from the table.

The man behind the card table bowed. "We'll hold your winnings for you, Lady Ariana."

She turned her head to the side, looking more at the floor than at him. "Thank you, Jason." Her smile was fragile, and a brilliant red bled into her cheeks.

Connor offered her his arm and she placed her hand in the crook of his elbow, her touch so slight it was almost imperceptible.

"I'd like to have a discussion with yer father," Connor said, speaking before she could offer an excuse.

There was pertinent information to discern before a lady was chosen. It was one of the reasons he had so few women under his instruction.

They walked at a slow pace toward the tables of wine and food.

"My father is dead. As is my mother." She smoothed a loose thread down on her gown, tucking it against the seam of her sleeve. "My brother as well," she continued in a nervous ramble, before he could respond. "He assumed responsibility of me for years after my parents' deaths. But now he's joined them."

"I'm sorry," Connor said solemnly.

"It was his heart."

She ran her fingers along the seam of her sleeve once more, as if ensuring the errant thread were safely tucked out of view.

"Who cares for ye now?" Though he tried to say it kindly, the question was blunt and, unfortunately, necessary.

He hated this conversation, and hated even more the necessity of it.

Her gaze trailed back toward the card table, where their seats had already been filled. "I care for myself."

As he'd suspected.

But it didn't lessen the tightness in his chest to know he'd been right.

After all, it was highly improbable that a noblewoman in an ill-fitting gown would be cheating at cards for the hell of it.

Ariana stopped walking. "I'm in considerable trouble, aren't I?" The words had been whispered softly, fearfully.

King James walked past then and met Connor's gaze, his eyes lit with a question Connor could read all too well. *Her?*

Connor nodded once.

James paused and Ariana dropped into an immediate curtsey.

He looked down at Ariana's bowed head and nodded approvingly. "I can always count on you."

Connor bowed low. When he rose, the king and his retinue

had passed. Ariana watched his departure and closed her eyes as if shutting out something painful.

"Might I still keep my winnings from tonight?" She opened her eyes and looked at him with all the imploring hope of a hound begging a meal.

Her audacity surprised him.

First cheating in public, now asking for her winnings despite having been caught.

"My staff," she said, and leaned closer into him. Unlike most noblewomen, she did not smell doused in perfume. Doubtless she could not afford such an expense. Her scent was light, like the taste of dew in the morning air. It was sweet and natural and enticingly feminine.

"They haven't been paid last week's wages," Ariana continued. "And if I'm to be...detained, they'll need coin to sustain them until they obtain new positions."

In her nervous chatter, she'd provided him with extra incentive to encourage her participation.

She was, without a doubt, the very girl he sought. And she'd be only too easy to convince.

Connor stared down at her, taking in her wide blue eyes, her porcelain-smooth skin, her cheeks tinged with the color of her shame. "Perhaps it's best we resume the conversation outside, aye?"

Ariana's mouth fell open and her gaze shot around the room, as if she expected to find someone obviously eavesdropping. "Yes, of course."

She allowed him to lead her toward the doorway to the gardens. A well-behaved lass, as most of true nobility were.

Lightning flashed silver-white against the windows and he knew it'd be miserably wet in addition to bitterly cold.

Ariana followed without protest despite the horrendous weather. He pushed open the door to the hissing shush of rain, and they stepped into the dark. The cold curled around him, but years in the Highlands left him immune to its bite.

He let the door slip closed. They were completely alone.

Lightning flashed once more, illuminating her in a blaze of light. She was thin, aye, but the shadows further highlighted her narrow face and called attention to the hollows of her cheeks.

For all her winnings, the girl was practically starving.

"What's to become of me?" Her breath puffed in a frozen cloud of steam in front of her.

Though they were alone, he stepped closer to ensure the privacy of their conversation. No one could be allowed to overhear. An eavesdropper would pay with their life, and he didn't want any more death than was needed staining his hands.

He met her wide-eyed stare and spoke the necessary words he'd been dreading to say. "What if I told ye there was a way out?"

• • •

Ariana couldn't breathe. The harder she tried to pull air into her lungs, the more breathless she became.

If only her heart would stop pounding so.

Her thoughts hammered in time with the unbridled beat, repeating over and over again.

Caught, caught, caught, caught.

Caught.

She stared at Connor in the darkness, a man who truly was a stranger. Light streamed from the windows and partially bathed him in a golden glow, leaving slanted jagged shadows over his face.

The garden was dark and cold and wet. Rain came in hard splats everywhere.

If she ran, he would catch her.

"Ariana."

She started at the sound of her name and jerked back toward him.

A knot formed in her throat, painfully hard.

Caught, caught, caught.

"Ye dinna have to be frightened of me." His voice was so smooth, so filled with powerful conviction.

She *wanted* to trust him, especially if he could make all this go away.

The king trusted him; he'd said as much only minutes before.

But she could not.

She took a step back. "Who *are* you?"

The cold air, thick with moisture, pressed into her gown, her hair, her burning face. She wished she could drown in it and be done.

"I'm the man who found ye cheating at cards."

Caught. Caught. Caught.

Ariana's knees went so soft she feared they might slip out from under her.

If only she could breathe. If only she could think.

"I'm the man who can save ye," he said. "Or see ye punished."

She pressed her hands to her skirt and gripped the fabric as though it could save her. The heavy silk was wet and cold against her stiff fingers.

Punished.

The world around her spun and she had to widen her stance to keep her balance on the stone beneath her.

"I could say you're lying." The idea flew through her mind in a wild burst of hope.

"Who would vouch for you?"

She scrambled through a sea of names and faces, all people who might have stood by her once. But no longer.

"And you would speak against me?" Her voice was small as she remembered the way the king had looked upon Connor with respect.

"The king doesna tolerate cheating at his parties. I'd be punished instead if he found out I knew and dinna tell."

"You said you could help me." She shook her head at the emotions and thoughts crowding inside her skull: confusion, fear, frustration, shame, desperation. "How do you threaten and offer aid in the same minute?"

"I can offer ye an opportunity to no' ever have to steal from others again."

Steal.

The word cut into her.

She wrapped her arms around herself and squeezed to keep from shattering.

"How?"

"By working for me."

She took an instinctive step back and hit the cold stone wall behind her.

He smirked. "No' anything like that. I need ye to get information for me. Most men never suspect women. I imagine it's why ye went the whole night without being caught. Several other women work for me as well in Scotland. They're trained on what to listen for, and how to defend themselves. Ye wouldna be alone in yer duties. Ye'd have a place to stay, food to eat, fine clothes, and a monthly stipend."

Ariana's mind raced faster than her heart. Could what he said be true?

"And what of the king?" she asked. "What if he finds out you've concealed my cheating from him?"

Connor tipped his head at a sly angle. "Who do ye think I work for, lass?"

Ariana sucked in a breath of cold air. "You want me to be a spy? For the king?"

She was a noble's daughter, raised only to become a wife. What he was suggesting was ridiculous, unheard of. The fraying of her nerves began to unravel everything civil and social within her.

She was a fox cornered in a hunt.

"Come to Scotland with me, and I'll teach ye things ye'll no' learn anywhere else." He held out his hand to her.

She stared down at his wide palm creased with lines. His long, thick fingers had seemed so graceful in candlelight but now appeared quite menacing.

"Even if I dinna tell on ye, it's only a matter of time until ye get caught," he said. "Without a way out."

He was right.

If he'd noticed her, someone else could too.

"If ye dinna come, I'll have to tell the king." The heavy note of disappointment in his rich voice made her open her eyes. His hand was still extended.

She looked up at him, at the lines of muscle showing at his neck, at the square set of his jaw. But for the hardness of his appearance, his regard toward her now could only be described as soft.

How long had it been since anyone had looked at her so?

Not for as long as she could remember.

Her throat tightened.

"The coin I left inside…?" She couldn't even form the groveling question. But she had to. She would not see the servants suffer for her actions.

He gave a simple nod. "Ye may have it delivered to yer servants."

The frantic gnawing of panic in her waned at his agreement. She drew a breath, a real, true one, for the first time since she'd been caught.

"Thank you," she whispered.

He lifted his extended hand higher, into her view. "Come work for me, work for yer king. Ye dinna need to live like this anymore."

The kindness in his eyes pressed deep into a dark place within her, and for a moment she felt as if he truly understood her.

A spy. For the king. Such a position was one of great power.

She'd had a taste of being powerful—when she sat at the card table and manipulated the odds into her favor. It melted on her tongue like a sweet.

Her breathing came faster at the thought. Never again would she have to slink helplessly through the card tables, securing just enough coin to see her through the next fortnight, nor would she go to bed with her stomach gnawing at itself in hunger.

Blood pumped through her veins with vigorous energy, an energy she tasted only when she cheated at cards. She placed her hand in his, and hoped to God she was not making the wrong decision.

• • •

Connor strode from the brilliantly lit hall, leaving the chattering noise of the party behind. He'd been successful in his mission.

Not only had Ariana agreed, but he'd also already delivered her into Sylvi's capable hands.

He tried not to think of how frightened she'd looked despite her composure. Her chest had expanded and fallen with the barely contained rapid breath of a snared rabbit, and she'd twisted her hands into the fabric of her skirts. Doubtless so he wouldn't see how they trembled.

But it was true. If he'd caught her, someone else would too, eventually.

At least the life he offered was better than most for a disgraced woman who cheated at cards.

That was what he told himself, to ease the tightness burning like hellfire in his chest.

Delilah appeared at his side from the shadows, exactly as planned.

She lifted her brows in silent question.

"Aye, she's joining us," he said.

"I've found another as well," Delilah said. "She's already with Sylvi. I discovered the woman by accident. She was threatening the life of a duke who tried to take more than she was willing to offer."

Another girl.

They didn't need any more. Hell, his soul was burdened by the ones he had already.

"She wouldn't have had anywhere else to go if I didn't encourage her to join us." Delilah spoke quickly, as if reading his hesitation. She picked at her thumbnail.

"What else?" he probed.

"Sylvi and the new girls will have to go to Scotland ahead of us." Her answer tugged his heart into his stomach.

There was only one reason he would be delayed from leaving. "The king wishes to see me."

She nodded, her eyes wide, almost sorrowful in her rounded face. "I know sometimes that means you must stay in England longer."

"Go on, then. Tell Sylvi to begin the journey to ensure the girl you found doesn't get caught. We'll travel faster than them on the return, and most likely arrive first."

He'd never divulged what the king asked of him, but Delilah had worked with him long enough to notice the shift in his mood after such meetings.

And he did loathe his rare meetings with the king, when he received his next private task.

When he would report on his findings in Scotland and receive the slip of paper, a silent communication conveying the name of another he would be forced to kill.

Chapter Three

Exhaustion pulled Ariana forward in her saddle, making her sag against the hard, creaking leather. Snow-covered hills rose and fell over the course of their travels through an endless sea of white. A dull white when the night came, and a piercing white when the sun reflected off its pristine surface.

White. White. White.

And so cold it gnawed at her sanity and threatened to break her.

Still, she was far better off than poor Liv.

She glanced beside her, where a bit of copper hair showed from between the folds of a tightly wrapped plaid. A single hand extended from the rough wool, limp and white where the reins rested against delicate fingertips.

Ariana edged her horse closer and tensed her body to catch Liv should the other woman fall. It would not be the first time.

"Do you need to stop?" The warmth of Ariana's breath passing over her lips was fleeting as she spoke, quickly replaced with the wet chill of late winter.

"So we can be spies now?" Liv slid her a bemused look.

It was a joke they'd shared. Neither one of them knew where in Scotland they were going, how they would be made into spies, or how any of it worked.

Or even if it was all a lie.

"You do too much for me already." Liv nestled deeper into her blankets and her response came out muffled. "I'll be fine."

Ariana's heart squeezed for her new friend.

Liv hadn't been quite so sick at the beginning of their journey. In the carriage from London, she'd introduced herself with a sardonic grin and proudly announced how she'd landed a blow on a duke. Every night when they made camp, they'd lain side by side in the dark and shared stories until they fell asleep. Both had been raised outside of court and placed there during their parents' attempts at an advantageous betrothal.

They were two women rejected by the court they'd once loved so much, two women who had lost everything and at least found friendship in one another. The first week or so of travel had been some of the most fun Ariana had had in almost her entire life.

But then Liv got sick. Nausea, weakness, and vomiting. The late-night stories and giggles had stopped and the bright smiles Liv gave had faded, like a sun hidden behind heavy clouds.

Ariana had tried to help, giving Liv extra rations from her own food and caring for her through the night. To no avail.

They'd lost track of how many days they'd traveled, how many times they'd changed horses.

"Does she need rest?" A woman's firm voice sounded behind Ariana.

She looked behind her toward Sylvi, who had escorted them from London to the frozen hell of Scotland. And escorted was all she'd done. She never answered their questions and gave them none of the information they so desperately sought.

Sylvi's hair gleamed white as the snow and had been pulled away from her face in a half a dozen small braids. Unlike Ariana and Liv, Sylvi did not cower beneath the flimsy refuge of a plaid. No, she leaned into the wind with little more than a fur mantle upon her shoulders and a simple dress, a challenge in the ice of her own hard blue gaze.

Ariana had once heard Scotland was wild and beautiful. There wasn't much beauty she could see outside of the wall of frozen misery she faced every day.

At least Scotland smelled a great deal better than London, where the streets ran with filth and the people lived atop one another. Especially near where she'd resided the past year. The small rented rooms, barely large enough for her and several staff, all paid for entirely with her winnings.

The thought of London stabbed at Ariana's heart. Not with longing, but with sharpness of memory at how she'd barely managed to scrape together a life for herself. At least the servants had been paid their final coin. Delivered by Sylvi, who had also collected Ariana's meager belongings.

Liv too had been eager to leave London. She didn't say why, but her eyes had filled with such sorrow that Ariana could not bring herself to press for an answer.

A savage wind stung at her cheeks and tried to pry the sodden plaid from her hard-knuckled grip. She clawed the blanket more tightly to her. Surely they would be stopping soon. They'd already traveled far longer than any day before.

"You're cold." Liv's horse came beside Ariana. "Will you take my extra blanket? I'm much warmer now."

She extended her pale hand with the blanket pinched between her fingers. It was the blanket Ariana had given her just that morning.

Ariana strengthened herself against the chill. "Keep it. I imagine we'll stop soon." She offered her friend a smile in an effort to convince her.

Liv gave her a fragile smile in return and her slender arm dropped as if she did not have the strength to hold it aloft anymore. She had wasted away so much during their travel. It pained Ariana to have watched it all unfold, and to be so helpless to stop any of it.

Hunger grumbled low in Ariana's stomach, no longer assuaged by the hard bit of crumbly oatcake she'd had earlier.

Sylvi's horse sidled up next to hers. There was a stern quietness to Sylvi, a strength so powerful it chipped away at Ariana's own resolve.

Was this how Connor would instruct her to be?

"We'll be arriving soon if she can make it a little longer." Sylvi's low voice carried over the wind. The ribbon tight around her throat lifted with the strain of raising her voice. The presence of the thin, delicate luxury seemed entirely out of place on Sylvi, who wore no additional adornment on either her simple blue gown or the thick gray fur mantle draped over her like a cape. And yet, there it was—a single black silk ribbon tied into a neat bow at the very center of her throat.

Though they'd traveled for almost a month together, Ariana found she knew nothing more of the woman aside from her apparent lack of sympathy for poor Liv, and the strange battle moves she executed each night when they finally stopped.

"We'll be arriving at our next campsite?" Ariana shifted in her saddle. A breath of cold air scurried around her legs and bottom, and the pinch in her back was no better off once she settled.

"At Kindrochit Castle. Where we live. Where you'll be living." Sylvi's reply was in her usual efficient, emotionless manner.

A spiral of hope curled hot and eager inside Ariana. "Truly? Truly we'll be done traveling?"

A little smile played on Sylvi's lips, the first Ariana had seen. "Truly."

They'd be in a castle.

Ariana could imagine the glow of a warm hearth and soft beds. Where the endless, rocking sway of a horse would stop.

"Did you hear, Liv?" Ariana leaned in her saddle to peer at her friend.

A pale face with lackluster gray eyes peered from a triangle of parted fabric. "I'll believe it when I'm there."

"Then you'll believe it very soon," Ariana said with as much encouragement as possible.

Liv gave a weak nod beneath her pile of cloth, and her eyes showed the smile all the blankets hid.

"There," Sylvi said. "In the distance."

Ariana searched the dulling skyline until she noticed a fleck of black in the distance.

It was far away, but noticeable nonetheless.

They were almost there.

No more sleeping on the cold, hard ground or facing the

winds with little more than sodden wool and chapped cheeks for protection.

A gurgling sound filled the air, soft at first and then louder, like the rushing of water.

And, indeed, as they approached, the snow fell away to a ribbon of churning river too large to cross.

The castle stood on the opposite side.

Each fall of the horse's hooves toward the bridge jarred her bones, each shift she made in the saddle cramped her muscles. Each step forward seemed so ineffective, they might as well have been stepping back.

Their entire journey thus far had not lasted as long as the final grueling hour.

Finally the darkened face of a castle rose before them, preceded by a stone bridge.

The muffled slush of the horse's hooves in the snow became hard clapping strikes upon the bridge, an almost deafening sound by comparison.

Mortar had fallen in large chunks from the sides of the bridge, leaving the boulders within seemingly loosely stacked rather than solidly constructed. The castle itself did not appear any sounder. Fractures were visible on its surface in dark, jagged lines, and several stones were missing altogether.

Ariana brought her horse close to Liv's. Her friend's pale hand came out and curled around hers. Liv's eyes were wide with worry. "Have we made a mistake?"

Ariana ignored the ball of unease tightnening in the pit of her stomach and shook her head.

"Murdoch," Sylvi shouted into the wind.

The sun had already begun to sink, dragging with it any vestiges of warmth.

Sylvi's cheeks and nose were brilliantly red in the fading light, the rest of her comely face little more than shadows.

A squealing creak rent the air and the gate opened before them, revealing a shadowed courtyard.

Ariana's temples thundered with the fluttering of her pulse and her breath came faster, puffing into the air in front of her. But she would not show her unease any more than she would reveal the discomfort of her saddle.

She might be a pauper and a cheat entering a castle that appeared to be falling in upon itself, but she was a still a noblewoman.

"Let us be strong." Ariana squeezed Liv's icy hands. "Like spies."

Liv gave a weak nod and her hand slipped away.

Ariana drew herself fully upright despite the screaming protest of her back, and rode through the gates with the grace of a queen.

She hoped.

The courtyard was little more than an empty field of snow and flecks of crushed grass surrounded by impossibly high stone walls. It was every bit the cage any debtor's prison would have been and, not for the first time, Ariana wondered if she'd made the right decision.

A large man with wild blond hair gripped her horse's reins, drawing her steed to a stop.

"Welcome to hell." Though he presented a jovial grin, his words shot straight to her gut.

"Enough, Murdoch," Sylvi said in a warning tone.

The man shrugged his shoulders. "Ach, I'm just toying with the new lasses. I'll no' be here long to share my winning personality."

Sylvi offered an unladylike snort and leaped gracefully from her own horse.

Ariana did likewise, except the act was far from graceful, and she landed on knees too soft to support her. When her legs buckled, she went sprawling to the cold, wet ground, no doubt staining her dress.

She shouldn't worry about her dress, she knew. After all, she'd lived in the garment for God knew how long, and only He knew how many stains the road must have already marked upon the once-fine velvet. But it was one of the few ones she hadn't been forced to sell, one of the few reminders of her former life.

And now even such a scant token was ruined.

Just like she was.

She lay where she fell, no longer possessing the motivation to rise, nor the fortitude to do so.

The harsh sound of retching met her ears, followed by a curse from Sylvi. Ariana lifted her head, wanting to rise to aid Liv, but her legs would not comply.

"Get Percy." An authoritative masculine voice rose above Sylvi's muttering, stopping it along with the beat of Ariana's heart.

She pulled in a hard breath, and the icy chill of it raked down her lungs. If only the ground would open and let her tumble away into its depths rather than let him see her thus. After all, it was the first time she'd seen him since he'd caught her.

Connor.

• • •

Connor rushed toward the pile of pale blue velvet on the ground.

"I'd rather ye took yer time arriving than show up with them half dead." He shot a hard glance toward Sylvi.

He bent over Ariana and scooped her up, the mass of skirts and velvet and all. The insignificance of her weight needled his thoughts.

She lifted a hand to stop him and shook her head, but he already had her in his arms. "Please." Her voice was a mere thread. "I can—"

"You made them my responsibility." Sylvi squared her shoulders and met his look. "And I saw fit to rush their arrival."

Despite her tone, her gaze darted with concern between both women.

"Please, I can walk." The sound came from the bundle Connor carried.

Ariana moved in his arms, attempting to extricate herself.

"Aye, but I can easily carry ye," he said softly.

She ceased her struggling. "And I can easily walk. I didn't anticipate my legs would be so tired from the longer ride today."

"I'll no' have ye falling to yer death on the stairs," he said, and strode toward the manor entrance with snow crunching under his feet.

A glint of defiance sparked in her gaze despite her drooping lids.

He shifted her in his arms, so her head rested against his chest and the stairs would be easier to maneuver. "Hush now, lass. Ye dinna have a choice in this."

Her protests quieted, and by the time he made it to the small room she would share with the other new woman, her deep, even breathing told him she'd fallen asleep.

The room was cold despite the fire crackling in the hearth. It'd been lit recently, when the riders had been spotted, but hadn't yet warmed the space.

He settled her in the bed and pulled the coverlet over her. Shadows danced across the areas beneath her cheeks and eyes where the firelight didn't touch.

Fabric rustled in the doorway. Connor looked up to find Sylvi watching him with more anxiety than she'd ever admit to.

"She's too thin," he said.

Sylvi crossed her arms. "I tried to get her to eat, but she was too attentive to the other one."

He rose and crossed the room. "Let's discuss this in private."

She followed without comment, her feet moving silently over the hard floor like she'd been taught.

He wasn't surprised. There wasn't a lesson in battle she hadn't mastered.

He waited to speak until they were behind the closed door of the solar. The musty, lingering scent of the books once held within was familiar, and a low fire crackled in the hearth. Shelves lined the back wall, gaping with emptiness.

"What were ye thinking, pushing them so hard?" he asked for the second time.

Sylvi's eyes flashed. "I told you, I made the decision. Liv vomited her way through England and Scotland and every damn place between." Her gaze slipped from his in a rare show of uncertainty. "I thought if I didn't get her here in time, she'd die."

Connor shook his head. "I've no' seen noblewomen travel as fast as ye pushed them. Delilah and I only just arrived yesterday."

"It was Ariana," she said with a lowered voice. "The one you carried upstairs. She insisted she was fine. She pushed Liv to go on and helped when she was sick. I think she held the same fears I did."

The skinny scrap of a woman he'd carried upstairs hardly seemed strong enough to have survived the trip herself, let alone have pushed to travel faster.

Sylvi widened her stance. "Why the hell did we do this now? It's nigh the middle of winter." An edge of her former baseborn accent slipped into her words, the roughness she'd worked so hard to smooth.

Connor lifted a brow and she lowered the challenge of her glare. A muscle worked in her jaw.

She was upset and had every right to be. He'd been unhappy with the timing himself, but had acted on the king's orders. King James didn't consider things like weather or how long the women took to train. He only cared that his orders were followed and those names Connor was given were eliminated in less than four months.

As it was, Connor only had three remaining.

"Traveling in this season doesn't make sense." She muttered it under her breath like a petulant child.

"There are more missions," he said. Two slips of paper sat on his desk.

Sylvi gave an exasperated hiss. "There are always more missions."

He wouldn't look at the papers right now. He wouldn't turn and see the two stark pieces of white parchment laid against the dark desk.

Overall, he'd had five names in his three years of service to the king. But always one at a time.

There'd never been two together before.

She drew a deep breath and let the air hiss out the way women do when they're displeased. In a house full of lasses, it was a sound he knew all too well.

The rigidity of her shoulders slackened. "I don't like this."

He didn't either.

"Go see to Liv, aye?"

She nodded.

"Let the poor girl sleep in the kitchen tonight for extra warmth." He clapped a hand on her shoulder and squeezed gently. "Ye did well in getting them safely to Kindrochit."

She nodded again and turned from the room.

He waited for some time to pass after her departure, until he could stand the scraping drag of time no more.

Then he turned toward his desk to do what he'd been dreading.

He lifted the first strip of parchment and snapped the seal. Waxy crumbles fell in several large chunks to his desk, but he paid them no mind. He unfolded the note with great care and read the single name written in the blackest ink.

Angus MacAlister.

A laird Connor had met only once as a boy, though he remembered little more than the name and how unruly the man's dark hair had been.

Connor closed his eyes against the memory and tossed the parchment into the fire.

After it had long since burned to ash, he reached for the second.

The seal made a soft click as it succumbed to the pressure of his large fingertips.

Two names.

Two, dammit.

As if the one weren't already difficult enough.

The paper crackled in his hands, loud as a shot in the silence of his room. His gaze skimmed the single name and his gut clenched.

Kenneth Gordon.

His hand curled shut, balling the paper in his crushing fist.

Kenneth Gordon.

A man he'd grown up with and once loved as a brother, who'd saved his life in the Battle of Glenlivet. The man who had then betrayed him.

And now the man Connor would have to kill.

Chapter Four

A subtle clink broke through the dark nothing of Ariana's consciousness. She squeezed her eyes shut, as if doing so might let her sleep longer.

Clink.

Like the sound of a lid being lifted from a jar.

Ariana wriggled beneath the covers, loving the caress of the mattress and the soft sheets beneath her battered body. Had she ever been so wonderfully comfortable?

She cracked an eye open and found a golden-haired woman kneeling beside her bed with a metal tray.

The woman turned and gave the most beautiful, bashful smile. Ariana felt herself stare and was, embarrassingly, unable to stop. It wasn't just the perfect white teeth showing between her full pink lips, but the woman herself.

Her large green eyes were rimmed with impossibly long lashes and her hair fell in silky waves around her porcelain face.

The woman was exquisitely beautiful.

Ariana's hair had not been combed in some time, and she'd fallen asleep in the very clothes she'd arrived in. Surely she looked a fright, especially compared to so lovely a woman.

"I hope you slept well," the woman spoke in a soft voice. The kind of voice Ariana's mother always said ladies should employ.

The woman's gaze drifted away before turning back to the jars littering her metal tray. Her fingers were slender and gracefully tapered, each nail a perfect arc of healthy white. She selected a small cup from the table and offered it to Ariana. "If you drink this, your body won't ache so terribly."

"What is it?" Ariana eyed the greenish brown liquid. "And who are you?"

The woman lowered her eyes. "Um…" Her tongue flicked between her lips and she offered an apologetic look. "It's a blend of different herbs and tinctures. The list is long and boring." She gave an apologetic smile.

There was a shyness about her, surprising for her considerable beauty, and it spurred in Ariana a spike of protectiveness, the way one might guard a fragile bloom in winter.

"And your name?" Ariana asked gently.

The woman's cheeks colored. "Oh, yes, I'm Percy. Well, not really Percy. It's Persephone, but it's such a long name, you see. So, well, everyone calls me Percy. And what's your name?"

"I'm Ariana Fitzroy." Ariana said her name with a considerable lack of pride. Her name meant nothing in this castle in the middle of snow-covered Scotland. Not like it once had when her parents were alive and had their noble connections.

"That's an enchanting name," Percy said with genuine kindness. "Oh, here—let me help you sit up."

She carefully eased Ariana into a sitting position and the soft scent of violets wafted from her golden waves.

Ariana accepted the drink once she was upright. The cup was warm against her fingertips, and she curled her whole hand around it to bask in the heat.

The room she'd slept in was large enough for two narrow beds with a hearth between. A small, well-used hearth. Flecks of stone had been chipped away and a large chunk was missing, leaving a hole in the mortar like the gap of a missing tooth. Regardless, it kept away the chill without filling the air with smoke. The flames of a strong fire licked merrily away at fresh-looking logs. No doubt Percy's doing.

Ariana eyed the empty bed across from hers. "Have you seen to Liv?"

"I saw to her first." Percy smiled, and again Ariana was struck by her extraordinary beauty. "I think she'll be fine after she rests."

Ariana released the tension creeping over her shoulders and regarded the drink in her hands. The perfume of rose and some other sort of flower greeted her. Surely it could not taste so bad if it smelled so pleasing.

"It will help," Percy said reassuringly.

Without thinking on it more, Ariana let the floral liquid wash into her mouth and swallowed quickly. It tasted as it smelled, with an edge of bitterness mellowed by a touch of sweetness.

Percy took the cup from her and handed her a bowl of pottage. "I put honey in it to make it taste a little better."

It was all Ariana could do to thank Percy before devouring the thick gray substance as daintily as was possible. While it was not the most appealing food Ariana had ever eaten, it was by far the most delicious. After days upon days of cold meat and bannocks, those hard and crumbling oatcakes, the gooey warmth of the pottage filled her stomach like a feast.

"Is my training to begin now?" Ariana asked when she was finished eating.

Sylvi had mentioned their training would start immediately. After displaying such an appalling weakness upon their arrival, Ariana was eager to prove her worth.

This was security, she reminded herself.

This was freedom.

Percy's mouth fell open. "Oh no, you must rest after your travels."

"What kind of training is it? I know nothing of what is expected of us."

Percy put a stopper back into one of the bottles. "No, I imagine Sylvi didn't explain much. The women do training every morning. It starts with a run, then they learn to fight with weapons. To defend themselves if need be. In the afternoon, there are lessons, if needed, to enable them to be better at gleaning information from others. It's rigorous, but beneficial."

"You say women." Ariana looked toward the empty bed. Would it be Liv staying with her, or would she have another roommate she didn't know? "How many women are here?"

"Five now, with you and Liv having arrived." Percy took the empty bowl from Ariana's hands. "Then myself, Sylvi, and Delilah. The only other person here is Connor. No staff; we do everything on our own."

Ariana nodded, taking in the information she'd been wanting to know all through the course of the last month. "Are Delilah and Sylvi resting now?"

Silence greeted her, as well as a telltale shift of Percy's lovely green eyes.

She wasn't sure if the women were training presently or not, but she refused to lie abed if they were.

She would not come across as weak again.

Ariana pulled herself from the bed, not an easy feat when the heavy exhaustion in her body begged her to follow Percy's request.

"Please, you mustn't," Percy said. "Connor doesn't like to be disobeyed."

"I refuse to rest if others aren't." Her conviction surged through her body, providing a burst of necessary energy. Her heart galloped in her chest and, like when she won at cards, she felt the dizzying wash of invigoration.

Of living.

Percy's hesitant expression blossomed into a grin, as if the eagerness flooding through Ariana were infectious. "If you're going to train, you'll need proper clothing. The women train most days with these garments, and then at least two days in dresses so they're used to fighting in all attire."

Within several surprisingly efficient minutes, Percy helped her out of the stained, travel-worn dress and into a pair of black trews with her breasts bound beneath a black léine.

Together, the two women made their way down the stone steps. Like the hearth of her bedroom, the stairs were in poor condition. Several cracks ran through the stone walls on either side, and the middle of each step had been worn into a dip. They seemed sturdy enough underfoot, which was what truly mattered.

The pants hugged her legs up to the crotch in a foreign manner, but were surprisingly comfortable, especially with the loose léine and jacket she wore over them.

"Connor won't be upset with you for letting me fight so soon, will he?" Ariana asked before they pushed through the large doors.

Percy shook her head, and the loose curls of her hair rolled against the velvet of her blue dress. "No, Connor never gets angry with me. He might not be too pleased with you though." She pressed the flat of her hand to the door. "Are you ready?"

Everything in Ariana hummed with a nervous excitement so powerful it made her jittery and weak all at once.

She nodded.

Percy pushed open the door, and they walked out into the icy, still air.

Connor stood not far away. His tall, lean body caught her gaze before she noticed two other women. She recognized Sylvi despite a large, awkward apron-like garment she wore on her body. Her hair was threaded back in several braids, and the black of her ribbon stood dark against the flush of her throat. The woman across from her was familiar as well. Hair somewhere between blonde and brown, a small freckle beside the lush mouth. The recollection struck Ariana like a blow. The woman from the card table in London when she had been caught cheating.

She too wore a cumbersome brown apron. They stood out against the bleak white of the snow blanketing the interior of the castle's curtain walls.

And there were swords in both women's hands.

Swords.

As if they were soldiers.

It was just as Percy had said.

Ariana stared at the length of steel gripped in Sylvi's fist, like an extension of her. The sun was hidden behind a smattering of clouds and yet it shone upon the metal like a beacon.

Sylvi opened her mouth and cried out before lunging toward the other woman. Their swords clashed with such ferocity, Ariana swore she saw a spark flash between them. The woman grunted and shoved back with her sword until Sylvi drew away.

This time Sylvi gripped the handle of her blade with two hands and swung it high overhead. She grimaced and arced the weapon down toward the head of the other woman.

Ariana winced as if she were the one about to take the blow. But before the blade could strike, the other woman cut her sword into the air and blocked.

Energy fired through Ariana's veins, raw and renewed.

She wanted to be like them, to be strong and powerful.

"What is she doing out here?" Connor's voice pulled her attention.

He strode toward them, his gait smooth despite the irate expression crinkling his brow. His nose and cheeks were bright red from the cold.

"I came of my own volition," Ariana said, before Percy could feel compelled to answer on her behalf.

His gaze shifted to Percy.

"She insisted," she answered in her soft voice.

His attention returned back to Ariana and fire seemed to burn in the depths of his hazel eyes.

Suddenly the memory of how he'd looked at her that fateful evening slammed into her. She'd been such a dolt for assuming his attention had been one of interest.

Her cheeks lit with shame, burning away all the chill of the morning air upon them.

But she had not come here to give in to the heart-sucking pressure of humiliation.

She had come to train.

• • •

Connor stared down at the small woman who dared defy him on her first day of training.

The trews sagged on her hips and the shirt hung from her shoulders as if it were set upon a line to dry.

Deep smudges of exhaustion showed under her eyes.

"Ye should take the day to rest. It may be the only one ye get," he said. "Ye look as though a strong wind could knock ye down."

"There is no wind, which makes your statement a wild assumption." She folded her arms over her narrow chest. "I'm quite capable."

He smirked. "If ye insist, but ye'll do well to remember I'm in charge."

Some of the defiant spark faded and she gave a nod.

"Percy, ye can go." He nodded toward the manor and gave her a pointed look. "I think ye've done enough here."

Percy gave a hesitant look at Ariana before she made her way back to the tower house. Connor watched her leave without guilt. If she'd been uncomfortable with Ariana staying, she shouldn't have allowed the lass to come down in the first place.

He turned to the other girls. "Enough watching. Get back to it."

Sylvi was a snake, coiled during the lull and waiting to strike. Delilah barely had time to lift her own weapon and block the blow.

The clang rang so sharply, it twinged deep in his ears.

They were good on their own. His attention went back to Ariana. "The first thing we need to do is get ye warmed up."

A shiver wracked through her. "I'm not cold." The lie came out in a fog of frozen breath.

"It's no' to make ye feel warm, it's to get yer muscles limber and ready for fighting. Ye take care of yer body so it takes care of ye. Do ye understand?"

She nodded sharply, and the muscles of her slender neck stood out like twigs beneath thin silk.

"Then we're going to run five times around the length of the wall."

It was a fraction of what they usually did, but he didn't want to kill the lass. He nodded for her to start and set his pace to match hers. They'd only done one lap when her breathing began to go ragged.

She'd wanted to train, he reminded himself.

By the second lap, her footfalls were heavy—a slow, staggered *crunch, crunch, crunch* against the ice-lined snow.

His body moved with ease, but he remembered a time long ago, when he'd been a boy and his father had done this with him. He'd gotten a stitch in his side so fierce he could only imagine he'd been stabbed. It was how one learned.

By the third lap, they were moving slower.

Still she had not stopped, not even to catch her breath.

On the fourth lap, she stumbled.

He lunged forward to catch her, but she righted herself and kept running.

Something inside him twisted. She was exhausted and there was almost nothing to her scrawny frame. He should have said two laps.

He should never have let her stay to train.

"I think ye've warmed up well enough," he said.

"No." She huffed a heavy breath. "One more."

Why the hell had he said five?

Because other women had been able to do at least five when they'd first arrived. After they were well rested. And of a decent weight.

Ariana lowered her head on the last lap and quickened her pace despite the rasp of her breathing. She didn't stumble again and did not stop until they reached the place they'd started.

Her small chest puffed in and out and sweat trickled down her reddened face, but she gave him a triumphant smile.

A slant of sunlight bathed her face, and he realized for the first time that her eyes weren't actually blue, but a deep blue-green. The color of the sea on a calm day with a ring of dark green around it, lending her eyes a feline look.

She truly was a beauty.

"Ye did well, Ariana." He patted her back and then wished he hadn't. The hard stab of her shoulders and spine against his palm struck him deep in the heart.

He'd be having a private conversation with Percy later to ensure Ariana ate more times per day than everyone else.

"You're right," Ariana said with her beautiful smile. "I feel much warmer, and my legs are hardly sore from yesterday's ride."

She looked as if she were about to fall over.

"First I'll teach ye to throw a dagger," he said. At least that task wouldn't be as exhaustive as fighting.

Connor wouldn't make the same mistake of training her too hard as he had with making her run those damn laps.

She followed him across the field. "Are we being trained to be warriors?"

He tugged the heavy round target from the pile of practice gear and set it up several yards away. She remained quiet, awaiting his answer.

"Something like that." He grabbed several sharp knives and put all but one on the frozen ground between them. The snow had melted somewhat and several limp strands of grass lay in green spears upon the muddied white surface.

Her gaze fell to the pile of blades. "When will I know?"

"When ye're ready," he said, and extended his hand so she could see how he held the dagger. "The key to this is ye hold the blade lightly between yer thumb and the knuckle of yer first finger."

Ariana plucked a dagger from the ground and mimicked his delicate grip.

"It's a light throw. If ye put power behind it, yer throw will go wild. Keep yer wrist relaxed." He loosed the dagger. It flew through the air and sank deep into the center of the target.

She worked her own dagger back and forth several times before releasing it. It clattered against the target and fell to the ground.

"Ye'll get it," he said. "Ye just have to practice."

She nodded and flung the next blade. It too sailed wildly through the air.

He let her continue to work on throwing daggers until the

salty scent of roasting ham wafting out from indoors told him their morning session had drawn to a close.

Connor put his hand over hers, stopping her from grabbing another dagger.

"We're done. Now ye'll eat something before attending yer lessons."

She straightened, and a line of worry creased her brows. "I need to check on Liv."

"Ye need to eat. Ye'll be no good to me being as thin as ye are."

For the first time since training, her gaze dropped and slid to the side in a show of obvious discomfort. She didn't speak, but instead gave a quiet nod.

Suddenly he found himself wishing for the irritated sigh women gave instead of this.

"I canna have ye getting sick," he amended.

She nodded again and lifted her beautiful eyes to meet his.

"After ye eat, ye'll have lessons with Delilah."

The troubled expression lit with excitement. "Sword lessons?"

"Gaelic," he replied. "And what Delilah likes to refer to as seduction."

Ariana's mouth fell open, and he anticipated a slew of questions.

Fortunately, Percy appeared between them, saving him from whatever it was Ariana intended to say.

"Your meal is waiting for you inside," she said to Ariana with a gentle smile. "Head straight back when you go inside and you'll find the kitchens. I've got a plate of food waiting for you."

"Go on, then," Connor said to Ariana. This time he made a point not to touch her skeletal back.

She picked up the daggers and deposited them into the weapons trunk before making her way indoors. Like a good soldier. Something akin to pride swelled in his chest.

He waited until she was out of sight before speaking. "The girl needs to put on some weight."

"I've already seen to ordering more supplies and will ensure she eats between meals." Percy tilted her head and looked behind

Connor's shoulder in thought. "I believe I have a tea I can make to strengthen her appetite."

He squeezed her shoulder and smiled down at her. "I dinna know what I'd do without ye."

"There's something else." She caught the end of a lock of hair and twisted it around her finger. "It's the other girl, Liv."

Everyone had been worried about the red-haired lass. Hell, even he'd been concerned at how pale she'd appeared when they arrived.

His gut tightened, like he'd been hit. "Is she dying?"

"Um…no." Percy released the lock of hair and bit down on her lower lip. "She's pregnant."

Chapter Five

The afternoon found Ariana seated on flimsy pillows in a room swathed with so many lengths of brightly colored silks, the stone walls beneath were impossible to see. Delilah wore a soft velvet gown of crimson and her hair was neatly swept back into a complicated style Ariana had only seen at court.

Her face was smooth with seriousness when she settled onto the soft cushions.

"This is an education on seduction," Delilah said in a reverent tone. "We know our beauty will aid us in gathering information and getting out of trouble. This tutelage is done in an effort to encourage us in feeling powerful enough to wield such a weapon."

Ariana shifted on the thin pillow. The chill of the flagstones beneath seeped up through the flimsy padding and left her bottom cold.

She didn't feel powerful. She felt silly.

And she wished Liv were well enough to be sitting beside her so they could laugh over the ridiculousness of it all together later.

Unperturbed by Ariana's lack of enthusiasm, Delilah gave a smile as if they had a shared secret. "When you ask for something, make sure you look at a man with incredible interest. Depending on how important the request or how close you are, you may want to look at him the way you'd regard someone you were about to kiss."

Ariana let her gaze skim across the silk wall hangings and shrugged. "I've not ever kissed a man."

"Haven't you?" Delilah stared at Ariana incredulously. "But you're so lovely."

Ariana already regretted having to waste her time on the lesson with Delilah. Images of the target board stood forefront in her mind and she tried to picture how exactly to hold the dagger between her fingers—the metal cool against her fingertips. Not too tight.

"You were at court for some time, correct?" Delilah's brown eyes searched Ariana's.

All imagined daggers disappeared from Ariana's mind. "Yes, for the last six years."

"Then how did you not kiss a boy in all that time? I remember them being most eager."

She was right. They had been eager. But Ariana had waited patiently for her parents to find the right match. Their attempts were unsuccessful, and when they died the responsibility passed to her brother, Caldwell.

She hadn't expected him to spend her dowry.

Later, she'd discovered her parents had spent far more than their lands generated, resulting in rumors of the family being on the brink of destitution. Only when it was too late to matter did Ariana realize the failed betrothal attempts were not due to ineptitude on her part, but to the very true rumors of their dwindling wealth.

In all her three and twenty years, Ariana had never kissed a man because she had obediently waited for the one she would marry.

"Had you?" Ariana replied at last.

Delilah accepted the change in subject with a pretty flush of her cheeks. "Yes, plenty of times. And men of all types, from an attractive stablehand to…" She leaned forward with a grin. "The king."

Ariana studied her, unsure if Delilah was trying to impress her or if she was being truthful. But then Ariana remembered how she had come to be here, and realized they all had their reasons for being brought to Scotland.

Delilah had not backed up from when she'd leaned closer, and the proximity was almost too much. "You've thought of it, at least?" she asked.

The muscles along Ariana's back tensed with the desire to draw away, but Delilah seemed so excited and Ariana did not wish to be rude.

Ariana shook her head.

Truthfully, she had not. She'd been so fixed on her attempts to placate her parents in the hopes they might pay her the slightest bit of positive attention, she had not so much as considered kissing any man.

Delilah's fingers touched Ariana's chin, feather light, and tilted her face toward hers. "It is the most delicious thing. Close your eyes and I will tell you of it."

Obediently, Ariana closed her eyes, hoping if she did as she was told, the lesson would end sooner.

It was an awkward sensation to sit in the ridiculous pillow-laden room with one's eyes closed.

"Relax," Delilah said in a velvety tone. "Listen."

Ariana let her muscles slacken.

"Imagine a man, tall and lean with muscle." Delilah's voice was quietly intimate. Hypnotic. "He's staring at you as if you were the only woman he'd ever seen. Truly seen. The only woman he's ever wanted. The desire for you burning in his eyes."

Hazel eyes rose to the forefront of Ariana's mind, a sharp jaw shadowed with a day's growth of beard.

Connor.

She swallowed.

"His arms come around you," Delilah continued. "So strong, so warm. They offer you a protection unlike anything you've ever felt and make you wish you could melt into his embrace for the rest of your life."

In Ariana's mind, Connor's arms wrapped around her. But she didn't shy from his touch—she welcomed it. The chill of the room ebbed into a pleasant heat.

"Your eyes meet. His fingers touch your face and his breath whispers over your lips. He lowers his head and you close your eyes just as his mouth touches yours, warm and demanding."

Ariana's heart quickened and her breathing went almost ragged. Her mouth was suddenly dry and she flicked her tongue over her lips.

"His body is a wall of strength against you, holding you upright, as your knees feel as though they will buckle. Then his tongue strokes yours, velvet fire and heady seduction."

Ariana drew a shaky breath.

Something pounded hard at the door.

She leapt and her heart lurched into her throat.

Delilah rose without issue and pulled open the door. A ribbon of cold air drifted in, exquisite where it swept over the blazing heat of Ariana's face.

Delilah murmured low, obviously talking to someone else before she spoke out again in a clear tone, announcing the lesson had ended for the day.

Relieved to escape, burdened with embarrassment, Ariana tried to pull herself upright from the pillows, floundering twice in a fluff of skirts before finally extricating herself from the lavish floor.

The hall outside was so starkly gray in comparison, it was like walking from daylight to darkness.

"Ariana," a deep voice sounded from behind her. "I'm sorry to have interrupted yer lesson. I needed to speak with ye."

She spun around and found Connor standing there, all stern authority and stoicism.

Only seconds ago, she'd been kissing him in her mind.

God, she'd had herself pressed against him, her body simmering with the most incredible burn. Everything in her had wanted him to kiss her, to hold her.

The door to Delilah's room closed and Ariana was left standing in the hall, her mind a wash of chaotic thoughts and scalded embarrassment.

Connor's brows lowered. "Are ye fine, lass?"

Ariana swallowed around her dry throat and gave a vigorous nod.

"Ye're red." He circled a finger in the air toward her. "In the face."

She pressed her hands to her cheeks, but her palms were just as hot. "I…"

He squared his shoulders. "I need to speak with ye."

Relief swept over Ariana with the same refreshment as the icy air of the hall now bathing her face. "Of course."

She would never think of her imagined kiss again.

Never.

What a foolish thing to have done.

"It's Liv," he said.

Ariana's heart sank in her chest, and she closed her eyes slowly against the sensation before opening them. The other woman had been deathly ill for too long. "Is she…"

"She's pregnant."

Ariana straightened in surprise.

She'd thought Liv so sick, but no, the whole time she'd been pregnant.

And it did make sense. The vomiting, the despondency, the exhaustion. Ariana had seen enough pregnant women that she ought to have realized.

Those women had been lucky. Those women had not only been successfully married, but had the promise of family swelling their bellies. And poor Liv had a babe in her belly with no husband to see to her.

"I can help care for her," Ariana said quickly.

"That isna necessary. Percy will cover the task." His jaw tightened. "I told ye because ye share a room and I thought it best for ye to know."

Ariana nodded. "Is there anything I can do?"

He put a large hand on her shoulder. The heat of his thumb brushed at her collarbone where the neckline of her gown did not cover.

Her pulse flitted faster.

"Sylvi told me how ye cared for her while ye traveled here, how ye encouraged her and kept her spirits up." His eyes met hers, a dazzling array of colors within the deep hazel. "The lass may be alive even now because of what ye did."

Ariana shook her head. "Liv is tougher than she looks, she—"

"Dinna underestimate yerself, Ariana. There's a courage in ye I dinna think ye can see." His free hand touched the underside of her chin. Soft and gentle.

Oh God.

He tipped her face toward his and her lungs stopped accepting air.

"I see yer strength and I believe in ye."

Her heart staggered erratically to find some clear rhythm and failed.

He gave her a firm pat on the shoulder and nodded once before walking off.

She spun away and grazed her cheek, where his touch still scalded, with shaking fingers.

And though she had promised herself she would not, her thoughts slipped back into the beautiful fog of that glorious imagined kiss.

• • •

Connor settled back in the chair that wasn't his and stared into the flames burning in the hearth of a solar that didn't belong to him.

The crumbling heap of a castle had been in the king's negligent hands for decades, if not centuries.

No one would want Kindrochit. Certainly not Connor.

As the promising heir of a laird so long ago, he never thought he'd grow up to have nothing.

Less than nothing.

Obligations he couldn't meet, a legacy he was so far from reclaiming it might as well be a legend. His people were dead. The only one still alive was Murdoch.

Connor's pact with the king only added weight to his mind, a scale forever tipping him further from the balance of morality. Then there was Cora, the sister he could barely protect, who resented him and whom he did not visit lest he face the fire of her disappointment. And now he had a sick woman with a babe to consider.

Not to mention those names.

Those damning names.

Angus MacAlister and Kenneth Gordon.

The muscles of his neck bunched, a knot drawn impossibly tight.

The betrayal tangled in the thorned web of what had once been a brotherhood.

Something thunked downstairs.

Most likely Sylvi going through her nightly routine.

Still, his shoulders rose with irritation.

He pulled in a deep breath and dropped his head back onto the velvet-covered chair.

When Murdoch returned from uncovering additional information on Angus MacAlister's whereabouts, Connor would send him to the village to see—

Thunk.

He lifted his head and turned toward the door. It stood slightly ajar.

Thunk.

With all the thoughts crammed inside his mind, the last thing he needed was a distraction from sorting them out. He heaved himself from the chair, strode across the room, and closed it with a satisfactory push.

A moment went by.

Two.

Silence.

His shoulders relaxed a fraction of an inch and he made his way back to the chair.

Thunk.

He wanted to roar like a beast, but flung the door open instead and followed the sound with the determination of a predator.

Light framed the kitchen door.

He shoved it open. "Damn it, Sylvi, a man canna think wi—"

Feline green eyes, wide with shock, stared up at him, a slender hand held aloft midair with a dagger pinched between her thumb and forefinger.

Ariana gasped. "Forgive me, Connor, I didn't know you could hear. I thought I'd been quiet."

He looked to the opposite side of the kitchen and there, much farther than he'd set it that morning outside, was the target with several daggers jutting from its scarred face.

He folded his arms over his chest and nodded appreciatively. "Well done."

"After I realized exactly how to hold them, light and easy. Like a card." A pleased flush colored Ariana's cheeks to the same red as her full lips, a bonny contrast to her fair skin and glossy black hair.

"Now ye just need to hit the center," he said. "Throw again."

She pursed her lips and closed one eye. Her arm pulled back, and the dagger slid from her fingers with incredible grace.

Thunk.

"Good, good," he murmured. "Do it one more time with both yer eyes open. And square yer hips."

She shot him a questioning look.

He reached out, grasped her hips and straightened her forward. She might be thin, but her hips were still round and feminine.

He nodded. "Again."

Both eyes open, she loosed her dagger. It sank into the very center.

Her chin lifted with obvious pride. "Thank you."

Connor shrugged. "It was yer own skill. I just showed ye what to adjust. Now let's get this cleaned up. Ye need yer sleep or ye'll be no good to me tomorrow."

Ariana immediately set to work scooping up the daggers.

There was a quiet grace to her, a gentleness contradicting her show of courage and fortitude. And under the layer of powerful determination, an innocence.

What the hell had Delilah said to her during their lesson?

Aye, Ariana needed instruction on how to use flirtation to escape situations and glean information, but he certainly hadn't wanted her being taught too much. Especially when Ariana had already demonstrated a habit of not backing down from a challenge.

"What did Delilah say to ye today?" he asked.

A dagger clattered to the floor. The color rose high in her cheeks. "Gaelic."

Clever girl. His mouth almost quirked into a smile. "I meant yer other lesson." He set to work lowering the target to keep her from feeling as if she were being interrogated.

Her tongue flicked out between her lips and she kept those large green eyes of hers fixed on him. "Kissing."

Kissing.

He almost laughed with relief. While he trusted Delilah's gentleness, he'd still have a talk with her to have a care with Ariana.

"We call the lessons seduction." He hefted the weight of the target into his hands. "But I want ye to know I dinna expect ye to seduce anyone. It's tutelage on using yer beauty to get where ye need to go, to get out of situations, aye?"

She nodded and suddenly looked more uncertain than he'd seen her that day.

He carried the target across the room and propped it against the wall. It could be returned to the chest in the morning.

"Ye know how to use your beauty already." Connor straightened and faced her. "I saw it the night I met ye."

Ariana's lips parted, as if to protest.

"Dinna try to lie and say ye dinna. Ye were quite good at it." He winked. "And I think Delilah will make ye a force to be reckoned with."

A small smile touched her lips. "Thank you," she said in a soft voice. "Not just for the compliment, but for teaching me to throw a dagger. For bringing me here."

A knot of discomfort lodged itself in his chest. "For bringing ye here?"

She nodded. "No one's ever believed in me. No one's taken a

moment to look at me long enough to ever consider me as anything more than a mere nobleman's daughter, a bargaining tool. Certainly never to assume I have potential for anything more. In all my life, you're the only person who has ever thought more of me." Her chin lifted a notch. "So, yes, thank you for bringing me here."

He stared at her, unsure of what to say. He didn't save women. He damned them. "I dinna think ye know what ye say."

"I do." She met his eyes with conviction. "We all are broken women. There is no place for us anywhere else." Her hand gestured to the kitchen door. "Every woman here is strong. Life may have ruined us, but you've saved us."

Then she jerked forward, pressed her lips to his cheek in a quick kiss, and swept from the room.

Chapter Six

MAY 1605

Connor's breath billowed out in front of him in great white clouds, and frosted grass crunched beneath the fall of his boots.

His muscles glided through their motions with familiar ease, and he reveled in the heat warming them. God, how he loved the morning routine of going for a run.

The sky was clear, his body so wonderfully alive and powerful, and for one blissful moment while he ran, his thoughts were finally without burden.

A black-clad figure ran past him. Her long, dark braid bounced against her back with each sure step.

He bit back a grin and quickened his pace to keep up with Ariana.

She'd surprised him with how quickly she'd adapted to training in the last two months.

How damn fast she'd gotten when she ran.

She'd plumped out nicely too, just as he'd imagined she would.

In fact, almost too nicely. His gaze slipped to her bottom, a luscious curve against tight black breeches. Shame hit him like a slap and he quickly jerked his stare back toward the bounce of her braid.

He was her trainer, her mentor. He was above ogling like some lewd tavern patron.

Instead, he lowered his head and pushed his body harder, making his legs burn with the effort of going faster, singeing away all vestiges of unwanted masculine appreciation.

He'd almost caught up with her when they reached their final lap. She finished mere seconds before him.

Ariana's blue-green eyes gleamed with victory. She wouldn't gloat though. She never did.

He wagged a finger. "I almost had ye."

"Maybe tomorrow morning." She winked and gave him a brilliant smile.

Delilah and Sylvi appeared around the castle wall together and drew to a stop. Their cheeks and noses were red from the cold, but sweat glistened at their brows. Their bright eyes and faces were lit with eagerness to train.

Connor motioned to the neat stack of practice weapons set upon a blanket. "Delilah and Ariana, practice with swords. Sylvi, we're doing hand-to-hand."

Delilah and Ariana gave each other an excited, shared smile. They were well matched. Delilah knew how to tutor Ariana while still challenging her, and Ariana didn't hit as hard as Sylvi.

All the women moved to comply, first tying on their boxy, padded armor and then taking their positions.

Sylvi braced herself with bent knees in front of him, her arms locked in preparation to fend off his blow.

Her pale blue gaze met his with a vehement determination that would throw most men off guard.

He punched. She blocked and spun out of his reach, her stare calculating.

The clang of swords and Delilah's careful instructions sounded to their left.

Sylvi ducked low and threw her fist at his stomach.

Connor jerked his hand down to block the hit just as she switched her hand's momentum, shoving it to the ground for support instead. Her leg swept at his ankles with the force of an iron pole and sent him crashing to the ground.

She was on him before the image of the sky even registered in his vision.

Her hands braced his shoulders and she glared down at him with the fierce anger she always showed when she fought.

"Show me how to break a neck." She panted around her words

with an almost bloodthirsty frenzy. "Show me everything I know your father taught you."

They'd had this conversation before. Too many damn times. "Ye know I willna do that."

She shoved off him. "And you know why I chose to come here." Her chest heaved with her frustration. "You know why I worked so damn hard to get here."

Connor rose to his feet. "It doesna give ye the authority to speak to me as ye do. Go run three times around the castle. I'll no' have ye hurting the others because of yer anger."

She gave a roar of frustration, but turned and obeyed his order.

He dragged a hand through his hair. She was getting more difficult to control each day, with each new skill she mastered. This morning was the first time she'd taken him down, and with too much ease. Her move had been a good one. He'd commend her on it when she cooled down.

Hell, he might even borrow it.

But no matter how much she disagreed with him, he knew she wasn't ready.

Connor's father, the Shadow, had been a famed warrior in the Highlands. He killed with a deft skill unparalleled by any other man in Scotland. He'd taught Connor many other lessons before teaching him how to kill. There was the responsibility, the appreciation, the impact of death, the understanding of what it could change—and what it could not.

For those reasons, Sylvi was not ready.

"I see ye're training hard, Connor." A masculine voice cut the air.

He turned to find a large man with a mass of blond waves and braids stalking toward him.

Murdoch.

"About damn time," Connor said with a grin. They locked forearms and embraced once before slapping each other on the back.

"Ye've got news, aye?" Connor asked in a low voice.

Murdoch opened his hands in a helpless gesture. "I wouldna have taken so long otherwise."

Connor jerked his head toward the castle. "Talk first, food later."

"Aye, that's why I ate a bannock on the way in." Murdoch flashed a smile, revealing a freshly broken front tooth.

Connor led the way to the castle entrance. "I see ye've gotten prettier since ye've been gone."

"And I see the skinny one has become a nice bonny lass," Murdoch mumbled to him. "If Delilah wants some help with teaching the girl some tips in the bedchamber, I'd like to volunteer my—"

Connor hadn't realized he was glaring at the man until Murdoch's speech stopped.

"She's bonny is all," Murdoch said with a shrug.

"She's a trainee is all." Connor led Murdoch into the castle, where the darkness of the stone walls left him near blind after the brilliance of the sun. His body prickled as his sweat began to cool. "These girls work hard and deserve respect."

"Aye, I know that."

Even though Murdoch had admitted to his mistake, Connor had the overwhelming urge to knock Murdoch's crooked nose farther across his face.

Connor didn't bother with idle chatter while they made their way to his solar. He'd never been one for it, especially not when such anger simmered in his blood.

Once they were inside, he folded his arms over his chest and counted through ticks of patience, a childhood lesson his mother had taught him. One he'd never outgrown, as he'd never seemed to acquire the patience age was supposed to render.

Oblivious, Murdoch warmed his reddened hands by the fire.

"What news do ye have?" Connor asked.

"Ach, I've been all over Scotland in the dead of winter. I'm thinking James needs to pay me more." Murdoch turned his head sharply to the side, and a deep, grinding pop sounded from the base of his neck. "First of all, I've almost found yer man. He moves fast, that one, so when he's found, ye need to act, aye?"

Connor nodded.

Angus MacAlister.

Connor had intentionally chosen the other man before Kenneth Gordon. In fact, he tried to not even think of Kenneth.

"MacAlister's a shite of a man," Murdoch said in gruff voice. "I wouldna mind killing him myself."

There was usually a reason Connor received the names he did. They were men too powerful for the king to reprimand, or who needed to be removed from society.

But with a diplomatic delicacy only Connor, the son of the notorious Shadow, could accomplish.

"I'm only staying the night, then I'm back out. I think MacAlister is in the area." Murdoch stepped away from the fireplace. Flames reflected off his pale hair, giving him an orange-cast glow. "Also, yer sister wants ye to visit."

Connor bit back a groan, and Murdoch grinned as if sensing his torment.

"Ye canna keep putting her off forever," Murdoch added. "She's only going to get more agitated."

Connor nodded toward the door. "Go get yer food."

Murdoch winked and was gone before Connor could sit back in his chair.

His friend was right. It'd been too long since he'd gone to see Cora. And he'd have hell to pay.

• • •

Two months had done little to ease the threat of death from Liv's features. Ariana smoothed the hair from her friend's pale cheek.

While Liv had at least stopped retching, the nausea kept her from gaining much weight.

Ariana had had no issues gaining weight. After mornings of

training, she was ravenous and had maintained a healthy consumption of all the foods she hadn't been able to afford in over a year.

Thick, crusty bread, fine cheese that stuck in her back teeth, and various game with roasted golden skin and tender, juicy meat.

When Ariana saw her reflection now, no longer were her cheeks gaunt and her chest sunken—no, she had a rosiness to her face and everything had plumped rather nicely.

She felt like a woman.

One who was healthy and strong and capable.

She wanted that for Liv too.

When Ariana trained, in the many moments when her body trembled with exhaustion and she felt she could no longer go on, she would think of Liv upstairs, trapped in the torment of her own body. And she would push that much harder—not for herself, but for Liv. As if making herself stronger might somehow be enough for the both of them.

Liv tilted back the cup of Percy's special tea and set it on her bedside table. Various glass bottles crowded the narrow surface.

Liv's skin had taken on a gray pallor and her gleaming copper waves seemed to have faded to a muddy, sallow brown.

Seeing her thus squeezed Ariana's heart.

She wished she could give some of the vitality of her body to her friend, to share the burning power, the incredible energy she'd never dreamed possible.

The best she'd been able to do was share stories of what she'd been going through with her training and the silly class on seduction. Omitting, of course, the imagined kiss with Connor.

"You don't have to look at me like that." Liv's lips barely moved as she spoke.

Ariana forced her face into an expression of impassivity. "Like what?"

"Like you're so worried." Liv pulled the shawl of blankets around her more tightly. Her fingers were thin white twigs against the dark fabric. "Everyone is so worried. I see it in their faces when they tell me everything will be fine." Tears glossed her dull eyes.

"But it's not fine. I can feel it. I can't stand for you of all people to look at me thus too."

Liv's hands cupped the sad little mound of her stomach, where her child fought to live with more desperation than its mother.

Sympathy clogged Ariana's throat. "We worry because we care."

Liv gave a subtle shake of her head, stopped, and clenched her jaw.

Ariana reached over the rumpled sheets and gripped Liv's hand. Her palm was cold and damp, her fingers limp.

An ache settled in Ariana's shoulder from where Sylvi had slammed into her that morning, but she did not move. Liv did not like to be touched. Her accepting the small semblance of comfort was indicative of the closeness of their bond and it warmed Ariana's heart.

"Wesley, my beloved." Liv's eyelids slid lower. Percy's tea was starting to take effect. "He's dead. And he never knew..."

She pulled her hand from Ariana's and curled her arms around her stomach once more.

Wesley? Ariana had never heard of him during their long discussions at night when they traveled.

"We all care for you," Ariana said. "This will pass and you'll be stronger. We're spies together, right?"

It was a pathetic comfort in light of the burden her friend carried, but it was all she could think to offer.

A smile touched Liv's colorless lips, and she closed her eyes with the corners of her mouth still upturned.

Ariana waited until her friend's breathing was deep and even before she rose from the bed, but she did not go to her own. Not when such sorrow burdened her mind and pain still radiated from her shoulder.

Percy would have given her a tonic had she asked, but stubborn pride had kept Ariana from doing so.

She regretted such pride now.

Rather than stay in the room and risk waking Liv, Ariana slipped into the hallway. She had to pause a moment to let her eyes adjust to the darkness. After being in the warmth of her room, the moist chill of the hallway pressed against her flesh.

Though she'd been in the castle for two months and had walked into almost every room and knew the layout, she suddenly had the disorienting sensation of being lost. Uncertain where to go, but certain where she did not want to be.

Perhaps the kitchen, where the hearth was still warm and the homey scent of baking bread hung in the air.

Ariana trod down the stairs and was just about to pass the second floor when a clink of glass from one of the rooms caught her attention. A light glowed down the long hall, framing the outline of a door.

The solar.

She ran a hand over her shoulder, gently probing to decipher if the pain was worth interrupting Percy from studying the books she always pored over. Even the careful touch was almost too much for her bruised flesh.

Yes, she would swallow her pride for one night and seek the aid, and companionable comfort, of Percy.

Ariana made her way down the hall and pushed open the door.

But it was not Percy standing over her bottles and her meager stack of precious books, as Ariana had expected. The light of the fire framed the back of a leanly muscled man with broad, square shoulders.

Connor.

"Come in." His voice was deep and rich, not stark with authority as she was used to.

She stepped into the room and her heart thudded a little faster in her chest.

This was the first time they'd been alone since she'd so foolishly pressed her lips to his cheek. She still recalled the prickle of his stubble against her lips, the warm, clean scent of him. How very close she'd been to the heat of his mouth.

She'd thought of it more times than she cared to admit and always a twist of humiliation following the memory.

He turned and his brows lifted. "Ariana."

Connor had traded his trews for a kilt after the most bitter of the cold had swept away with winter. He now wore the pleated plaid slung around his narrow hips, the wool stopping just above his knees and revealing finely sculpted legs. More so in the firelight, with the way the golden glow teased out the shadowed lines of sinewy flesh.

Ariana forced herself to pull her gaze from his legs. "I thought you were Percy."

"Is something wrong?" Concern pulled at his brow.

She shook her head quickly, realizing he most likely thought something was amiss with Liv. "No, nothing. Liv is fine." The warmth of the large hearth beckoned her, especially with the chill of the hall still at her back. "I couldn't sleep and didn't want to wake her."

A small smile teased the corners of his full mouth and he nodded. "In that case, ye're welcome to join the sleepless." He tilted the cup he held in his hand toward her. "Close the door behind ye. It's colder than a witch's soul tonight."

Ariana did as she was told and strode into the room. Though she'd been in the solar several times, it looked different during the daytime, when light touched the dark wood shelves and turned the overstuffed green chairs the color of a lush meadow. Now shadows lingered in corners and left everything dark with the unknown.

Connor strode toward a small table with a decanter set upon it. She noticed then his feet were bare. Somehow, seeing him thus lent an intimacy to the large room.

He poured a splash of liquid into a second cup. "Come in and warm yerself by the fire."

Ariana walked deeper into the room, toward the glow of the hearth. Its heat enveloped her skin and eased away the chill with such expediency, she almost sighed.

Connor appeared beside her with a metal cup extended. "I canna sleep often myself."

She closed her fingers around the cool surface and glanced at the dark liquid within. A sharp scent hit her nostrils.

"Whisky," Connor said.

He was perfection in the firelight. Shadows etched his jaw while the light softened his face, his lips. The powerful lines of his chest were visible at the neck of his léine, as well as a dark peppering of small curling black hairs.

"Whisky," Ariana said with a forced stare at the cup instead of him. "Of course. I drink this all the time."

"Aye, I knew that about ye. When I first saw ye, I thought, 'Now there's a lass who can handle her whisky.'" Connor winked at her with disarming playfulness. "It'll do ye some good. Take off the chill and settle yer thoughts."

"Why do you assume my thoughts are unsettled?" she asked.

He took a swallow from his cup. "Because sleep comes easily to those without weight on their minds."

Ariana took a careful sip from her own cup, the way she'd seen men at the card tables drink. The liquid burned like sin down her throat and caught in her chest.

She gritted her teeth and swallowed hard several times to keep from sputtering.

Though she'd hoped to keep her reaction discreet, the grin on Connor's face told her he saw through her guise.

"It's good." Her voice came out in a croak and Connor laughed. It was a warm, rich sound and she found it terribly pleasing.

His eyes crinkled. "Now that we've discovered yer love of whisky, why dinna ye tell me what's got yer thoughts heavy?"

Uncertainty warred in her thoughts. This was the man who trained her in combat, who pushed her harder and demanded toughness. And now he was asking her to be vulnerable, to share her innermost thoughts.

Could he mean it?

Those hazel eyes of his rested on her, fixing her with his full attention.

Yes, he did.

Heat stirred in her chest and made her stomach flutter.

Part of her wanted to open up to him. It was the part which

had imagined his kiss in her mind and made her think on it far more often than she should. But there was another part of her, one which wanted his respect and demanded the world think her stronger than she thought even herself.

Could she let herself open up to him?

Chapter Seven

Connor watched the emotions play out over Ariana's face, the furrow of uncertainty on her brow, crinkling a small line where her face had been smooth and honest before. Ariana didn't trust him.

But then, he didn't blame her, considering the circumstances which had led her into his care in the first place.

He had taken her from everything she knew, everything she wanted.

Guilt was a familiar companion to him.

Connor was about to tell her she didn't need to speak when she pulled in a soft breath.

"It's Liv," she confessed. "Percy tries so hard to help, and I do too, but I don't think it's enough."

"Why do ye say that?"

Ariana lifted the cup to her lips and took a sip of her whisky. This time she did not flinch. "She's not getting better. She's getting worse. No one's saying it. But deep down, we all know." A pained look pinched her brows. "*She* knows."

What Ariana said was true—there was no denying it. But Connor said nothing. He'd been around women long enough to know they needed time to say what lingered on their minds, and once they were no longer burdened, they felt better.

If only it were so easy for men.

"I've seen women with child before," Ariana continued. "They're plump and glowing with excitement. But not Liv. She fades more every day, grows weaker every day. The little bump where her baby grows…" Her gaze lowered. "It's so pathetic and small."

Connor placed a hand on her shoulder, but Ariana shifted away.

"You asked me to be strong for her." The look in Ariana's eyes went hard. "But nothing is working."

Guilt cut into him. He'd said that to encourage her, not to tear her down.

"Percy is the best healer I've ever known," he said. "And ye have been strong, extraordinarily so. That's all ye can do, lass."

Her jaw clenched and she swallowed hard. "I've seen people die and never has it struck so deep. My parents and my brother, they all died. But I didn't—"

She stopped speaking and turned sharply to look into the fire smoldering in the hearth. Firelight played over her features, the smoothness of her skin, and the rounded arc of her cheekbones.

"But ye dinna what?" he asked.

When she did not answer, he touched the cheek facing away from him. She was warm beneath his fingertips, her skin silky.

He gently turned her face toward him, her eyes large and lit with something he realized he wanted desperately to know.

He dropped his hand from her face, but his fingers tingled with the memory of the sensation. "But ye dinna what?"

She lifted her chin with her usual determined strength. "When my parents and brother died, I didn't know them well enough to *feel*." Her free hand clenched into a fist. "This is different, Connor. I know Liv. I care for her. I worry about her every day."

Her compassion was palpable and it pulled at something deep inside him. "Percy would let ye help more if ye like. Yer lessons can be shortened."

He'd meant to reassure her, but Ariana's shoulders sagged in defeat. "It's not that. I've tried to help more, but end up underfoot. It's just—every day I grow stronger and every day Liv grows weaker. I wish I could do something more than sit by and watch her waste away. I feel so helpless."

Her eyes glowed with emotion and her smooth brow puckered. It made him want do whatever it took, say whatever she needed to hear, to soothe her.

"Being helpless is difficult," he admitted.

"I can't imagine you ever being helpless."

"My sister was ill once," he said. "No' like Liv, but verra sick." He drank from his cup and let the burn of liquor warm his throat and insides. "With the plague."

"Did she...?"

"Survive? Aye, but she was verra bad before she got better. Like ye, I could only stand by and watch. I couldna fight the sickness for her, I couldna make her better, and though I wanted it more than anything, I couldna take her place."

The unwanted memory of Cora rose in his mind. Her small body had been so still, her lips and cheeks without color as death cradled her ever closer. Helplessness had raged within him, like a clawing beast writhing to be free from a cage with no doors.

"I'm glad you still have her," Ariana said.

The thought of Cora, her long mane of wild brown waves and her laughing brown eyes, touched a smile to his lips. "I'm glad to still have her too. My ma died giving birth to her and it was as though all the kindness of my ma passed into Cora."

He didn't know why he'd shared that about his mother, but the quiet look on Ariana's face compelled him to continue. "I was a lad of ten and though I knew I should be a man about it, my ma's death devastated me. I wanted to hate Cora for having taken her from me. But then I saw Cora. She was a bitty wee thing and she smiled at me, all sweetness and love, and I knew then I'd no' ever hate the lass."

Aye, Connor was glad his sister was still alive, and he'd done a poor job of showing it. Murdoch was right. He needed to see her again.

Ariana watched him with a quiet smile on her face and the realization of just how much of himself he'd shared struck him as sure and quick as lightning.

"Ach, ye need to get yer sleep," he said with a gruffness he hadn't intended. "It'll be another hard day tomorrow."

"I'd be disappointed otherwise." Ariana handed her cup to him and had started to walk away when she stopped and turned back toward him. The firelight played across her beautiful features, on the delicate curl of her dark hair where it fell around her shoulders.

On the bruised skin visible just under her dress on her left shoulder.

"Thank you, Connor. Good night."

He nodded absentmindedly, unable to pull his gaze from her discolored flesh.

She turned and strode from the room, her slippers silent on the floor.

He wanted to stop her, to demand she tell him who'd hit her with such force. But he already knew the answer.

Sylvi.

• • •

Ariana tightened her grip on the pole in her hands. The wood was cold beneath her fingers, but her body was warm. Ready to fight.

Delilah stood in front of her, her face calm and her dark eyes watching Ariana with matched intensity.

"Go," Delilah said sharply.

Ariana's coiled muscles fired into action, propelling her forward. The pole whistled in the air and smacked harmlessly against Delilah's padded armor with a muted *thwock*.

Delilah grinned. "Perfect." She swept a hand over her apron, smoothing out the puckered dent as if the fabric were a fine gown. "Again."

Ariana's shoulder glowed with pain, but she whipped the pole around again and slammed it into Delilah's side with all the strength she could muster.

Delilah staggered slightly against the blow. "Even better." An errant curl slipped from her perfectly pinned hair and fluttered against her cheek. "You're picking this up far quicker than even Sylvi did."

She leaned closer and the floral notes of her perfume surrounded Ariana like a friend's embrace. "But don't tell her I said that." Delilah's doe-like brown eyes twinkled.

"Oh, never," Ariana agreed in a conspiratorial whisper.

Delilah grinned. "Now let's get out of this ugly armor and see what Percy's made for us to eat. I wanted to ask you about the masquerade balls you attended."

"Of course." Ariana felt herself smile in response. Delilah was full of questions about court. What gowns were being worn, what food was being eaten, what dances were being done.

From what Ariana had gathered, Delilah had spent her life dreaming of attending court. While she finally had made it there, something had prevented her from staying very long.

Ariana was sure it was the reason she was now at Kindrochit.

They were both almost out of their padding when the clangs of a weapon against steel rang out, sharp and in quick succession.

Delilah's head jerked up and her mouth fell open.

Ariana plucked the last tie of her armor loose and looked up toward where Sylvi and Connor were training.

Sylvi was a bolt of lightning, lithe and fast, striking at Connor, making him step back and back and back. She moved with such haste, Ariana would never have been able to keep up with her. But Connor matched the speed of her blows, smooth and graceful.

"Teach me what he taught ye." Sylvi's voice exploded from her with the same force as her blows. "Ye know how to kill and ye willna show me." Her strikes matched her words, which were heavy with a rough lilt Ariana had never noticed in her speech.

Tension snapped in the air and alarm jolted down Ariana's spine.

Delilah uttered a soft curse and ran toward the two with Ariana following closely behind, but they both stopped short against the whipping of Sylvi's blade.

"Sylvi, stop this," Delilah hissed.

But Sylvi did not stop. Her blade lashed out at Connor, but he blocked it with his own.

"Ye dinna know what ye ask for." Connor parried and ducked smoothly.

Ariana's body tensed watching the two. Connor was strong, yes, but Sylvi had never been so out of control, so reckless.

"And ye dinna know what I saw. I want to kill them, every last one of them." Sylvi's bellowed words were raw with unmistakable pain, her attacks blind and wild. "Ye never knew what I had to endure to be here. Ye'll never understand."

Connor leapt at her then, like a cat descending on its prey. He dodged the flash of her sword and slammed her back to the ground, where he pinned her.

The breath was pulled from Ariana's chest, but she forced herself to stay where she was.

"I understand far more than ye think," he said in a low growl. "Killing them willna make the pain go away. Nothing will ever make the pain go away. That is what ye need to understand before ye're ready."

There was something unguarded in his voice, something hoarse and hurt. Ariana knew she should turn away from the exchange, but found she could not.

Sylvi glared up at Connor. "My Lady never would have held back."

He scoffed. "Ye'd be even more heartless if ye'd been under her this whole time." He shoved off of Sylvi. "If this continues, or if I see one more of the girls with another injury from yer rage, ye're gone."

Delilah gasped and ran toward Sylvi, mumbling something to her in soft words.

Sylvi's ribbon lay crooked on her neck and revealed a bit of smooth pink skin beneath. A scar?

Connor stalked off across the field to where the shadows left the grass tipped with fuzzy white frost.

Ariana stood awkwardly for a moment, unsure where to go, what to do. And then, before she could think on it further, she chased after Connor.

He stood with his hands on his hips and his head lowered.

"Ye dinna need to check on me," he said. "I dinna lose control so easily."

"I know you don't." Ariana stepped closer. "You were there for my heavy thoughts. I'd like to be here for yours."

He turned toward her. His face was grim, a tired line etched deep in the center of his forehead. "Lass, if only ye knew how heavy my thoughts truly were."

She reached out and touched his shoulder. The muscle there was impossibly hard, his flesh hot beneath the thin fabric of his léine.

"You could tell me." She said it softly, half hoping he would hear her sincerity, half hoping he might not, lest he think her a foolish girl.

He stared down at her, and though he said nothing and kept his face impassive, something in his eyes burned deep to the pit of her own burdened soul. And she welcomed it as readily as he'd welcomed her words the night before.

She moved her hand from his shoulder, her action thoughtless and automatic, and touched his cheek. His whiskers prickled against her palm.

He closed his eyes.

Brazen and breathless, she curled her fingers slightly to caress the hard line of his jaw. He swallowed and opened his eyes once more before wrapping his warm hand around her wrist.

His gaze lowered to her lips.

Ariana's pulse ticked faster and heat rose in her cheeks.

But he pulled her hand from his face and unfurled his fingers from her wrist. "Ye have lessons to attend."

Ariana nodded mutely and turned from him with great hesitation. But it was not pity tugging at Ariana's heart as she left him in the darkness of his own shadows—it was then she knew he understood pain so much better than she'd realized.

Connor, for all his bravery and strength and all the women he'd saved, was just as broken as her.

Chapter Eight

Connor waited until he'd passed over the stone bridge above River Clunie before urging his horse into a full run. The wind shoved at them, its merciless edge leaving a burning cold sensation tingling at his face.

He welcomed it.

Let it numb his flesh and erase the memory of Ariana's touch.

God, but her touch had been sweet.

And he did not deserve it.

Where he was everything evil and wrong, she was everything innocent and right. Even her downfall from court had been born out of necessity.

Her gaze lured him with the promise that somehow just holding her, kissing her, would make him feel right—if only for one blissful moment.

He tightened his grip on the reins until his muscles ached and he rode as hard and as fast as possible to clear his mind of Ariana.

Only when he saw the small gray frame of the nunnery did he begin to slow. It had been the perfect place to put Cora, nearby enough to see her, and remote enough to not warrant many visitors. While he would have liked to have placed her in a wealthier convent, the poorer ones were more likely to escape notice.

As Connor made his way up the narrow trail leading to the entrance, a man on a large white destrier emerged from the small courtyard. He did not seem to notice Connor.

But Connor noticed him.

Wild, dark hair and a familiar face now lined with the effects of age and war… Angus MacAlister.

And within the walls of the abbey, where Cora was supposedly safe.

Fear gripped Connor in a chilling embrace.

He forced his pounding heart to slow and did a careful sweep of the courtyard, seeking evidence of nearby warriors waiting to ambush. Seeing none, he eased his boots from the stirrups of his horse for easy dismount. Just in case.

But there were no other warriors. Not that he could see… None hidden in the shadows, no fearful-looking nuns attempting to continue in their duties in a rigid pass at appearing normal.

Surely MacAlister would not travel without a retinue.

Connor leapt from his horse and handed the limp reins to an aging nun he'd seen before. "Where is she?"

The nun turned her head toward the small garden. "Where she always is."

Connor nodded a stiff thanks and stalked toward the large plot of dirt where a pathetic show of plants coiled low to the warmth of the ground.

Every scenario spiraled through his mind, each one ending in the garden absent the one person in the world who mattered most to him.

But no—there, safe, and kneeling in the dark soil, was his sister.

Relief washed over him with such poignancy, it threatened to choke him.

"Cora." It came out strained, but saying her name, seeing her safe, all of it eased the spike of fear jammed into his heart.

She looked up, then jumped to her feet and ran toward Connor as she'd done when she was a girl, arms wide and with fearless speed.

He caught her before she could slam into him and squeezed her in so fierce an embrace it lifted her feet from the ground.

But if MacAlister hadn't taken Cora, then why the hell had he been there?

Connor set Cora on her feet and tried not to stare too hard at her. "What was MacAlister doing here?"

She brushed some dirt from Connor's jacket and only succeeded in smearing more into the wool. "Who?"

She wasn't looking at him, which made it impossible to tell if she was lying or not. Which she well knew.

"MacAlister," Connor repeated. "The man who just left."

Cora gave a nonchalant shrug. "I dinna know a MacAlister."

Connor's insides tightened. With fear, and frustration, and rage, and all those helpless feelings he'd discussed the very night before.

"How did he find ye? How did he know ye were here?" Connor clenched his fists at his sides in an effort to control his desperate, protective anger.

"I dinna know what ye're talking about." The warm happiness cooled from her eyes and an angry line showed between her brows. "Ye finally come here and ye want to accuse me of something?"

Cora never got angry, unless she was feeling defensive.

"I'm accusing ye because I see it in yer eyes. I see it in the way ye're acting now. Ye're lying and I know it."

A gust of wind shoved her hair into her face. She pushed it back and crossed her arms over her chest, mute.

"Ye were there that day, Cora," Connor said, trying to keep his voice level. "Ye saw what they did to Da. Ye know what they almost did to ye."

Cora closed her eyes slowly, as if the action pained her, and nodded. "I know," she said.

"There could be others still seeking us out." She looked so small with her petulant stance, and he was reminded of when she'd been such a wee, innocent thing. Like the time he'd told her she couldn't follow him around all the time, and she'd put her fists on her hips, declaring she only did it because she loved him.

Pulled toward her by such memories, he put his arms around her and hugged her to his chest.

Her hair smelled soft and sweet, like chamomile flowers, the same as it always had. The familiarity warmed him. "I keep ye here so ye'll be safe."

She pushed away from him, and the warmth they'd shared went cold. "But what is a life that isna being lived? I havena any friends. I have ye, aye, the few times ye come to visit. Look at me, Connor."

She'd once been a proud laird's daughter in fine clothes, a happy girl with a ready smile on her lips. But her gown was a dull brown, muddy with black dirt from where she'd knelt on the ground. There were lines on her face he'd never seen before, and the glint of her eyes had faded.

Even the gleam of her hair was not as he remembered.

Like all of the life was draining from her.

She looked like Liv.

His heart went heavy.

"I canna let ye die like Da," he said softly.

"And yet ye canna let me live," she replied.

He knew what she wanted—placement in a castle where she could be restored to her former glory. Hell, Connor wanted that too. But it wasn't safe.

Perhaps he might be able to find another abbey, one with more wealth. "I'll find ye another place," he conceded. "If ye tell me why MacAlister was here."

She gave a hard smile—an expression he'd never seen cross her sweet face. "Another abbey, I'm sure," she said. "Where I'll be safe." The last word was cold and brittle.

Desperation tightened Connor's chest. "I need to know why he was here. I need to know who else has been here."

Damn it, there was a reason MacAlister's name had come to him, why the king wanted him dead.

What the hell had Cora gotten herself into?

She looked up at him. "No one else has come, and no one else knows I'm here. I'll say no more."

Her face was open and honest. And characteristically stubborn. He'd never get the reason for MacAlister's visit from her. The realization was like a blade being driven into his gut.

Connor reached for her, but she stepped away from him and grabbed a sack from where it lay propped against the fence. The clink of tools sounded from within.

Their visit was done.

He didn't want it to be. He wanted to make this right, to promise she could live a life with fine gowns and a home and a clan again. He wanted to see the gleam of happiness in her eyes and the smile restored to her face.

But he was helpless to do so.

Seven more years.

"I only want to see ye safe," he said. "I love ye, Cora."

She slid him a look from the corners of her eyes. "Just go."

Then she turned her back and walked away.

He waited until she had sunk to her knees in the dirt and begun working before he turned away. Why he waited, he had no idea.

Perhaps for her to turn to him, to be grateful for the dismal position he was leaving her in.

Perhaps for her to tell him she loved him with the same exuberance she had when they were children.

But they weren't children anymore, and the life they knew then, all the safety and happiness and wealth, had been shattered. He'd clearly done a shoddy job of repairing it.

The abbess approached him as he emerged into the courtyard.

"Good day, laird." She nodded respectfully.

He hardened his heart against the title, the one that had once been his. The woman insisted on calling him laird out of respect for his father.

"How did MacAlister find her?" he asked.

The nun straightened, clearly affronted by his curt tone.

"She's supposed to be safe here," he said, more softly. "Yet I see a man leaving. How did this come to be?"

"By accident." Her thin mouth turned downward in a slight frown. "She was in the garden when he came to see about a place for a cousin of his. He has come to visit several times and..." The old woman tapered off.

"And?" Connor said with measured patience.

The lines of her face crumpled deeper in a heartfelt look of sympathy. "And I hate seeing her youth and vibrancy fade here. She's happy after she sees him, aye? He's an ally to my clan, and a good man."

Connor drew in a slow, deep breath. "Ye're to keep her safe."

"I would no' ever do otherwise." She pushed her gnarled hand against his and something warm and heavy settled against his palm. "I have this for ye too."

He looked down to find a gold signet ring shining in his palm, the etched burning hill more deeply grooved than he remembered. It'd been three years since last he saw this ring.

It had been collateral for the coin he sent every month to see Cora safe. He'd been saving to buy it back and had almost accumulated enough to do so.

"I kept it for ye, like ye asked." The nun said. "MacAlister has been sending coin for her. I think he intends to marry her."

She smiled then, so widely it bared her fragile teeth and all the hope for goodwill only a nun could possess.

But Connor was not smiling. The insult was a slap in the face. "Had I no' been sending enough?"

"Nay, it's been fine. But he wants to see her in fine gowns."

Fine gowns garnered attention. And attention did not always come from good places. And sure as hell not from MacAlister.

The nun's face fell. "Forgive me, I'd sent a message and dinna hear back. I assumed ye were fine with it."

"There was no message," Connor said. "She's to see no one but me."

The nun nodded, but he did not miss how her shoulders slumped.

The time had come to move Cora from the small abbey.

And the time had come to kill MacAlister.

• • •

Ariana knelt in front of the door with a narrow tool in her hand, seemingly too small for her task.

Still, she held her breath to keep her fingers from trembling with nerves, and slipped the pick into the dark cavern of the lock.

The bit of metal moved blindly inside. She traced the outline of the invisible parts within, seeking out the little latch Delilah had described.

Sweat prickled at Ariana's brow despite the cool room.

Where was the latch?

She moved the piece carefully once more, pressing harder this time.

Something gave, just the slightest bit.

But it was enough.

She tightened her fingertips on the pick, sacrificing dexterity for strength, and pushed.

A victorious click sounded from the large metal lock. Ariana tried the handle and the door swung open with ease. Delilah sat on a bench within the room, fingers buried in her thick light brown tresses.

She gave a mock pout. "I didn't even get to finish plaiting my hair." The pout gave way to a wide grin. "That was fast."

A shadow fell over Ariana.

"Connor wants to see us in his solar." Sylvi's brisk tone sounded over Ariana's head.

Ariana looked up in time to see the other woman stalking down the hall. Sylvi's shoulders were squared out like a warrior's, and the small braids framing her face had been twisted into a mass of blonde hair at the back of her head.

Delilah raked a hand through the beginnings of her own braid, which slipped free and left her hair falling around her shoulders like a silk curtain. "Connor probably has a mission for us."

Ariana's stomach did a little flip. Two months of training and now she might finally use what she had been learning. Her heart thudded a little faster.

Delilah got up from the bench and took the pick from Ariana. "Put that in your hair and we'll put it up after we go see Connor."

"In my hair?" Ariana asked.

Delilah took the pick from her hands, folded it in half, and handed it back.

It did resemble a hairpin. The side where Ariana had held her thumb earlier was etched with a series of whorls and flowers. She slid it into her hair with the patterned side out.

Delilah adjusted it slightly and smiled. "Perfect. Percy really is amazing with her creations."

Before Ariana could ask more, Delilah caught her hand in hers and pulled her toward Connor's solar. Not that Ariana needed pulling. It was all she could do to not run up there.

This...this was what she'd been waiting for.

And yet curiosity dragged her back.

"What happened with Sylvi at practice today?" she asked, giving voice to the question wearing a hole in her mind.

Delilah stopped, but did not drop Ariana's hand. "Sylvi is very different from us. She..." Delilah pursed her lips. "She is here because she found out about the woman who used to do what we now all do together, before Connor came here and found us to aid him. Sylvi wanted to learn."

"Why?" Ariana whispered to keep her voice from carrying through the pitted stone walls of the hall.

Delilah's eyes went wide, making them appear all the more like a fawn's—overlarge, deep brown, and fringed with thick black lashes. "It's horrible, Ariana. Her entire family was killed. The men who killed them tried to kill her too, they slit her throat, but they must not have gone deep enough. She heard and saw *everything*."

The horror of it flashed through Ariana's mind, staining her thoughts with an image she didn't want to see. An image she could not imagine ever witnessing. Even though she hadn't had a strong connection to her family, the idea of seeing them murdered in front of her and being unable to help them—it was too much.

Her stomach twisted at the very idea.

It all made sense now.

The way Sylvi had acted at practice and her drive to kill. She wanted vengeance.

And somehow Connor had already had his.

By the time they arrived in Connor's solar, Sylvi was already there, standing by the fire with her arms crossed over her chest. The black ribbon gleamed, reflecting the firelight.

It made sense now too, the ribbon, and what she now knew for certain what it covered.

A scar.

A reminder.

Ariana's heart squeezed in empathy.

Connor stood on the other end of the hearth in a mirror image of serious contemplation. He didn't speak until the door was closed.

"We need to go out and gather some information." There was a heaviness to his tone Ariana hadn't heard before. "We're looking for a man named Angus MacAlister and his retinue. There are several nearby towns where he could be."

"Is there any information we need to listen for specifically?" Delilah asked.

The muscle in Connor's jaw flexed. "Aye, if ye hear anything about a lass in a nunnery being wed. And, of course, the usual treasonous activity. The man moves fast. We'll need to head out tonight."

He nodded toward Delilah. "Ye go with Sylvi to the east toward Castleton, I'll take the west toward Auchendryne."

Ariana waited for her orders, but they did not come. Suddenly she felt like an outsider standing in a conversation not meant for her ears.

"And what of me?" she asked.

Connor's gaze flicked over at her. "Ye're no' coming."

Indignation jerked her back ramrod straight. "I've been training for two months now. I can do this."

Delilah stepped forward. "She can. And you know I wouldn't speak up if I didn't believe it."

Connor's forefinger tapped against his bicep where his arms

were folded. He was quiet for a long moment. "Verra well, but ye come with me so I can keep an eye on ye, and if ye slow me down, I'll send ye back."

Ariana's heart tamped out an erratic beat and her cheeks went hot with excitement.

She was going on a mission.

"Of course," Ariana replied with measured calm.

He stared at her a moment more and his finger tapped a few more times. "We'll do taverns tonight. Get some food in ye and ready yerselves. We leave within the hour."

Chapter Nine

Ariana and Connor stepped into what appeared to be the middle of a dark forest.

Connor led the horses to a crude stable, secured them, and closed the door. "We'll have a ways to walk, but at least we willna have to worry about the horses."

Whether he'd built the stable after years of coming to the small town or had happened upon it at some point, Ariana did not know, and it seemed a pointless thing to ask.

She pulled the velvet drawstring bag from her pocket and let her fingers sift through the lumps of the three vials within, all from Percy.

The shortest one for masking the color of her eyes, the long, slender one for making a man appear more drunk than he was, and a round stoppered one if she found herself in a situation she could not escape.

She had been warned enough times about the last one to make her hesitant to even touch it.

Careful not to loosen her blonde wig, Ariana leaned her head back and poured a drop or two from the shortest vial into her eyes.

The liquid stung slightly and her eyes welled with tears. She blinked until the sensation ceased. A heaviness warmed over her vision.

Connor secured a ragged coat atop a pair of trews and a stained léine. His hair was mussed and somehow he'd managed to black out a front bottom tooth.

The effect was startling. Never would she have recognized him.

"Do I appear as different as you?" she asked in Gaelic. He'd insisted on it since they left. For practice, he'd said.

Fortunately for her, she'd picked up the difficult language with ease. Her parents' attempts to match her to a wealthy man had included rigorous lessons. She'd had to learn several languages in anticipation of the husband who never came.

Connor looked down at her, studying her face.

Delilah had taken care to line her eyes with kohl and put a smear of carmine on her lips and cheeks. The way most wenches wore their faces at night, she'd said.

"I'd no' ever recognize ye in a thousand years," he said.

She nodded, relieved.

She was even more relieved when her wig stayed locked in place despite the movement.

"The town isna far." He nodded to the west, where lights glowed through the trees. "When we get to the clearing, ye go first. We'll be going to a tavern called the Lamb's Tail Inn, aye? It's the busiest in the area and it will be full."

Ariana's pulse skipped and raced a little faster.

This was it.

"I remember," she said.

He smiled and rubbed his thumb over her cheek. "Ye'll do fine, lass."

The affection took her aback, but before she could react, he'd already turned and begun walking through the wet forest. She followed suit and repeated in her mind what she was to do: Enter the Lamb's Tail Inn and make her way through the crowd. Talk and flirt, but without intent, until Connor arrived and could point her in the right direction.

It was an easy enough task.

All too soon, Ariana found herself at the clearing and stepped out on her own. The weight of Connor's gaze settled over her back like a sable mantle on a cold day.

There was a slight tiredness to her eyes from the tincture she'd put in them, and the low lights from the taverns she passed seemed overly bright.

Several men stared as she passed, openly and lewdly.

Her breath came harder in her nervousness, but she forced it to slow.

Men had never stared at her so. She had always been a lady and warranted respect, but she did not appear a lady now. Not with the carmine painting her lips or the way her cloak lay open to reveal the exceedingly low-cut bodice beneath.

Several men loitered outside a dingy white building, leaning against the walls and several barrels set in the thick mud. The sign above the establishment indicated it was the Lamb's Tail Inn.

A bald man grinned at her. "Can I get ye somethin' to slake yer thirst, lady?"

She forced a little laugh and waved him off, answering back in Gaelic. "I haven't even made it in yet."

His hard lean against the barrel did not indicate he'd be moving from it anytime soon. "Ach, maybe on yer way out then?"

"Mayhap." She spoke in a lowered voice, trying for a husky timbre. With a wink, she pushed through the door and was met with the heat and odor of at least a hundred bodies. Her breath clogged in her throat, and she fumbled with the clasp at her neck a moment before liberating the latch.

Sweat prickled at her scalp beneath the wig. Where outside it had been so cool, inside was like standing near a blacksmith's forge. She swept the cloak from her shoulders and slung it over a peg on the wall.

The scent of stale beer was pungent in the thick, greasy air, but she forced herself further inside. Large wooden tables filled the room, and bodies crowded side by side upon the benches. With the barmaid navigating the narrow aisles, it would be almost impossible to move.

Connor had been right. It was indeed busy.

A woman with two pints in hand aggressively pushed her way between two men and threw a comment over her shoulder. They laughed and one swatted her on the bottom.

Ariana followed suit and forced a path through the crowd.

A hand caught at her arm. "I've always liked a fair-haired lass."

She looked down to find an impossibly large man with black hair holding her. He gave her a friendly smile. "I havena seen ye here."

"I'm just passing through," Ariana said in Gaelic.

"Why dinna ye sit beside me?"

She looked at the crowded bench. "There isn't room."

He grasped the back of the man's léine beside him and jerked him upright. Beer sprayed from the hapless man's mouth and he staggered backward into the bench behind them.

Laughter rose up from the nearby tables.

"And now there is," said the large man.

"Aye, but only for a moment." Ariana sank into the newly available spot.

Out of the corner of her eye, she watched for the man who had been vacated from his seat. The men on the other bench made room for him and he slunk down into the narrow gap.

A hand landed on her thigh.

Her upper thigh.

She jerked her attention to the large man and found him staring intently at her. "Ye're a bonny lass." He grinned beneath his full beard. "And I'd like ye for more than a moment."

A little warning tapped at the back of her mind and suddenly she found herself grateful for all the training she'd done with Delilah. No matter how powerful this man before her was, her skills at manipulation were stronger.

The door opened and in walked a beggar with shaggy hair and one missing tooth.

No one noticed his arrival.

No one but Ariana.

Yes, it was good she knew how to pry herself from this man.

Something told her she'd need to do it soon.

• • •

It was almost impossible not to stare at Ariana.

Connor navigated the narrow aisle between the benches, the backs on either side so close they brushed his body as he passed.

Despite how often he tried to force his gaze to those he passed, he found it repeatedly returning to Ariana.

Not that it mattered.

He was hardly the only one.

True, she'd worn the same low-cut gown as any other tavern wench did, and Delilah had covered Ariana's natural beauty with smears of carmine and rice powder as they did, but she was not one of them.

Her beauty shone like a candle in a dark room and her confidence burned even brighter.

She was the kind of woman men couldn't help but want.

And it made something inside Connor want to fight every damn one of them.

Conversations buzzed around him, and only then did he realize he hadn't been paying attention to what was being said.

He'd been too distracted.

He gritted his back teeth.

They'd be there all night if he didn't focus, and the last thing he wanted was to keep Ariana in the ring of all these men.

He skulked through the crowd, head lowered with a gait meant to suggest he'd already had a few pints of ale before his arrival. A man no one noticed despite his upturned hand in a show of begging coin. He shuffled his way down the long lines of tables, listening intently to every word spoken, sifting through what was useless and what held potential.

"Aye, I hear she's a fine one," a man said on Connor's right. "The kind of lass that shouldna be in a convent."

Connor moved closer and tried to listen when Ariana's soft laughter sounded behind him.

He turned, slight enough to be imperceptible, but enough to see the man's hand resting on Ariana's inner thigh.

Rage heated Connor's body, leaving him boiling beneath the

thick cloak he wore. A cool coin pressed into his palm, pulling at his attention once more.

"And why's the lass in a convent?" asked another voice in the same conversation.

"I think it's her brother who's put her there."

Connor's heartbeat thundered in his ears.

Ariana's back was only several feet away. Her flimsy sleeve had slipped from its place and revealed the delicate curve of her shoulder, her flesh flawless and naked.

He felt the sudden urge to trail the pad of his middle finger over the graceful line arching from her neck to her arm, but instead placed his hand fully upon her.

The skin beneath his palm was warm and soft.

"The men behind ye were generous." He spoke in a cracking, aged voice. He knew Ariana would understand he meant for her to get information from them. "Would ye be so as well, lovely lass?"

The large man beside Ariana grabbed Connor's wrist and flung his hand from her. "Dinna touch her, ye filthy lout."

Connor measured the man in a quick glance: an overly sure beast who would be taken down easily.

Ariana lay her hand in a graceful gesture on the man's chest. "We must be kind to those less fortunate." She rose from the bench and he stiffened.

"Where are ye going?" he demanded.

Ariana continued to rise. "To see if the other table will aid me in helping to buy a meal for this poor man, of course."

"If I kill him, he won't need to eat."

Connor fought to suppress an eye roll at the arrogant show.

The man's hand wrapped around Ariana's wrist and Connor's body went tight, his muscles ready to spring into a fight. Connor knew men like the one holding Ariana now. They did as they wanted, they took what they wanted. They did not accept no as an answer.

"Tut tut," she admonished gently. "Surely you aren't afraid I won't come back." Her tone was coy.

She leaned toward the man's ear and said a few words before

easily extracting herself from his grip. She left with little more than a wink and received not a word of protest.

Whatever the hell it was Delilah was teaching, she knew what she was doing.

Ariana had no trouble finding a place among the men who'd been speaking of the nunnery, and within minutes, Connor was set against a rear table with a plate full of steaming food.

Once more, she was magnificent, like she'd been at the card tables months ago. The men leaned toward her, like budding plants stretching toward the heat of the morning sun. But despite their eagerness, she kept herself at a distance with flirtatious reprimands and witty somethings that left the table all laughing at one red-faced man.

A mug of ale settled before Connor. He tore his gaze from Ariana and found a barmaid standing beside him, her breasts sagging in her half-laced bodice like a tired sigh.

"The barkeep thought ye'd want something to wash yer food down with."

Connor nodded his thanks and turned back to the table, mug halfway to his mouth.

He stopped short of putting it to his lips, and his heart punched down into his stomach.

One of the men from the table was missing, and so was Ariana.

Chapter Ten

Ariana had never followed a man to his room before.

The stocky form in front of her stumbled his way up the narrow flight of stairs to the row of rooms above. Already he swayed on his feet.

Percy's vial had worked quickly.

"Are you well, Cuthbert?" Ariana asked innocently.

He straightened. "Ach, aye." His brows furrowed with a concentration his eyes could not seem to match.

Perhaps she had given him too much from the slender vial. Percy hadn't specified an amount.

If nothing else, Ariana hoped he'd make it to the room and she wouldn't have to guess which was his.

He staggered toward a door with heavy feet and managed to unlock it in a series of bumps and scraping shuffles. She followed him inside and the odor of stale rushes filled her nose. Still, it was a reprieve from the overwhelming stench of too many bodies below.

Cuthbert hiccupped. "Join me on the bed." His words were so slurred, Ariana had to pause a moment to even decipher them.

She made a humming, acquiescent sound and closed the door.

The thud of his body upon the small bed was followed by a deep, even snoring. She let the breath she'd been holding whoosh out. Perfect timing.

Quick as she dared, she made her way to the simple table by the window and opened the shutter to allow the moonlight to cast its glow upon the papers there.

A gust of wind swept in and she found herself gulping down

a lungful of pure, delicious air. The rush of desperation racing through her veins calmed and she was once more able to focus.

A snort from the bed lanced through the serenity and set Ariana's heart pounding once more.

She froze and looked back at him.

He did not move.

She fingered the outline of the round bottle in her skirt pocket, reassuring herself of its presence, even if she was not much inclined to put it to use.

A sharp breeze swept in and brushed several papers to the floor. Ariana scooped them up and leaned over the desk, ever mindful to listen for a break in the even, sawing snores behind her.

The heavy sensation in her eyes had not bothered her downstairs once she'd grown accustomed to the light. Now though, no matter how hard she squinted or craned her neck over the page, the slanting words blurred.

She held the parchment farther away and could make out the larger of the letters.

Land was evident on one, a name she did not recognize on another, marriage on yet another.

Her heart beat a little faster.

This was why she'd followed him up. The scribe snoring in the bed had bragged about drafting a marriage contract for the girl in the nunnery.

Despite the ale consumed, they'd all been guarded in their speech. No names were mentioned.

Ariana stretched her arm in front of her in an attempt to read the name and could make out nothing.

Her fingers tensed on the parchment.

She could take it. Read it later.

Surely then the man would know she'd stolen from him and would be on the lookout for her.

But then, she was disguised.

She folded it quickly, before her guilt got the better of her.

The heavy parchment crackled in her hands. She shoved it into her bodice.

The man would no doubt pay the price for the missing document. She winced at the thought and almost pulled it from her bodice once more.

But she did not.

This was her first mission and she would not fail.

She opened the window wider and the mid-May night air rushed in with its usual frigid chill and lifted several sheets of paper from the desk. They scattered across the floor in haphazard piles.

Perfect.

It all looked very natural, just as the missing page would.

Or so she hoped.

Then, before the sleeping man could possibly have a chance to wake, Ariana slipped into the hall.

The paper against her breast was stiff, and the corners bit into her tender flesh, as if punishing her for her misdeed.

She pushed aside the weight of her own guilt and made her way down the empty corridor toward the stairs. A quick glance over the railing confirmed Cuthbert's friends still occupied the table.

An oath she'd heard Sylvi once say burned hot in her throat.

Surely they would question why Ariana returned without their friend.

Something warm covered her mouth and nose and a solid wall of a body stood at her back.

Ariana's heart leapt to life, thundering in her chest.

She'd been caught.

• • •

It was obvious Connor had surprised Ariana.

He kept his hand over her mouth to keep her from crying out. The last thing they needed was more attention.

Her body tightened and something sharp jabbed into his ribs, so hard and fast it caught his breath. He relaxed his hand and Ariana spun around, knife in hand.

He'd underestimated how well she'd done in her training.

Connor held his arms up in surrender despite the pain in his ribs where her hit had landed.

Recognition passed over her face and she relaxed her stance. He held a finger to his lips before she could say anything.

Relief washed the tension from his muscles.

He knew he'd find her, of course. He just wasn't sure what predicament she might be in.

What the hell had she been thinking, disappearing up here?

And who the hell had been in the room with her?

Connor waved for her to follow him and led her toward the narrow stairs the staff used. The floorboards squeaked under her footsteps.

He'd need to teach her how to walk without sound.

For next time.

His chest tightened uncomfortably and he realized he didn't want there to be another time when she might be at risk.

He wrestled the thought away. This was what she had been brought in to do.

The aging stairs swayed slightly beneath them, but in a quick moment, they were in a darkened alleyway. Outside, the air was thick with the threat of rain and left the odor of rotting food heavy around them.

A surreptitious glance confirmed they were alone. Connor pulled Ariana's cloak from his shirt and handed it to her.

"What the hell were ye thinking?" he whispered harshly.

He should have waited until they were in the woods, but the thought had been singed into his mind the whole damn time she'd been gone.

She took her cloak from him and pulled it over her shoulders. "How did you get this?"

He'd stolen it, like any other beggar would have considering where she left it, but that wasn't what he wanted to discuss.

And here was not the place to discuss any of it.

The deep baritone of several male voices sounded on the street outside the alley, their only exit.

"Lean on me and act drunk," Connor said.

A lazy smile lilted over Ariana's lips and her lids slid a little lower over the wild blackness of her eyes, where her pupils covered the beautiful blue-green—an effect from the tincture to further mask her identity.

She sagged against his proffered arm and her delicate, fresh scent teased at his senses despite the putrid stench of the alley. Though he was not a tall man, her head rested just below his shoulder, and he had to put his other arm around her waist to keep her secure against him.

Together they walked onto the street. Try though he might, he could not ignore how the curve of her hip moved in a graceful swaying motion under his hand.

What he could at least ignore was the way he wanted to trace her shape with his fingers, with the sensitive flat of his palm—down her slender back to the dip of her waist and the rounded swell of—

He swallowed hard and focused on the street in front of them.

Seventeen.

There were seventeen men and one woman in view. Most in front of the Lamb's Tail Inn.

Connor steered Ariana from the inn, toward the edge of town. Urgency pressed at his back. While it was a sensation he never ignored, he wondered how much it had to do with a possible threat and how much it had to do with Ariana.

The crunch of coarse sand sounded under someone's boot nearby.

Behind them.

Connor didn't turn to look, instead he nudged Ariana toward the nearest wall and pushed her back toward it with his own body.

She moved with him, allowing him to shift her as if she were drunk, even letting her feet stumble slightly.

He pressed himself against her as lovers might do, holding her upright and shielding her all at once. They faced one another, chest to very exposed, very tempting breast.

Ariana stared up at him in the darkness, her gaze locked on his, her lips parted, her chest rising and falling.

His gaze lowered to the lush shape of her mouth and his breath came a little faster.

He could kiss her.

The thought came quickly and was altogether too damn tempting.

That was when he realized he'd forgotten the footsteps.

That was when he realized he'd stopped paying attention.

That was when something hard and heavy slammed against the side of his head.

Chapter Eleven

Ariana bit back a scream.

Connor did not fall from his place in front of her despite the hard hit, but he didn't move either.

The large man behind him, the one who'd struck him, was the man she'd first sat next to at the inn.

"Ye said ye'd be back." His words came out in a low growl. "And I find ye out here wi' him."

The handle of her blade was hot in Ariana's palm and now she was grateful for having not slipped it back in its sheath.

Connor's head lolled, and a cold tightness gripped her heart.

The other man was too big. One solid hit and he might actually kill Connor.

"Ach, I drank too much," Ariana said, slurring her words. "I thought I met ye last night. Was that this night then?" She squinted at the man.

Connor still was not responding.

Ariana steeled herself with determination.

She would defend him.

"Aye, it was tonight," the man said, and leered down at her. "And I intend to have ye fulfill yer promise."

His large hands fell on Connor's shoulders and spun him around.

Before Ariana's heart could even lurch, Connor came to life.

He thrust up with the heel of his hand under the man's chin, snapping his head upward. Connor kicked out at his opponent's chest and delivered a sharp blow with his elbow to the man's temple.

The large attacker fell to the ground with a great and heavy *whump*.

And did not move.

Ariana stared in shock. Connor's movements had been so smooth, so fast. She'd never in her life seen a person move with a grace so sleek, so lethal.

A shout sounded from somewhere near the inn.

Connor grabbed her hand. "Follow me and keep to the shadows. We dinna have much time before he wakes."

So, the man was not dead after all. She realized then her shoulders had crept closer to her ears with tension.

While she was glad the man was incapacitated, she certainly had not wanted him dead.

She wanted to glance back at him one more time to confirm for herself, but Connor was already ahead of her and moving quickly. Faster than the sound of the footsteps approaching them.

Ariana pulled her hood over her face and slipped into the darkened alcoves of the shops and homes, skimming her body against the coarse walls as Connor did before her.

Her feet, she noticed, were not as quiet, no matter how hard she tried to let her shoes land softly against the ground.

Connor was quick and silent, like he'd been during the attack. This was a different man than she had ever seen in the course of their training.

The shouts of concern behind them had died down, and though no one gave chase, neither Connor nor Ariana slowed.

The buildings became more spaced out and the shadows broadened.

They were almost free.

Ariana's breath came in smooth, even huffs, the same as when she ran in the morning. Now she understood the true purpose of incorporating the activity into their warm up.

The gravelly sand of the village gave way to soft grass, and both she and Connor opened into a full sprint to the tree line.

They did not stop until they reached the crude stable among the trees.

Ariana's breath did not come so smoothly now. With each ragged gasp of breath, the folded parchment at her breast jabbed against her skin until they reached the makeshift stable.

They readied their horses without speaking. Connor's face held a tight expression and he did not once look at her. The silence thickened between them.

Though she willed it not to, realization swelled ugly and heavy in her chest.

He was disappointed.

In her.

• • •

The impatient edge Connor had worked so hard to smooth was now jagged and hot.

Ariana had put herself in danger, and almost compromised the mission with her impulsive decision to follow the man upstairs.

"What the hell were ye thinking?" he asked for the second time.

"I did nothing wrong." Her defense was simply stated and without the pitch of a whine.

He expected nothing less.

Still, he slowed his horse and looked hard at the woman who spoke with such clear confidence.

Moonlight washed over Ariana, casting a bluish sheen over the blonde hair of the wig and leaving her fair skin glowing like a pearl. Even though she wore the attire of a tavern wench, she kept her back straight like a highborn noble.

Damn it, she was beautiful.

"Nothing wrong?" he countered. "Why did ye go upstairs with the man?"

"Cuthbert." She slowed her own horse, but did not stop, so he was forced to urge his forward once more.

"What?"

"His name was Cuthbert."

Rage simmered inside Connor, like a kettle of water near boiling. He didn't want to know the fool's name.

He counted a slow, steady stream of numbers in his head in an attempt to gather patience. "Why did ye go upstairs with Cuthbert?" he asked in a level tone.

Ariana tilted her chin indignantly. "You asked me to find information on a nunnery. I went to the men you'd indicated and found they were indeed speaking of a woman trapped in a nunnery. Cuthbert was none other than the scribe who had drawn up her newly contracted marriage negotiation."

Marriage negotiation.

The words punched him low in the gut.

The old nun he'd spoken to had mentioned MacAlister's interest in marrying Cora.

Connor squeezed the reins in his hand until the leather strap pressed hard into his palms.

Perhaps it was true, then.

"I tried to get them to say the woman's name," Ariana continued. "They would not. I slipped Percy's vial into Cuthbert's drink, waited until he appeared drunk, then I lured him upstairs." She gave Connor a long, considering stare before adding in a gentle voice, "I did everything I was trained to do."

He shifted in his saddle, agitated by his own ire. She'd done what she was expected to—exactly the sort of thing Delilah and Sylvi did regularly.

"And what did ye find?" he asked.

Ariana reached into her bodice and pulled a folded square of parchment. "I believe it's a marriage contract. I tried to read it, but the words kept blurring."

Connor took the document from her. "Aye, the tincture Percy gave ye. We dinna expect ye'd be needing to read anything at a tavern."

His heartbeat came faster, more desperate, with each section of the parchment he unfolded.

It was indeed a marriage contract.

His gaze fell to the two names and the tension bled out from his shoulders.

He didn't recognize either name. Which meant the bride was not to be Cora.

Ariana watched him expectantly.

A whip of frustration lashed at him.

She'd put herself at risk for nothing.

He folded the page once more, following the original lines on the page, and tucked it into his own shirt.

Ariana still stared at him. "Was it what you needed?"

"It's not common to find exactly what ye're looking for on yer first mission." He tried to keep his patience tethered, but knew from her wrinkled brow he had not succeeded.

The opaque mass of clouds in the distance flickered with the brilliant blue glow of lightning. The storm was coming.

Kindrochit Castle came into view, and they both hastened their horses.

"You're disappointed." She spoke over the churning roar of River Clunie.

Connor led the way over the stone bridge and turned slightly in his saddle to regard her. "Ye did everything as ye should have."

The wary concentration on her face told him she didn't believe him.

They entered the courtyard and made their way to the stable. Inside, the stable was blessedly free of the wind, and warm in the absence of the biting chill. The sweet scent of the rushes lining the stalls was oddly comforting after the stress of their time at the tavern.

They worked in silence together, caring for the horses and putting them in their stalls for the night.

His quiet rage, Connor knew, was directed at himself. For being distracted, for putting them both in danger, for letting himself feel too much for her.

"Should I have done something differently?" Ariana's voice clattered into his thoughts.

He turned and found her staring up at him, her eyes still wild with the effects of the drug. The carmine of her lips stood out brilliant red in the golden light of the stable.

She lifted her chin with a determined slant he'd come to know almost too well. "If I can be better, then I want you to tell me how."

"Ye did verra well tonight," he said earnestly. "Far better than I expected for a first mission. Ye were right, ye did exactly as ye'd been instructed and ye've succeeded in what ye've been trained to do." He patted her on the shoulder, mindful to do so on the good one. "I'm proud of ye."

A pleased glow lit her face. "Then I look forward to another attempt tomorrow evening."

Tomorrow evening.

Connor almost groaned aloud.

Unless, of course, Sylvi and Delilah had found something in their venture farther north.

And he hoped to God they had.

• • •

Sleep would be difficult when Ariana's thoughts were still racing with the thrill of the night's adventure.

She climbed the long staircase toward the room she shared with Liv. Patches of the plastered white wall were either cracking or missing altogether, revealing the mismatched stonework beneath.

The hour was late and the energy firing through her body had leeched away, leaving her limbs heavy with exhaustion despite the excitement of her thoughts. Each step taxed her and burned at the tops of her thighs in a way she was unaccustomed to.

Such a simple climb had always been so easy.

At long last, the door appeared before her. She pressed her weary body to its cool surface and felt as much as heard the click of it opening.

Something prickled at her senses and shot a streak of wakefulness through her before the door opened wide enough for her to see.

An odor wafted toward—a metallic, fetid smell.

Ariana's body tensed with renewed energy.

Blood.

She pushed her way into the room and her heart crumpled into her stomach.

There, in the flickering light of the hearth, lay Liv, in a bed stained dark with blood, her face pale, and her body unmoving.

Chapter Twelve

It was not an easy task to clean spilled blood.

Dawn lit the sky gray and then pale blue long before Ariana and Percy had ceased working.

Liv lay on a clean pallet, her face smooth with a drugged sleep meant to help her heal. The breath Ariana had sworn she'd never see again now rose and fell in shallow bursts from her friend.

The blood had all been washed away, but still its scent lingered and its rich russet color stained the skin around Ariana's fingernails.

Liv's head rolled from side to side on the pillow and an almost inaudible moan sounded from somewhere deep in her throat. Percy's tonic was wearing off.

Ariana darted across the narrow room to Liv and sank down beside her bed.

Liv's eyes opened in a squint and her brow creased. As if she knew something was not right. "What happened?"

"You were very sick." It was all Ariana could allow herself to say.

Liv's hand lifted weakly from her side and trailed toward her stomach, fingers trembling.

Ariana's throat went tight. She wanted to grip Liv's arm and still her efforts, but all she could do was watch, helpless, while her heart pounded.

Liv's thin, pale hand came to rest atop her empty womb. Her eyes were fully open now, her emotions playing out over her face with heartbreaking clarity. Her eyes widened first, thrust open in desperate realization, the soft gray of her gaze searching the ceiling for understanding while her fingers patted with a frantic base need only an expecting mother would know.

Ariana pressed her hand to her mouth to stifle the aching sob growing in her throat.

Tears welled in Liv's eyes until they passed the brim of her lashes and slid in silent agony down her cheeks. "Ariana." Her whisper cracked with her pain.

Liv turned her head on her pillow and met Ariana's gaze. "Please." The horror of her realization drained the little bit of color from Liv's already pale face and her brows pressed hard together. She shook her head, denying the painful reality of it all.

Yet seeking confirmation from Ariana.

"Oh Liv," Ariana breathed. It was all she could manage around the squeezing pressure in her throat.

But Liv didn't need more.

Her face crumpled and a low keening came from that place in the chest where one's heart breaks.

Tears burned in Ariana's eyes and her knees could no longer support her own weight. She fell upon them to the hard floor beside the bed and gathered Liv in her arms.

Liv did not fight the touch, whether through weakness or overwhelming sorrow, and let herself sob like a child against Ariana's chest.

Percy appeared in the doorway with a mug in hand, her comely face a mask of sympathy.

"I heard her." Her voice caught and her eyes were brilliant with open anguish.

Percy's broken composure snagged at a deep part of Ariana and soon her own tears were almost impossible to keep at bay. They built in her throat like a swelling river against a dam until her entire neck ached from the effort.

Still Ariana fought them.

She had to be strong.

Percy helped Liv sit to receive the tonic, and the keening started once more, a dagger's edge scraping at Ariana's heart. The tears on

Ariana's clothing sat heavy and cold against her skin like a shroud sucked tight to her breast.

Percy tried to give Liv the contents of a mug, but Liv turned her head to the side.

Ariana should help, she knew. But her limbs were immobile, her body paralyzed by the pressure in her chest, in her head, in her heart.

Percy was there now. She could be the strong one. Because the only thing Ariana felt was helpless. She hadn't been there when Liv's child died, and there was nothing she could do to make any of it better now.

Liv's cries rose and raked across a rawness within Ariana. It made her want to curl onto the floor and cover her ears.

If she could not hear, then she would not feel.

If she could not feel, then she could not break.

Already cracks were forming, and she trembled with the need to flee, to give into the swell of tears smearing the world around her.

Percy spoke to Liv, coaxing her to drink.

Perhaps it was those soothing tones which helped Ariana stay long enough to see Liv fade into sleep once more. But once her eyes were closed, once Percy gave a confirming nod, Ariana's limbs leaped to life and carried her from the room.

She ran blindly down the stairs and halls, stone and light all smearing into a gray blur of tears. Her body burned with energy now, carrying her fast and frantic away from all the suffering.

She burst through the doors of the castle and the brilliant light of day stabbed at her poor, throbbing head. Still, she did not stop, not until she found a quiet area in the rear of the castle grounds.

Where no one would see her.

Where no one would hear her.

A sob choked from her, the rupture of the swollen ache of her throat loosing the flood of tears she'd dammed for too long.

She buried her face in the heat of her palms and sobbed. Never had she cried so. Not when she'd learned of her destitute state, nor when her parents had died, nor when her brother had died.

Yet now, as a woman who had attained power, at the peak of her own strength, so too with it came the pain of her weakest moment. At least there was no one nearby to bear witness.

• • •

Connor should have backed away from the window. Or so he told himself several times. His feet refused to obey the order his mind issued.

Ariana's red gown stood out like a berry among the brush near the rear of the castle where the solar overlooked. Her rounded back faced him and her head bowed forward, no doubt beneath the same burden weighing upon them all.

Thanks be to God Liv had survived, though the loss of her child had disturbed the household.

Well, those who knew.

A note sat on the desk behind him, one penned in Delilah's carefully curling hand. Connor and Ariana might have found only a marriage contract with no worth to them, but Delilah and Sylvi had uncovered something potentially treasonous.

Their note, carried in the hands of an illiterate adolescent, indicated they would not return until they had all the necessary information.

Doubtless Sylvi had made the decision.

Delilah, of course, would have most likely wanted to pack several more gowns and perfumes before their departure.

He would have smirked in amusement were it not for the shapely red back still turned toward him.

A gentle knock sounded on his door and he turned from the window with the speed of the guilty before bidding his visitor enter.

The door cracked open in so quiet a manner he knew it was Percy before his eyes could confirm it.

She wore a clean blue dress and her hair fell down her back in a long, blonde braid. Smudges of darkness showed under her eyes, where exhaustion bruised her delicate flesh. She carried a linen-covered trencher.

Connor strode toward her and took the tray.

"You haven't eaten since your return," Percy said.

"And ye havena slept," he countered.

Percy gave a gentle, acknowledging smile. "I will."

Connor set the surprisingly heavy trencher on the table. The briny scent of roasted pork mingled with the sweet, homey aroma of oatcakes. His mouth watered, but he swallowed and turned away from the food.

"How is Liv?" he asked.

Percy folded her hands in front of her waist. "She will recover, though it may take some time. Her heart is broken from what she's lost." She pursed her lips before speaking. "I believe Ariana's may be as well."

It was all Connor could do to keep from turning toward the window and peering through the brambles, to where Ariana stood in the desolation of her grief.

"We are all quite saddened by what happened, of course," Percy continued. "But it is in my heart to believe Ariana has never before cared for someone, not to the extent she cares for Liv."

The conversation he'd had with Ariana several nights prior rose to the forefront of his mind, how she said she'd never known her own parents well enough to feel their loss.

And, in the light of having witnessed her sorrow, he didn't know which was worse—to experience the pain of loss, or to never have loved enough to know it.

Percy wavered on her feet, but steadied herself before Connor could reach out to her. Still, he settled his hand on her shoulder, helping to support her willowy frame.

"Ariana will be fine, lass," he said. "As will Liv. Ye need to get rest or ye willna be of help to anyone."

"I have to ready things for tonight first. It's—"

"I'll no' be going," Connor lied in a firm tone, trying to avoid the way his gut twisted. Lying to a woman as gentle and kind as

Percy was as abysmal as kicking a puppy, and he suddenly felt like a monster. But if she knew...

"Ariana needs her rest," Connor said. "And so do ye." When she said nothing, he met her eyes once more and raised his brows. "Aye?"

She gave a resigned nod.

"Go on then." He pressed a hand to her back. "Though I do appreciate ye feeding me."

Percy tossed him a smile and left as he'd instructed.

But he didn't make his way to the food. He returned to the window and peered out.

Ariana was gone.

The weight of her pain pulled at his heart like a stone.

He'd been uneasy with bringing her on another mission and risking her distracting him, but not at this price.

At least he did not feel guilty for leaving Ariana, not when it was obvious she needed time to recover from the horror she'd witnessed.

Finally he settled himself into the great chair behind his desk. All the aches and stiffness of having been on his feet too long eased from him like a sigh and a veil of exhaustion whispered at his consciousness.

He would sleep after his meal, but he knew it would not be for long. Not with the discomfort of the day's events settling so heavy upon his mind, his soul.

Soon he would ride out to the northernmost village to glean what he could about MacAlister's whereabouts.

This time, though, without Ariana.

• • •

All the tears had dried and been scrubbed away from Ariana's face, and all the exhaustion had been purged from her mind by a deep sleep of nothingness. But when she finally woke, she realized the ache in her heart had not abated, and she sought out Connor after ensuring Liv still slept comfortably across the room.

The crumbling halls of Kindrochit Castle were unusually quiet.

But it was not others she sought. It was Connor.

He was not in the solar, nor in the kitchen.

Dusk had faded the brilliance of day to a shaded glow of blue and orange. She had not slept long enough to miss the time of their departure.

Urgency prickled along Ariana's spine.

Surely he had not left without her.

She fought down the swell of panic rising in her chest and made her way to the stable. The long grass hissed against her feet in protest of her quickened pace. She did not slow, not until she'd reached the stable and saw the empty stall where Connor's horse had once resided.

He had left without her.

The hope for distraction, the anticipation to leave and for one moment not think of the hurt within the walls of Kindrochit all crumpled in her chest until she was left hollow.

She leaned her back against the wall near the horse she'd ridden the previous evening. The beast looked at her with dark, gentle eyes and nudged her arm.

"It would appear we've been left behind." Though she spoke softly, her voice seemed too loud in the quiet of the stable.

She reached up and absently stroked the animal's large, velvety nose. If anything, Ariana wished she could at least ride—even just for a bit. To escape for only a moment.

The horse huffed out a soft breath of warm air.

No doubt Connor would be displeased if she did so.

Of course, if she anticipated causing him displeasure, then she might as well do it to the fullest.

Her pulse fired in her veins and charged her with a renewed energy for the first time that day.

She knew how to saddle a horse and how to take care of herself. She was no longer a helpless woman, and had wasted far too many years fearing the disappointment of others.

A moment of hesitation held her back. Kindrochit was a relatively remote castle. No doubt it was why they trained and lived there—away from prying eyes. But it also made finding neighboring towns more difficult.

Outside, the sky was streaked with the cooling hues of sunset and Ariana steeled herself.

She could do this. She was capable.

Connor may have left her behind, but she would still go on a mission this night.

Alone.

Chapter Thirteen

Venturing out alone was not as unsettling as Ariana might have initially thought.

And finding a town nearby had been easier than anticipated. For that she was grateful. While she didn't have a stable like the one they'd used outside Auchendryne, the surrounding woods provided ample trees where she could discreetly tie her horse. After all, no one would believe a wench owned her own horse.

The heavy, smoky scent of burning peat hung in the air. The houses of this town were more spread apart than the ones in Auchendryne, fewer in number and smaller in size, but all well cared for.

She scanned the narrow dirt road running between the neat row of buildings.

No sign of Connor.

Then again, it was hard to find a man who made it a point never to be seen.

Still, the tension in her shoulders ebbed. He did not appear to be in the same town as she. He couldn't catch her sneaking out alone.

What she was doing was risky. She had the round vial remaining in her pocket from the night before, but not the narrow one which had made Cuthbert overly drunk, nor the eye tincture. Not that she'd ever use it again. The mere memory of her difficult vision left a strain in her temples.

A tall man with wild blond hair and braids caught her attention. He moved in powerful strides, with all the confident strength of a warrior.

A gait she knew well enough to recognize.

Murdoch.

Instinct made her flinch from view, but curiosity lured her out once more.

He had not been back to the keep for several days and no doubt was performing his own task for Connor.

Rather than guess which tavern to place her luck, Ariana waited for him to duck into a doorway, then followed closely behind. Her eyes adjusted to the light with far more ease without the eye tincture.

Several guests milled about the room or sat at the large, wooden tables. It was not nearly as populated as the Lamb's Tail Inn, but it did not make breathing any easier.

Instead of the stench of too many unwashed bodies in a small space, the thick, greasy odor of the sputtering tallow candles clogged her throat.

"Would you get me something to drink?" The highborn lilt of feminine English nobility sounded just behind Ariana.

She turned to find a woman with long red hair watching her with carefully tethered patience. The woman's yellow silk gown stood out in the tavern like a rose in a patch of scraggy weeds.

She pressed a gold coin into Ariana's palm. "Wine if you have it."

The precious metal was warm against Ariana's skin, as if it had been held for some time before being relinquished.

A blonde wench stopped in front of them and cocked a hand on her rounded hip. "She in't one of us. She don' work here."

Ariana's heartbeat came a little faster.

She hadn't anticipated one of the women would have taken the time to disprove her. In truth, Ariana had expected this town to be as busy as the previous one, where she could have easily blended.

It was a foolish mistake she would note and ensure she did not make again.

Before she could stagger out a pathetic lie, the noblewoman spoke. "If I'd wanted something from you or your women, I would have asked. I want her."

The wench did not attempt to shield her irritation. She rolled her eyes heavenward with such exaggeration, the whites of her eyes were easily apparent. With a slight huff, she turned toward a table of men and altered her rigid steps to more of a saunter.

"I'll see what I can do," Ariana offered with a smile.

After several inquiries, Ariana procured a hearty pour of wine for the woman who had taken a seat at a table by herself. Murdoch was at the table beside hers, engaged in conversation with a dark-haired, older man.

Ariana stared hard at Murdoch in an attempt to get him to see her before she approached the noblewoman. To no avail. He'd glanced at Ariana once, but without recognition. Doubtless due to her blonde wig.

It was quite apparent she would not be able to coordinate anything with him as a result.

Her efforts were rewarded with the noblewoman's smile, a pretty expression displaying a mouthful of straight, white teeth.

She took the wine and indicated the bench across from her. "Please keep me company."

Ariana hesitated. It was one thing for a wench to join a table of men. But a lone noblewoman?

"My maid died on our journey here," she said with a sad smile. "I'm in sore need of a reprieve from the onslaught of male companionship."

There was something pleading in her pale blue eyes, something lonely.

Ariana understood loneliness all too well, all the stark times in London after her brother had died when the flow of friends and visitors had ceased, and she found herself on the hard bench despite what dictated propriety for a serving wench.

"I'm Isabel," the woman said. She lifted the cup to her lips and muttered, "MacAlister."

The name MacAlister snagged in Ariana's consciousness.

But there were many men with the last name of MacAlister.

Suddenly she was glad she had taken Isabel's offer to sit. Perhaps she knew who Angus might be.

Isabel had set her glass on the table and was staring plaintively at Ariana. "I assume you have a name as well?" The smile hovering on her lips was not malicious despite her teasing tone.

"I'm Bess, my lady." Ariana spoke with a Scots-laced accent, but while she was confident in her ability to pull it off, her pulse pounded with the lie.

She'd been instructed on how to deal with men in taverns, men who were distracted by too much bosom or flirtation, but not women of high birth.

Isabel raised a brow. "Just Bess?"

Ariana wanted to collapse in on herself until she was small enough to disappear. "Bess Mackay, my lady." She'd once heard the name in court and knew it to be a Scottish surname.

Both Isabel's brows raised this time. "You're a long way from your clan, Bess."

"My husband's clan, my lady," Ariana amended. "But he's long since passed."

"You must have been extraordinarily young when you wed. Doesn't surprise me. Men often take what they want." Isabel's gaze wandered toward the dark-haired man speaking with Murdoch. "I find myself envious of you, Bess."

Her candid reply startled Ariana. No lady ever spoke so openly to a servant, especially when others were within earshot.

"Have ye been married long, my lady?" she asked.

"A fortnight, but it's been enough." Isabel's stare hardened, then she ripped her gaze from the dark-haired man and settled once more on Ariana. "Why do you do this job?"

"My lady?" Ariana said with feigned confusion. The room squeezed in close around her and her muscles tensed. She had known it was foolish to come out alone—she knew better, and now she paid the price.

"You serve patrons, at a tavern not your own." Isabel drank

from her cup, but did not break her cool gaze from where she held Ariana's captive.

"I've little money and no other trade to ply." Though Ariana only played a role, her cheeks went hot. She knew too well the position of having little coin and no skills to gain more. Nothing save cheating.

Several men rose from the table and half carried another man out. His head, dark with greasy hair, hung between his shoulders, obviously ill from too much drink.

Both women watched their shuffling departure before Isabel flicked a finger toward Ariana's hands.

"Your nails are very well kept for a wench," Isabel said. "It's why I insisted you get my wine."

Ariana looked at where her hands rested on the table, her nails were trimmed low and clean. An oversight to her costume. "The tavern where I usually work is far more fastidious, my lady."

She inwardly winced and immediately knew she'd slipped on her reply.

"Fastidious." Isabel's lip curved into a smile. "You've quite a grand knowledge of words."

Before Ariana could flutter out a reply, Isabel continued. "And your posture is immaculate, as is your clean hair and skin, despite all that rouge and kohl you've applied. Your husband may have been from the north, if you ever had a husband, but the London dialect glaring through your Scots would suggest you are not."

The world around Ariana wavered. She glanced to where Murdoch had been and found him missing. He could offer her no assistance.

No words tumbled into her mind. There was nothing to say when everything the woman spoke was the truth.

For the second time in her clandestine endeavors, Ariana had been caught.

• • •

Connor latched the stable door and headed for the keep. The nearby town he'd gone to had proved a waste of time.

Urgency crept over his shoulders, tight and clawing.

Every day that passed was another Cora might be in danger, and there were no nunneries he found acceptable. Either they were too short of coin to even feed their cloister, or too heavy of it and cast a grand shadow on the landscape all were sure to notice.

Bringing her to Kindrochit was out of the question. Cora would be too eager to join the other ladies, and he could not have her doing so. He could not put her at risk as he already was forced to do with the women he trained.

MacAlister wanted Cora for something, and Connor didn't like it. The sooner the man was dead, the better all this would be.

Connor pushed through the heavy castle door with all the force of his frustration. It swung as though it were a thin sheet rather than heavy hewn wood, and slammed against the stone wall with an audible bang.

Percy regarded him from the stairs, a small tray set atop her splayed hand. "Windy night?" she asked, offering a polite excuse he did not deserve.

Her sweet countenance eased the raging torment in his mind and replaced it with the weight of guilt.

Not only for his poor display of frustration, but for the lie she so obviously knew he'd told.

She wouldn't ask, he knew, but that did not assuage his self-placed guilt.

He turned and closed the door behind him, more quietly this time. She knew. He might as well be truthful with her. "I dinna find anything." His voice was gravelly from a night breathing in the thick black smoke from the tallow candles.

Percy descended the stairs and gave him an encouraging smile. "Perhaps tomorrow?"

He nodded and tried not to let her see his resignation. MacAlister was not a man to stay still.

"Liv is feeling better." Percy's voice was hopeful and light. "Please tell Ariana when she gets in from stabling her horse."

Connor furrowed his brow at Percy. "Ariana isna stabling her horse."

"You went alone?" Accusation burned bright in her gaze for a quick moment before she turned her head to the side, as if doing so could keep him from having seen the flash of anger.

"Aye," he conceded. "I'm sorr—"

She turned back to him, her eyes so wide and hurt, it actually stung at his heart. "You promised no one would ever go alone again. Not even you."

He hated the pain lingering in her gaze, the memory he knew was playing out in her mind.

It'd been his fault.

He'd sent Percy out alone a year ago. He thought she'd been ready. And now Ariana—

"What of Ariana?" The tension of the night clenched at his shoulders and neck, tightening. "She's no' here?"

Percy shook her head and her braid rubbed against her right shoulder. The quiet of the house pressed against Connor's ears and made them ache with the desire to hear Ariana's voice.

Only silence answered his wish.

"How long has she been missing?" he asked.

Percy's cheeks colored and she set her tray down on a small table. It rocked slightly under the weight of the laden platter. "Um... I'm not sure." She shook her head. "I shouldn't have slept. But I did, and when I woke, you were gone. Both of you." Her fingers plucked anxiously at one another. "I assumed you'd decided to go and took her."

And didn't go alone. The unspoken words thickened in the air between them.

A hearty knock banged upon the door and set Connor's heart pounding. He jerked it open and found Murdoch standing there, his blond hair more wild than normal.

He grinned. "I've got something ye're going to want to hear."

• • •

Despite all of her training, Ariana found herself just as paralyzed at having been discovered false by Isabel as she'd been the night Connor exposed her cheating at cards.

Ariana's chest went tight and the air was suddenly too thin to breathe.

Isabel leaned forward, the coy smile on her lips declaring her victory. "I know you aren't who you say you are, but I don't care. In fact, I envy your freedom."

She slid a look in the direction of the dark-haired man who now watched them with deep intensity. "I've recently come from London, a place I had no desire to leave, to wed a man I had no desire to even know. It is an unhappy union, as I suspected it would be." There was a note of bitterness in her soft voice.

Ariana studied the woman, trying to find some recognition she might recall from her own time at court. The years prior came back in a flash of faces and places and names, yet this woman did not appear familiar. But then, the last year, Ariana had been too focused on cards to truly notice anyone else.

Someone gave a bark of laughter at a nearby table and Isabel shot them an irritated look. "As I said," she continued. "My maid died early in my voyage and I've been without female companionship among these men. I don't know who you are or what your past is, but I'll never question it so long as you agree to be my lady's maid."

Ariana opened her mouth to decline, but Isabel held up a hand. "At least, promise me you'll consider the request."

"I can consider it," Ariana said finally, still speaking with the thick Scottish accent she hadn't perfected as well as she'd thought. While she felt silly continuing to do so, she knew she needed to, lest she call even more unwanted attention.

"I won't be here long. Tomorrow we leave for a place called Loch Manor. I'm not sure how far it is from here, but I can be found there." Isabel's face softened into a gentle smile and her shoulders

117

relaxed slightly. "I do hope to see you and will gladly reimburse you for any travel expenses you incur."

The opportunity broke through Ariana's thoughts like a shaft of sunlight through cloudy skies. Her mind raced with possibilities. If she'd been invited to the manor, she could take advantage of the offer to locate MacAlister. She could help Connor find the information he needed.

"Is the manor on MacAlister land?" she asked, with as much finesse as she could muster.

Isabel tilted her head. "You truly don't know Scotland at all, do you?"

Heat singed Ariana's cheeks at her folly. In her next lesson with Delilah, she would be bringing up the layout of Scotland and which clans belonged to which areas to prevent future mistakes.

"I was seeking someone and wondered if I might find information on him there." Her heartbeat came fast and hard once the words were out of her mouth. There had been no careful diplomacy to her statement, no crafted disguise.

"Who are you seeking?" Isabel asked.

Ariana swallowed. She'd already blundered thus far, she might as well broach what she needed. "Angus MacAlister."

To her great surprise, Isabel laughed, a lilting sound filled with genuine gaiety.

"Well, you've found him, my dear." Her eyes danced with mirth. "He's my husband. And if you'd like to warm his bed, I'm sure he'll talk endlessly about himself and you'll get whatever you wanted out of him. In fact, I'd be most grateful."

She rose from the table in a graceful, sweeping motion. "I think we can work out a private discussion on my husband if you come into my employ. I do hope I'll see you again, Bess."

Ariana nodded. "Aye, my lady, I'm sure ye will."

It was not until she was finally free of the tavern did she realize her great victory.

Not only did she know Angus MacAlister's location, she also had a way to get to him.

Her first lone mission had been a success.

Chapter Fourteen

Ariana had the information Connor needed and she wouldn't waste a moment in getting it to him.

She raced up the stairs of the keep, her heart slamming in time to the quick, steady slap of her feet upon the worn stone.

She'd done the mission completely on her own, she'd gotten what she set out for and she hadn't gotten lost on the way back.

Victory warmed her from within and kept the cool night air from touching her.

She stopped at the landing and her pulse quickened.

Light framed the door of the solar.

Connor was still awake.

She made her way down the dark hall in a rapid succession of bouncing steps. Her excitement was far too great to be contained. It was like trying to capture the brilliance of the sun between one's hands.

She didn't stop when she reached the door. She placed her hot palms against the cool, smooth surface and pushed it open.

The room was darker than usual, the hearth little more than a red glow of fading embers outlining Connor's body in front of it.

He did not turn around. "Close the door."

His voice was quiet with a tone she couldn't name, but it curled around her heart and snuffed out the brilliant sun of excitement she'd so eagerly held.

She pushed the door closed.

His shoulders lifted and fell, as if he were taking a deep breath. "Come here." Again, too quiet, too ominous.

Ariana swallowed, her throat tight, and walked toward him on stiff legs. Deep within, she bristled at her own obedience.

What she'd done had been the right thing.

Surely he would understand once she explained the information she had.

He didn't turn to her even when she stood directly beside him. The wavering light of the hearth bathed the front of him in a reddish glow—his folded arms, the seriousness of his carved expression, the way his forefinger tapped against his bicep.

It was never good when his forefinger tapped.

It was a familiar movement at practice when someone made the same mistake too many times, or when Sylvi challenged him.

He stared intently into the hearth, where molten red with black bits of bark crusted along the glowing surfaces of the logs. "Where the hell were you?"

Ariana pulled in a steadying breath, one she hoped was discreet enough to not be heard. "I went to one of the nearby villages."

Connor tilted his head slightly and angled his gaze on her. "And who did you go with?"

She squared her shoulders the way she'd seen Sylvi do. But it did not strengthen Ariana's resolve—she knew she'd done wrong. "Alone."

Again his forefinger tapped.

Silence settled between them, as cold and as dark as the shadows untouched by the meager fire.

Tap.

Tap.

Tap.

Ariana tried to swallow again, but her throat was too dry. "I found the information you were looking for."

Her breath came faster with anticipation. He would hear her news and forgive her.

"I already have the information I need," he said.

The firm set of muscles between Ariana's shoulder blades slackened. "What?"

"Murdoch came here tonight and told me MacAlister would be at Loch Manor in the next several days."

The heady elation of her victory deflated from her chest in a slow exhale.

"I saw Murdoch," she conceded. "And wondered if he'd managed to track Angus MacAlister there."

"Ye were in the same village?"

Ariana nodded. "I went into the same tavern and saw him talking to MacAlister. I don't think he recognized me, though. And I didn't know the man was MacAlister until his wife told me."

"MacAlister's wife?" Connor's jaw flexed. "He's married then," he muttered to himself. He drew in a long, slow breath. "Ye shouldna have gone by yerself. And ye shouldna be following Murdoch around. Ye could ruin all his work by interfering—"

"I only followed him into the tavern. I did not interfere," Ariana said in a hard tone. A flame of anger flickered to life inside her.

"It was dangerous to go alone. Sylvi doesna even go alone."

"I was careful." Ariana's hand moved to her pocket where she'd placed the round vial, for reassurance. And met nothing but fabric.

Her thoughts scattered for a distracted moment, torn between the sudden fear of having lost the vial and her frustration at the current conversation.

She pressed her dress between her palm and her thigh, confirming the vial's absence.

"Are ye listening to me?" Connor put a hand on her shoulder and she almost snatched her hand from her dress. "It doesna matter how careful ye are, Ariana. Murdoch wouldna have been able to help. He didna even notice ye. If he had, I know he would have mentioned it when I told him ye were missing."

"MacAlister's wife offered me a position as her lady's maid." She threw the words at him like she was presenting a winning poker hand. "We have an opportunity to arrive on invitation and get the information we need."

A line showed across Connor's brow. "We dinna need such an opportunity. I need ye to do as ye're told."

"To do as I'm told." Her cheeks blazed with indignation. She stepped back, freeing her shoulder from the weight of his resting hand. "I've always done as I'm told," she continued, her voice as low and quiet as Connor's had been when she first entered the room.

He took a step toward her, but she put up her hand.

"I did as my parents bade and it ended in one failed marriage attempt after another." Her body trembled inside with the force of her admission, with the heat of all the pent-up rage now cracking the facade she'd hid it behind for so many years.

"My obedience won me nothing. Not the husband and children I wanted, not the respect I worked so hard to obtain, not even their affection. Nothing." She said the last word through gritted teeth. "I obeyed my brother and got nothing in return but rumors about why no one would wed me."

The scalding resentment within her singed away all the embarrassment at her rejection she'd once felt. Now only raw, ugly fury took its place. "And after all that humiliation, after all those years of obedience, he spent my dowry and died, leaving me with nothing but debt and the scraps of my good name."

Connor watched her with eyes so intent, it was as if he could see the soul she'd so passionately bared.

"Ariana." His voice was soft now, not threateningly so, but velvety, affectionate. It worked into a deep, wounded part of her she'd shoved aside for so long she'd forgotten it existed.

Words caught in her throat, but she forced them out. "I thought it would be different here."

She turned to go, but he caught her forearm in a firm yet gentle grip.

"It is different." He turned her to face him and set both hands on her shoulders so she had nowhere to go. Immediately he pulled one hand off, from the side where she'd received the bruise from Sylvi. It had mostly healed already, but it was endearing to know he'd remembered.

He met her gaze. "The rules are to keep ye safe."

"To protect the investment of your time and training?" It was a petty, childish thing to say, a final bitter note of scorn she wished she could recall once it left her lips.

She looked away, unable to meet the openness of his gaze. Her fury was now spent and the petulance she'd unleashed heated her with shame.

He stepped even closer, so his broad chest filled her vision. His léine lay open at the neck, revealing the muscular flesh beneath and a few scattered black hairs.

Though their proximity should have unsettled her, she found she could not move. Nor could she tear her gaze from the visible lines of his naked flesh, or stave off the ache of her fingers to stroke it.

"Ye couldna be more wrong." The passion in his tone pulled her attention from his chest to his face.

He gazed into her eyes and she found herself drawn to the myriad flecks of green and black and gold in those hazel depths.

He leaned over her then, as if he might—

Ariana's breath snagged in her dry throat.

As if he might kiss her.

• • •

Connor held Ariana still by the shoulders, but though her cheeks were still flushed with the effects of her ire, her body was no longer tense.

"Then if you're not protecting your investment, what are you protecting?" she asked, an edge to her tone.

Her breath was sweet and mingled with her fresh, delicate scent.

He should turn from her now. He should walk away and keep his distance.

Yet he knew he could not.

"Ye," he said. "I'm protecting ye. I care about ye, lass."

Her lips parted with her surprise. "You do?"

"Aye. Too damn much." His voice came out rough and hard. "I care."

Her breathing came faster, evidenced by the repeated rapid swell of her breasts against the low-cut bodice.

Before he could let his thoughts circle around once more, he cupped the elegant line of her jaw in his palm.

Her eyes widened.

"Are you going to kiss me?" she whispered.

Instead of answering, he lowered his mouth to the luscious warmth of hers.

A soft intake of her breath brushed between them and he gently swept his tongue against the seam of her mouth. She made a little humming sound of delight. Encouraged, he deepened he kiss and brushed her tongue with his.

This time she gave a soft whimper. Her hands slid up his arms, holding him to her.

Connor's body lit with a heat he hadn't known in far too long and with such force he could only barely restrain it. He wanted to pull her up against him, to run his ravenous hands over every inch of her body.

Ariana tilted her face upward with a moan and widened her mouth. Her tongue skimmed against his with the tender hesitation of the untried.

A reminder of her innocence.

He shouldn't be doing this, not with one of his girls. Not one who trusted him and looked to him for guidance.

But this wasn't just any one of his girls. It was Ariana. Beautiful, determined, fascinating.

No.

He groaned and tried to pull back, but Ariana leaned forward, following him so no space was made between them.

Her hands had, at some point, slid from his arms to the back of his head and now she tightened her grip to keep him from withdrawing.

God, she was so sweet, all silken temptation and heat.

And he was so damn weak.

Her mouth widened and now the stroke of her tongue was bold, hungry.

A flame to tinder.

He groaned again, this time in resignation, and gave in to the burn of his desire. He cradled her head in his palms and kissed her with all the pent-up passion and longing he'd harbored in the months he'd known her.

Her lips were soft, her tongue hot and eager. Their breath came in quick pants and time lost all meaning.

Her hand stroked his chest where only the fabric of his léine kept her from his skin.

Every part of him was lit with an incredible awareness, every-thing sensitive and greedy for her touch. His cock pounded with an ache he hadn't known in years, swollen to the point of bursting in the most exquisite torture.

Ariana's curious fingers crept up his chest until the warmth of her skin touched the blazing heat of his own. Her moan hummed between their lips and her fingernails gently raked down his exposed flesh.

The tingle of pleasure was more than he could bear. He acted without thought, grabbing her hips and pulling her against him, against that insistent, aching throb.

Her moan was louder this time, on the breath of an exhale. She arched her hips forward so their pelvises were locked against one another. The slight friction sent bolts of pleasure sizzling through Connor.

His hands were restless on her body now, exploring the span of her narrow waist, the curve of her firm bottom beneath the flimsy dress she wore, the swell of her breasts where they strained over her bodice.

He gripped the laces of the bodice and tugged, unleashing its merciless hold on the softness he wanted.

Ariana's own hands moved with abandon over him, touching with the same excitement and yearning. Every connection sent strokes of encouraging heat through him.

He tugged at the criss-crossed laces until her bodice hung open, then slid his hand around her waist where the shapeless sark hung from her shoulders.

Ariana caught his mouth in a savage kiss, their teeth almost grinding together between their lips, as if no amount of closeness were enough to sate their shared lust.

His palm glided over her ribs, where the delicate muscles of her stomach flexed with her movements. He did not stop until he met the firmness of her breast. It was heavy in his hand, round and full. He groaned and let his thumb brush the fabric of her sark where the hard nub of her nipple stood out.

She gave a sharp intake of breath and stilled her hands on his back, where her fingernails gently dug into his skin.

He shoved aside the flimsy fabric with impatience and slid his hands against warm, silky flesh. A low growl of appreciation rasped from his throat.

Everything in his body cried out for more. Desperate. Hungry. Wild.

He trailed kisses from the plushness of her beautiful mouth, down the length of her graceful neck, further still to her chest, where the swell of her breast met his lips with heavenly softness.

Ariana's fingers threaded through his hair, holding him to her. And he knew she wanted more.

His mouth went dry with longing. He caressed her bared breasts in his hands and brushed the tightness of one of her nipples with his lips.

Ariana cried out and arched toward him. Connor flicked his tongue over the little nub before sucking and gently teasing it with his teeth.

Her fingers clutched him now, and her body writhed with a frustration he knew all too well.

He wanted her.

Now.

Here.

He straightened and edged his hand up her skirt, drawing the fabric upward. Her legs were long and shapely beneath, etched with a line of feminine muscle. She watched him with heavy-lidded eyes, her lips red from the force of their desperate kisses.

The passion that had left them frenzied slowed then to something careful and tantalizing, a taste of being lost within the moment, lost within each other.

He skimmed his fingertips up her thigh. She flicked her tongue over her full lips and her heavy breathing filled the quiet between them.

The skin of her inner thighs was impossibly soft. He let his fingers inch higher, higher and higher until her flesh grew hot near the apex and then he stopped.

Ariana's eyes searched his, as if wondering what he might do.

And then he swept his middle finger between her delicate slit. She gave a sharp gasp and gripped the back of the chair she stood near.

She was slick beneath the bluntness of his finger, swollen with longing and so hot.

His cock lurched to attention with mindless want.

A thunk came from outside the door, like the sound of a book slamming the flat of its cover against a hard surface.

Ariana and Connor both leaped apart and looked toward the closed door.

Someone was out there.

Chapter Fifteen

There were worse things than being caught half-dressed while in the throes of frantic passion.

Ariana just couldn't think of a single one at the moment.

Her skirt swayed against her ankles, her body still humming with an incredible longing despite the discontented pounding in her heart.

She met Connor's gaze with a shared look of concern.

Already he was grabbing his dirk from his belt. She knew it was there. She'd felt it when she'd been running her hands over him so shamelessly.

Her cheeks burned with the memory.

Connor made his way toward the closed door with soundless footsteps and Ariana quickly laced her bodice.

It was a feat not easily done when her fingers trembled so, and the billowing sark kept getting tangled in the cords.

What if they'd been caught?

The only people in the castle now were Liv, Percy, and Murdoch.

Surely it couldn't be Liv.

She hoped it'd been Murdoch. He was seldom there and was always courteous when he was.

Her heart flinched.

How could she face Percy's sweet face daily when she knew the other woman had heard her cry out in pleasure?

Connor had made his way to the door and stopped.

Ariana gave a final tug at her bodice cords and tied a hasty knot that would fool no one in its lopsided state. Her heart hammered so loudly in her ears, it was a wonder she could even discern the creak of the door opening.

But open it did.

Revealing a dark hallway.

A dark, empty hallway.

Whoever had been there was now gone.

Connor chuckled then, a rich, warm sound. He bent and came upright with something gray and fluffy in his hands.

He closed the door before speaking. "We've a wee visitor."

Ariana strode toward him, drawn by curiosity and the blue eyes peeping at her from the mound of fur. "How precious! Where did she come from?"

Connor shrugged, his large hands cupping the kitten. "Most likely one of the cats in the stable. I'm no' sure how she got in here."

"Do you think she needs her mother?" Ariana leaned against him for a better look and placed her hand on the swell of his muscular arm. He was so firm beneath her fingertips, so powerfully strong.

The warmth between her legs went hotter with a renewed intensity.

"Ach, no, she's no' that young." Connor turned toward her and the smiling lines around his eyes smoothed. "We shouldna have been—I shouldna have kissed ye. We're lucky it was only this wee thing outside the door."

He handed her the kitten, which she readily accepted. She tried to focus on the decadently soft fur she cradled against her breast rather than the ache beneath.

She had not regretted their passion.

It appeared he did.

"There's too much at risk," Connor said. His tone was almost apologetic. He took a breath to continue, but Ariana cut him off, not wanting to hear any more.

"I know," Ariana agreed quickly. As if saying it fast might make it easier to endure the hurt.

The little kitten climbed up her bodice with needle thin claws she didn't feel beneath the thick fabric. She followed its body with cupped hands lest the poor thing lose its grip and tumble to the ground.

"I assume you leave soon to follow MacAlister," she said. "I want to go with you."

Connor watched her with an unreadable expression on his face. She wished suddenly she could hear his thoughts as she heard the beat of her own heavy heart.

"It's a three-day journey there." He said it as if the statement might actually dissuade her. "I'm no' sure how long I'll be gone."

"I rode the whole way from London, except when we were on the boat." She tried to keep the pride from her voice. "I'm stronger now and even more able to keep a quicker pace."

The kitten curled up against her cupped palm, its warmth settling just above her bodice. The vibrations of purring hummed against her skin and she couldn't help the smile stretching over her lips.

"And I know Isabel MacAlister," she continued. "I can get us inside the manor."

"That isna necessary."

She pulled her gaze from the kitten and looked up at Connor. "Then let me come with you."

His jaw flexed. "Ye know why I hesitate."

Her heart fluttered a little faster.

Because he cared.

About her.

"Then it's all the more reason to let me come," she said gently. "If you truly care for me, you will let me join you. We can work together."

He went silent, and she turned her attention to the sleeping cat to keep the awkward tightness from growing between them.

"If I let ye come, we canna do this again."

Her cheeks burned.

She knew what he meant by "this."

"Ariana, I'm no' a man like those ye knew at court. I dinna have that kind of freedom. There's just too much at risk. I'm no'…"

"You're not what?" she pressed. But she didn't have to look up to know his silence was all the answer she'd get.

And she wasn't about to beg.

She could only guess what he'd been about to say—that he wasn't willing to take the chance of ruining the freedoms he did have for her.

"I understand," she said.

And truly she did. She'd been in her own dire circumstances before, with her own fears and her own calculated risks. He was right. She didn't know about what freedoms he had or didn't have.

He had mentioned a sister once, and there was much more below the surface than he'd said. It was in his eyes when he'd lowered his guard enough for her to see the pain there, like the day he'd fought with Sylvi.

Ariana didn't know much more about him than the little bit he'd shared.

"I understand," she said again, and looked up at him. "And if that is your condition, then I accept."

He nodded, his face achingly unreadable. "We will ride out at dawn then, once we've slept and eaten. But yer new friend will need to remain at Kindrochit, aye?"

Ariana stroked the warm gray fur. "I'm sure she won't mind. Mind if I keep her in the castle? I've just the thing in mind for her."

"Aye, ye can keep her here." Connor stared down at her for a long time, as if he meant to say something else. A quiet intimacy hovered in the silence, or perhaps it was restraint.

"Sleep well," Ariana said, and departed the room before he could reply.

She strode up the stairs with the small sleeping kitten cradled in a warm, soothing ball at her breast.

Connor had agreed to let her come.

Her heart thumped in her chest—with excitement for the upcoming mission, with the memory of his hot and hungry kisses, with the fear of never experiencing them again.

But she'd made a promise.

And she would not be his undoing.

. . .

As with everything Ariana set her mind to, she'd been correct in saying she was an easy traveling companion. For that Connor was exceedingly grateful.

The sun, once high and bright in the cloudy sky, had begun to sag toward the earth. He surveyed the forest they rode through, seeking a clearing of trees large enough for them to set up camp.

"We should stop soon," he said.

"I can keep going," Ariana replied. Exhaustion shadowed her eyes and her ready conversation had begun to fade.

He couldn't help but smile at her determination. "That isna necessary. We dinna want to be riding through the woods at night. It's best we stop."

"This isn't nearly as difficult as coming to Scotland." A smile eased some of the weariness from her features.

"I imagine it was a difficult journey," Connor said. "Did ye enjoy the snow?" He winked at her, and she laughed.

Though he didn't want to admit it to himself, he loved the sound of her laughter.

The trees thinned out and an expanse of soft grass revealed itself. The perfect spot for setting up camp.

Connor stopped his horse and swung from it. Ariana did likewise, but he noticed a slight stagger following her landing.

He quickly came around to help her, but she shook her head. "I'm fine."

"Ye'll feel better once ye've moved around a wee bit." He said it more to himself than to her.

If he were being honest, he'd admit that he wanted the excuse to touch her, to hold her. He balled his hands into fists. This was not how he was supposed to be thinking.

"Oh, I remember." She smiled at him. "Moving around always helps. Might not be a bad idea to spar." The smile unfurled into a grin.

He arched his back and was rewarded with several gratifying pops. "It wouldna be such a bad idea."

"Maybe then you'll have a little more confidence in my fighting ability. After all, we've never sparred before." She arched her eyebrow, as if challenging him.

He thought back to the many training sessions they'd been through. "Haven't we?"

She shook her head.

"How do ye like fighting in skirts?" He indicated her riding habit. Dust and creases lined the full green velvet skirts.

She shrugged off the fitted jacket, revealing the simple green bodice beneath and a white sark. "My trainer has prepared me to fight in anything."

He couldn't help but smirk at her reply. "Verra well, but no bladed weapons."

She slipped a hand into the pocket of her skirt and removed a dagger. He knew well where the blade had been only moments before—down through the pocket with no seam and strapped to her slender thigh, hugging her impossibly soft skin. Doubtless the metal was still warm from the heat of her body.

Her fists came up into a blocking positon in front of her and she sank several inches lower, no doubt bending her knees beneath the weight of all those skirts.

"Unless you brought practice weapons, I'm assuming hand-to-hand?" Her eyes narrowed with focus.

He mirrored her stance. "An astute assumption."

They circled one another. Her gaze was sharp with concentration, her lips tight, and he realized with absolute certainty she was right—they had not yet sparred.

This would be interesting.

No sooner had he tensed his body for a fight than her small fist flew toward him. He ducked to avoid it and would have been struck on the opposite side had he not dropped low enough in time.

"Good move," he commended.

Ariana's features did not relax. "Delilah was a good teacher."

"She must have had a good teacher as well." He kept his face equally stoic.

This time he did not allow Ariana to be on the offensive. He lunged toward her, intending to grapple her to the ground where he could easily trap her and declare his victory.

Rather than dart from his attack, she ran into it and shoved against his chest with the flats of her palms.

His balance was offset by the move, but he managed to stay upright and locked his arms around her head.

With a grunt, she spun free and lurched backward, out of arm's reach. Her narrow escape left her hair wild, with strands loosened from the carefully twisted knot she'd secured it in that morning.

She inched forward and he threw his fist toward her, though with the restrained strength he used in practice.

Again, she stepped into an offensive position, so his fist flew past her ear and she had access to everything his attack had left exposed.

She grabbed his arm and pulled while lowering her body to the ground. He flipped over her and landed on soft knees with enough surety to pop up once more.

Ariana was right. She was tougher than she looked.

And he was damn glad for it.

Dusk tinged the sky a somber blue, and he knew they didn't have much time before a cloak of darkness fell over them.

Again Ariana inched closer to him, encouraging his attack. This time he knew better.

He moved to charge toward her, but when she attempted her own maneuver, he was ready.

He caught her narrow waist with his right hand and nudged her legs from behind so her knees bent and buckled. They both fell to the ground.

She went down like a cat shoved into a barrel of water, all elbows and fists and legs shooting out in blind determination to hit a target.

Unsuccessfully.

The weight of her skirts kept her kicks from being as effective and bared too many inches of tempting flesh.

Shapely and smooth and creamy.

He locked his body over hers to tame her struggle and win once and for all.

Memories from the night before fogged his mind. The huskiness of her moan, how incredibly wet she'd been.

Her hips bucked upward and she forcefully shoved him off.

She sat down hard atop him in a straddle, and her skirts lay over his legs like a thick blanket, as though her weight were substantial enough to hold him down. Her chest heaved with the labor of her breath and her cheeks were red in the fading light.

"I think I won." There was a slyness to her tone the warrior in him could not abide.

He grabbed her wrists and rolled them both over once more, so that he was the victor.

She looked up at him, eyes twinkling with excitement, hair spilling from its constraints.

His large hands trapped her small ones. She was at his mercy.

How he wanted to use that to his advantage—one he knew she would enjoy based on the previous night's engagement. He could trail his mouth against her neck, her bosom, even lower to where she'd been so damn wet.

The very thought almost made him groan. To taste her.

To enjoy all of her and slake the lust burning through him once and for all.

Chapter Sixteen

Ariana wanted nothing more than to give in to the lure of hot temptation in Connor's stare.

She was locked under him, beneath the grip of hands she knew would soften at the sound of a single word.

But she did not wish to utter it.

She wanted instead to feel the heat of his lips press to hers, the scorch of his searching tongue.

His body ached for her as well, as evidenced by the same insistent hardness now pressing against her hip that had been present the night before.

His hands tightened and his eyes searched hers, as if seeking permission.

It was so enticing, so beautifully, tangibly enticing, to submit, and fall into the passion together. Where overloud thoughts were quelled by pleasure, unmarred by the reality of consequence.

He sank lower upon her, his face softening with intent.

To give in, to give in, to give in.

Oh God, to give in.

But she'd given him her word.

"Connor." She fixed a stern expression on her face. "No."

The word dragged from the pit of her heart and leeched away some of the pain of having to reject him.

He stopped and cleared his throat—a loud, grating sound in the otherwise silent forest.

He got to his feet and thrust his hand out to her. "Forgive me."

She accepted his offer and found his naked palm hot against her fingertips. "There's nothing to forgive. You've won."

Though she offered him a bright smile, the tension drawn across his face did not ease. Perhaps he could see through her facade to the darkness of her own disappointment at having to deny herself of what she so deeply longed for.

But had he not stopped at her word, he would not be the Connor she loved, would he?

She stilled at that thought.

The Connor she loved.

Did she truly love him?

The air she breathed struggled to reach her lungs, like she'd been running too hard for too long.

Connor handed her several twigs. "Start the fire while I get more wood."

She looked up at him in surprise. The fading light played in his hazel eyes, turning the colors to an array of green and brown and gold with flecks of black.

Connor's gaze turned thoughtful. "I'm sorry."

She blinked and shook her head.

He cleared his throat again and his brow furrowed. "I shouldna have taken advantage of having won earlier."

"You didn't," she answered, and turned before he could say anything else. She bent over her task, eager for something to distract her from the ache her realization had placed in her heart.

The air between them was no less strained with awkwardness once the fire was lit than it had been when he first handed her the kindling. They ate in silence, neither looking at the other, before finally settling in to sleep on the hard, cold ground with the blazing fire between them.

Though Ariana had looked forward to the blanket of slumber and the momentary reprieve from the discomfort of her current situation, sleep did not come.

She'd slept in many a forest in her travels to Kindrochit, and on even colder ground, but she'd had the heat and comfort of Liv beside her to curl against. She missed her friend now and tried to tamp down the swell of pain in her heart at the thought of Liv lying so weakly in her bed back at the castle.

Something rustled out in the woods beyond.

Leaves, most likely.

Or squirrels.

But possibly wolves.

Yes, wolves would make such a sound while brushing through the foliage.

In her mind's eye she saw yellow, ravenous eyes glinting in the darkness, the beast salivating for the meat of her body, the heat of her blood.

She sunk lower into her makeshift bed and pulled the rough fabric over her scrunched-shut eyes. It offered little solace and only pushed her thoughts down deeper, more macabre paths.

Her hand curled around the cold comfort of her dagger.

Wind pushed against her, ruthless and wild. It bit through her simple blanket and teased the marrow of her bones until she was left trembling.

She pushed her face free and sucked in a freezing breath of air. The moon shone bright overhead, full faced and mocking her fear.

Just over the fire between them, Connor slept. His deep breath came even, like the slow, steady beat of a calm heart.

How she longed for his warm security. To feel the strength of his embrace.

She tucked her legs against her stomach in an effort to ward off both the chill and her childish, foolish fears.

To no avail.

A snuffing sounded in the woods beyond, followed by a howl so close it cut through the thin shield of her bravery and pierced her fears beneath.

She leapt to her feet and bunched her blanket up at her breast.

The moonlight shone down on the empty clearing.

Ariana's heart still tapped out a rapid beat.

Foolish.

She was foolish.

But she could not convince her heart of it.

She glanced at Connor's sleeping form once more and her decision was made before she allowed herself to accept.

Her feet moved of their own volition.

She laid her blanket beside his, careful not to wake him.

"What is it?" His voice was gravelly with sleep.

Ariana pursed her lips, unwilling to give voice to her ridiculous unease.

"It's cold," she said finally.

When he did not protest her proximity, she smoothed her blanket and slid in beside him. His arm came around her, covering her with the wide expanse of the plaid he usually wore slung over his shoulder, securing them in the length of wool together.

His heat and his strength hugged her in a glorious cocoon. Warmth seeped in through her chilled skin and heated everything frozen within her. A hum of contentment vibrated in her throat and sleep lured her closer.

She had Connor at her side.

And she had him in her heart.

Of that, she was now certain.

• • •

It was far warmer than any other April Connor had experienced.

The scent of dew roused his senses with its freshness, its delicate feminine quality.

He cracked an eye open and found a dark lock of tousled hair tucked beneath his chin.

Ariana.

Though he should not, he breathed in once more, and plucked her fragile scent from that of the earthy forest floor beneath them.

His arm lay draped over her slender body, and she held it to her breast like a lady clutching her sable in a windstorm. The night had left him impossibly hard, but it wasn't just the normal press of a full bladder. The ache extended to the tip of his cock where it nudged against the sweet curve of Ariana's rump.

It was almost impossible not to strain his hips forward and press against her softness.

He shifted in his makeshift bed, defying desire and forcing himself from her. A channel of cold morning air bled between their bodies, dispelling the heat once shared there.

Ariana gave a soft whimper and rolled toward him. Her hands caught blindly at his chest, where she rested her head and sighed in contentment once more.

Her scent was more pervasive now, teasing and tempting.

And damn it, he was only a man. He could take no more.

Connor eased himself from her touch and turned a deaf ear to her sleepy protest.

The chilly morning air was damp with the promise of rain and made his body creak. Soft light from the slowly rising sun colored the forest a quiet blue-gray, the early hour finding everything still.

He found his gaze fixed upon Ariana's sleeping form. Her long dark hair trailed behind her like a proud banner caught in a defiant wind. The innocence of slumber tinged her cheeks and lips pink and left her alabaster skin porcelain white in comparison.

She truly was beautiful.

And altogether too alluring.

He'd been close the night before. Too close.

She had been the one to stop him.

He was grateful to her for having done so, for surely he hadn't had the strength to stop himself.

She shifted in her sleep, and her hand reached toward where he'd slept. Her fingers fanned over nothing for a moment before falling still.

He would not make the same mistake again. He would keep his lust in check.

For that was surely all it was—lust.

With the thought firmly lodged in his mind, he decided to

let her sleep several moments more while he cleaned up in the nearby stream.

That was when the rain started.

The trickle from the skies was slow at first, little flecks of moisture dotting his skin. By the time he came back to camp, the hiss of a hard rain filled his ears.

Ariana peered at him from beneath a plaid she had thrown over her head with only her face peeking out.

Her sigh fogged in the icy air and she gave him a ready smile. "At least the company will be good."

But the company was not good those next two days, nor did the rain abate.

Ariana had tried to offer conversation, but Connor had not been receptive and eventually her lighthearted attempts had faded into silence.

Talking to her made him want to know too much about her, hearing her laugh only made him want to encourage her joy, being closer to her only made him want to be nearer still.

His heart was heavy knowing he was the cause of the severe silence, but he was not strong enough to endure the temptation of Ariana Fitzroy.

He knew she too was miserable. Her white-knuckled grip on the plaid under her chin only loosened when they stayed at the inn the second night. It was a modest place, clean, with good hot food and an owner who asked no questions.

It had been easy to secure two separate rooms without issue.

The final day of their journey was just as wet and, if possible, even colder.

The scenery had given way to the gentle rolling swells of hills with a blue loch beyond.

Home.

He had not been back in over three years.

His heart thundered in his chest at the prospect and he suddenly found himself wishing simultaneously that it was further away and closer all at once.

Regardless of what he wished, Urquhart Castle came slowly into view, powerful and stoic, set in a protective bit of land jutting into Loch Ness.

Visible windows on the castle's face stood dark, like the gaping empty sockets of a skull. Urquhart Castle, a place which once held such life, such memories of love and happiness, now stood cold and dark and dead.

"Is something wrong?" Ariana's voice jarred him from his mental lamentation. She peered at him from beneath her plaid, her face little more than a circle of white against the dark, rain-soaked wool.

He had not realized he'd stopped the horse.

His throat had grown tight and he had to swallow before speaking. "We'll stay here tonight. It's near Loch Manor."

Thinking of Loch Manor made his thoughts stray toward his impending mission to kill MacAlister. And it made Connor think of Cora and the question which had been plaguing him. If MacAlister was already married, what the hell was he doing with Connor's sister?

Ariana's gaze was drawn toward Urquhart Castle. "Are they expecting us?"

The drawbridge, he noticed, was lowered, but the grid pattern of the portcullis was dark against the darkness beyond.

At least someone had left the castle secure.

"There isna anyone to expect us." He urged his horse across the drawbridge. "The castle is empty."

The bridge was firm under the hearty thunk of their horses' hooves, a relief considering the poor state of the moat. Debris dotted the crevice of earth and thick puddles of murky water churned with the driving rain.

Doubtless nothing had been cared for in his absence.

Connor stopped beneath the wood-beamed structure in the center of the bridge. It wasn't much of a cover, but it would be better than nothing.

He leapt from his horse. "I'll need ye to stay here while I scale the wall."

Ariana slid from her steed and accepted the reins of his horse from him. The leather was heavy and swollen with rain. She turned an assessing gaze toward the wall. "I could do it if you show me how."

He pulled a grappling hook from his pack and slung the heavy coil of rope over his shoulder. "Perhaps a lesson when there's no' as much rain and we're dry."

She gave a nod from the depths of her plaid and he made his way toward the castle.

Ariana's gaze went with him, heavy on his shoulders, but he paid her little mind. All he could think of was what lay before him.

Urquhart Castle.

His castle.

And all the ghosts suddenly welling in his thoughts.

Arrow slits dotted the face of the castle. Were the castle full, he would have several dozen arrows trained on him.

Connor stopped at the entrance and swung the hook over the lower wall to his left. He climbed it in three quick kicks while holding the rope. He could have attempted to climb the main front of Urquhart, but that would have required more rope. The side curtain wall was considerably lower.

Breaching the castle was no easy feat considering its heavy fortification. He crossed the grassy front and the thought swam in his head, around and around, the same as it had for years.

Someone must have been helping from the inside.

A traitor.

Surely the Gordons could not have acted on their own.

He stopped just under where the curtain wall dipped lower and pulled the coil of rope from his shoulder. It landed on the sodden ground with a wet *whump*.

Though the rope was slippery and waterlogged, he held it snug in his fist, the way his father had shown him, and let it spin to gain momentum.

The weight of the hook pulled it faster and faster through the air overhead. His father's voice was deep and rich in Connor's mind, as if they stood side by side.

Steady, lad. Steady.

Now!

Connor let the hook fly from his fingers. It arced high into the air before landing with a clank somewhere over the crenellations.

A solid yank on the hanging rope in front of him gave only a fraction of a moment before the spines of the grapple snagged on stone and caught.

Hand over hand on the rope, he stepped up the wall of the castle. Rainwater slapped at his face and the muscles of his back were burning with effort by the time he reached the top.

The courtyard stood below him, stark and open, and suddenly his heart was as vulnerable as the raw pink skin of a wound not yet healed.

Rain drove against his face and ran down his chin, emulating the tears he had never allowed himself to shed.

His father had stood in the courtyard that day, tall and proud, hands bound behind his back.

Still he had not kneeled.

Men surrounded him... Gordon men.

Connor jerked his head from the courtyard.

He could not think about what came next.

Instead he jogged down the stairs toward the gatehouse, where the winding contraption to the portcullis was housed in the constable's lodging. Ariana was waiting on him and he would not let ghosts keep her in the rain.

The musty smell of disuse permeated the small living quarters of the former constable. A fine layer of dust left everything muted and clad in soft gray.

Without the deluge assaulting his ears, the room was disconcertingly quiet, holding tight to all the secret horrors it had once witnessed.

The way to open the portcullis was just up the stairs. Then he could leave.

He took the stairs two at a time until the solid door came into view and the memory of the room beyond tugged at Connor. The various objects neatly arranged on the large wall-mounted cupboard, the pair of chairs often set before the fireplace where the constable was often found sitting with his only child, Murdoch.

The constable's death had been a hard blow for Murdoch, and they'd never discussed it as a result. Just as well. Connor hadn't wanted to bring up his own father's demise either.

Connor drew in a breath of musty air and pushed the door so it eased open despite its long, protesting groan. He entered the room and stopped.

His heart slid like ice into the recesses of his belly.

What was once orderly was now flung about the room in a haphazard display of chaos. Of struggle.

One that led to great violence and the dark patches still staining the aged floor.

Blood.

Chapter Seventeen

Somehow the rain was as cold as the persistent snow had been two months before.

Ariana pulled the plaid tighter around her shoulders and tried to press against her horse in an effort to share warmth. The beast turned his head back and gave a little grumble, but did not pull away.

Rain sluiced from the thick bands of wood overhead and splashed over them in several great spouts of water. Perhaps standing under the structure was actually worse than being in the rain itself.

Ariana huffed at the white knuckles of her fingers where they rested in balled fists under her chin. The warmth of her breath whisked over her skin for barely a moment before being replaced with cold wetness once more.

She stared at the wall Connor had disappeared over. He'd climbed it with such grace, he'd made it appear easy—though she was sure it was not.

A loud screech wrenched her attention back to the portcullis in front of her, which gave way to a squeal of aged metal against aged metal, and slowly the great bars began to lift.

The horse shuddered beside her and flicked his ears back.

Without waiting for Connor to appear, Ariana urged the horses toward the great arched entryway of the castle. Underneath, it was as thick as three men were tall, and finally shielded them from the rain.

Her sigh of relief slipped out in a white curl of frozen air.

The loud screech sounded again and the portcullis closed with a heavy bang, locking them within the confines of the castle.

Connor appeared then, his shoulders hunched against the

onslaught of the storm. He took the reins of both horses from her without speaking and strode into the open courtyard.

A large part of Ariana did not wish to follow. True, she was cold and so hopelessly wet, a few more drops would hardly matter. But finally being out of the driving rain only to have to plunge into it once more was more than she could bear.

She didn't want the rain to plaster her hair against her face and trickle into the scant warmth of her bodice like cruel fingers of ice.

She didn't want to expose herself to the merciless wind sweeping through her skin to leave her very bones raw with chill.

And she didn't want to enter the darkness of the massive castle and feel its clammy press of stories she did not want to hear told.

But Connor walked into the assault of all these things with his steady, sure pace, and she would rather die than appear a coward.

She followed behind him with quick steps.

Fortunately the walk was not long, and soon they were within the stable. The stalls were empty and the entire building was dark. The hollow cold suggested neither man nor beast had been within its confines for some time.

A shiver ran down her back, though this time it had little to do with the wind or rain.

They worked in silence, settling their horses in for the night. Queries about the castle and why it was empty were on the tip of Ariana's tongue, but the hard mask of Connor's face kept her silent.

There had been a change in him since the night they'd sparred. Since she told him no.

She did not regret it. In fact, she did not even think her refusing him was what had angered him.

A great part of him was similar to her. If she was correct in her assumption, she knew him to be angry with himself.

And she would not fault herself for his personal castigation.

They finished securing the horses and once more had to plunge into the rain. The sky had darkened to a low purplish hue that cast the castle into shadow.

Despite the dreariness of the place, Ariana found herself wishing to be behind the solid walls, protected from the cold and the wet. Her jaw ached from clenching her teeth against the cold and every part of her was so stiff, she was sure she'd never be able to unfold her fingers from their balled fists.

She wanted dry clothes and a reprieve from the angry, lashing wind.

They passed several buildings without pause. Some doors remained closed. Others remained open in a manner that was becoming almost welcome. Connor led her to the massive towering structure she'd noticed to the left when they'd entered the courtyard.

Another drawbridge stood before them, open. They rushed across it and stopped at a door. Connor tried the latch, but it held against his attempt with a solid clunk.

Ariana's hope, her roaring desperation to be inside, withered in her chest.

Connor pulled a key from his pocket, and it was then she noticed he wore a gold ring on his finger. One she had not seen before. He must have only recently put it on, but where had it come from?

He slipped the large iron key into the door and twisted. It gave way with a metallic click.

He pushed the door open, and Ariana followed him into a large room. Shadows darkened the corners, leaving the vast chamber gloomy. But it was dry.

Their footsteps, light though they were, echoed in an eerie reverberation which seemed to come from all sides.

"Connor." Her voice repeated back at her from the high stone walls. "Where *are* we?"

He closed the door, but even though he'd done so quietly, the sound was almost explosive and afterward left the room drenched in the same reverent silence as a tomb. Their breath whooshing in and out was the only sound remaining.

"Whose castle is this?" She spoke more softly this time, disconcerted by the echo, by all the open emptiness.

"It belongs to King James." There was something bitter in his voice.

He turned to look at her for the first time since their arrival. His features were drawn tight with the kind of lined concentration he exhibited before fighting.

"It belongs to King James," he repeated. "But this castle is mine."

• • •

Coming to Urquhart had been a mistake.

Connor hadn't realized how much would be dredged up.

Ariana waited for him to say more, her stare level from beneath the makeshift hood of her plaid. He knew she waited and yet he could not bring himself to speak.

His throat had gone tight with a mix of emotions. There was anger, aye, blinding and hot, at all he'd lost. There was the burn of injustice that the king should hold Connor's inheritance over his head to keep him biddable.

And there was sorrow.

Sorrow for the lives lost. Not only his father's, but all of theirs.

"I don't understand," Ariana said softly. Her eyes searched his for answers he was not yet ready to give.

He swallowed. "I will explain more later."

Perhaps.

For now, he led her up the narrow spiral stairs of Grant Tower, climbing up, up, up to the fifth floor where the rooms were smaller and would be more easily warmed.

The floors there were blessedly free of stains, as he had hoped. Perhaps he might have the courage to explore the rooms below later. As it was, he would not have been able to sleep in a room scarred with death.

Better still, several logs lay piled beside the hearth, dry from three long years of being closed off from the world.

A large cabinet stood to the opposite side of the wall as the hearth—too cumbersome to carry down the stairs, too large and thick to easily chop, too plain to be of any worth.

Doubtless most other pieces of furniture had not been afforded the same reprieve.

"Get into yer dry clothes." He looked at the small water-proofed sack in her hands and nodded toward another room. "I'll get the fire lit."

Ariana left with her face still swaddled in the plaid and the rest of her body little more than a huddled mass beneath.

The fire was easily lit with such dry tinder and blazed with a brilliant red-orange glow. Its heat bathed his skin and the light chased shadows from the darkness of his thoughts.

A strangled cry came from the next room.

Connor's heart caught and he slid his sword from its scabbard on instinct. Not wasting time to call out, he ran into the adjoining room where he found Ariana's back hunched toward him.

A quick scan of the empty room revealed nothing, save the orange flicker of the fire's light reflecting from the room he'd just left.

His body nearly shook with the release of an explosion of energy. He'd been ready to fight.

Ready to kill.

"What is it?" he demanded in a low growl. His muscles strained as he rose from his crouched stance.

"It's nothing." Ariana's voice was tight.

His body knotted with incredulous irritation. "Nothing?"

Ariana's breath drew in slowly and then released in a long, sighing exhale.

"I'm stuck. I'm stuck and I'm frustrated because I'm so..." She spun around. "Because I'm so *damn* cold and wet that my fingers won't work properly."

The curse left her lips with the vehemence of any warrior he'd ever met, and hearing it spew from her beautiful mouth almost made him laugh.

Her brow crinkled and her lips parted. "Are you laughing at me?" she asked with a note of indignation.

Though anger flashed in her eyes, she did look a sight with her slender fingers gnarled in a twist of bodice cords.

He welcomed the change of his thoughts, altogether too eager to cast aside the slew of emotions Urquhart Castle had dredged up. He let a smile ease the tension of his face.

"I've no' ever heard ye curse."

Ariana lifted her head, still obviously incensed. "I haven't actually done it before now."

"And ye look a wee bit like an old woman with yer plaid wrapped around yer head like a kerchief." He knew he shouldn't have said it, but he couldn't help himself.

Her mouth fell open and she propped her hands on her hips. He laughed then, for truly she did look like an old woman and it only fueled his mirth.

"Come, lass, get yerself by the fire and I'll help ye." He put his hand between her shoulder blades and led her from the room. The fabric of her clothing was soaked through, much as his was.

It would be good to get out of wet clothes and into the dry ones within their bags. Percy, God bless her, had devised a special mixture of wax which she rubbed upon their traveling bags and kept the contents dry despite the torrential rains they'd encountered.

Connor didn't know where the hell she got her ideas, but he was glad she did.

Ariana stood near the fire, the plaid from her head noticeably absent. Her hair fell around her face in lank, black locks. She faced the fire with her eyes closed and her generous mouth curled at the corners in a look of pure euphoria.

He had the sudden urge to cup her face in his hands and sample the sweet warmth of her lips.

It was tempting to offer his assistance with her bodice ties. He remembered how easily the cords had given under his hands several nights before, and how silky and full her breasts had been in his hands.

The memory of her soft cry of pleasure baited his thoughts and made his cock tense.

He could lose himself in her and forget his soul-deep hurt.

Instead, he took a step back, putting even more distance between them. "Yer hands should be thawed enough now to untie yer laces, aye?"

Her eyes opened and found his, her brows lifted. "Depends. How quickly do an old woman's fingers thaw?"

She rubbed her hands together and laughed.

He'd missed that sound, he realized, the soft tinkling of it, the sweetness of it.

He'd done neither one of them any favors by keeping his silence these last two days.

"Get into yer dry clothes, then we'll eat and get some sleep." He turned away.

"Why here?" she asked.

Something wet slapped to the floor, followed minutes later by another splat of sodden fabric on wood.

"What do ye mean, why here?" He counted the items in his head.

The woolen plaid.

The jacket.

The bodice and skirts.

The petticoats.

The sark.

She stood behind him, fully nude.

An image rose forefront in his mind. Ariana naked with firelight dancing over her body and the delicate sheen of rainwater.

He could lick the droplets of moisture from her smooth skin. Cold silk ready for him to warm.

He breathed deep and jerked his léine over his head, intentionally forceful to throw his thoughts from anything but her beautifully naked body.

"Why are we staying here?" Her voice was muffled by something against her face. Her sark, perhaps.

The rustle of dry fabric sounded this time and he knew she was pulling her clothing on.

And waiting for an answer to his question.

"The castle is near Loch Manor, where MacAlister will be stay-ing," he replied. "I assumed staying here would keep us from being recognized, but put us nearby."

His own sodden kilt dripped to the floor like a puddle of wasted wool. He knew it would dry well enough, but for now it was in sorry condition.

The clothing in his bag was gloriously dry and he quickly pulled it on lest Ariana turn to find him still naked.

Not that he'd mind.

He gritted his teeth against the thought. This was not what the trip was for. This was not why they were at Urquhart.

The last reminder was a splash of vinegar against a fresh wound.

No, he was not here to seduce Ariana. He would never do any-thing of the like regardless of where they were. But he was allowing her to remove his mind from the pressing ache of pain.

Surely a distraction was not so terrible a thing.

Connor turned and they met each other's gaze across the small room, which suddenly seemed much smaller. Her sark and gown were rumpled from being packed so tightly into the bag, and her hair hung in thick wet ropes down her back.

Somehow it all only made her appear even more beautiful, more real, her face sweeter and lovelier against the rumpled mess.

They'd been naked in the same room together only moments before, and the knowledge of that hummed in the air between them.

It was in the atmosphere of shared intimacy when they ate their dinner of hard cheese, made all the harder by the cold, and bannocks washed down with some ale.

The entire time, Connor was extremely aware of her proxim-ity—the grace of her fingers when they held the skin of ale, the small, delicate bites she took from her oatcake, the decadent flicker of firelight playing upon her smooth skin.

He'd felt her gaze on him as well and let it stroke his conscious-ness with gluttonous appreciation.

"Where will we sleep?" Ariana asked, after the last of the food was gone.

"On the floor on a blanket," he answered.

She surveyed the room. "Only one is dry."

Indeed, only one was dry. He'd already considered as much. They would have no choice but to sleep next to one another.

He spread his plaid on the floor and offered a wink. "I promise to behave myself."

She settled onto the floor beside him and lay down with her back against his chest. "I'll hold you to that, Connor Grant."

He pulled the blanket around both of them and immediately the warmth melted them against one another. They lay together like lovers after their passion had been spent, limbs caught around the other's, seeking closeness and heat.

She was perfect in his arms, as she'd been on the forest floor the first night of their journey. Her nearness was a balm to his senses and he reveled in the moment.

He let his mind empty of weighing thoughts, of MacAlister and his impending assassination, of Urquhart and the massacre, of the knowledge that the only way it could have fallen was through treachery.

All of it he let fade from his mind and instead focused on Ariana, realizing that, were it not for her, he could never have faced the nightmare of returning to Urquhart.

He enjoyed the moment of respite for what it was, for the following day he would have another face to haunt his nights.

That of Angus MacAlister.

Chapter Eighteen

The scent of savory meat wafted into Ariana's dreams. A juicy bit with the skin roasted golden brown by the lick of open flames.

Her mouth watered, but swallowing left her empty stomach angry, and a snarl rumbled from its depths.

She turned in her sleep. Her bed was hard. Too hard.

It dug into her hip bone and left her back aching.

She woke and breathed deeply. The delicious aroma was no dream.

She opened her eyes and found the fire burning low and bright in the hearth with a small, skinned animal skewered over it.

Though she couldn't tell what it was exactly, she realized she did not entirely care.

Sunlight bathed the room in a brilliant glow, and she immediately knew she'd been asleep late into the morning.

She looked toward the window to confirm the hour and found Connor with a shoulder propped against the frame of stonework, staring out at something she could not see.

His gaze was distant, and she knew him well enough to know he'd become lost in his own thoughts. Though, as usual, his face revealed nothing.

Ariana rose from the floor to join him. Her body ached with the effort. Despite her many hours training and all the time spent on the road and on horseback, nothing could have prepared her for the repercussions of sleeping on a hard floor.

Connor glanced at her as she approached. A sliver of sunlight played over his face and made the amber and green flecks in his eyes seem to glow.

An anxious little knot tightened in Ariana's chest and she suddenly felt almost shy under his stare. "Thank you for letting me sleep."

"Ye needed the rest." He glanced back toward the fire. "And I figured the smell of food would wake ye in time."

Her stomach gave an embarrassing grumble of agreement.

She placed her hand over her middle and tried to keep the blush from her cheeks with willpower alone. "Obviously your ploy worked."

Connor's eyes crinkled at the sides and he gave a low chuckle. "Aye, it would appear it did."

The room was cooler by the window, but by no means cold. The small space and well-tended fire had kept everything blissfully warm.

There was something about the moment which made her want to lean her body against the strength of Connor's, to let his arms enfold her while they stared into the great beyond together.

Instead she stood at his side and glanced through the thick glass to see for herself what he'd stared at with such intensity.

Outside the skies were brilliantly blue for the first time in two days and the sunlight reflected off the loch below as though off dozens of sparkling gems, all framed by two swells of lush green hills on either side.

It appeared no more real than an artist's depiction of heaven, a thing no mortal could truly know.

And yet here she stood.

"Oh, Connor," she said softly. She let her gaze settle on the landscape and fill her vision, only to find herself inclined to stare even more. "It's the loveliest thing I've ever seen."

"The loveliest land," he amended in a quiet voice. "I've been thinking..."

She turned and found him watching her. Heat flared in her cheeks. "Yes?"

"Yer idea to speak with Lady MacAlister is a good one." He

nodded, as if confirming it to himself. "We should go into town today. I will go with ye to see the layout of the manor. Ye'll ask after Lady MacAlister to see if she's arrived and I'll try to beg a bit of food from the keep. Sometimes they'll allow a beggar entry into the kitchens to sup."

Pleasure rose warm from her toes up to her cheeks. He had liked her idea after all. Perhaps her first attempt at working on her own had not been such a failure.

"Lady MacAlister will be traveling by carriage, no doubt." Ariana left the obvious unsaid. Carriages traveled far more slowly than did horses, and ladies more slowly still.

"Aye, but MacAlister may be there. Ye'll be using yer excuse to see Lady MacAlister as a means of getting into the castle. Besides, MacAlister moves quickly. If he intends to have his wife at his side, she too must move with haste."

He strode toward the fire and lifted a poker to the meat. "But first, we eat."

Two hours and a bellyful of rabbit later, Ariana strode into town with Connor on her right. Gray clouds had infiltrated the skies with the promise of more rain. She only hoped the impending storm waited until she'd been to the manor. The last thing she wanted was to arrive appearing drenched and disheveled.

At least her nails would be clean.

Her heart hammered louder in her chest the closer she got to the towering manor. Even its appearance of stoic gray stone and thickly guarded walls seemed to offer a battle cry of intimidation.

This was the first time she'd gone out in the light of day with only the cover of the same blonde wig she'd worn the night she met Lady MacAlister. The wig had been in a sorry state after being crammed in the bag, but it had been blessedly dry and brushed free of tangles with some patience.

Ariana wore a simple dress, one a servant might wear, but she'd put no kohl or carmine on her face. It left her feeling exposed, as though even the hidden light of the sun blotted from the clouds still managed to highlight her and her alone.

A man stepped in front of her. The dagger at his side glinted beside the butt of a pistol jutting from his hip.

"Where do ye think ye're going?" he asked in a gruff voice.

Ariana's heart smacked hard inside her ribs. Regardless, she lifted her head with the purpose of someone knowing where they intended to go.

"To see Lady MacAlister by her invitation," she answered. This time she did not bother to hide her English accent beneath the veil of Scots, though she had been practicing to improve.

Several people nearby turned toward her, their gazes probing and immediately laced with unfriendly distrust.

"She's no' here," the guard said with disinterest. His small eyes darted to where Connor stood behind her. "Beggars are no' welcome here. Move on."

Ariana positioned herself between the guard and Connor, intentionally grabbing the man's attention once more. The way any woman who intended to be in the employ of a lady would.

"Lady MacAlister is expecting me." She met the man's gaze levelly. "I'm here expressly on her invitation."

Irritation flickered over the man's brutish features. "I told ye, she's no' here." Again, his gaze settled on Connor.

Again, Ariana thrust herself back into his line of sight. She crossed her arms over her chest in a show of impatience. "Well, when will she be back?"

"She's no' arrived yet."

Ariana sighed in the snobbish way the ladies at court did when dealing with those they found insufferable. "Then when will she arrive?"

Someone pressed past her and bumped her sideways, knocking her into Connor. Before she could right herself, a man's aged voice whispered toward Connor in a fierce tone.

"I recognize ye. Many of us do."

She had to force herself to not jerk her head in the direction of the man who had spoken. What had he meant by what he'd said to Connor? Who was the "us" he referred to?

The guard did not reach out to help steady Ariana after she'd been jostled and she gave him a look of reproach. "When will she be back?" she asked, louder this time, to mask the voice which had just spoken.

But her mind was not on his answer. She knew Lady MacAlister would not arrive until the evening at the earliest. A coach with a noblewoman inside could not travel as fast as she and Connor had on horseback. But she hoped it was enough of a ruse to get either herself, or Connor, into the manor.

"Very well," Ariana said with a dismissive wave of her hand. "I'd like to see Laird MacAlister, then."

The guard gave her an unmasked glower of irritation and turned his gaze toward Connor. "Is this man with ye?"

Ariana put her hands on her hips. "He was hungry and I expected your household would see him well-fed."

The guard smirked. "We dinna take beggars. And ye'll no' be seeing Laird MacAlister."

Ariana had trusted in the nobles to see their poor fed and had assumed she could get Connor inside with the ploy. But their apparent lack of interest in keeping their paupers from going hungry turned her stomach. Whoever owned the manor had immediately lost her respect.

"I'll ensure Lady MacAlister hears of this," she said sharply.

The guard did not seem at all bothered by her threat. The lout.

"Is Laird MacAlister arrived yet? I expect you to show me to him posthaste." She stated her demand with precise indignation.

"Aye, he's here, but he'll no' be seeing ye." The guard gave her a triumphant look. "He'll no' be handling his lady's business."

"Very well," Ariana snapped. "You'll be seeing me tomorrow, and I'll ensure her ladyship hears of your lack of manners and your obvious disinterest in helping those in need."

She spun away before the man could respond, if he'd even meant to do so.

She had the information they needed, even if she hadn't been able to get inside.

Laird MacAlister had arrived and was in Loch Manor.

• • •

Connor had been recognized.

But by whom?

He pulled the hood lower over his face and glanced toward the market from his place in the shadows of an alleyway.

Everything still looked as it had three years prior. The same small, neat rows of cottages with their thatched roofs, the same wares being sold in the same luckenbooths.

Only the people had changed.

Most of them.

A chill coiled up his spine.

I recognize ye. Many of us do.

He may have recognized Connor, but Connor had not recognized him. There'd been too little time to see the man's face, and he'd blended into the crowd of people behind them before Connor could get a second look.

Even the man's tone had been indiscernible. There had been no note of threat, but nor had there been one of hope.

Connor stared through the cluster of people to where Ariana moved through the market and placed purchased goods in the basket strung over her arm. Provisions for the next few days.

The idea of being here another few days left his muscles tight.

He searched the crowd for a familiar face. Perhaps if he could find someone he recognized from the castle, someone he trusted who had not been slain, he could ask after the others.

But had there been others?

He thought back to the day when he'd returned to the castle to find it bathed in a river of blood. It had been a massacre.

And when it had all ended, the only movements he saw were those of the men surrounding his father.

But he hadn't checked. A little voice in his head reminded him of this.

There hadn't been time to check.

But the Gordons had stayed in the castle. Surely anyone alive would have been dealt with. Then there were the people of the village. Connor hadn't gone through the village. He was too concerned with keeping Cora safe. Murdoch had told him all the villagers were dead.

Murdoch would have located the survivors if they were alive. He'd been searching too.

Everyone was dead.

From what Connor knew, only himself, Cora, and Murdoch had survived.

"I've finished." A feminine voice sounded beside Connor and nearly made him part with his flesh.

Ariana studied him with an amused glint in her sea-colored eyes. "Did I scare you?" Her full lips parted in a coy smile.

He tried to give her an expression of boredom. "Of course ye dinna."

Her smirk told him she didn't believe the lie. "I'd tried to get your attention, but you were so lost in your thoughts, you didn't see me."

Irritation coiled through him.

First being distracted by Ariana back in the town near Kindrochit, and now being lost in his musings over the potential survivors of Urquhart Castle's massacre.

The weight of his thoughts pulled him to a point of sleeplessness, save the rarity of the previous night with Ariana.

The burden, the exhaustion—it was all catching up with him.

His father would have been disappointed by his performance.

As soon as it'd come, Connor knew the thought to be a lie. The Shadow had never found fault in his son.

"Meet me on the outskirts of town," Connor said. "Stay where ye can be seen." Her light-colored gown would be too conspicuous and she was safer if she continued to pretend to be a woman out gathering household wares and food stores for her mistress.

Ariana nodded and slipped back out into the busy marketplace.

Connor made his way through the shadows, moving with the invisibility of a beggar.

A strong part of him did not want to return to Urquhart.

Unease prickled along his scalp.

There could be an ambush.

Or his people could be alive and in need of their laird. The idea of them needing him and him not being there crushed inside his chest.

But first he needed to see to his obligation to the king and ensure Cora was safe, which meant eliminating MacAlister.

The rows of houses gave way to several trees and an open grassy field. Ariana appeared beside him and held up her basket to show bundled vegetables and small wrapped parcels.

"Tonight, we dine well." The anticipation for such a meal was evident in her wide smile.

"We'll dine well, but we'll do so early. We have much to do tonight."

Ariana lowered the basket and her eyes sparkled. "Will I be scaling a wall into the manor with you? If so, you'll need to teach me."

"Nay, lass. Ye'll be standing guard while I do it." He started walking toward Urquhart before he could let himself see her disappointment. This was always the difficult part—performing the assassination without the girls knowing.

His hands were stained with blood. Theirs did not have to be.

He would protect their innocence at any cost.

No matter how they begrudged him for it.

"What I need from MacAlister is something only I can attain." His absent reply was the same he gave the other girls as they'd unwittingly assisted with each of his missions. "I'll need ye to be a distraction. Nothing more, aye?"

A low rumble sounded overhead, promising more rain. He thought of Urquhart and reaching the safety of the tower.

His people had not seen safety there.

They might not have known safety for some time.

"Lady MacAlister appeared to be quite knowledgeable," Ariana continued. "If we ask tomorrow, I can help."

Several drops of rain spattered the top of Connor's head. "We have what we need. This is something I prefer to do on my own. What I seek is highly sensitive." He flicked the excess length of his plaid over his head and increased his pace.

The sooner they finished this task, the sooner he could devote himself to seeking out the surviving members of his clan. Gordon could wait a few more days for his death. Connor wanted to know of his people's fate. But not before he'd killed MacAlister and secured Cora's safety.

Perhaps even with Ariana's aid.

"But Lady MacAlister might be more willing to part with information the laird will not," Ariana said.

The constant interruption of important thoughts ground at Connor's patience and made him spin around to face her. "We'll go tonight—before Lady MacAlister arrives."

Ariana was silent for a moment. "I'm perfectly capable."

Connor shook his head.

"I won't mess things up. I've been trained—"

"I know ye've been trained." Connor's control snapped like a thread drawn too tight. "Ariana, we need to return to Kindrochit. Ye either obey my orders without question, or ye stay behind and I handle the task on my own."

She quieted then, and a part of him winced with guilt for having spoken harshly.

Deep down, despite his remorse, he knew he'd done the right thing. She would keep her hands and her conscience clean, and he would perform his duty to his sovereign, which might one day release Urquhart to him once more.

Chapter Nineteen

The cover of night was always the best cloak for killing.

With stomachs full of a hearty meal, Connor had set out with Ariana at his side. The sun had dropped away during their trek and a thick blanket of fog had spread over the land in a smoky film.

The manor was not far from the castle. It was a brisk walk of perhaps half an hour, but they didn't have to worry after they tethered their horses. Horses weren't discreet, especially ones belonging to a beggar and a whore.

Fortunately for them, the rain had ceased long before supper.

Together they crouched behind a thick bush with waxy green leaves. In addition to the fog, it offered a sufficient amount of coverage.

Connor's heart thudded in a hard tempo low in the pit of his stomach. He'd brought his knife with him, though hopefully he wouldn't have to use it. Of the men he'd killed, he'd had to slit very few throats. It was a messy death and absent the discretion King James insisted upon.

But in some cases, it couldn't be helped.

Connor filled his lungs with a deep breath of cool air. The rich, moist scent of the earth underfoot blended with the faint aroma of something spiced roasting within the manor. The large stone tower was filled with life, and soon he would take one of those lives.

That knowledge twisted in his gut like a hot blade.

He let his gaze dart over the multiple guards positioned at various points throughout the manor wall. Not all were visible due to the heavy fog, but of those he could see, he knew the manor to be heavily fortified. He'd noticed as much earlier that day.

Getting inside would be difficult, but not impossible.

He found Ariana's determined gaze in the shielded moonlight. "There are a lot of soldiers on guard," he whispered.

She nodded and looked over the bush once more.

"I'm going to try to go in through one of the side windows. Ye'll need to stand guard and offer distraction if needed."

Again she nodded. She would have no issue distracting the men, Connor knew.

To avoid being recognized from when she'd been in town earlier, she'd left off the blonde wig and worn her own beautiful dark hair like a crown. Her servant's attire had been easily modified with flimsy fabric and a few notches of her bodice left undone.

Connor pulled his gaze from Ariana.

It was time.

His mind screamed at him not to go and his limbs felt too heavy to push forward. The same reaction, every time. Regardless of what he knew of the person, no matter how corrupt or cruel they were.

Even this man, who put Cora's security at risk.

It was another life he would be taking, another ghost to add to the collection surfacing in his nightmares.

Ariana looked at him with a blank expression and he knew she wondered at his delay.

Her suspicion was unwelcome.

He took another deep breath and slipped around the bushes without making a sound.

The blade was cumbersome where it was tucked against his belt.

God save him, using his blade was one of the worst options.

No, breaking the neck would be ideal. A sharp snap when the man least expected it. Connor flexed his hands in preparation for the vibration of the sickening crack he'd experienced more times than he cared to count.

An open window glowed at the side wall of the castle. A bit of a climb, but the stonework had given way in its age and the surface was uneven enough to grip. Another thing he'd noticed earlier.

His stomach tightened into a hard ball of ice.

Break the neck and then make the body tumble down the stairs. Like usual.

For Cora. For Urquhart.

For his people.

The tension in his chest was squeezing, squeezing, squeezing.

He was at the base of the stone wall with the golden glow of the window above like a beacon.

One hand over the other, he began to climb the wall in the concealing cloak of darkness and heavy fog.

Tonight, he would kill.

• • •

Time stood breathlessly still.

Ariana semi-rose into a poised crouch, her gaze darting between Connor's dark form against the castle wall and the figures shadowed in the thick veil of fog.

Connor moved with the incredible grace she'd come to expect from him. He had been almost invisible in his sprint up the grassy hill and though he'd only just begun the short climb toward the window three man-lengths high, his movements were nimble and silent.

Something showed through the fog to the right of where Connor climbed.

Ariana's heart skipped, a quick thudding in her chest. She strained her eyes against the wispy gray fog.

A man.

Someone was approaching.

She hastily stood on legs grateful to be straight once more and made her way toward the man.

"Sir," she called in Gaelic. "Sir, can ye help me?"

The man stopped and turned toward her. "I'm sure I can do something to help ye," he said.

Their exchange had not impacted Connor's steady pace.

"What's a bonny lass like yerself need on an awful night like this?" The guard stopped just under Connor's feet and looked down the gentle sloping hill toward her.

She did not make her way to him, hoping to lure him down. "I canna find the entrance to the manor," she said.

"Ach, 'tis easy. Ye go back that way." He pointed to the left. "It'll be right there."

Connor was near the window now.

So close.

The guard's neck craned upward ever so slightly.

"What if I stay here a moment longer?" Ariana asked hastily, perhaps too hastily.

But the guard returned his attention to her with a quirked eyebrow. "Surely ye'd rather be inside with all the young men."

She walked up the sloping hill toward him then and slipped her fingers through the open pocket of her dress, where her dagger was strapped to her thigh beneath.

Just in case.

"Perhaps I'd rather be here," she said in a low voice.

Eight more steps would close the distance between them.

The guard turned abruptly and looked up.

Her heart froze mid-beat. He was looking directly at Connor.

The guard's chest swelled with the hearty inhale required to call out, and Ariana acted without thinking.

She jerked her dagger free of her pocket and sent it sailing through the air toward the man before he could ever even suspect he was in danger.

True to her aim, the blade sunk deep into the man's neck. Blood spurted out, an eerie purple red in the dark of night.

He spun back toward her with a gurgling choke she knew she would never forget, and he pitched forward, rolling toward her.

She stepped backward on instinct, but the slope of the hill had not registered in her shock and she fell onto her back on the cold, wet ground.

A solid weight landed atop her and punched the air from her lungs. Something hovered over her face and wetness covered her neck, her chest, and the hands she had instinctively pushed out in front of her.

Don't scream.

She twisted to free herself, her panicked mind firing rapid, confusing thoughts with one screaming above all others.

For the briefest of moments she was dazed, before she recognized the weight as the man, the shadow over her face as his, and the wetness as his blood.

His wide, pale eyes stared at her without seeing, hauntingly devoid of life.

The metallic odor of blood filled her nose and was salty hot where it had gotten into her mouth. Her stomach lurched and the panic, once only in her mind, pumped down to her body.

She twisted to free herself, wild with helpless abandon. She had no thought of her training, no thought of proving herself. Only freedom.

Freedom and blood.

So much blood.

Don't scream.

The voice in the back of her mind was small, but she held the breath she'd pulled in.

She pushed hard, but her fingers only slipped beneath the weight of his body. Another gush of blood washed over her, hot and stinking.

Don't scream.

Focus.

Ariana squeezed her eyes shut to block out the man's face and concentrated. If she were being attacked on the ground like this, what would she do?

The coppery odor of the man's blood lay thick in her throat, choking, but she put it from her mind and focused.

She put herself mentally in the grassy courtyard at Kindrochit with Delilah where she'd trained. The air was cool and fresh and Delilah had wrestled with her on the ground.

Ariana dug her heels into the soft, wet earth and thrust her hips up and toward the downward slope of the hill.

The man rolled off her like a limp doll, his arms, legs, and neck all flopping unnaturally until he came to a stop several feet away from her.

Her skin immediately chilled in the absence of the last of his body's warmth. The blood on her gown was cold and wet against her flesh the way the rain had been.

Ariana gulped a lungful of sweet, fresh air and the harrowing panic quickly ebbed.

Something settled on her shoulder.

She jerked toward the touch to find Connor leaning over her, his finger at his lips in a silent shushing motion.

The baritone of male voices nearby carried toward them, their words indiscernible.

Ariana bolted upright on shaky legs and almost collapsed. Her entire body trembled as if she'd just spent days training without sleep.

Someone was coming.

Energy fired through her veins and pumped into her exhausted limbs, but she could not move. Her brain staggered over itself in an attempt to formulate a plan, to come up with something except to run.

And so she stood, staring up toward where the voices had emerged.

They were getting closer.

Her breathing came faster and though the air burned in her lungs, she did not feel the effects of a breath well taken. The world spun around her.

Something jerked at her cloak.

She looked forward and found Connor in front of her. He had tugged her dark cloak over her bloodstained clothing and his lips were moving.

His hand came to her shoulder and he met her eyes, recalling her full attention. "Follow my lead," he whispered.

He made his way to the dead man. A final, weak trickle of blood trailed from the guard's neck. The leather handle of her dagger still jutted from the mortal wound.

Connor pulled off his own dark cloak and jerked the man upright by his shoulder. The man's back sagged and his head lolled to the side in a grotesque display.

Ariana rushed forward and assisted in holding the man well enough to secure the cloak over his shoulders.

The voices were louder now. Too close.

Anxiety prickled through her veins like needles of ice.

Shapes were beginning to materialize in the fog.

Faster.

The word echoed in her head over and over as they worked. Surely it only took moments, but in her mind, it seemed lifetimes had passed.

Connor indicated she should pull the man's arm over her shoulder. The man's limb was oddly heavy and noncompliant. She had to grip his skin hard to keep his arm drawn across her back.

No sooner had they propped him between them than two soldiers appeared above.

The figures stopped and one pointed toward them. "What are ye doing here?"

"Coming to get my drunk friend." Connor's voice slurred as though he'd consumed far too much whisky himself. "He fell asleep here in this ditch. I figured ye wouldna want him staying..."

"Aye," said the second man. "Ye figured right. Get him out of here."

Connor started to turn them and Ariana leaned farther forward to ensure the dead man's weight did not tip him backward.

"Wait." The first man spoke, his voice hard and authoritative.

Both Connor and Ariana stopped.

"What happened to yer face, lass?" the first man asked.

Her face?

Ariana resisted touching her hands to her cheek, realizing it was no doubt covered in a smear of blood.

Connor snorted. "This bastard punched her in the face. He's lucky as hell she's even helping him now and no' leaving his arse for the beasts."

Ariana lowered her head to hide her face lest any expression give them away. She only hoped they took her action for shame.

One of the guards chortled. "Ach, well, make sure ye punch him well and good when he rises to teach him a lesson."

Connor gave a grunt of agreement and then they were turning, away from the manor and the soldiers and the threat of danger.

Ariana's relief was short-lived. The farther they walked, the more reality sank into her awareness. A swell of panic washed over her in suffocating waves until she was drowning.

Her heart pounded too quickly.

Her lips were too numb.

Her breath too shallow.

Don't scream.

The voice was getting harder to heed. Pinpricks of moisture gathered on her forehead.

"Ariana." Connor's voice sounded on the other side of the man.

The man.

His hand was no longer warm against her grip.

Oh God, the man.

She'd killed him.

Something whooshed in her ears.

Her own breathing.

She'd killed a man and he'd landed on her, bleeding on her.

She was covered in his blood.

A low whimper bubbled up from her throat and she pitched forward.

Chapter Twenty

Ariana was not well.

Connor observed her with concern. She stood by the fire, her eyes staring wide and blank at nothing in particular, her hands folded serenely in front of her despite the dark stains of blood.

He dipped his fingers into the pot of water over the fire. Still cold.

He flicked the excess water from his hand and regarded Ariana once more.

Her expression was entirely empty.

"Ariana," he called.

She did not respond.

A hearty crack of thunder sounded overhead, so powerful it nearly split Connor's already aching head.

Ariana did not flinch, nor did she blink. She issued no response whatsoever.

His heart hammered harder in his chest.

This was worse than when Percy's mission had resulted in her killing an innocent man, and almost herself as well. She'd been upset and had refused to ever do another mission.

While losing her as a spy was difficult, he understood too well the burden of guilt and had acquiesced to her request.

He had known what to do to help heal Percy's body. Her own knowledge of herbs then had been basic, but she knew enough to help him see her well.

But then, wounds were more easily healed than what Ariana

faced. Percy slept through most of her pain in those first few weeks while she recovered.

A hard knot of angry frustration burned in his gut.

He didn't know how to make this right.

"Ariana." His voice sounded strained, even to his own ears. He approached her and took her hands in his.

Her skin was warm under his touch, but she stared without seeing despite him being directly in front of her.

Like the dead.

A cold chill prickled over his flesh.

What if she never recovered? What if she never moved again, spoke again, gave that beautiful laugh of hers again?

It tore at something vulnerable inside him to see her lacking the determined glint in her gaze and the triumphant smile following all her victories.

What if he never saw those again either?

Panic licked at his usual calm resolve and seized him in a hard grip.

Action. He needed action.

He practically leapt across the room toward the cold water on the fire and plunged a small bowl into it. Heedless of the drips raining from his hands and onto the floor, he set it next to Ariana and dipped a cloth into the water. His movements were sloppy and hurried, but he ran the cloth over her cheek.

The dried blood did not come away easily and left an orange-red streak on her skin.

She did not acknowledge his action.

"Ariana," he said in a thick voice. "I'm going to clean ye up and then ye should feel better."

He wiped again and more of the blood smeared away.

"I dinna tell ye this earlier," he said. "But I havena been back here since my da died. This was the first time." He stared into eyes that did not stare back and his throat went tight. "And I couldna have done it without ye."

His heart ached at the thought of facing the pain of Urquhart without her, of having only ghosts to keep him company in the empty, cold rooms.

And he thought of how he'd treated her with an unjustified indifference on the ride here. She'd given him so much—her joy, her companionship, her strength—and he'd repaid her with solitude and no explanation.

His list of sins was already so great, and this only added to it. The crush of it left him almost unable to draw breath.

He kept his gaze fixed on her while he dipped the cloth in the bowl. "I was upset with ye because I was upset with myself after we sparred. I'm no' a good man, Ariana."

It was true. He wasn't.

Never had he said those words out loud, and the admission sliced through him.

"I'm no' a good man," he repeated hoarsely. "I kill men. I destroy the lives of women by training them into something they werena meant to be, and I do all of it for the selfishness of seeing myself a laird."

The words choked him and fell on deaf ears.

"The hurt of many for the accomplishment of one." His movements were repetitive and unthinking, dip and wipe, dip and wipe, anything to keep from focusing on what he'd confessed to her. His words came in the same manner as his actions, no longer a confession, but simply telling her of Urquhart, of the joy he and his family had found there.

But he did not speak of Kenneth Gordon. Even that was still too painful.

One childhood story after another. Her face, neck, and chest were clean of any blood and the water had finally warmed.

Still Ariana stared out at nothing. It struck Connor how similar she looked to the glass doll Cora had gotten from their father once when he'd gone to France. Lovely and unnervingly still.

The action of cleaning the blood was not helping Connor the way he'd thought. It'd been a fix for a while, a meaningless distraction, but it wouldn't change a thing.

Not a damn thing.

He gritted his teeth against the swell of angry frustration.

He'd lost too much in his life.

There was no damn way he was going to lose Ariana too.

He cupped her face in his hands and looked into her clear, unseeing eyes. The pupils were still mere pinpricks of black in a sea of deep blue-green.

"Ariana." He searched her gaze like a drowning man seeking land. "Ariana, please. Please look at me. Look at me."

His thumb brushed over her smooth cheek. "Ariana, it's Connor. Connor Grant. I want ye, nay—I *need* ye to look at me."

The narrowness of her pupils swelled slightly.

"Ariana." He spoke her name as if her were issuing a command. She flinched.

Good.

"Ariana, ye need to look at me," he ordered. "Now."

Her eyelids flickered shut and then, finally, those beautiful sea-colored eyes focused on him.

"Connor." She'd spoken so softly he would not have heard were it not so quiet in the small room.

But he had, and it was the most beautiful sound ever to caress his ears. Relief flooded him in a frenzied, exciting rush and he understood then why lasses cried when they were happy.

Not that he was going to cry, of course.

He pulled in a loud, shaking breath. "Ariana, my God, lass, ye gave me a fright."

She looked around the room and a little wrinkle appeared on her smooth brow. "How did we get back?"

Her body began to tremble slightly, and he remembered he'd cleaned her mainly with icy water. Of course she'd be cold.

He grabbed a dry plaid and threw it around her shoulders. She hugged it against her and the slight trembles turned into shakes.

He gripped her hard at the shoulders with his hands, as if he could stop her tremors himself.

"How…did we…get back?" she asked through clenched teeth.

Connor opened his mouth to speak and stopped. After she'd fallen outside the village, he'd helped her up and they'd gone about the task of removing the guard's gear for their return trip and burying the body. Ariana had assisted him through everything, though she'd been entirely silent, her face expressionless.

Granted, Connor had expected her to cry or fret, but she'd done nothing more than what he asked and then watched him when she was not needed.

Perhaps it was best not to remind her of what had been done.

"We walked," he said finally, and rubbed his palms up and down her arms to help create some heat.

Her trembling seemed to quell, but a slight frown tugged at her full lips. "I don't remember walking." She shook her head. "I remember being behind a bush and watching you climb the wall."

"We dinna have to talk about this," Connor interjected quickly.

"No." She shook her head again. "I can't remember. This isn't like me." Tears welled in her eyes and she dropped her head down.

Her sharp gasp punctuated the air and she lifted her hands in the air.

Dried blood flecked her skin, lining the creases and flaking from her knuckles like bits of rust.

Connor's heart sank deep into the pit of his stomach. He hadn't yet had a chance to clean her hands.

Her fingers plucked frantically at the plaid wrapped around her. The wool peeled away and revealed the blood-soaked gown beneath.

Connor tried to pull the shawl from the iron grip of her hands to cover the sight once more. "Lass, ye dinna—"

"You climbed the wall and almost got caught." Her breath was coming faster and her eyes had a wild shine to them. "I called to the guard and I had his attention, but then something made him look at you. I didn't think, I just grabbed my dagger and threw it."

Her eyes shut and a tear leaked from beneath her pressed-together lids. "Oh God, I killed him."

She opened her eyes and looked down at her hands in silent horror.

Her eyes widened and shifted back to him. "I killed a man." She held her palms out to him, putting the evidence of her act on display.

Connor grabbed the bowl of water and sloshed the cloth over her hands. Orange-red water trickled from her hands and pooled unseen against the dark floor.

She did not stop his efforts.

"He would have killed us," Connor said, as gently as he could.

A choked cry came from deep within her chest and cut through his heart as sharp and sure as any blade.

Her hands were clean now, but she continued to stare at them as if they were still creased with blood. "No, no. I should have waited. I should have called to him. Surely there was more I could have—"

He dropped the rag and gripped her by the shoulders. "Ye did what ye had to."

Her lower lip quivered and her eyes were lit with the gleam of unshed tears. She looked so painfully tortured, he did the only thing he could think to help—he pulled her into his arms and let her bury her head in his chest.

Her sobs came then, in great racking gulps.

As he stood there, holding her trembling back and bearing witness to the sound of her innocence breaking, he knew he'd been correct in not teaching the girls to kill.

It was best left to him, the one whose hands were already stained with blood.

• • •

Almost all the blood was gone.

Small flecks of maroon dotted Ariana's knuckles and formed narrow lines in the creases of her palms, only visible if she stared hard enough.

Which she did now.

She dragged a fingernail across the sensitive pad of her hand, ignoring the discomfort in the interest of clearing her hands of their guilt.

For surely her soul would forever be stained.

The fire blazed with deceptively merry energy to her right and dried her freshly washed hair. Scrubbing her skin and changing her clothing had only made her feel physically more comfortable.

Connor sat across from her with a stick in his hands, whittling with feigned concentration. She didn't have to look up to know his concerned gaze fell on her periodically. She could sense it the way a patient felt an overprotective nurse hovering over them in their sleep.

Ariana watched the flames in the hearth as they licked and danced over one another in a greedy tangle upward before wicking away into a curl of smoke.

Connor was looking at her.

"I'm fine, Connor," she said softly.

"It concerns me when ye stare like that." He hesitated and did not speak again until she pulled her gaze from the fire toward him. "Ye stared like that earlier, as if ye couldna hear me or see me. Do ye remember?"

Ariana tried to think and frowned. There was much she didn't remember. She could recall everything until she fell when they were on the outskirts of town, then nothing until she saw Connor's panic-stricken face in their small room at Urquhart Castle.

Her face went hot with the memory. What a fool she must have looked, to have cried so. It made her plunge deeper into misery to know she had obviously exhibited more weakness she could now not even remember.

"I can't recall," she said honestly.

She didn't necessarily know if she wanted to.

"Ye were there before me, but ye werena. I dinna know if ye could hear me." A sheepish smile showed on his lips and it transformed his face from that of a hard man of authority to something far more boyish and charming. "I spoke to ye while ye were like that in case ye could hear."

The look on his face was pleasant on a night where little was. "What did you talk to me about?" she asked, simultaneously curious at what might make a man like him sheepish, and regretful at not having been in her right mind to properly hear.

Connor shrugged. "Ach, no' anything of interest, really." He slid the blade of his small knife down the stick until a sliver of pale wood coiled up and fell away to join several others strewn upon the ground below. "Silly stories about trouble Cora and I got into together as bairns, memories of my ma—no' anything special."

She was all the more poignantly regretful now to have missed his speech now that she knew its subject.

Through the course of their trip, and in spite of the silence for the latter two days of their journey, she had learned much. All the pieces of him she knew were falling into place and creating a picture she was desperate to see the whole of.

She put her weight on one hand and leaned closer, hoping her eagerness would not be too apparent. "Would you tell me more now?" she asked.

His brow furrowed and then went smooth with the warmth of his laugh. "What would ye possibly want to know?" He swept the blade down the stick and another curl of wood joined the others.

She sat back on her heels and thought the matter over. Surely at this point she had as many questions as the night sky had stars.

"You said this was your castle," Ariana said. "How is it your castle and why does it now belong to King James?"

The smile on Connor's face faded. At first she thought she'd ruined this one opportunity, but then he spoke: "It is mine because it has been in the family for generations. It belongs to King James because the man who took it from my father died and the king confiscated all his belongings."

"How did they take it from your father?" She thought of the castle's front, the height of the walls, how thick they were, how solid everything seemed.

Connor set his whittling down and regarded her with a long, wary stare. "There was a great betrayal from those we trusted. It's a gruesome story, one I dinna think is appropriate, given—"

"Please." It was begging, she knew. She knew too she ought

to be above that. And on any other night, she would be—but not tonight. "Please tell me. I want to know."

He tilted his head to the side.

"I'd like the distraction," Ariana added quickly.

His lips pursed and he studied her a moment longer. "Verra well."

Something warmed through Ariana at his resigned agreement to share. He was trusting her with something far deeper, far more significant than ever before.

Chapter Twenty-One

Connor did not often let his thoughts trail back to the fateful day of his father's death. The memories were far too taxing.

Far too painful.

Ariana waited patiently in front of him, the focus of her wide eyes fixed steadily upon him.

"I was away from the castle when it was first attacked," he said. "There was a valid reason for it, but that's for another time, aye?"

Now was not the time to get into the betrayal, nor the brotherly affection he could not deny—even after all these years.

Kenneth Gordon.

Damn him. Even after Connor had vowed not to mention him, not to think of him, the image of the dark-haired man Connor had considered a brother was forefront in his mind.

Ariana nodded. Connor pushed aside Kenneth's image and continued on. "I had Cora with me. We heard the sounds of battle before we saw it."

Cora's hand was hot in his, and even in his anger he worried he might be clamping down on her slender fingers too hard. He loosened his grip and opened his mouth to speak when a loud pop sounded in the distance, like the blast of a pistol. The wind blew against them and carried with it the raucous cry of men's voices and the acrid odor of gunpowder.

All coming from Urquhart Castle.

Connor's muscles bunched along the back of his neck. He remembered too well when they had finally seen the castle. "Urquhart was under attack by another laird, a trusted friend to our family."

Kenneth Gordon's da, laird of the Gordon clan.

Connor didn't say his name, though. It meant nothing to Ariana, and meant far too much to him.

"I tried to leave Cora in a safe place so I could help defend the castle. But the lass always had too much spirit for her own good and followed behind me to join the fight." He shook his head. "I dinna know she'd do it. I should have, but I dinna. I was thinking only of the battle. It was…"

He trailed off, remembering.

Blood bathed everything in a wash of thick crimson. It left the ground underfoot slick and seasoned the air with its metallic odor.

Connor slid his blade free and let his body explode toward the attackers, his rage building with all the bodies he ran past. Soldiers and unarmed men alike struck down by blades.

The women and children were somehow blessedly absent, most likely sequestered in the church.

It was then he caught sight of the structure, and its gaping door.

And the grisly shadows moving within.

The women and children were not being spared after all.

"It was chaos," Connor concluded. Divulging details to a woman recently horrified by violence was hardly wise.

"I was fighting among my father's men, but we were severely outnumbered. I'd been determined to stay and fight until my dying breath when I heard Cora cry out." The scream echoed in his mind like a nightmare. The hairs on his arms rose. "That's when I knew she'd followed me. My castle needed me, but so did she. I had to make a choice." He clenched his fist. "And I chose her."

Ariana said nothing as he spoke. She nodded in quiet appreciation.

She knew.

She understood.

As he knew she would.

"I managed to fight the men off Cora," he continued, "and dragged her away from the castle."

Rage pumped through his body like liquid fire. He didn't remember killing the men in his blind fury, but they lay suddenly dead at his feet and their blood spattered the stonework around them. Cora allowed herself to be pulled up and dragged away without protest.

Together they ran from the castle until Connor's legs burned from the effort. Until he was comfortable she was far enough away.

"This time ye dinna move, aye?" His demand came out in a growl. He'd never spoken to Cora so, but did not wait for a reply. He turned back toward the castle below, intent on returning to help—and stopped.

He was already too late.

Connor had to swallow before he could continue. "In the short amount of time it took to get Cora to safety, the Gordons defeated the Grant men and captured my da." He squeezed his fist tighter, until his knuckles ached. "There were at least twenty men surrounding him. My da never stood a chance."

Connor was too far away to help, unable do anything but watch in helpless horror. The men closed in on his father's proud form like a circle of vultures. Their blades flashed in the weak sunlight and then emerged red before plunging in once more.

Cora cried out behind him, but he swallowed down the sound of his own grief. He needed to be strong. For Cora.

Ariana's mouth parted in shock. "They killed him?"

Connor nodded. "Aye, and then shoved his body over the edge of the castle near the water. I went back that night—"

A warning tingled in the back of his mind and made him cut off his words.

He'd said too much.

"What happened when you went back?" Ariana asked. Concern shone in her eyes. The fire had started to die and left the glowing embers to emit their fading light into the room. "Did they capture you?"

"Nay, I was too careful."

"Then what?" She slid closer to where he sat on the hard wooden floor and placed her hand on his. Her palm was warm and soft, as was her gaze.

Connor stared at her a long moment. He'd never told anyone about that night. Not even Cora knew.

But then, Cora didn't know a lot of things.

No one did.

"I found his body," he said. "And buried him."

Connor stood in the shadowed forest on a night with no moon and stared into the freshly dug hole where his father's twisted body lay. Death had petrified his limbs in the awkward shape he'd lain in after the fall. The famed Shadow, so strong, so proud and capable, now a twisted corpse buried in the forest like a thief.

Coarse grains of salt still clung to Connor's palm from the small pile he'd set upon his da's chest.

"Forgive me, Da." But what he wanted forgiveness for, Connor did not know. His failure to protect the castle, the crude burial for the father he could not save, or for the weight of the coin and signet ring laying heavy in his pocket.

Even now, three years later, the pain of his loss crushed Connor's heart.

He shouldn't have shared as much as he had, yet now he couldn't stop. Part of him wanted her to understand how awful he really was, to know the extent of his crimes against his own family. "Before I buried him, I took what coin he had on him as well as his signet ring."

Connor's head dropped forward with the burden of his many wrongs.

"I needed it to care for Cora," he added. "To see her safe in a world where I trusted no one."

The justification did little to quell his own stifling guilt. He had robbed his father of all his worldly possessions before burying his crooked body in unconsecrated ground.

Ariana squeezed his hand. "You were looking after your sister. He would have understood. In fact, I think he would have been grateful you'd even taken the risk to bury him."

Connor thought of his father then, the towering man with dark hair and eyes crinkling at the corners. The burden of guilt had always been so present, he'd never truly thought of what his father would say.

"Nay," Connor replied decidedly. "He'd have thought me daft for risking myself for something so foolish as a man who was dead."

He gazed down at Ariana, wishing he could see himself as she did. Somehow she managed to find the good in him and overlook the bad.

And there was much bad to see.

He slid his hand over her cheek, intending just to touch.

But she was so sweetly soft against the pads of his fingers, he found himself caressing the curve of her cheek, the line of her jaw, the supple swell of her lower lip.

Her eyes fluttered closed.

And though he lowered his mouth to hers, intending just to kiss her, he knew there would be far more.

• • •

Ariana was selfish.

She knew she should not allow Connor to kiss her, that he might be angry at himself later for having done so, and yet she reveled in the touch of his warm lips on hers.

The horror of the evening hovered in her thoughts and swelled up in her mind. She wanted the odor of blood blotted out with his spicy, outdoor scent. She wanted the clammy skin of a cooling body burned away by his touch.

She wanted Connor to be the one to make her forget.

His kiss was tender, gentle.

It left her wanting more.

She brushed her mouth against his, back and forth, once, twice, letting the heat of their lips taunt one another.

He'd shared much with her when he told her what happened at Urquhart, far more than she'd expected to hear. Her heart ached for him. Not with pity, but with the need to heal.

They were both hurt. She'd known as much long before he spoke.

Perhaps together they could find solace. At least on this one night.

Connor pressed his mouth to hers and stilled her teasing with a solid, hot kiss.

A moan vibrated in her throat. She brushed her tongue against his lips in silent demand for more.

This time she would not be shy.

She knew what she wanted now and would be bold enough to get it.

His mouth opened, and his tongue swept against hers.

Excitement prickled over her flesh and her heartbeat thrummed faster.

Connor's fingers threaded up through her hair and he tightened his grip at the nape of her neck. Tingles of pleasure shot through her scalp.

Their breath came harder with their eagerness to kiss and taste.

Ariana flicked her tongue against the velvety smoothness of his. Connor caught her lower lip and bit it gently between his teeth.

As he'd done with her nipple the night at Kindrochit.

Oh God, that... She wanted that again.

And more.

She tugged at the lacing of her bodice in brazen invitation. One Connor readily accepted with a groan. The sound was low, like a growl, primal. It left heat throbbing between her legs, more powerful than before.

She was a maiden, yes, but she'd been at court long enough to hear the talk of what happened between a man and a woman.

And that was what she wanted.

Now.

With him.

The simple cord of the bodice made a quiet *pop* as it was pulled free of the fabric. The tension of it around her torso eased and the warm air in the room whispered against her skin.

Connor's hands cupped her breasts and his kisses turned hungrier, desperate almost, and they fueled her own desire for more.

His fingers rolled against the tender little nub of her nipple and she cried out against his mouth.

He trailed his mouth down her neck in a sprinkle of kisses, down lower, as he'd done before.

Her heart slammed in her chest with anticipation.

Yes.

She may have even panted the word. She couldn't be certain.

The heat of his mouth closed over her tender skin and she whimpered in husky pleasure.

She pulled him toward her, her hands gliding with greedy longing, sampling the rippled hard flesh beneath the léine.

Connor pulled away from her for a moment and jerked the clothing over his head. She saw him for a brief second, a flash of sculpted flesh in the low glow of the fire, before he had her in his arms once more.

The naked skin of his chest was warm against hers and the coarse hair there rasped against her sensitive nipples. Her hands roamed without thought, without shame, traveling over soft skin stretched taut over hard muscle.

Connor leaned over her and eased her back onto the ground. Ariana obeyed silently, her entire body alight.

More.

More.

More.

He lay on top of her, his strong body stretched over hers. She skimmed her fingers up his arms where he held himself up to avoid putting his full weight on her. Deep etches of beautiful muscle met the pads of her fingertips.

She curled her hands up his back and pulled him down to her. Evidence of his desire lay hard and heavy against her stomach. Her hips flexed toward him on instinct in a movement both foreign and natural all at once.

Connor gave another growling groan and eased a hand up her leg, pulling with it the fabric of her skirt.

Ariana's mouth went dry. His fingers brushed over her inner thighs, easing higher, higher, to the source of her frantic hunger.

And stroked.

Heat and pleasure tightened through her and whet her appetite. Like the first bite of food when one is starving.

She eased her legs apart like a wanton woman and rolled her hips against his hand.

He watched her with a hot gaze and let his fingers glide against her slick yearning, over and over and over until Ariana's body hummed as if it were going to explode.

And then she did.

The ball of pleasure drew tighter, tighter, until she felt she could take it no more, then pleasure tingled and burned through every part of her. Her own cries were loud in her ears, but she could no more help them than she could the press of her legs around Connor's hand.

Her body went languid and she lay there a moment while the vestiges of bliss lapped through her.

She slowly opened her eyes, unsure when she'd even closed them, and found Connor still watching her. He wore his kilt still, but was naked from the waist up.

Naked and beautiful.

The firelight etched deep shadows into his muscled torso. He felt so strong beneath her fingertips, so powerful.

His desire jutted up from his kilt and a need thrummed through her once more, pulling her body from its lazy relaxation.

She got to her feet and slipped her overdress off, easing it from her hips into a pile on the ground. He stayed crouched on the ground, one arm casually slung atop his knee, his gaze intense.

The sark belled out around her in a blanket of shapeless fabric. She pulled the cord free of its bow, widening the neck until she could pull it over her head and let it flutter to the floor to join the dress.

Nervous excitement left her pulse ticking through her veins with almost enough energy to leave her trembling.

She was naked in front of Connor Grant.

Not as she'd been before, with her back to him while they both quickly dressed, but slowly, carefully. And with glorious intent.

Chapter Twenty-Two

Ariana was even more beautiful in the nude than Connor had imagined.

And he'd imagined it many more times than he should have. Still, nothing could have prepared him for what he saw.

Hours of training had left a hint of muscle along her flat belly and her long legs. Her body was firm and supple all at once with the softness of a woman and the evident strength of her determination.

Never had anything been more exquisite than the beauty of Ariana Fitzroy.

Her cheeks flushed a deep red and her eyes sparkled with desire. The stubborn tilt of her chin remained, even in the absence of her clothing. As if she were daring him to find her anything but stunning.

Connor rose to his knees and caught her hands in his. Her fingers trembled, belying the facade of confidence she so defiantly wore.

Her skin was flawless in the low light and pulled him toward her with the temptation to run his palm over its silky surface.

He brushed his lips over her lower stomach, close to her sex, and breathed in the heady scent of her arousal. Its tantalizing lure made his mind swim and left everything hazy with lust.

He wanted to part her slick folds with his tongue and lose himself in her taste.

And he would.

In time.

For now, it'd been too long since he'd had a woman. Hearing

the sultry cries of her climax again might very well undo him before he even had the chance to enter her.

It was all he could do to keep himself above the cloud of his lust. He circled her navel with the tip of his tongue and kissed higher and higher, while rising to his feet.

Ariana responded to his kisses with soft sighs of appreciation, minor mirrors of the husky sounds she'd made earlier.

He wanted to hear those again.

While inside her.

He rose completely to his feet, heedless now of how his cock pressed against her body. Nay, not heedless, for he reveled in it. The teasing pressure of her against the head, so swollen with want, it pained him. The coarse wool of his kilt rasped against the sensitive flesh like nails.

His hands moved to remove his belt and found hers already there. Her fingers jerked at the buckle, freeing it from the leather so it fell to the floor with an audible *clank*.

His kilt followed suit, though it made considerably less noise.

Or so he assumed.

In truth, he wasn't paying much mind to sounds, only to the beautiful woman standing in front of him and the burning hot desire in her eyes.

She didn't sit there and stare at him wide-eyed or suddenly become shy, as he'd heard most virgins were wont to do. Not his Ariana. She dragged her hand down the edge of his stomach, her touch so tantalizingly slow that his stomach instinctively flexed.

Her fingers still trembled, but evidence of any apprehension or nervousness was not apparent on her face. She leaned forward and kissed him. It was an aggressive kiss, with tongue and the slight grinding of teeth against lips amid heavy breathing.

Then, finally, her fingers wrapped around the length of him and squeezed.

Pleasure fired sharply and echoed through him like a pistol's report.

He couldn't think anymore, not when the only thing in him was want.

A sound rumbled low in his throat. He returned her passion with his own, echoing her need. His hands roamed over her body, all soft curves and lean lines, and pulled her gently to the floor.

He lay over her, his cock aimed toward the heat of her sex. She watched him with half-lidded eyes, her lips parted.

He shouldn't do this.

She was one of his girls.

A maiden.

And too damn good for the likes of him.

The thought flashed through his mind before she flexed her hips toward him and brushed against the head of his cock.

All protests in his mind died away.

Ariana cradled his body between her legs and he carefully arched forward until the blunt edge of him nudged against the wet heat he so desperately sought.

"Yes," she said. It was a whimper strained by the same longing he felt.

He needed no further encouragement. His mouth came down on hers and he kissed her deeply while he thrust into her, quick and sharp to pierce her maidenhead without drawing it out and making it more painful than it had to be.

She flinched, but made no sound.

She was so tight, the impossible pressure around him the most uncomfortable bliss he'd ever experienced.

He had to fight the urge to pump his hips. "I dinna want to hurt ye," he managed.

He hadn't meant it as a challenge, but her lips quirked to one side as if she had just accepted one. "I told you." She arched her hips and slid them toward him once more. "I'm tougher than I look."

The friction of movement made desire coil and knot inside him.

He shifted to position himself directly over her, and flexed his hips forward, penetrating her slowly.

Ariana's lips parted and she gasped softly at the intimate contact.

She watched him through slitted eyes, her gaze so languid and erotic, he couldn't make himself stop staring. He thrust again, and her lids fluttered with euphoria before her eyes opened and found his once more.

Her hips rocked up and down with his, hesitant at first, a student learning a new technique, and then faster, harder, with the same determined force of spirit she applied to all her training.

Her movements glided in time with his and the tension was building, greater and greater.

Tight.

She was too tight.

The friction was too much.

Connor grit his teeth against the pleasure, against the hot swollen throb of his body's insistence.

He caught her hands in his fists and pushed them to the ground in an attempt to still her so he could enjoy her even longer.

Her breasts arched upward, and he slowed his pace, gliding in and out, teasing his climax back. She did not fight his restraint.

He flicked his tongue against one tempting nipple before closing his mouth over it. Her soft whimper of pleasure was more than he could take. His cock jerked in appreciation and he plunged harder, deeper into her, riding the wave he could no longer hold at bay.

Her cries were husky and loud in his ear and her hips quickened their pace with his. He held her hands tighter and lost himself to the force of his own undoing.

His energy exploded from him in a roar of pleasure so great, it left stars dancing in his vision. His heart thundered in his chest and every part of his body tingled with the effects of intense euphoria.

He stayed within her while they caught their breath, both panting, then finally slid himself from her.

She smiled up at him, a shy smile he was unused to seeing from her.

The warm hum of spent lust waned and was replaced with a chill.

He had taken her innocence.

He had nothing to offer Ariana, save the hope of an empty

castle when he'd finally fulfilled his service to King James in seven years, that and a lot of failed dreams.

An uncomfortable moment of silence fell between them. Perhaps he ought to say something.

"I'm sorry," he offered.

The languid expression on her face tightened to something else—disbelief? Anger?

Either way, it was not good.

"You're sorry." Her brows knit together.

She studied his face for a brief moment before turning away from him. He reached an arm over her. She did not resist his touch.

He hugged her to his body, and again she did not reject him.

She fit so well against him, better than he cared to admit. He could see himself like this every night too easily, his blood hot from their lovemaking, her body curled in the embrace of his.

And every morning he could wake to find her sweet face, rosy with slumber, before she woke and gave him one of her beautiful smiles.

But that couldn't be.

He *was* sorry. Not for him, but for her.

She had her good name still, and her reputation, since they'd kept her cheating at cards silent. He had no idea if King James would ever release the women, but if he did, Ariana would have been able to find a place back at court.

Doing so would not be impossible, but she wouldn't be able to wed now, not with the absence of her maidenhead.

The warm, lulling aftereffects of their coupling had long since cooled. He would not see her harmed further. Not after what she'd already been through with the man she killed.

Of one thing he knew for certain—he could not implicate her in MacAlister's death.

Tomorrow, he would wake before her and he would kill MacAlister alone.

• • •

Ariana was awake long before she opened her eyes. The ground was hard beneath her and Connor was no longer there. She hadn't expected him to stay.

Heat burned her cheeks and she wished she could clench her eyes tight enough to somehow make herself disappear. It'd been so special to her. So beautiful and passionate and the most incredible thing she'd ever experienced.

The soreness between her legs warmed at the thought, but she jerked her thoughts away from her enjoyment.

Connor had obviously regretted it. Knowing that left her feeling hollow.

And embarrassed.

How could she face him today knowing what they'd shared?

Should she act as if it hadn't happened?

Her cheeks flamed hotter still.

She could not.

Her heart galloped in her chest. She needed to face this. Lying on the floor would solve none of her problems.

She opened her eyes and sat up, her body tense and ready for what she'd already spent too much time in dreaded anticipation of.

The chamber was empty.

She twisted around and surveyed the room.

Connor was not there.

Neither, she noticed, was his cloak, which had hung on the wall the night before.

Rage flared through her.

He had left her.

Again.

They had enough food after she'd shopped at the market the day before, and plenty of other supplies. There could be no reason for him to leave. And then she realized exactly where he'd likely gone.

Ariana dressed in a rush, purposefully ignoring the bloody clothes balled up in the corner of the room. A chill crept over her flesh. She could ignore the evidence all she wanted, but it would never make the memories go away.

Even after having saved Connor, he still left without her.

Once dressed as a servant, she made her way down the stairs, her feet slapping angrily against the smooth stone and ringing out on the circular walls surrounding her.

Too much had happened the previous night, and the memory of all of it settled like rocks in her stomach.

There would be no cowering against the reality of any of it. She would face it here and now.

Ire quickened her pace and made her arrival at Loch Manor come sooner than expected.

She'd left her blonde wig and held an empty basket propped on her hip. The guard was different than the previous day, and for that she was grateful.

"What's yer business here?" he asked.

"Seein' to the laundry," Ariana answered in Gaelic with bored disinterest.

Inside, she was anything but bored or disinterested.

Looking at him reminded her of the man she'd killed. Had this guard known him? Did he know if there had been a family left to mourn? A wife and child who wondered if he'd ever return home?

Her heart crushed down into her stomach and she had to force herself to look away.

"Aye, go on then." His attention fixed on someone behind her when she looked back toward him. She was no longer of interest to him.

Her pulse ticked a little faster.

She'd made it inside.

Now what?

The crowd of pressing solicitors disappeared behind her, as did the chatter of their many conversations. She entered a long, quiet hall made quieter still by the heavy roll of carpet muting her steps.

The furnishings were rich and stung her with the memory of having once lived such a life. A large manor, gilt-thread tapestries hanging in colorful arrays over the stonework, glossy masterpieces of carved wood chairs and tables throughout.

None of it had made her happy then, especially when she'd been so blissfully unaware of debt and its bite. But she knew for sure that none of it would make her happy now.

She found a side set of stairs and made her way up. If Connor was within the castle, no doubt he'd be inside the solar, or perhaps one of the upper chambers, finding whatever it was he sought from MacAlister.

Several doors met her at the top of the stairs. All closed.

She'd have to open each to discern what lay beyond. Then again, she doubted any conversation Connor might have with the laird or any of the servants would warrant an open door.

Thankfully, having dressed as a servant would keep her from appearing out of place.

She opened the first door and found a large bedchamber with several trunks and bags piled near the massive bed.

No one appeared to be inside.

She slipped out and closed the door.

"What are ye doin'?" A harsh female voice sounded behind her.

Ariana's heart lurched into her throat. She spun around to find a large woman with a frown creasing deep grooves in a fleshy face, like an apple left to wither in the sun.

"I—I was gathering sheets to launder." Stammering the statement like a young servant was an easy feat, what with the fright the older woman had given Ariana.

The woman's small brown eyes squinted and she craned her head toward the basket Ariana held. "We collected them yesterday."

Ariana gripped the handle of the basket tighter to keep her nerves from showing. The woven wood crackled against her palm. "I was told Laird MacAlister needed me to take his."

The older woman's scowl deepened and her thin mouth all but disappeared. "Ach, I canna say I'm surprised." She muttered something under her breath. "But that isna Laird MacAlister's room."

Ariana ducked her head. "Forgive me, I'm new."

"Aye, I havena seen ye before." The woman jerked her thumb over her shoulder. "His room's the last one on the right. Mind ye hurry up though. I've need of ye in the kitchens helping for the feast tonight."

Ariana nodded.

The woman didn't leave, though. Instead she leaned closer, enveloping Ariana in the mingled scents of soap and sweat. "Whatever ye find in there, ye keep it to yerself, aye?"

Ariana nodded again, this time in agreement to the whispered threat.

Apparently satisfied, the woman pulled out of Ariana's personal space and bustled in the opposite direction.

Ariana rushed down the hall with as much haste as she dared and tried the handle of MacAlister's door. It gave beneath her fingers and swung silently open.

Quietly, save the pounding of her heart, she slipped inside. The shutters were closed, but the rising sun outside still lit the interior of the room.

Ariana glanced toward the bed and everything in her went still.

There, in the bed, were two sleeping figures, Laird and Lady MacAlister. But that wasn't what caused her heart to cease its erratic beat.

Wearing the clothes of the dead guard from the night before and leaning over the man, hands poised to strangle, was Connor.

Chapter Twenty-Three

Connor had been caught.

He stared at Ariana across the room.

Her eyes darted from his outstretched hands to MacAlister's sleeping form and back to him. A look of horror parted her lips.

His heart went heavy as lead and slid deep into the pit of his stomach.

Of all people to catch him, it had to be Ariana, the woman who had consumed his thoughts through the night and all morning.

And to think he'd come alone to keep her safe, to keep her from being involved. Now she was here, witnessing him in his true form. As a killer.

He wanted to call out to her and offer some form of explanation. But nothing could be said to make this right, and even if it could, now wouldn't be the time.

Already he was surprised MacAlister hadn't woken. Most would have suspected someone standing above them by now and woken on instinct alone. But he'd been there more than a few moments already, and still MacAlister's face remained relaxed in slumber.

Ariana backed toward the cracked door. Her skirts swayed and bumped against an iron rack. It tipped backward and crashed to the hard floor with a reverberating clang.

Everything in Connor froze and his attention darted toward the bed.

Neither Laird MacAlister nor Lady MacAlister had stirred.

Their faces remained still.

Too still.

Too pale, now that he looked closer.

An icy tendril of realization spiraled through him.

They were both already dead.

The door clicked closed and a key turned in the lock.

Connor jerked his gaze toward the entryway, expecting to find Ariana gone and the door locked tight behind her.

But there she stood with her hand firmly planted on the door latch, her chest rising and falling with her rapid breath. There was a wild look in her eyes, like a trapped animal.

She wandered closer and looked to the figures on the bed, her gaze lingering on the sleeping form of Lady MacAlister.

The woman's brilliant hair splayed across the white sheets in a violent splash of red. The covers had fallen low on her torso, revealing one full breast lying against her ribs.

"They're dead." Ariana said it as a statement, not a question. As if she already knew without having to ask.

"You killed them," she amended. Angry tears shone bright in her eyes. "Lady MacAlister, too?"

Connor grabbed her arm, stilling her rage before it grew too loud. Already anyone could come to the locked door and force entry. At any moment, they could be caught.

He knew his luck couldn't last forever, no matter the skills his father had taught him. Eventually, he would be caught and Cora would receive wealth he'd been saving to see her free and happy.

But not like this, not with Ariana.

He could easily face his death beneath the burden of his sins, but he could not subject her to such a fate.

Ariana jerked away and stared at him with horror.

"We need to go," Connor said.

She did not move from where she stood an arm's length away. Accusation burned bright in her eyes and seared him deeper than he thought possible.

"You killed them," she ground out.

"I dinna kill them. They were dead when I arrived."

"Then why were you standing over him like that?" She swallowed. "Like you planned to kill him."

Connor didn't say anything. Silence was better than confessing his original intentions, however apparent they so obviously were.

She didn't belive him. He could read as much on her face.

Ariana's hands balled into fists at her side. "Did you have to kill her, too?"

Footsteps sounded on stone nearby. Someone was coming.

A flicker of panic flared within Connor. He shot his hand out toward her and caught her arm. "I dinna kill either of them. We need to go."

The shuffle of footsteps was coming closer.

"Get out of here." His voice came out in a growl in his desperation. "Get out of here and pretend like ye never came in here to start with."

He shoved her toward the door, but did not move to follow her. He intended to stay. He would face the repercussions of murder— ironically for people he hadn't killed.

Ariana hesitated and he could see loyalty and fear warring on her lovely face—the shift of her gaze from him to where Lady MacAlister lay on the bed.

A door creaked open and it took Connor a moment to realize it was not the locked door at the front of the room, but a concealed partition in the wall shifting outward.

A hidden door.

They were both caught.

Ariana's hesitation had cost her freedom.

Connor moved to stand in front of Ariana and faced the woman who pushed her way into the room.

A tall, graceful woman with brilliant red hair regarded him with a note of noble disinterest, leaving him to wonder who the hell she was and why she was in there.

• • •

They were killers and they would die.

Together.

Ariana had heard the footsteps approach, and while she appreciated Connor's attempt to protect her, she would not allow him to take the burden alone.

After all, it was she who'd told him Lady MacAlister would eventually be there. It was she who had put both people at risk.

The realization churned sourly in her gut.

She hadn't understood how much danger she'd placed them in. She hadn't known Connor's intent wasn't to get information on MacAlister.

It was to kill.

The very action which had left Ariana horrified the day before when she'd taken the life of the guard, he was doing it now. Willingly.

What was worse, he continued to deny to her he'd even done it.

And she did not believe him.

Connor.

The man she trusted and let love her the previous night.

A murderer.

No longer could she consider herself a spy helping a good cause. She had been assisting a murderer. A man she had trusted to be good and just, a man she had thought she loved.

A man she had given her virginity to and whose quiet anger she had endured afterward. And now Lady MacAlister, a woman who had offered her kindness, was dead.

Her nose tingled with the burn of impending tears, but she willed them away.

She would not hide from the person who had found them. Though she had not killed the couple in the bed, she was as guilty as Connor, regardless of her ignorance.

"I don't know you." The voice addressing Connor was a woman's. "Who is behind you?"

Ariana peered around Connor's broad shoulder and her heart stopped beating for the briefest of moments.

Lady MacAlister, the woman she'd assumed to be lying dead

beside her husband in the bed, stood before them in a regal blue gown with an icy countenance.

"Lady MacAlister," she breathed.

The noblewoman arched an eyebrow. "Bess? Is that you?" She tilted her head. "I must say, brown hair suits you better than that garish blonde." She waved a hand toward Connor. "Who is this?"

Ariana paused, uncertain what to say. Had Lady MacAlister seen her husband yet, or the woman who had died beside him?

And who *was* the woman beside him, if not Lady MacAlister?

"A friend." It was all Ariana could manage. She couldn't give away Connor's name when she hadn't even supplied her own.

Lady MacAlister nodded in obvious satisfaction and approached the bed with curiosity. "Do call me Isabel," she said. "And I'd prefer to know your real name as well."

To Ariana's horror, Lady MacAlister—Isabel—touched her husband's neck with the press of her fingertips. She regarded the other woman with a pensive expression then turned to Ariana once more.

"Did you wish to accept my offer as lady's maid?" Isabel asked her.

Ariana frowned slightly, not understanding the question nor why Isabel appeared entirely unperturbed by her husband's death.

Isabel pulled the ribbon at her bodice and began unlacing the long satin ties. "I'll need you to help me put her in my clothing, then make me look like a whore." She stared down at the woman on the bed. "Like her."

The world had gone entirely mad, and Ariana was left standing dumbly there to bear witness.

"What are you getting at?" Connor demanded.

Isabel narrowed her eyes at him, the glare in her gaze sharp and spiteful. "This pathetic excuse for a husband I was forced to marry takes whatever he wants, whether it be land or coin. Or me." Her lips curled with unmasked loathing. "I won't tell you what he did to me, but I couldn't stand the thought of living with him anymore—even the idea of his very touch."

She shuddered.

"And the woman?" Ariana asked, finding her voice.

Isabel's face softened. "The woman was guilty only of being the unfortunate girl to bed a wealthy, married man in the hopes of gaining glory later. It was to my benefit that she happened to look very similar to me. Apparently my husband—" she spat out the word "—enjoyed women with red hair."

Isabel jerked the last of the ribbon through the bodice and it sagged away from her body. She did not pause in pulling it off and letting it land in a heap on the floor.

Connor turned away.

Ariana caught the fine garment and lifted it lest it get dirty. "Why are we putting it on her?"

Isabel paused and faced the dead woman. "Because she will be buried a noblewoman."

"As you," Ariana surmised.

"Yes." Isabel pulled the tie of her brilliant blue skirt. It belled around her waist before pooling on the floor. "And I thank you for the poison you gave me. I had no idea how potent it was until I saw how quickly it killed off the rats in my room that night. Perfect, considering I had my own rat to see dead."

Ariana snapped upright. "My poison?" So, Connor had not been the source of their demise. She had unjustly accused him. Her cheeks went hot and she glanced toward Connor.

His back tensed, a slight action Ariana did not miss.

"The one I took from your pocket. I knew you were more than just a lowly wench." Isabel gave her a conspiring grin.

The round vial.

Ariana had thought she'd lost it on the ride back to Kindrochit. But it had been stolen. Percy, who had warned her time and again to be cautious with the vial, would be horrified to learn how her potion had been used.

Ariana's stomach knotted with disgust at herself.

So many deaths.

Had she known prior to coming to Scotland, she would have

accepted her fate in prison, or whatever punishment the king saw fit for a card cheat.

At least it would have only been she who suffered.

Isabel's cold hand touched Ariana's cheek, and eyes as clear and blue as an endless summer sky stared at her. "Do not think me cruel. Do not judge one whose life you have not lived."

"We must hurry." Connor's voice broke the connection, and Ariana was grateful for the interruption.

He was right. They could not be caught.

"What will you do now?" Ariana asked while Isabel removed the remainder of her clothing. "Return to London?"

"I can't return to London." Isabel peeled her shift over her head and stood unabashedly naked. "I'll be sold off into marriage again."

Though Ariana tried not to look at the naked woman, it was impossible not to. Her body was slender and curvy with breasts much larger than Ariana's. But it was not that which caught Ariana's attention.

Bruises marred Isabel's pale skin, in various shades, from the deep purple black of those freshly received to the sickly yellow of those many days healed. Several scratches showed on her ribs and waist, angry and red. They must have been horribly uncomfortable against the tightness of Isabel's corset.

The woman met her horrified stare with a hard look. "He won't touch me again."

She grabbed her clothes from the ground with a jerk and made her way to where the woman lay in the bed. Together she and Ariana worked to dress the dead woman and make her appear as if she were Lady MacAlister.

The body had not been long dead, as evidenced by the pliable warmth of her skin. Ariana moved quickly to dress her, not wanting to witness the transformation of life to cool death with her fingertips again. The dead woman had similar bruising and scratches on her body as well.

Once the dead woman was dressed, Isabel bent over her and pressed a kiss to her waxy brow. It was an odd thing to do and, somehow, Ariana felt as though she should not have been there to witness the strangely intimate action.

Dressing Isabel as a common whore was far easier, and she was ready within a quick moment.

"It's done," Ariana said to Connor, who turned around, great relief evident on his face.

Isabel led them toward the hidden door, but stopped and turned to face them. "Let me come with you."

"No." Connor's answer was quick and firm.

A look of panic fluttered over Isabel's otherwise composed face. "I have nowhere to go. I thought I could figure it out, but—"

A voice boomed outside the locked door. "I told her to come in here to change the sheets, but she's been there for ages. New girl. I'm sure she'll be needing help."

A prickle of fear skittered over Ariana's skin.

"Please," Isabel hissed. "Or I'll let us all get caught."

"No," Connor repeated. His gaze shifted from the door to Isabel, and Ariana knew a plan was already forming in his mind.

"Please," Isabel whispered with a pitch of desperation. "I'm the king's cousin."

Chapter Twenty-Four

The skies were roiling with gray angry clouds, a perfect mirror to Connor's own mood.

He stalked through the courtyard of Urquhart Castle with Ariana and Isabel trailing behind him.

Escaping from the manor had been easy. A beggar, a servant, and a whore—all unseen to uncaring guards upon their exit.

And here they all were, in the castle which should be his, but didn't belong to him.

He'd wanted to look for his people, damn it.

Now he had to figure out what the hell to do with Isabel. The king's cousin, of all damn people.

But it hadn't been that declaration which had changed his mind, a decision he now regretted—it had been the imploring gaze from Ariana.

Ariana.

God, she knew now. He'd have to explain it all to her and hope she understood.

His temples ached with the raging pressure inside his skull.

He couldn't keep Isabel with them. He couldn't be responsible for the king's cousin, especially against the king's knowledge. Too much had already been sacrificed to secure his inheritance. He would not see it all come to naught because some lass wanted to escape being married.

"Ye can stay here tonight," Connor said, finally breaking the silence the group had held since their departure. "But I canna let ye stay with us permanently."

Isabel looked toward Ariana, obviously knowing who best to implore. "I don't want to go back to court. I don't want to be another pawn in another marriage. Please. I can help you. I don't know what sort of role you play, but I can help. I'm skilled in many areas. I can help make your accent more believable and can teach you many languages." Her words came faster and her pitch shot up with determination.

She begged with her eyes, and Connor gritted his teeth at the softening of sympathy upon Ariana's face. "I helped James all the time when he needed information from someone," Isabel said. "I could do the same for you. Please."

Through it all, she kept her stance proud as any English noble, a strange combination with her whore's attire and her begging desperation.

She was in dire need.

Connor opened the door to Grant Tower and addressed Isabel. "Get inside and get the fire lit so ye can get into decent clothing. We'll be up momentarily."

Isabel shot him a grateful look and scurried through the doorway.

Rain spattered them, but he didn't want to speak inside the large tower house. It was too empty. Even if they were on the bottom floor, their voices would echo on bare walls and carry their conversation up to Isabel's waiting ears.

Ariana watched him through a curtain of damp hair, her arms crossed in a determined manner.

He nodded toward the inner close of the castle. "Follow me."

He led her through the doors of the kitchen. As with all the other buildings, it now stood empty, devoid of life, its furnishings carried away. Several long counters still stood intact, as did the massive hearth with a hearty band of iron stabbed through it. The same sad coating of dust layered the room, masking the fond memories the building had once held. It had once bustled with activity and had always been warm no matter the season. The cook had smuggled him bits of browned fat when he came in and declared he needed to eat more to be large like his da.

Was the cook still alive in the village?

He couldn't think about that now. Not when there was the issue of Isabel to figure out. It was one thing to seek out his people when only Ariana was with him. To do so with the king's cousin nearby, a woman the town would assume dead—it would be impossible.

Ariana entered behind him and cast a glance around the empty room. She pulled her shawl more tightly around her shoulders. "We should let her come with us."

"I need to see if anyone is still alive from Urquhart," he said, giving voice to the argument pounding his brain.

Her brows furrowed, then lifted with realization. "The man from town? The one who recognized you?"

He nodded. "Aye, I think there are members of my household who are still alive."

She stepped toward him and stopped abruptly, her hand extended between them.

It was the first time they'd been alone since their coupling and since she found him over MacAlister and correctly assumed what he was.

Her expression softened, as if she too were realizing all of this. "Connor," she whispered. "What were you doing at Loch Manor?"

The rain spattered the cobblestones outside the open door and little splats echoed through the cold, empty kitchen.

She moved closer to him. The wet air heightened her fresh scent. It caressed him and made him want to pull her into his arms, where she couldn't look at up at him so imploringly.

How could he answer her question honestly?

The truth clogged in his throat and left him momentarily mute.

Her hand came to rest on his forearm, feather light and warm. "I know Lady MacAlister killed her husband, but I don't believe you knew that." She paused and searched the air, as if she might find the words she needed to say there. "I know what I saw, but I need to hear it from you."

His heartbeat thudded faster in his chest. She knew. Of course she did. There could be no denying it.

She deserved to know who he was at his core. He had nothing to offer her and nothing would prove it to her more than the truth.

"I was going to kill Angus MacAlister," Connor said at last.

Her fingertips flinched on his forearm, as if she had intended to draw away but forced herself to stay where she was.

The rain came down harder outside now and the sound of it roared inside the room. Or perhaps it was the roaring in his ears.

"And Lady MacAlister, too?" she asked.

He shook his head. "Only Laird MacAlister. I've done it before, killing a man as he slept beside his wife." His stomach clenched at the memory. "If one is quick and silent, it's not impossible."

"You've done this before," she repeated. Her expression was unreadable, but the delicate muscles of her neck stood taut against her creamy throat.

There was no more for it, but to let her know—to let her see him. The real him. "Yes."

Five times. Men he'd killed for the king, their faces blending with those of men Connor had slain in battle.

This time she did draw her hand away. Tears gleamed in her eyes, making them seem to glow in the muted light. "Connor, why?"

His stomach knotted and his muscles drew tight. Everything in him went on high alert. He couldn't stand the way she looked at him, with a mixture of horror and desperation.

"Because I dinna have a choice," he said in a rough tone. "Because it's the only way to get all this back, and to help Cora."

He turned from her and braced his arms over the massive fireplace. Black streaks of scorched stone and the sediment of ash long since cold greeted his misery.

Ariana did not make a sound, but he knew she was still nearby. He could sense her as surely as he could sense the heat of the sun on a clear day.

"I dinna tell ye everything about my da's death." He hung

his head forward, dropping it between his outstretched arms. The weight of so many memories so difficult to bear.

"Will you tell me now?" Ariana asked quietly.

Connor drew a deep breath and nodded.

After all these years, he would finally confess the extent of his sins, and how he'd somehow secured a deal with the very devil himself.

• • •

Connor's story was indeed one of heartbreak.

Ariana listened as he told her how he'd secured a convent for Cora with his father's signet ring. He'd left both beloved things in Scotland and went to England on the coin stolen from his father.

To seek an audience with the king, or so he'd thought.

But then he had been refused.

"I broke into his rooms that night." Connor turned from the hearth with a mirthless grin on his face. "I surprised the spit out of him. He'd thought his room impenetrable."

Ariana moved closer to keep from missing anything. His voice had gone softer and the rain louder.

"I got permission to kill Laird Gordon, who had taken Urquhart, but had to promise the king wouldna be implicated were I caught." He smirked. "Apparently I did so well, the king wished to appoint me as his personal assassin."

Ariana imagined him, younger, burdened with sorrow, ready to reclaim his inheritance once more. "Did you refuse?"

"Aye, of course I did. But it was then the king informed me he'd assumed ownership of the property to minimize the chance of war in the Highlands."

He sighed and looked down at his hands, which were braced against the hard counter. Dust had smeared over his palms in a pale, chalky coating where they met the stone. "The king told me if I agreed to be his personal assassin for ten years, he'd give me Urquhart. And if not, he'd find Cora."

The muscles clenched at the sides of his jaw.

Ariana moved toward him, but he put up his hands to stop her. "Nay." His voice was a low, threatening whisper. "Ye dinna know the things I've done. The life I've led. The sins I've had to commit."

Everything in her pulled at her to go to him, to wrap her arms about him and let his pain bleed into her so he would not suffer so much alone.

But he did not want her—he'd made that much clear.

"How?" she asked.

"I get names from the king on a bit of parchment I burn after reading them. This time there were two names." His gaze was distant when he shook his head. "There's never been two names."

Ariana drew the cold air into her chest, but it seemed too thin to breathe. "MacAlister," she guessed.

"Aye." Connor still didn't look at her. His haunted expression shot through her heart and left it chilled. "And another man, Kenneth Gordon."

"Gordon?"

"Laird Gordon's son." Connor pressed his thumb and forefinger against his eyes as if it hurt to see. "He was as a brother to me. He killed for me once, at the battle of Glenlivet. We were on opposing sides and both new to battle. I slipped—" He gave a thick swallow. "I slipped and he was there, killing the man, his own brethren, who sought to kill me."

She said nothing, too afraid to speak lest he stop. His pain was evident in the hoarseness of his voice, how he pinched at his eyes.

"I trusted him," Connor continued. "But the day Urquhart was attacked, the bastard laid hands on Cora. I found them kissing. We fought and I landed a punch. I took Cora and left. But he knew. He knew and he never told us."

Connor wrenched his hand from his eyes and stared at her, his gaze hard. "I trusted him." His words were said so loudly they rang out against the stone wall and made Ariana jump.

His vehemence echoed around them for a brief moment before she could quiet her frantic nerves. Never had she seen Connor so agitated. It tore at her heart to know his pain, and to finally understand his plight.

What would she do in such a situation?

What would anyone do?

Exactly as he had done.

"And now you're torn because you know you should kill him," she said, moving closer. "You know you should hate him."

He stared up at her with a wounded wariness most would know to avoid. But she kept moving forward, her hand extended toward him.

"But you can't," she said finally. She touched a hand to his back and the tension of his shoulders melted with a defeated sag.

Her arms came around him and she held the strongest man she had ever known, understanding the hurt plaguing him more than he could possibly know.

Or perhaps he did know. Silence wrapped around them for a long moment, settling comfortably between them.

"Isabel has been hurt too, Connor." She spoke softly and in soothing tones. "She's been wronged. You can help make it right."

A rumble of thunder sounded in the distance, a low, menacing growl.

Connor straightened and looked down at Ariana, his eyes seeking something in hers. "Ye want me to bring Isabel to Kindrochit, to let her become one of us."

She nodded. "It's what's right, Connor. We have to help her." Her hand found his and she gripped his hard, callused fingers. "She's broken, too."

"I dinna heal the way ye think I do. We are no' a house for lost women." He shook his head. "Ye see the world differently—"

"She has information on the king. And if Kenneth Gordon was involved with MacAlister, she would know that too," Ariana added.

Connor's eyes narrowed.

"You can decide what to do with whatever information she gives you." Ariana hoped she was right, that Isabel did have information on Kenneth. "And once you have the information you need, you can decide if Kenneth truly needs to be killed."

Chapter Twenty-Five

Connor hoped like hell his decision to bring Isabel to Kindrochit would not be one he regretted.

Where their travel to Urquhart had been long, the trek back would be difficult, and the thought of it sat in his gut like a stone.

Their first day saw them cover only a fraction of the distance they had previously. He hadn't been able to locate an inn, but they had found an abandoned hut without too many leaks in its thatched roof.

While there hadn't been wood inside to burn in the small hearth, there were several slabs of peat. Enough to keep them warm through the night. It smoldered now in front of them where they sat on the floor, the gray-white smoke spiraling upward and its thick scent permeating the room.

Isabel put a crooked forefinger under her nose and blinked. "That's rather pungent."

"Have ye no' smelled peat burning before?" he asked with a dull note of incredulity.

Peat was often burned for warmth and cooking—not just during the winter, but year round. Its scent reminded him of being a boy and going through the village with his father.

"I've smelled it before." Isabel's eyes squinted in exaggeration to the smoke. "Just not so close."

Connor shrugged. "It's warm."

Ariana sat silent beside him with her hands held toward the fire, palms out.

The subtle light played over her face and reminded him of how impossibly soft her skin had been. The urge to stroke her cheek made his fingers twitch with longing. He wanted to kiss her cool flesh warm and tease moans from her lush mouth. He wanted to have their usual, easy conversation and hear the beautiful sound of her laughter.

"Are ye looking forward to being back at Kindrochit?" Connor asked.

Her gaze slid toward Isabel and she gave an uncertain smile. "Yes."

A simple, singular answer. Disappointment threaded through Connor.

Isabel's presence had lodged a cold, uncomfortable wedge between them. Awkwardness seemed to cling to every move, knowing they were being seen, and to every word, knowing they were being overheard.

As they had only two horses, Isabel had ridden with him, as his horse was meant for heavy warriors and heavy gear. Ariana's small palfrey would have gone even slower with two women atop it. As a result, Connor's back ached like a knot being drawn tight. He stretched in front of the hissing fire and his back gave a deep, gratifying pop in several places.

"We'll see about getting ye yer own horse tomorrow." He nodded toward Isabel before reaching for the small bag of food. Tomorrow they would venture through a town and all could be replenished.

He handed a roll and chunk of cheese to each woman.

Isabel took it with some hesitation. "Is there no meat for a stew?"

Annoyance prickled along the back of Connor's neck, and he had to remind himself for the hundredth time that Isabel was a noblewoman. She'd been raised in court and had known only luxury.

"When we arrive back at Kindrochit, aye, there will be many stews and freshly baked bread. But for now, this is what we have."

He lowered himself to the floor between the women once more and bit into his own roll. It was hard and cold and squeaked against his back teeth when he chewed. Not that he minded. It would soothe the angry hunger in his stomach and allow him to get by until morning, when he'd dispense the last of the rolls, which would be all the harder.

He decided not to divulge that bit of information to the noblewoman.

"You're the king's cousin," Ariana said suddenly. "How?"

Isabel stared at her for a moment. "I'm a bastard. My father is Charles Stuart and my mother was the daughter of advantageous nobodies who landed their pretty girl in an earl's bed." She gave a bitter smile. "I'm not precious enough to fear stealing the crown, but royal enough to be an encouraging proposition for marriage negotiations."

"And if you go back, you'll be set for another marriage," Ariana said.

Isabel nodded. "That's why I can't go back. I could try to run, say I'd been compelled by witches or something. James seems to think they're rampant in Scotland and is deathly afraid of them." Isabel gave a snort of laughter. "But knowing him, I'd end up dead for the mere association." She sighed. "Makes me wish I'd faded into the background at court more, away from view, that I'd spent my time in the circles you did."

Ariana's mouth parted in surprise.

"Yes," Isabel confirmed. "I recognize you from court, though it took me a while to pair you with who you really were. I didn't realize it until I saw you without that hideous blonde wig."

Ariana cast a quick glance in Connor's direction and she pursed her lips, obviously not intending to ask for further information. But Connor wanted more, to know Ariana's life before he taught her to spy, before she had to cheat and steal to live.

"What circles?" he asked.

Isabel rolled her eyes. "The stuffy ones. Where manners were always exhibited with immaculate perfection and rules were tediously followed. I could almost cry at the sheer boredom of it all." She looked baldly at Ariana. "Truly I don't know how you could have dealt with it. But now you're anything but a bargaining chip and traveling alone with a man and staying together in an old abandoned castle. How curious."

215

It was odd to imagine Ariana leading such a quiet life. He knew the enjoyment she got from accomplishing new tasks, from even the simple run they always completed before their training sessions.

"How much do you know of MacAlister's dealings?" Ariana asked in an abrupt change of subject.

Isabel gave a noncommittal shrug of her shoulders. "He did not share much with me."

Of course.

Disappointment weighed on Connor's aching back. He'd hoped to learn information from Isabel, as Ariana had suggested. Something he could use to determine what MacAlister had been doing with Cora.

He hesitated a moment before asking a question he needed the answer to, but was uncertain if he truly wanted to know. "Did ye ever hear the name Cora Grant?"

Isabel nibbled on her bread with her sharp little teeth, a thoughtful expression on her comely face. "No," she said finally. "I've never heard of her before."

Damn.

"What about Kenneth Gordon?" Ariana asked.

"Now *that* name I know well," Isabel said with a quirk of her eyebrow. "And I can share a lot of information."

She went quiet and let the silence drag out in a way Connor did not like.

"It involves conspiracy." She stared down at her hair and carefully plucked apart the wet strands with maddening disinterest. "Tomorrow evening I'd like to stay at an inn. Every night, for that matter. And I'd like better food than what we have here. A hot meal."

Connor's gut knotted in aggravation. He wouldn't be told what to do by some nobleman's brat—royal blood or no.

"Then ye can stay here and fend for yerself," he said in a quiet voice.

Her gaze flicked from her hair to his face. "What?" She narrowed her eyes with a look of incredulity.

"I willna have ye giving orders and making demands of us." His tone was hard, as was intended. "I'm no servant of yers and neither is Ariana. We'll continue to help ye after we know everything, but I willna be extorted for information."

Isabel stared at him for a moment, her face blank. Surely no one had ever spoken to her as he had.

"Very well," she said after a pause. "My former husband made an alliance with Kenneth Gordon to depose the king of Scotland."

She said those damning words as if she found them boring, but Connor felt as though he'd been punched in the throat.

Kenneth Gordon.

Aye, Connor knew he was no longer the boy of their youth, but treason?

Kenneth had tried to take advantage of Cora and had played a role in Connor's father's death—for those things he could never forgive him.

But never would he have suspected Kenneth would go through with something as dangerous, as foolhardy, as treason.

"Is that why ye killed yer husband?" Connor asked. "To protect yer cousin?"

Isabel cast her gaze toward Ariana before looking back at him, her back stiffening to a regal, if not affronted, manner. "No."

Connor didn't need to know the reason why, but he did know one thing for certain—he would ask every necessary question, note every subtle look and every shift in her voice. He would get the entire story by the time they arrived.

The sooner he had what he needed from her and had deposited her at Kindrochit, the sooner he could return to Urquhart and seek out his people.

• • •

Once again, the journey was cold and wet, but this time Ariana found it far more miserable.

She hunched over her horse in an effort to borrow some of its warmth and breathed out in a slow, steady exhale. Her breath fogged in front of her, swelling against the pouring rain before dissipating.

Irritation clawed at her insides. It raked against her nerves and left her throat burning with the need to scream.

The cold, the wet, the discomfort of every part of her body from so much riding.

She could scarce stand another second.

The trip, which had only taken three days on the way to Urquhart, had taken five on the way back. Perhaps six if they did not reach the castle by nightfall.

Already the sky was beginning to cast the pallor of dusk upon the surrounding forest.

Connor had said they were close, but how could one discern one forest from another?

She looked several feet in front of her to where Connor rode beside Isabel, who sat on the small brown mare he'd purchased for her. They'd been side by side almost the entire journey, their heads bent toward each other to conceal Isabel's secrets. Such nearness made them look like lovers.

Pain sluiced through Ariana's heart, just as fresh and painful as it'd been the first time she had experienced it. A foolish emotion, when she knew Connor needed information from Isabel. And yet, Ariana could not tamp it down.

Surely after several days, the discomfort would have diminished.

But, no, it had not. And she found her gaze wandering periodically to the two, like touching a wound to see if it still ached.

It did.

She knew the feeling for what it was and hated herself for it.

Jealousy.

She wrenched her eyes from them, but still the pain throbbed, hollow and hot in her belly. The stab of discomfort was entirely unwarranted.

Connor had given her no promises. She'd had no expectations when she'd lain with him.

Had she?

Thoughts swirled in a dizzying whirl in her head and tangled with the fragile web of her memory from that night. So much had happened then.

If anything, Ariana should have been grateful for Isabel, and truly, deep down, she was. While Isabel had slowed their pace considerably, she had also tried to help where she could and had readily answered all questions she was asked. From her, they'd learned Kenneth had been promised a betrothal from MacAlister, though Isabel didn't know to whom, and that Kenneth had been forced to find more allies for them. The plan to depose the king was simple— unite the Highlands and overwhelm the Lowlands. Take Scotland back, as its own entity, free of the rule of England.

Isabel had been kind and helpful. Impossible to hate.

Not that Ariana wanted to hate her. And so she hated herself and the jealousy burning inside her—an ember of pain fanned by each innocent interaction between Connor and Isabel.

Connor looked back at her over his shoulder and smiled. Her poor, stupidly bruised heart flinched.

She cared for him too much.

The way she'd once tried to love her parents, and her brother— when she was far too young to understand they would never even warm toward her.

And, like Connor, they had never returned her affection, no matter what she did to please them with her wasted life.

Isabel was right. Ariana had been stuffy, boring. She'd lived her life by the rules set for her and received nothing for her efforts. Not a husband and children, nor a household of her own, nor even the slightest show of affection.

Connor slowed his horse to be side by side with her. "No' much longer now, lass."

Ariana forced a smile. He shifted in his saddle and the low creak of leather made the silence between them all the more apparent.

Isabel rode several feet ahead, too far away to hear a quiet conversation. This was the closest they'd come to being alone since Ariana had convinced him to bring Isabel to Kindrochit.

Whatever he'd approached her for, the air seemed to thicken with his obvious discomfort.

"That night." His brow creased. "Between us."

"What happened at Urquhart need stay only between us." The words fell from her mouth with all the decorum of a polite dinner request—a beautiful facade for the ugly wrenching emotion tearing through her.

"I canna—" Connor raked his fingers through his hair and scrubbed at the back of his head before dropping his hand. Never had she seen him look so unsure of himself, so regretful.

A fresh dagger of pain sliced through her chest.

"I dinna want anyone to know." His gaze was almost pleadingly apologetic.

"I understand." She said it quickly, as if doing so might make his words hurt less.

And she did understand. She'd assumed as much from the start. He'd acted on lust, nothing more.

Hadn't she done the same?

Wasn't it she who had so selfishly continued on the night she'd killed the guard? She'd wanted his comfort and had reveled in it.

This was the price she paid.

"I'm sorry," he spoke softly. He reached out and settled a hand over where hers clutched the sodden reins. Somehow his palm was warm despite the wet, bone-freezing chill, and yet it brought her no comfort.

Anger chipped away at her control. Anger at herself for having given him her innocence, and anger at him for having taken it only to cast her aside. She had been a fool, gambling for high stakes when she didn't have a good hand.

When she didn't even have a card hidden up her sleeve.

Once she'd had a respectable name and her innocence. Now she had only her respectable name, however scuffed it might be.

Her heart dragged and scraped on the hard reality of her situation.

If there'd ever been a chance to go back to King James's court in London, there was little hope for it now.

Connor removed his hand from hers and the air bathed her skin with a refreshing chill.

"Thank you," he said.

His gratitude only fed the flames of her anger, and it flared with greedy force.

Perhaps anything he'd said then might have done the same. Silence passed between them, long and awkward enough to make her feel as though she ought to say something more.

Before she could, however, he returned to Isabel's side and left Ariana alone to wade alone through the deepest pits of her dark thoughts.

A knot fisted in her throat, ugly and aching.

She'd felt like this too often before—when her constant attempts to please her parents had resulted in the continuation of their cold indifference. When her fragile hope for a new life with her brother had wilted under the reality of that same lack of affection their parents had afforded her.

And so there was nothing to do but hide, as she'd done then.

She could almost feel the stoic defense sliding a shield between her and the burning heat of her pain. A hardness curling around the wounded place in her heart like a sheet of iron—powerful and impenetrable.

She knew that shield well. She'd held it locked tight around her heart for most of her life. It had gotten her through a lifetime of disappointment and hurt.

And now it would get her through this.

Chapter Twenty-Six

If Connor had had much weighing on his mind when he left Kindrochit, he now had even more.

Kenneth's involvement in the plot to overthrow the king lodged in his thoughts like a stone caught in a boot. The idea was reckless and dangerous. Not that Kenneth was above being those things, but it was also stupid, and Kenneth was anything but that.

Connor only hoped he could quickly see everything to rights at Kindrochit and rush back to Urquhart. If Delilah and Sylvi had returned, he could send them to seek out Kenneth, to ascertain proof to support Isabel's claims. Doubtless the potential treason they followed had been part of MacAlister's plot, if it was truly as large a conspiracy as Isabel had stated.

The sooner Connor could get back to Urquhart, the better. His people needed him, just as he needed them. They were his legacy. All these years, such a concept had remained dormant. Until the man in Loch Manor.

I recognize ye. Many of us do.

If any of his people were truly alive, then he'd left them alone and defenseless.

If that man was one of his people, they knew he was alive. They would be looking for him, seeking his counsel.

The roar of River Clunie announced their arrival before Kindrochit rose into view, but Connor did not feel the comfort of returning home. This was not his home. This was the place he was made to stay, where he was forced to twist women into something unnatural. Where he was forced to abandon the life he loved.

He glanced beside him where Ariana rode in silence, her face betraying none of the happiness and affection he so wished to see.

Kindrochit was a place where he had no future, even with the woman he wanted.

A palpable longing ached in his chest.

He hated telling her to keep what they'd shared silent, but he hadn't wanted to bring her further shame by having anyone know. It was bad enough he'd taken her maidenhead, but it ached his heart to think she would be embarrassed were the others to know.

"This is it?" Isabel asked. "It looks…old." Her nose wrinkled.

Connor suppressed a sigh. One thing he'd be glad for was freedom from Isabel's constant complaints. Going from a luxurious life of royal nobility to that of a weary traveler had doubtless not been easy for her. Over time, he would see her toughened up.

Until then, he was at the mercy of her displeasure.

"It is old," Connor answered simply. "It was abandoned before we took up residence, but it's remote and people don't assume it's inhabited."

Isabel offered him a small smile, at least making an effort to be amiable. "Remote is good."

He led the way across the crumbling bridge of Kindrochit when a *clang* sounded from within. Every muscle in Connor's body went tight.

He knew the sound well—the striking of blade against blade. Perhaps it was Delilah and Sylvi back, but if not…

He rushed into Kindrochit to find Liv and Percy facing one another in the large courtyard, both dripping wet from the rain and wearing the padded armor. Each woman brandished a sword.

He stared for a moment at the delicate way Percy prodded the air with the tip of her blade. Never had he thought to see her with a weapon in her hands again.

"Liv!" Ariana's voice broke through the silence.

Percy dropped her sword and Liv spun around.

Ariana raced across the small courtyard and embraced her friend with obvious care.

For the first time since Liv had arrived at Kindrochit, Connor saw color warm her cheeks and brightness in her eyes. Even the copper of her hair shone brilliantly in the fading light.

"It's good to see ye about, Liv," he said with a smile.

"It's nice to finally be feeling better." Liv returned his smile, but there was something soft and sad to the lift of her lips.

Doubtless the lass still had much healing to do.

He regarded Percy. "I dinna think to see ye with a sword in yer hand again."

Percy's cheeks went red. "Um…Liv asked me to show her. I warned her I wouldn't be much help."

Connor nodded. "Then Delilah and Sylvi havena yet returned."

Percy laid her sword in the box of practice weapons. "No, but Murdoch arrived yesterday. He was fair exhausted and has been abed since."

Perfect. Just the man he needed to see.

"I'll see him when he's rested, then," Connor said.

Percy nodded.

Isabel appeared at Connor's side, her head arrogantly cocked as she waited to be introduced. "This is Isabel," he said. "She'll be staying with us for a while. I'd like ye to show her around a bit while Ariana and I see to the horses."

"Of course." Percy was the first to step forward. "Welcome to Kindrochit."

As expected, she immediately took charge and set Liv to putting away the remainder of the practice equipment while she ushered Isabel inside.

Connor was alone with Ariana once more.

Together they walked the horses to the stable.

"I'm sorry," he said softly to her. He knew he wouldn't have to say what it was he apologized for.

She unfastened the saddle from her horse. "I had no illusions."

There was something about how she said it, so accepting, so understanding, so emotionless. It made him want to crush his lips to hers, push her body against the wall, and have her again right there, so the passion glowed bright in her eyes.

The image worked in his mind, building and growing, until he could think of nothing else while they cared for the horses after the long trip.

It was the first time they'd been truly alone since Ariana had convinced him to bring Isabel with them—a decision which had already proved beneficial. Isabel had been a wealth of knowledge.

But he'd never been able to get the night he'd spent with Ariana out of his mind, nor the way she'd so readily accepted him after he'd confessed everything to her in the empty kitchen at Urquhart.

The air was thick and warm, and every part of him became increasingly aware of the movements she made, each graceful sweep of her hand, the very breath passing between her plump lips.

She glanced at him when they finished, and he could take the silent togetherness no more.

"I know I shouldna, I know it isna fair, but I still want ye." The words were out of his mouth before he could stop them.

Before she had a chance to answer, he pressed his mouth to hers. Her lips were warm despite the cold night, warm and soft and lush.

He let his tongue stroke hers, teasing the fiery passion he wished to unleash.

"We can still see each other." He spoke between kisses, hurried and hungry for her. "In the solar while the others sleep."

Ariana pushed herself back and stared up at him. Her fingertips hovered over his chest in a move to keep him away from her. Her mouth and chin were pink from the force of their kiss and her hair had somehow come loose from its simple knot.

She should say no. He had taken everything from her and had nothing to offer her in return. Less than nothing.

And yet the idea of her rejection rent his mind and left him hopelessly desperate.

Her fingers fell away from him and his heart sucked down into his stomach. He knew her answer before it fell from her lips.

"No."

He exhaled the breath he'd kept trapped in his chest. She backed up, watching him, before she turned and was swallowed up by the dark, cold night.

He'd once thought there wasn't anything else he could possibly stand to lose.

He stared into the darkness and realized, for the first time, how very wrong he had been.

• • •

Ariana's heart thundered in her chest with each step she climbed toward the room she shared with Liv. There was a nervous tremor in her legs and her lungs felt as if they no longer fit in her chest. But, no, it was a giddy excitement.

She had told Connor no.

Despite the way he'd looked at her and the way her own longing still hummed warm and tempting in her blood, she'd said no.

Her external strength had been obvious to her for a while now, but her internal strength had been severely lacking.

The trip to Urquhart had taught her as much.

But the man she'd killed, and the other man she'd loved, both had taught hard, fast lessons about how soft her heart had truly been.

No longer was that the case.

She had told Connor no, and now the power in her left her in a rush of dizzying excitement.

Her footsteps tapped and echoed around her and her breath came harder.

The door stood before her. Its image sobered her thoughts and calmed the heady rush of her pulse.

Liv.

How many times had Ariana climbed the stairs as silently as possible only to enter and find a pale and mournful Liv in a fitful state of slumber?

Now she did not slow in the interest of trying to quiet the

sound of her ascent. Now she wanted haste, to see the friend she loved so dearly and ensure she was still alive and healthy.

She lifted the door latch and the door flew open, all her eagerness near bursting within her.

Liv sat before the fire, dangling a bit of string in front of a fluff of gray and white fur. Her head snapped up and she gave so dazzling a smile, Ariana swore the room became brighter.

"Ariana." Liv spoke her name in a soft, breathy voice and attempted to rise from her place on the floor.

"No," Ariana said quickly, and fell into place beside her friend. "You needn't rise."

Color warmed Liv's face unlike Ariana had ever seen before. Her cheeks were a soft pink and the gray of her eyes shone brilliantly in the firelight.

"It's fine," Liv said. "I'm stronger."

She set the string aside and grabbed Ariana's hand in a tight grip, as if trying to put to proof what she'd so boldly declared. Indeed, her hold was firm and her palms warm.

But Ariana could not remove from her mind the last time she'd seen her friend, when Liv's face had been as pale as wax and as unmoving as the dead.

Questions crowded in Ariana's mind and clogged her constricting throat.

She'd feared her return to Kindrochit would bring with it news of Liv's death. But now her friend sat before her, fully alive, with brows drawn together and eyes sparkling with unshed tears. "Please don't cry."

"How?" Ariana choked out.

Liv placed her free hand over her empty womb. "I had been so sick for so long with…" She tucked her lower lip into her mouth and looked away. "With the baby." Her voice caught.

Ariana shook her head. "You don't have to—"

"I want to." Liv's voice was firm. "When I lost the baby, I confess, I wanted to die too. I'd lost everything. My betrothed, the child we'd made together, my parents, my reputation, my life at court. I had nothing."

The small gray and white kitten wiggled her bottom and lunged at the abandoned bit of string with zeal, her little needle-like nails drawn like daggers.

A smile warmed the sorrow from Liv's face, shining through her tears.

"One morning, I woke and found this little girl curled up on my stomach." Liv stroked the small kitten. "Right where my sweet child had been."

Ariana's heart gave a hard, wrenching beat.

Liv lifted the cat to her chest and kissed the downy fur of her head. "It was her who got me through this fortnight. Her and Percy. And you."

Ariana swallowed against the tightness in her throat. "Me?"

"Percy healed me. She sat by my bedside night and day and held a rag to my head as diligently as even my own mother had." Liv squeezed Ariana's hand. "She healed me. And you gave me strength. I know something horrible must have happened for you to end up here, and yet you never appeared anything less than strong to me. I wanted that same determination." The color in Liv's cheeks darkened. "I wanted to be like you."

Tears tingled in Ariana's eyes and her protest balled up tight in her throat.

In the time she'd been gone, she'd killed a man—a man who had been buried in the woods, who may or may not have had a family, who may or may not be missed by ones who loved him. She'd given away her virginity to a man who now wanted only to ensure no one knew of their tryst. She'd helped a woman murder her husband and his lover, and used the lover's corpse to make others assume the king's cousin was dead.

Ariana might have just moments before reveled in the power she had over her own emotions, but she was no woman to admire.

Shame cast its shadow over what would otherwise have been pride.

She gave a weak smile and suddenly wished she could shield herself from her friend as easily as she'd done with Connor.

"I've named her Fianna, if you don't mind," Liv said with a sheepish grin.

Ariana had fallen too deep into the dark spiral of her own thoughts. "What?"

Liv stroked a fingertip over the cat's small head. "The kitten. I've named her Fianna. I had a dream you'd given her to me and, when I woke, I couldn't remember if it'd been real or not. I wanted to be sure you liked the name, just in case."

Ariana had indeed settled the small animal in the rumpled sheets of her friend's bed. She'd hoped they'd find camaraderie with one another, and it appeared they had. Warmth blossomed over the ache in Ariana's chest.

"It's a beautiful name," she said softly.

She released her hand from Liv's. Their palms had begun to sweat against one another, and the absence of heat left Ariana's skin clammy. "The hour is late."

Liv gave a slow nod and settled a kiss on the sleeping kitten. "I'm sure you're tired." She rose with Fianna in her arms, cradled like a babe. "Will you train with me tomorrow?"

"Nothing would give me greater joy." Ariana couldn't help the smile spreading over her face.

She would, of course, be gentle—the way Delilah had been when she'd given Ariana instruction.

Weariness drew at Ariana's eyelids and left her limbs feeling heavy. She slid into bed and reveled in the cool slide of familiar sheets against her skin.

But despite the embracing comfort of the stuffed mattress beneath her, her mind remained agitated by memories—Connor asking her not to say anything to the other women, Connor still expecting her to be with him, tempting her with the promise in his stare and the fierceness of his kiss.

For the countless time, angry thoughts tumbled through her mind and careened into everything calm.

She wasn't hurting from a lack of affection.

No, she was used to that.

Her fingers curled into fists.

She was angry.

She'd done everything right and ended up with nothing. She'd given her heart and seen it rejected. Her throat tightened against the rush of emotion and she squeezed her fists until her arms shook with the effort.

Years of obeying her parents and brother—all of it had been for naught.

There in the dark, with anger pulsing and swelling within her breast and thrumming in her temples, she lay wide awake, feeding the savage rage coming to life within her.

She didn't need her parents or her brother or Connor. She'd survived a year in London, at court no less, on her own.

Her heart raced a little faster, frenzied at the memory.

Such freedom and independence. Granted, the life had been hard, but never had she needed to kill someone.

Never had she needed to guard her heart.

She could be on her own again. Her skills were uncommon. Surely she could find someone willing to hire a woman skilled at gleaning secrets. Finding the right clients would be almost too easy. Even the amount of coin she'd saved already would easily afford a small place to stay and enough food to eat. She could supplement with cheating at cards if need be—if clients were not found quickly enough.

Surely cheating at cards was better than having to kill, and being made to feel as unloved as she had with her parents. The hollow hurt of it filled her, empty and aching.

Liv would get stronger. She didn't need Ariana anymore.

And then the word rose in her mind, floating to the surface of her dark, roiling thoughts of rage and unfairness.

Escape.

Chapter Twenty-Seven

Ariana woke to a sliver of sunlight jabbing into her eyes. She squeezed her eyelids shut and rolled over in her bed, desperate to slide back into sleep.

The desire for more rest pressed at her body, but her mind had already passed into awareness. Not hurt, not sorrow, but the raw, bruised anger left over from the night before, sore from overindulgence of thought.

She'd stayed awake late into the night, allowing herself to be haunted by rage while planning how she could escape and where she might go.

She would stay in Scotland, venturing into the Lowlands, where she could easily win secrets and cards and opportunities to spy for high-paying noblility. Last night, she had figured it all out. Everything seemed so *possible*.

Still, the meager sleep she'd scavenged had not been enough to clear the shadows from her thoughts.

The savory scent of oatcakes and some kind of salted meat edged its way into her conscience with an insistence she could not ignore. Perhaps food might improve her mood.

She dressed quickly and made her way to the great hall, where Liv and Isabel were already sitting.

Connor, she noticed, was absent.

What was also impossible not to notice was Isabel.

She wore the same drab men's clothing for training as both Ariana and Liv, but she'd rimmed her eyes in kohl, lending them an unnaturally bold feline appearance, and her lips were glossy and red with carmine.

"I once made a man leap into the Thames for me." Her voice was so silky smooth, it came out like a purr.

Liv cast her a skeptical look as Ariana took a seat at the large table beside her.

"It's true." Isabel's eyes widened beneath the kohl.

"And how, pray tell, did you accomplish that?" Liv asked and cocked her head to the side, a slight tilt denoting her disbelief.

Isabel leaned forward and licked her lips before speaking. "Because men are malleable. They will do anything you want so long as you know how to ask."

"And I take it you know how to ask?" Ariana interjected.

Isabel's sky blue eyes slid toward her. "Yes, I do. And I can teach you as well." She winked.

A snide comment sharpened on Ariana's tongue, but she clamped her teeth against it. There was no need to subject others to the foulness of her mood.

A helping of pottage sat mostly eaten in Liv's bowl and little Fianna rested at her feet. Despite Ariana's foul mood, she could not help but feel warm at the sight of her friend's recovery.

Footsteps sounded in the doorway behind Ariana and the skin along her back tingled with the eager desire to turn around.

"We already have a teacher for such things," Connor's voice sounded from where the footsteps had come. Rich with a familiar timbre she could not ignore.

And it only served to scrape at her nerves all the more.

She tightened her fist under the table with resolve. She would not turn around.

Isabel gave a little grin. "Then perhaps I can assist with such lessons."

Connor's footsteps sounded, coming closer to Ariana until he appeared beside her and plucked a bit of bread from the trencher with his large, graceful hand.

He shrugged. "Ye'll have to speak with Delilah when she returns. For now, we've got training to do, aye?"

His hand came down on Ariana's shoulder, warm and firm, and he gave her a gentle squeeze. The scent of him teased a spiral of languid desire through her like smooth honey.

It was unwanted.

Ariana rose with the other two women, but the hold Connor had on her shoulder prevented her from leaving along with them.

She shifted her gaze from the table in front of her to his chest, where his léine lay open just wide enough to show the top of his muscular chest. The memory of how warm and strong that very spot had been against her lips whispered over her mouth like a kiss.

He stepped closer with his hand still on her shoulder, his grip soft but still holding her in place. "Ye dinna need to come downstairs. Feel free to rest more."

The show of concern rankled all the more. "I don't need the rest, and they're all waiting for us."

He was too close. His scent too familiar, too intimate.

She shifted her weight, putting the scantest of space between them. But it was enough to allow her to breathe once more.

He watched her with a steady gaze, one altogether heavy and intense. As if he were studying her.

And she didn't like it.

She arched an eyebrow. "Was there something more?"

His stare did not abate, and she tried to pretend she didn't notice the flecks of green and black in his hazel eyes she'd once found so fascinating.

"There's no' anything more."

She needed no further encouragement. She turned her back on the suffocating weight of his observation and left the room.

The other two women were opening the trunk of practice gear by the time she arrived downstairs. The cold morning air nipped at the heat of her cheeks and laced their breath into wisps of white.

Connor had not followed her.

"First we run," Ariana said, indicating the path between the castle walls and the curtain shielding it from view. The grass there was still fuzzy with the morning's frost.

She jogged toward the narrow alley, taking the same path as so many times before.

Isabel and Liv followed at a slow, cautious jog, as if they didn't know what to do.

Ariana remembered too well her own trepidation when she'd first come to Scotland. Being exhausted and hungry and confused as to what would happen in her world.

What would happen to her.

Now she knew.

Her muscles warmed as she ran and energy exploded through her, fueled by the toiling of her thoughts and the lingering anger.

She ran so hard her muscles burned like fire, until sweat lay cool and moist on her brow and the deep insides of her ears ached from the brutal cold. Liv and Isabel were both walking, but their breath fogged thick in front of them.

"That's enough." Connor's voice carried around the castle to where she had finally relaxed into a slow jog.

Something tightened within her. Dread. She didn't want to see him.

And yet she had no choice, and she refused to allow herself to be cowed by her emotions.

She rounded the corner and found him helping Liv and Isabel into their padded armor.

"Hold these blades." He handed each woman a sword. "And lift them repeatedly like this."

He speared the blade out in front of him. Both women did likewise.

An easy enough feat, but Ariana knew how many times they would have to repeat the motion. Until the blazing ache in their arms and backs faded from pain to such a weak numbness they could scarcely raise a cup to their lips later.

Ariana's shoulder burned with the memory of having done the

same thing herself. She'd hated the effort at the time, but it had strengthened her to train properly in the future.

Connor looked directly at her. His lips and cheeks were red from the cold. "And ye." He bent his knees in a bracing stance and his body tensed perceptively. "Ye'll train with me."

• • •

There was a ferocity to Ariana Connor had never seen before.

He stood across from her, both taking a quick break from combat to catch their breath.

The chill of the morning had faded and the sun had warmed the grass back to a lush green. Behind him came the grunts of the other two women in their sword training, lifting the blade first with their right hand until they could no more, then switching to the left.

Ariana wasn't looking at him, but he knew she was aware of him watching her.

And he couldn't help but watch her.

Her blows had been delivered without her usual restraint. They were hard and unhindered and damn accurate. She was powerful, her movements smooth and calculated.

She watched the other women, her face unreadable and her back tall and proud. The sun had risen behind her and limned the curves of her body in a brilliant outline.

Her blue-green eyes settled on him with a hardness he found unwelcome. "Again?"

He braced himself for the impact he knew would come. "Aye."

The word hadn't even fled his lips completely before she lunged at him. But she didn't plow into him like before.

He'd been pushing his weight toward her in expectation and almost pitched forward when she didn't strike.

Instead she rolled between his wide-legged stance and knocked at the backs of his knees. He staggered, but caught his balance and turned.

Her fist flew at his face, but he managed to block it just in time so only the tip of her knuckle grazed his cheek. Her eyes flashed. A huff of air escaped her mouth and her leg flew up toward him.

It would have caught him had he not jumped backward to avoid it. Ordinarily he tempered his own attacks on the girls lest he hurt them. The only one he had never done so with was Sylvi.

And now Ariana.

He swept his leg toward hers and knocked her feet from under her. She fell to the ground with a grunt but quickly popped back up.

Her arms rose in front of her, ready to block and ready to strike. "Again."

He prepared himself, but this time she did not attack. They circled one another, their gaze fixed on the other. Predator stalking prey and waiting for the perfect opportunity to pounce.

"Ye've been doing well, Ariana," he said. "I havena seen ye train so hard."

Her eyes narrowed. "Maybe you've underestimated me."

Then she flew at him and caught him in the gut with her fist.

Indeed, he had underestimated her.

Not only her strength, but also her emotion. What had transpired between them at Urquhart, what had happened with the man she'd killed, it had all had changed her.

Guilt twisted inside him and further drew his breath from his lungs.

He had done it. All of it.

He'd taken his own damaged past and ruined her too.

The soft squeals and grunts of effort behind them had ceased. Liv and Isabel could doubtless no longer raise their blades.

"Enough," Connor said. "Practice is over."

Ariana's gaze flicked toward the sun, which was not yet fully overhead. "It's early."

"Aye," he agreed. "But no' all are as tough as ye."

She nodded. "I'll help them put everything away."

He wanted to stop her as she walked past. He wanted to catch her by the arm and meet her angry gaze so she would understand the depth of his regret for the many things he'd done wrong.

But he knew from her clipped gait, even if he did do such a thing, it wouldn't make a difference.

The door to the castle burst open and slapped against the stone wall with a crack. Connor turned to see Percy running toward them with a box in her hand.

"Percy, what—"

"Delilah and Sylvi are coming," she shouted. "They've got someone injured. Throw open the gate."

Connor sprinted toward the portcullis and triggered the contraption to raise the gate, which ascended with painful slowness.

Percy danced from foot to foot with uncharacteristic impatience. "I saw them from the window. At first I didn't recognize them."

"Who is with them?" Connor asked.

Percy shook her head. "I'm not sure. Murdoch is in his room—I already checked. He's still sleeping." She craned her neck in an effort to look impatiently under the slowly raising gate. "I will check on him when he wakes."

When the widening gap in the gate had reached about three feet, Percy darted forward and ducked under the heavy wooden structure. Connor did likewise and raced behind her to where Delilah and Sylvi approached.

An extraordinarily large man was slung over Sylvi's horse, facedown.

"We found him on the road not far from here," Sylvi said. Her face was set and deep shadows showed beneath her eyes.

Percy waved her hand toward Connor. "Help me pull him down."

"Save your herbs, Percy. They're not needed." Sylvi leapt off her horse and pressed a hand to her lower back before stretching forward.

Delilah slid from her own horse and cast a worried glance at the man. Her dress was rumpled and stained from having worn it often. Even her hair fell limp around her face. Never had Delilah been such a mess.

"He's already dead." Delilah's voice was as wan as she looked.

"Are you sure?" Percy asked.

Connor grasped the man's shirt to pull him down. The skin beneath the cloth felt waxy and cool.

"His throat was cut," Sylvi said. "And not many can survive that." She fingered her own neck, where the skin showed pink beneath the ribbon she wore. Her gaze flicked to Connor, and her hands dropped when she obviously realized he was watching.

He slid the man off the horse, hefting him carefully to keep the body from slamming to the ground. The head fell backward. Too far, as if it meant to roll off. Connor shoved his shoulder forward and braced the weight before it could fall further.

Percy gave a horrified gasp and pressed a hand to her mouth as though she were squelching a scream.

The man's throat had been cut with such savage strength, his head was nearly shorn off.

Connor lowered the man to the ground.

"Don't look, Percy." Sylvi's voice sounded from behind Connor, and the grass rustled with their retreating footsteps.

But Connor did not lift the man to follow their departure. He could not tear his gaze from the face on the ground.

The dark hair had thinned some since Connor had last seen him, but the thick brows and the scar down one cheek was unmistakable.

Connor knew this man.

Renny. Renny was his name.

He'd been the blacksmith.

At Urquhart.

One of the many men Connor assumed had died three years ago. And now he was truly dead.

Something hot and tight coiled in his chest.

If he'd stayed at Urquhart, this never would have happened.

And if Renny had only recently still been alive, so too were others.

Connor would leave for Urquhart immediately.

His people had need of him.

Chapter Twenty-Eight

Connor refused to return to Urquhart without Renny's body.

He couldn't allow one of his men to be buried anywhere but at home. Nay, Renny would be buried at Urquhart, near his parents and the young wife he'd lost so early in their marriage.

Connor had begun mentally preparing the list of items he would need for his journey, especially since he'd need to travel quickly. The urgency of his impending departure raked at his nerves, but not nearly as much as the urgent issues needing his attention before he left.

Sylvi and Delilah were both waiting for him in his solar. Sylvi's back was ramrod straight despite her obvious exhaustion. Delilah, who had taken the time to change into a soft pink gown, slumped in the seat beside her.

"We've uncovered a plot against the king." Sylvi spoke before the door had even closed.

Connor came around the large desk and regarded them. Grime lined Sylvi's face from their journey, but her pale eyes were bright.

"Where did ye hear about this?" he asked.

"The night we went to seek out MacAlister. We didn't find him, but we heard some men talking about trying to raise coin to buy gunpowder." Her brows raised. "A lot of gunpowder. I sent Delilah to them to get more information."

She looked to where Delilah sat beside her.

Delilah's cheeks were red and her face shining where she'd obviously scrubbed her skin clean prior to their arrival, but she hardly appeared refreshed. "They weren't loose with their information, so we stayed at the inn near them long enough to get their trust. This has been a plot going back over two years now. Something having to do with Englishmen on Scottish soil."

Sylvi shook her head. "No, it's about religion. King James would happily kill all the Catholics, but knows he can't. They, however, feel they can kill him for his beliefs regardless. An Englishman, Thomas Percy, approached the king in Scotland to convince him to change his philosophy on the persecution of Catholics, but the king refused. Some Scots slipped words in his ear and incited his rage."

The irritation squeezing at Connor's chest knotted further. "How does this have to do with a plot against the king?"

Delilah waved her hand dismissively. "These Englishmen are angry and want to blow up the king. During the State Opening of Parliament."

Which would not just kill the king, but also the queen, the entire House of Lords, and any other men or women standing nearby.

Though ruthless, Connor had to admit it was brilliant. Not only would the entire country fall into a state of fear and turmoil, but James's young daughter would sit on the throne with Catholic influence.

While it did not separate Scotland from England, it did reduce the religious strife in the Highlands, and a young girl would be more easily influenced than her father.

"Do ye have names?" Connor asked.

Sylvi shook her head. "Not all of them. Just a few." She handed a folded parchment to Connor. "These are the ones I have thus far. I'm in the process of securing more. The Englishmen are trying to enlist Scottish financial support for all the gunpowder."

Connor unfolded the list and saw several English names. While he did not recognize them, he was sure the king would.

"We'll be going back out," Sylvi added. "We needed to come back for supplies. And someone needed clean clothes." She shot Delilah a hard look.

Delilah folded her arms over her chest and returned a defiant stare of her own.

"It's good ye came back." Connor nodded. "This is valuable information ye already have, but ye have to have a care for yerselves as well. Get some good rest, take all the supplies ye need, and ensure ye have enough coin to see ye through yer mission."

The women nodded in unison and rose from their seats. Connor walked to the door with them, intending to leave, when he was met by Percy. An anxious line creased her brow and blood creased the front of a white apron she wore over her simple pink dress.

A spike of alarm jabbed up through Connor.

"It's Murdoch," she said. "He's been stabbed."

Connor followed her quickly down the hall toward the small room where Murdoch stayed. "Where? When? How did this happen?" he demanded.

"In the stomach. He's fortunate to even be alive. He said it was at a tavern near Inverness." She pushed open the narrow wooden door to reveal Murdoch's large form laid out on the bed. The clean scent of steeped herbs scented the air with a medicinal smell.

Connor approached the bed. "Sleeping off drink is easily done, but ye canna sleep off a stab wound." The jest came out hollow.

Murdoch's light hair looked dark against the paleness of his skin. "Ach, ye know it'll take more than a little stab wound to drop me." His words came out slightly slurred.

"I've given him some valerian root for the pain," Percy said softly.

"Why dinna he tell ye he'd been stabbed?" Connor asked.

Murdoch waved a hand in the air. "It wasna deep. I thought it'd be fine. I used to do this when I was younger."

Connor shook his head. "Ye're no' so young anymore, my friend." And it was true. Murdoch was several years older than Connor, but he seemed to have aged over a decade in the last three years.

Murdoch looked up at Connor with a glassy stare. "Gordon was at his castle, at Glenbuchat, only recently returned from Loch Manor, or so his staff said."

Connor's mouth pulled into a grimace. Murdoch, ever the true and good friend, had brought back the necessary information even as he lay in a fog of valerian root and pain.

"Ye're a good man." Connor gently squeezed his friend's arm. "But dinna be a stubborn one. Get some rest, aye? We've enough information for now."

Murdoch nodded and his eyes slid closed.

Connor glanced at Percy, silently seeking confirmation the large man would be fine. She met his gaze and nodded.

Together they left the room, but Connor did not speak until the door had sealed closed behind them. "I'm going to need some supplies for a few days, as will Sylvi and Delilah."

Percy's brow furrowed for the briefest of moments. "You'll be joining them then?"

He shook his head. "I'll be going back to Urquhart and bringing the man Sylvi and Delilah found with me. I believe he's from that area." He offered no more information on it, and knew she would not question it. "I dinna know how long I'll be gone."

"Then I'll ensure I get enough for Ariana as well." She turned to go.

"Ariana willna be coming," Connor said.

Percy spun back around. "She's the only one of us strong enough to go. Liv is only just recovered and Isabel hasn't had any training."

He did not answer at first. He didn't want to, not when he knew how she would take his answer.

But she already knew.

Her hands wrung together, and he regretted the words before he spoke them: "I'm going alone."

She jerked back as if she'd been slapped. "You know how dangerous it is to go alone." She shook her head. "You can't. I won't allow it."

It wasn't ferocity sparking in her words, but fear.

"Ye dinna have a say." He spoke harsh enough to echo in the narrow hallway, but gentle Percy did not so much as flinch.

"No," she said. "But I have experience." Tears shone in her eyes, turning the soft blue brilliant. She pressed a hand over her chest where a blade had once barely missed her heart. The pale line of a silvery scar peeked over the neckline of her plain pink dress.

Percy, who had always been so acquiescent and understanding, now stood before him with her hands clenched into fists at her sides. "You swore we would never go out alone after that day."

Guilt tore into him. "I dinna mean myself."

"And what of us?" Percy said in a harsh whisper. "What if you go and you don't come back? Where will this band of cast-aside women find refuge? We have no home but here. We have no skills but those you've given us. We have nothing to sustain a true life."

She took a deep breath and placed a hand on his arm. Her touch was light and soothing, the way it always was. "We care for you too much to lose you, Connor. Please take Ariana with you."

The words he needed to say stuck in his throat, but Percy was patient and waited with only her eyes imploring him to explain. "Ariana killed a man at Urquhart."

Percy's eyes softened and she breathed out a slow, painful exhalation. "Is she all right?"

"She wasna injured."

"Then it's all the more reason to bring her with you. Watch her, guide her as only you can." Her head tilted and a lock of blonde hair fell over her shoulder. "I often wonder if I would have had the strength to continue as the other women have, if I'd gone out again soon after."

Connor frowned. He'd been so sure giving in to Percy's request to never go on another mission had been the right thing to do. Her doubt made him question his own long-ago decision.

"I don't know for certain," Percy said quickly, as if she knew how her words had twisted into his heart. "But there's one way to find out. Take her with you."

There was never any arguing with Percy. Her gentle insistence and large blue eyes were impossible to rage against.

Connor gave a heavy sigh and nodded. "Verra well. I'll bring Ariana."

And this time he swore to himself things would go differently.

• • •

Ariana made her way down the hall to Percy's room for a few lock-picks to use in training Liv and Isabel. Instructing them had made Ariana realize how much she truly had learned since she'd arrived in Scotland.

How much she'd be able to use on her own when she was free.

The other women had listened with rapt attention to her instructions on preparing for a mission. What to expect, what to do when something bad happened. Certainly she knew too well how difficult it could be when bad things happened, but had avoided sharing the details of her last botched mission.

She tried not to think of the slow, sardonic smile Isabel had given at the mention of the round vial of poison.

Sylvi came out of Percy's room and closed the door quickly behind her. She had something in her hand Ariana could not make out.

Ariana gave Sylvi a nod, not wanting to engage in small talk any more than Sylvi likely wanted to.

The woman was fascinating, though. She possessed the greatest skill of any of the other women there, but she did not venture out on her own.

Sylvi's brows furrowed together and she gave Ariana a discon-certed look. "What?"

Ariana gritted her teeth. Evidently, she had been staring. She could have kicked herself for it.

"Why do you stay?" Ariana let the question slide from her lips and tried not to regret it.

Sylvi smirked. "I'm not going to go until I find who I'm looking for." Lines of white along the sides of Sylvi's eyes stood out against the duskiness of her dirty skin, as if she'd been squinting during her ride. "Besides, I get training here."

"More than you have already?"

Sylvi shrugged off the compliment. "There is always more to

learn. Until I find who I'm looking for. And when I do—" She drew in a deep breath, as if to calm herself. "And when I do, I'll be ready."

There was a coldness to her tone, like the razor-sharp edge of a dagger. A chill skittered over Ariana's skin.

Sylvi narrowed her eyes and the white lines around her eyes disappeared in the creases of grit. "You act as though it's easy to leave, Ariana. No one just walks away."

Ariana felt as if she'd been doused with a bucket of melted snow.

She gave a nod, all she could muster, and then Sylvi was gone.

Had that been a threat?

Ariana opened the door to Percy's room and slipped inside, grateful her encounter with Sylvi was over, and grateful to be once more blissfully alone.

The light inside the room was so brilliant, it left Ariana momentarily stunned. Where the hallway had been dark, the room was brighter than the day outside. Sunlight shone in through the narrow windows lining the back wall, but surely it was not enough to fill the entire room.

Mirrors dotted the room, on walls and on tables and in sconces. One in particular reflected a dazzling shard of sunlight directly into her eyes. It was then Ariana realized the mirrors were responsible for the incredible amount of light.

Several silver lockpick-hairpins glinted at her from a table across the room, where they were neatly lined up alongside one another. Exactly what she needed.

Ariana plucked three from the table, all with a delicate rose design etched into them, and slid one into her hair. There was another table next to her, one with the small vials she'd received from Percy the night of her first mission. The dreadful eye tincture Ariana would never use again, the slender tube of the concoction which left a man incapacitated. And the round vial.

Her gaze flitted from the round vial. After having witnessed its effects, she wanted nothing more to do with its contents.

But the slender tube… Her hand lifted of its own accord and hung in the air for a brief moment.

There were many possibilities with the slender vial, many ways it could aid her in escaping.

No one just walks away.

Sylvi's words pounded in her head.

The enticement flared up inside Ariana, greedy and entitled. She had always played by the rules, always done as she was told. Barring her time at the gaming tables, of course.

Her fingers settled over the slick glass. This was her opportunity to make her own rules, to live her own life.

That was when the door clicked closed with a softness that might as well have been a slam.

Ariana's heart near burst from her chest and she spun around.

She wanted to be angry at the intrusion, to let it feed the fire of unfairness burning through her. And perhaps she could have—were the person anyone else.

Percy stood in front of the closed door, her blonde hair falling around her face like an angel's. A soft smile touched Percy's lips and her expression was as gentle and beautifully open as it always was.

It was impossible to begrudge Percy her beauty as much as it was impossible to feel anger toward her. It was possible, however, to feel guilt—and its weight pressed hard against Ariana's soul.

She had stolen. From Percy.

Shame scorched Ariana's cheeks.

"I assume you've already been informed, then?" Percy asked.

Percy was not at all suspicious of what Ariana was doing, and somehow that made Ariana feel all the worse for her actions.

"I've been informed about what?" Ariana forced a casual tone to her voice.

Percy was closer now, bringing with her the delicate scent of violets. Her hand settled against Ariana's arm, the grasp so light, the touch of her cool fingers was almost indiscernible.

A tingle of alarm hummed in the back of Ariana's mind.

Percy's brow flinched together in an almost sympathetic

gesture and her kind blue eyes met Ariana's. "You're going on another mission."

The words clotted in Ariana's ears and made her head swim.

Another mission.

So soon?

"Will I be leaving with Delilah and Sylvi, then?" Ariana asked.

Percy shook her head. "You'll be leaving with Connor for Urquhart."

Ariana's fingers tingled as if they'd been raked over ice. "When?"

"Tonight." Percy took a deep breath and softly blew it out. "Connor told me what happened when you were there last."

Ariana had to fight to keep her eyes from going wide. Now her entire body felt like it'd been dragged through snow and ice and everything else chilling and awful. Everything went cold and prickled with horror.

Surely Percy didn't know about what Connor and she had shared at the castle...

"I killed someone once, too," Percy whispered. "I had to, or he would have killed me. He almost did."

The blue of Percy's eyes already stood out against the subtle pink of her dress. Now tears lit them to the dazzling deep blue of a sapphire. Those tears tore at Ariana's heart and made her want to put her arms around the other girl, to share the pain of a lost life.

But before Ariana had the chance, Percy moved away and opened a cabinet. "It was because I went on a mission by myself. It was what I'd been ordered to do. I made Connor promise two things—to never have any of us travel alone again, and to never send me out. He has honored that promise. But there are days I regret telling him to take me off missions, days I wished I'd pushed on instead." She pulled a pair of brown shoes from an unseen shelf and settled them on the table with a thunk.

She strode across the room. "I don't want you to regret not going out again."

Going out again.

Those words drew tighter, like the knot of a noose around Ariana's neck.

"You said tonight," Ariana said. "When specifically?"

Percy pressed a small dagger into Ariana's hand. "Within the hour."

The noose went taut.

An hour. She'd only just seen Liv again, and helped Isabel get comfortable at Kindrochit.

"So soon?" Ariana's question came out in a breathy exhale.

Percy stopped moving around the room and came to Ariana with a whispering swish of her skirt. She clasped Ariana's hand in hers. "I know you don't want to do this, but you know how dangerous it can be when you're alone. Connor is strong, yes, but I still worry about him. I worry about all of you."

But it was not the quiet plea in Percy's desperate gaze which swayed Ariana's heart. No, it was a far more selfish reason.

Opportunity.

It would be too hard to leave from Kindrochit. Liv might feel as though Ariana had abandoned her. There were too many in the castle who knew to track her steps. She would be found quickly.

Or maybe she wouldn't be able to stay away and leave the others hurt at her absence.

But to leave on a mission… No one would feel the burn of offense, save Connor. And it was apparent he felt nothing for Ariana but lust.

In their travels to Urquhart, they would be three days out from Kindrochit. Ariana could easily find a way to slip the draught to Connor one night and then, while he slept, she could quietly slip away and begin a new life.

"Yes," she said finally. "I'll go with him."

Percy pressed a hand to her chest with a relieved smile.

And Ariana tried her best to avoid the burden of guilt for what she planned to do.

Escape.

Chapter Twenty-Nine

The angry flush on Ariana's face told Connor all he needed to know about how she felt traveling with him. She held a pair of shoes pinched between her fingers and one of Percy's travel satchels loosely slung over her forearm.

Her eyes flickered to him, then back to the hall. She hadn't even bothered to slow down as she passed.

He wanted to call out to her, to get her attention and hope he could somehow right all his wrongs.

And he had so damn many.

"Ariana," he said.

She stopped and waited a brief moment before turning back toward him.

The apology sat heavy on his tongue. There was no use in apologizing again. But he was sorry.

The light coming in from the window lit her skin and the beautiful clear blue-green of her eyes. She'd been like silk under his hands. He longed to touch her again.

She arched an eyebrow in silent inquiry.

"I'll keep ye safe this time," he said finally.

Her chin notched upward. "I can take care of myself."

There was a cold edge to her voice, one he'd never heard before. One he never wanted to hear again.

He liked the sweet feminine confidence with which she spoke.

This, he realized, would be a long trip. He regretted having promised Percy he would take Ariana with him. Things would be so much easier without her.

He followed her out to the stable and found her with her hands on her hips. Her gaze snapped toward him when he entered. "You didn't have to start preparing my horse. I'm perfectly capable of doing it myself."

"I know ye're capable." He dropped his own travel items to the straw-covered floor. "Which is why I dinna do anything with yer horse."

The mare dipped her head toward Ariana, who absently rubbed the large velvety cheek with her free hand. "Then why is she in a different stall?"

Connor looked at the stalls in front of him. "Are ye sure?"

He remembered being in the stable with Ariana all too well. He'd burned so hot with longing for her.

And she'd so readily rejected him.

He certainly wouldn't make that mistake again.

From what he remembered, her horse had been closer to his. She had been closer to him.

"I'm almost certain." Doubt faded the conviction from her voice.

"We were tired when we arrived," he added. *And distracted.* But he didn't speak the additional thought.

She frowned slightly and set her items on the floor beside an already stuffed bag.

Connor lifted the metal links from the wall to attach the loop which would connect the cart to his horse. They clinked against one another in a metallic jingle. Ariana's horse gave an annoyed swish of her tail.

"What's that?" Ariana asked.

He grabbed the Y-shaped bar used for keeping the cart sturdy as they rode. "A piece of a cart."

She regarded him from the corner of her eye. "Why do we need a cart?"

"For the body," Connor replied.

Ariana's eyes widened. "You can't mean we'll be traveling with him being carted behind us."

He nodded. "Aye, I do. If anything, it'll decrease any chance of a robbery. Funeral parties are seldom attacked. It's bad luck."

Ariana opened her mouth as if she wished to say something more, but then let her lips close.

The cool air between them had grown hot with friction.

Connor straightened and regarded her with a hard stare. "Ye dinna have to come, Ariana. I can go alone."

She gave him a narrowed expression that could only be described as shrewd. "I said I'm coming."

"It'll be a hard trek." He realized he wanted her to back out of the trip with him, to find it too daunting. "We need to get there in as short a time as possible, but we canna travel as fast. That means less sleep, less rest."

On their last trip to Urquhart, Ariana's presence had made the return to his family's home more bearable. The connection between them had been strong then, her regard toward him so sweet, so caring, so accepting—even after he'd told her about his da's death.

Even after his confession about what he did for the king.

But now the connection had been snapped by his own hand, and her warmth had gone cold. It was better this way.

"Ye dinna have to go, Ariana. Ye can stay here with Liv and help her train." His tone was urging.

"I said I'd go." Her cheeks flared with a flush of red. She snatched up her bag from the ground and shot him a challenging look. "You can't get rid of me that easily, Connor Grant."

Somehow he knew she referred to more than just her involvement in this personal mission.

And somehow he knew she was entirely correct.

• • •

The body complicated everything.

Ariana let her gaze glide to the flat cart trailing behind Connor's horse. He'd been correct. They could not travel as quickly, and they had sacrificed sleep to cover the same amount of ground. A lot of sleep.

Even more so, the body made it difficult to come up with an ideal time to slip Connor the draught.

Leaving Connor to sleep off the effects in safety while she slipped away was one thing. Leaving a body unattended was quite another.

It was the beginning of the third day, if it could even be called "day," as the sun had not yet risen. There hadn't exactly been ample opportunities to slip him the drug, as most of their meals were taken quickly and in painful silence. Still, had there been a moment she could have dumped the contents into his drink, her conscience wouldn't have allowed her to.

Not until the man was buried.

Whoever he was.

Ariana's eyes were gritty with lack of sleep and a fog of exhaustion clouded her thoughts with a milky haze.

At least this time they hadn't had the rain. The sun hung high above them now and lit the world around her in glowing emerald green. If her head did not ache so, she knew she would have found the effect beautiful.

As it was, the brilliance shattered in her mind like shards of light from a glinting gem.

Connor did not much care for those moments of sunshine either, and he'd urge the horses to move with more haste over the rugged terrain.

She expected their return to Urquhart had more to do with the man who had recognized Connor than the man they were burying.

While Connor hadn't explained the reason they were coming back to Urquhart, he had on more than one occasion looked at her. Sometimes a quick glance, other times a long, contemplative stare.

She'd noted them all.

Though the silence between them was a cool salve she embraced, she needed information on what to expect when they arrived. Especially if she would need to hold off on her escape until they were no longer in possession of the body.

She regarded the plaid-covered shape on the cart once more, the outline beneath so distinctly human, the lack of movement so disconcertingly devoid of life.

The cart lurched over an unseen object and the body jerked with the rough-hewn wood structure before settling stiffly once more.

She looked at Connor and found his jaw clenched. He knew who was beneath the plaid.

He knew and he cared.

"Who was he?" Ariana asked.

She hadn't been next to Connor when the man's head had almost plunged from his body, but she'd been close enough to see the carnage. And to witness the hurt crack Connor's stoic exterior.

"Ye're talking to me now?" He didn't look at her when he spoke.

"I don't have to." Ariana fixed her own gaze forward and stared out at where the grass was starting to warm into a more vibrant green on the path before them.

The silence settled over them again, but this time it did not feel like a cool balm. This time it was hot and tight and oppressive.

Her pulse simmered with a rebellious fire where all the pain—all the aching, soul-sucking pain she never wanted to acknowledge—curled into ash. If only it would blow away and leave her with nothing.

"I knew him," Connor said, interrupting the torment of her own thoughts. "From Urquhart. His name was Renny, our black-smith. I thought he was dead." He frowned. "I mean, I thought he'd died that day when Urquhart fell. I thought they all had. Yet how could Renny have found me where I was? How could he be so far from Urquhart, unless he knew I was alive and sought me out?"

"Now you want to go back to see if anyone else lives?"

"If there are people still alive..." He focused on something unseen in the distance. "Then I abandoned them to pursue my own selfish endeavors."

She wanted to console him, to offer her support to carry the weight of his burden. But to give her sympathy would be to open her heart, an act she could ill afford to do.

She reminded herself of the hurt he'd inflicted upon her when he'd rejected her. It was pressure against a fresh wound, and brought up the shield around her heart.

"What do you expect to find when we return?" she asked.

"I'm no' sure."

"If they are alive, what do you intend to do?"

"I'm no' sure."

Ariana remembered the additional items Percy had given her before they left Kindrochit. Not just food to tide them over for at least a week, but also a small dagger to hide in her bodice, and a pair of plain brown shoes with false bottoms.

The shoes were quite extraordinary. One need only to press one's weight on the heel and twist to slide loose the trap door, revealing the single compartment. Within was another slender dagger which was sheathed under the foot, and a narrow slit on the side held a spare vial.

The shoes, which Ariana currently wore, were surprisingly comfortable.

The mix of items meant Percy hadn't known what to expect either.

Neither Connor nor Ariana spoke again until it was well into the night and they'd made their way into the silent walls of Urquhart Castle.

Connor wasted no time preparing the grave, though the moon rose as high above them as the sun had that afternoon. Ariana would not offer him consolation, yet she did not leave him to bury his friend alone.

She grabbed an extra shovel and worked at his side, plunging the wide head into the soil until the earthy, moist scent surrounded them and the hole was deep enough to bury Renny.

Together they slid his stiff body into the waiting grave and shoveled the dirt back over him. When they were done, the mound of broken earth marked all that had once been a man. Like Connor's father buried somewhere, hidden from his enemies. Like the guard they'd buried in the woods.

Her heart flinched at the thought.

Connor stayed for a long while, staring at the grave, and Ariana did not move from his side. Her arms ached to hold him, but she knew she could ill afford the attempt to comfort.

Finally, at long last, he turned to her. "Thank ye for yer help."

Deep lines and shadows were visible on his face, his exhaustion as evident as hers felt. He opened his mouth, as though he intended to say more, and then stopped. "We should go to sleep. Tomorrow I hope to find the survivors of the massacre at Urquhart."

She followed obediently behind him and hardened her resolve for what must be done before his people could be found. Renny was buried now. The corpse would no longer be left unattended.

Her footsteps were heavy with exhaustion, but her heart raced with a heady rush.

Tomorrow. She would escape tomorrow, after she'd had sufficient rest.

At her first opportunity, she would slip him the draught and leave.

Chapter Thirty

Connor stared out the narrow window at Loch Ness and tried not to let his gaze slip from the dazzling flecks of light dancing over the water to the bonny woman sleeping on the floor. The same as the last time he'd been at Urquhart with Ariana.

It was difficult for him not to stare with her sleeping so close, her black hair around her face like a silk curtain.

Since they'd returned to Kindrochit, he'd only seen her face either a hard set of determination or completely devoid of any emotion.

But now…

He let his gaze slip from the sunlit swells of hills framing the loch to Ariana, and unabashedly began to study her beauty.

Now her face was soft, her lips slightly pouted, her brow smooth.

She gave a heavy-lidded blink and he shifted his gaze back toward the loch.

"I'd almost given up on ye." He'd meant it as a light jest, but the words fell flat.

Irritation niggled at him, though at himself or her or the situation, he had no idea.

Maybe a little of all.

"Are you wearing that?" Her voice was husky with sleep.

He hadn't opted for his usual beggar's attire of rags and the musk of horse manure. Usually he meant to discourage people from getting too close. But a laird could not approach his people thus, and so he'd donned his finest léine and newest plaid. He'd scraped his face with care by the loch. He even wore his father's ring, though it sat heavy against his skin.

His stomach tightened at the idea of seeing his people again.

If he found them. If they wanted to see him.

So many damn ifs.

"Aye, I'm wearing this," he answered. "We'll break our fast in town once ye're dressed."

Ariana dressed quickly in a separate room and emerged wearing a simple green dress of good quality, also unusual attire for a mission.

Their trek into town was silent and uneventful. The same could not be said of their arrival.

The echo of cheers and cries carried on the wind and greeted them before their feet touched the hard-packed streets of the town. One man's voice rose high above the others, then another round of cheering.

Connor put a hand out to stay Ariana. It was a leader's instinct to protect those he was responsible for, but she did not take it as such. She shot him a frown and made her way past him toward the crowd, her shoulders squared with a soldier's confidence.

On the street just behind the first several buildings was a crowd of people gathered around something. Or someone.

"This is the reason we have disorder here," a male voice called out. "For the rich have more and the poor have less."

The crowd gave a roar of assent.

Ariana pushed her way through the crowd and disappeared from view.

Alarm buzzed in the back of his mind. It was not typical for her to stray from him. He knew she was trying to prove her ability to care for herself, but the price could be foolishly high.

Frustration knotted at his shoulders. He shoved into the crowd after her, his gaze sweeping the faces—not only for Ariana, but also his people.

He found neither.

A man in the obvious cast-off clothing of a noble stood with an air of pretension in the center of the crowd.

"MacAlister and his wife were killed by their own wickedness." The man's hand curled into a fist. "And many more like them will pay if we dinna get what we need."

The crowd shifted around him, agitated.

This—this was what happened when a king stripped a laird of his lands and passed the care of them to nobles who took turns at a manor as if it were a hunting lodge rather than a manor managing the lives of its citizens.

Even if Connor did not locate his people, he'd need to find a way to reclaim Urquhart before everyone killed each other in the impending riot, the anticipation for which crackled in the air.

A flash of green caught his eye. A slip of a lass with dark hair who disappeared into the shadows with far too much ease to be anyone but Ariana.

He forced his way from the crowd and ignored the stares prickling at his back. A grunt sounded from the dark space between two buildings where Ariana had disappeared.

A male grunt.

Connor quickened his pace and arrived just as Ariana swung her elbow up high enough to catch the man in the jaw. The man collapsed to the ground.

She spun toward Connor with her arms bent in front of her face in preparation to attack.

She dropped her hands when she recognized him and gave a little half smirk, obviously pleased with herself.

On the one hand, he wasn't especially pleased with her, but on the other, he knew the bloodlust of crowds could whip into frenzy. And her approach had been flawless.

The man gave a low groan.

"We need to go," he said sharply.

Together they fled the alleyway and headed toward the first tavern opposite the crowd.

"They're using MacAlister's death to incite a riot," she said.

Connor's jaw set. "Aye, I know. They havena had a strong leader here since my da. The king owns the manor, but so many nobles come and go, it isna enough to maintain order. They've got a king, one who pays them no mind. They need a laird."

A wooden sign with a boar's head etched into it hung over the scarred door of the tavern. Connor pushed it open and they both entered the stuffy room.

The small windows along the wall did little to let in light, and most of the rows of tables seemed to fade into the darkness. Tallow candles sputtered out streams of thick, greasy smoke at several tables. The place was almost entirely empty.

But there was an underlying scent to the heavy odor of burning grease—the savory, tantalizing aroma of roasting meat.

"Two ales," Connor told the woman who watched them from across the room.

Another woman appeared beside her, a brunette whose face looked entirely too familiar to ignore.

"Wait here," he murmured to Ariana.

He made his way quickly across the empty room to where the other woman stood. Up close he was even more certain he knew her: the point of her nose, the small notch dimpling where the point of a chin would be. "Ye look familiar," he said.

The woman glanced toward where Ariana sat before turning a coy smile on him. "I get that from all the lads."

"I think I've seen ye before. At Urquhart."

The upturn of her lips wilted and her eyes narrowed slightly. "Ye must be mistaken. I havena been to Urquhart in some time. No' any of us have."

There was something guarded about the way she crossed her arms, as if in stubborn defiance. The movement was even more familiar and gnawed at his memory.

He didn't remember her name, but he knew one thing for certain—she would not be talking. Not with what his people had suffered.

But it did not dampen his spirits. If he'd found one of his clan, he would find more.

• • •

The throbbing in the pit of Ariana's stomach had been present since she'd woken. Now, it was near pulsing with an almost frenzied excitement. She knew immediately what it was—dread.

The barmaid approached Ariana's table and placed the two cups of ale before her.

Ariana nodded her thanks and glanced around the woman's retreating frame to where Connor still spoke to the brunette on the opposite side of the room.

He was occupied.

This might be Ariana's only chance.

She pulled the slender vial from the pocket in her dress, where she'd tucked it for accessibility and discretion. The clear liquid inside caught the meager light from the windows.

With one last glance toward Connor to ensure he was occupied, she tugged the small stopper from the vial. A bit of liquid splashed onto the heel of her palm. Not enough to matter, but enough to betray how badly her hands shook.

She emptied the contents into one mug with an almost imperceptible splash and pushed the offending mug away from her, to where Connor would likely sit.

Another glance confirmed he still had not turned toward her.

Her heart fluttered in a rush of panic and doubt.

Perhaps she should just ask him if she could leave.

Throughout their journey, the idea had rolled its way smooth by the constant churning of her thoughts. But Sylvi's words always came back to her.

No one just walks away.

If she was correct, and there was no way to quietly leave it all behind, then Ariana was better off not asking Connor. He was a perceptive man and far too intelligent to trick if he knew a blow was coming. Her asking would be all the warning he'd need of what she intended to do. And she didn't intend to hurt him—just leave him quietly sleeping.

Somehow the thought did not untangle the knot in her stomach.

He turned from the woman and made his way back to the small table where Ariana sat.

His gait was confident and a slight smile showed on his full lips. He sat down across from her. In front of the laced ale.

His sharp jaw was so smooth, her palm ached to brush it, and he'd put on a new léine and plaid—fine ones. She'd never seen him like this before, looking every bit the laird he should be.

Looking so very handsome and noble.

"It'll be nice to have a good ale after three hard days' travel," he said with an earnest smile.

The guilt rose like bile in the back of her throat, but she swallowed it down with her own ale and gave a weak nod. She should have been more convincing, but it was all she could force herself to muster.

"That good, huh?" He winked at her and put his cup to his lips.

Ariana's chest squeezed.

If she was going to stop him, now would be the time. The world around her seemed to shrink back and slow down.

He tipped the cup.

Everything faded away but him and the strong flex of his throat as he swallowed.

She could scarce draw breath, or even think.

He set the mug to the table and nodded in appreciation. "Now that is some good ale."

Ariana smiled, but it felt as if it were stretching her face into something foreign and unwanted. How soon would it begin to work?

She tried to remember the last time she'd used the vial. Her nerves had been so frayed then, her whole body so on edge. She'd been far too distracted to count time.

Outside came the sound of the crowd shouting something indiscernible.

Indiscernible, but close.

Connor narrowed his eyes and looked past her to the small windows set against the front of the tavern. "I think there might be an uprising if the king's nobles can't get a handle on that crowd."

His gaze returned to her and his brow puckered. "Surely ye are no' worried."

Tears stung in her eyes and her throat clogged with guilt.

"Ariana." His voice was tender. It might have been soothing had she not felt so awful.

He covered her hand with the warmth of his. "Ye can talk to me, lass."

"I want to leave." She'd practiced the admission in her mind a thousand times over. Always it'd come out confident and insistent. Now it emerged a whisper.

He stared at her a long moment without speaking. But not without feeling.

She could see the pain burn bright in his eyes, in those beautiful hazel eyes she'd spent far too much time studying.

He cleared his throat and his gaze shielded his emotions.

He had his own defenses, and he was clearly using them on her.

"I dinna want ye to leave," he said finally.

His hand still rested atop hers and his palm had begun to sweat. It was apparent the draught was beginning to take effect. Connor blinked slowly and shook his head, as if he could shake off the feeling creeping over him.

Ariana knew it was a useless gesture.

"You don't have a choice," she said.

"What have ye done?" he ground out.

She had to swallow down the hard knot in her throat before she could answer. "I'm sorry, Connor."

"Ye're sorry." He repeated her words with a bitter edge.

"Sometimes sorry is not enough, is it?" It was her turn to let bitterness seep into her tone. "You were sorry, and now I am too. There is no better way to end this than that."

Connor lifted his drooping head and eyed her before letting it fall forward once more.

Ariana rushed to the barmaid. "My friend is tired," she said in Gaelic. "I'd like a room for him."

After the exchange of a precious coin, Ariana had secured a

room on the small second floor and hefted Connor slowly up the stairs. His arm was draped over her shoulders and his footsteps were heavy and labored, dragging more than walking.

Somehow she managed to keep him propped upright—herself as well, which was a small miracle considering the burden of his body weight—and open the door to the narrow room.

It was simple, with little more than a bed within, but it appeared clean enough. She shuffled her feet across the floor, careful to never let herself lose her footing, and managed to ease Connor onto the bed.

Something hard and firm clasped over her wrist as she turned to go. She spun around and found Connor's hand locked on her and his eyes slitted open.

"I trusted ye." He swallowed. "Ye know more about me than anyone. Like Kenneth."

Her tears threatened to choke her now. She pulled her hand free and backed away before she lost her nerve. "I'll never betray those secrets or compromise your mission." It was a promise she meant to keep.

Then she locked the door behind her and fled the room.

The streets outside churned with unrest and it bled into the chaos of her own mind. People shoved against one another, incensed with rage. There were so many more than the original group of people they'd seen on the street. And so much more anger.

The loud group from the streets was quickly turning into a mob.

Ariana tried not to think of Connor sleeping on the bed.

Helpless.

She'd locked the door, of course. But then, the door was as flimsy as parchment.

The green swells of hills just outside of town were her free-dom. Away from the grip of hazel eyes, away from Connor, to a life of her own choosing. Away from a life that once again required she keep herself from feeling to avoid being hurt.

The sound of a gunshot rang out behind her. People surged for-ward with a cry, scattering as vermin do when light falls upon them.

They bumped and bustled past her, but she held her ground—no longer moving forward, but moving back.

Toward Connor.

Her breath came hard and fast in panicked, panting breaths. She needed to be there, to protect him while he slept.

Oh, God—what had she done?

After all these months he'd protected her, and she abandoned him to danger.

She shoved through the crowd streaming past her, ducking wild blows and sidling around swells thick with people. She didn't stop until the swinging tavern sign came into view.

Relief choked off her breath until she was almost dizzy.

She shoved through the inn door to find the place completely empty. The candles still flickered on the table, but not a soul emerged from the door to the kitchen.

Ariana didn't wait to see if they eventually did. She charged up the stairs and stopped.

The door to Connor's room stood open.

Her heart lodged itself in her throat. She tried to swallow it down—to no avail.

No sound met her ears.

The fine hair along the back of her neck stood on end.

She slipped the dagger from her thigh through the false pocket of her gown and cautiously approached the room. A cry burst from her throat.

Connor's bed was empty.

Chapter Thirty-One

The nausea threatening to overtake Connor was even worse outside.

The street was thick with people, and the odor of so many together mingling with the stink of their fear was almost more than he could bear.

He braced himself against the wall and let the rough exterior scrape over his cheek. The more he could feel, the more aware he was.

And the more aware he was, the more easily he'd be able to find Ariana.

His heart constricted around what she'd said.

Sometimes sorry is not enough, is it?

He knew too well what apology she'd been referring to. When they'd arrived at Kindrochit with Isabel and he'd told her to keep their coupling a secret. He grimaced at the memory.

She was right. Sorry wasn't enough.

And he'd be damned if he made the same mistake again.

If he had the chance.

Frustration bunched across his shoulders. He needed to find her.

The world blurred and he shook his head yet again. His neck had begun to ache from the repeated action.

Not that it did much to help.

He pushed himself from the building and staggered forward.

Strong hands grasped his shoulder and pulled. Connor lurched backward and tried to swing out his hand, but his arm was too heavy to lift.

"I have ye, laird. Dinna worry." There was a soothing quality to the voice in his ear, and the person seemed to be propping him up rather than shoving at him.

Laird.

His delayed thoughts repeated the word back to him.

He lifted his gaze and found a woman looking back at him. The woman from the tavern who'd insisted she didn't look familiar. He concentrated on her face while the rest of the world spun around him. Her name peeled away from the fog of his mind.

"Anise."

She nodded. "Sorry I acted as though I dinna recognize ye earlier. I dinna want unwanted people to hear. Ye dinna know who is listening." Her lips lifted in a kind smile. "Yer people have waited a long time to see ye again."

His people were waiting for him.

Ariana.

He hadn't found her yet.

But he'd abandoned his people once before. He could not so again.

And he was so, so damn tired.

"Where's Ariana?" he asked on an exhale.

"The lass ye came in with?" Anise shifted his weight, and only then did he realize he was drooping toward the ground. "Dinna worry, laird. We have her too."

• • •

After asking the girl from the tavern, Anise, if she'd seen Connor, Ariana was led to a room behind the inn. She'd been given food and drink and the promise of Connor's safe return, but it was not enough.

Anxiety rippled through her. She jerked away from the small table and paced the room while keeping her gaze fixed on the only door to the room, and the two men who stood near it.

The door still had not opened.

Connor had not been found.

Anise could have lied. But then, Ariana had been too desperate to care.

Now though, Ariana studied the two men who stood on opposite sides of the door. For her protection, Anise had said.

They were both large. Taller than Connor and thickened with fat over muscle, lending them a bulky show of more strength than they likely possessed. They both wore their dark hair unbound over their shoulders and matching indifferent expressions.

Right now, it felt more like they were there to ensure she didn't leave. Like their presence was meant to intimidate rather than reassure. The whitewashed walls around her seemed to press in.

She'd left her lockpick hair pin back at Urquhart. She could have kicked herself for the oversight. The men would be difficult to take given their size, but she could have done it. The solid oak door however, which Anise had locked when she left, would be difficult to open without the proper tool.

She'd been so close to freedom.

She never should have returned.

And yet…

Connor.

Her gaze crept unbidden toward the door.

This time it opened.

Her heart leapt into a staggered beat. Anise shuffled in, and Ariana's "protectors" rushed forward to pull Connor from where he stood slumped against her. He pushed stubbornly away from the men and lifted his head, eyes squinting in her direction.

"Ye're here," he said in a slurred voice.

Shame made her cheeks hot. "I came back."

His face relaxed into a smile, the kind that might have melted her heart had she let herself be susceptible.

She went to him, but kept herself from reaching out to comfort—either him or herself.

"Why are you not sleeping?" she asked.

He squinted at his palm and held up an empty vial held between his thumb and forefinger. "Percy gave me this to use if I ever found myself poisoned. It's slow working, but it kept me awake."

"Why did you leave the room?" she asked.

He looked at her with piercing honesty. "To find ye."

"I'd planned to leave," she confessed.

"Aye," he said seriously. "And I'd hoped to change yer mind."

Anise held up a mug of ale between them. "Drink, laird. There's much to discuss." Up close, she was even younger than Ariana had assumed. Her face was untouched by the lines of age and her eyes held a helplessness only the young possessed.

"Did my da find ye?" Anise asked.

"Renny." Connor's voice came out in a deep scrape of gravel. Only Ariana knew it had nothing to do with having been poisoned.

Anise nodded, and the white cap she wore fluttered over her brow. "Aye, he saw ye in town and said he'd follow ye, so ye'd know we were here." Her eyes were rimmed with emotion. "All this time, we'd thought ye were dead."

Ariana glanced toward Connor, but he did not meet her gaze.

"Renny followed me, but I dinna know." He drew his palm down over his face and let his hand fall away. "Anise, I'm sorry to tell ye this, lass. He's—"

"No." She shook her head and her eyes went wide. "No. It couldna be. He was too strong, too brave."

Ariana backed slowly away to give the young woman her privacy. But the obvious pain on her face pulled at something deep down in Ariana. The woman had clearly loved her father. She'd mourned his passing in a manner Ariana had been unable to, yet always wished she'd had the opportunity to.

Connor put a hand on Anise's shoulder, as he often did to all the women at Kindrochit when he wanted them to know he was being serious. "We brought him back with us and buried him at Urquhart."

Anise lifted her head and offered a brave smile. "Ye're a good laird. Even after all this time."

Ariana winced inwardly, knowing Connor would disagree with the statement and how deeply it would cut him.

He paced the small room, like an agitated beast stalking the length of its cage. "I'd assumed ye were all dead. I dinna…" He pursed his lips. "I dinna come check myself. I couldna stand the pain of discovering what I thought I knew. I left ye to fend for yerselves."

Anise shook her head. "We havena had to fend for ourselves."

"But the people outside," Ariana interjected. All eyes in the room turned toward her. "The crowd of people who were starving and in need of clothing."

"No' us," Anise replied solemnly. "We've been well cared for all this time."

Connor stopped pacing and turned toward her. "By whom?"

Anise regarded him with surprise, as if she assumed he already knew the answer. "Why, Laird Kenneth Gordon, of course."

• • •

Kenneth Gordon.

Connor stared at Anise, his thoughts momentarily paralyzed by the name which had haunted him the last few months.

The friend, the betrayer…and now the savior of the very people Connor had failed.

Kenneth Gordon.

He did not have to turn to know Ariana was staring at him intently. The weight of her gaze was too heavy on his back. He could not bear to face it head on.

"The Gordons were responsible for the fall of Urquhart," Connor said. The disbelief he'd tried so hard to mask came through far too clear.

"His da, the late laird—he was the one who took Urquhart." Anise nodded toward the guards.

They stepped forward, almost as one. For the first time, Connor noticed they were identical. Tavin and Tavish, the brewer's sons who were once the scrawniest fourteen-year-old lads Connor had ever laid eyes on. The past three years, and the harrowing circumstances, had clearly turned them into men.

"We dinna want to believe it at first either," Tavin said.

"But he's helped us," Tavish finished his brother's sentence the same as he always had. "He wants to help those in this town as well. It isna easy with politics."

Connor grimaced. He knew politics too damn well.

Emotions clashed within him. Anger for having not come to check on his people himself, shame for having abandoned them, and frustration at how they had been saved by the very man who had betrayed him.

He needed to see Kenneth, and not just because his name was next on the list to kill.

Connor needed to speak with him, to ask the question plaguing him all the past three years: Why?

"He thinks ye're dead as well." Anise's gentle tone pulled Connor from his reverie. "I think it'd do his heart good to see ye survived."

This time he did turn and meet Ariana's gaze. She nodded slightly.

"There's a feast in two days' time at Glenbuchat Castle in Kildrummy," Tavin said.

"Aye, English and Scottish alike," Tavish interjected. "A ball of sorts."

Tavin nodded enthusiastically, belying his youth. "Ye'd have enough time to get there."

The two looked at each other and shrugged simultaneously.

Ariana turned to Anise. "Could you secure a gown for me?"

Anise cast a reverent glance toward Connor. "Aye, anything ye need."

The lass was putting on a brave front, but the red tip of her nose and the hollows around her eyes gave away the grief threatening to break her facade.

"Ye've done well, Anise," he said. "Thank ye. I'll have ye go home now and Tavin and Tavish can coordinate what we need."

She nodded.

"Please let me know if ye need anything," Connor offered before she slipped out the door. "I'm indebted to yer family."

"It lightens our hearts to know ye're alive, laird." Her voice broke and she quit the room before any of them could see her tears.

Renny would have been proud of his daughter.

The subtle fresh scent he'd come to associate with Ariana tickled his awareness. He turned and found her at his side.

Close, but not touching.

As was her way now.

"I'll go with you," she said softly.

A swell of hope warmed through him. "Ye're no' going to leave, then?"

"Not until after." She gave a smile so wry, it did not curl her lips or touch her eyes. "When you no longer need me."

He wanted to tell her there would never be a time he wouldn't need her. But with Tavin and Tavish in the church-quiet room and the brittle cloak of bitterness Ariana wore slung over her shoulders, he knew the words would be wasted.

He had her for two more days and two more nights.

It would have to be enough time to meet with Gordon and convince Ariana she did not need to leave.

Kenneth.

Connor pulled in a deep breath, but it did little to release the strain of the tension knotting his back.

After all this time, after all the betrayal, he would be seeing Kenneth again.

And would have to kill him.

Chapter Thirty-Two

In another life, Ariana might not have felt so impressed by the ball at Glenbuchat Castle. But that other life was long cold in her thoughts, and to her, the night sparkled like magic.

The buzz of conversation filled the air like the melodic hum of a violin, and the many flickering lights glowing around the castle reminded Ariana of a sky lit with a million stars.

She wore a lovely gown of jewel-green silk, the kind her parents would have had made for her in preparation for the meeting of a new suitor. And she'd met many—all fruitless endeavors, of course.

But this was different.

Connor exited the carriage and held his arm out to her in silent invitation. She'd been talked into the idea of playing at husband and wife lest she appear a whore on his arm, as she had no lady to attend her.

Her hand trembled somewhat and she slipped it quickly into the crook of Connor's arm lest he notice. Deep down inside her hummed a lightheaded thrill at pretending to be his wife, and the quiet suggestion of intimacy hung in the air like sparkling cloth of gold.

Connor rested the warmth of his hand over hers and smiled down at her the way a man would gaze upon his wife. His eyes were warm and tender, his chest puffed out with pride at the woman on his arm, a slight smile curving the sensual line of his mouth. Ariana's pulse thrummed faster and her palm began to sweat against the fine sleeve of his jacket.

He leaned closer to her and the delicious scent of him brought images fluttering through her mind she'd rather not be thinking.

"Pretend we like each other tonight, aye?" His whispered words were a caress against her ear and the sensitive side of her neck.

A delicious wave of chills glided down her back. Her cheeks went hot.

"I think I can do that." She spoke without looking at him lest she fall into something from which she could not be free.

Tonight was not for stabbing herself with the memory of painful words and acts. Goodness knew there was far too great an arsenal of those floating in her mind.

No, tonight was for celebrating the nearness of her freedom.

Together she and Connor made their way toward the large stone entry of Glenbuchat Castle. He stopped before they could walk in and touched the underside of her chin, tipping her face toward his.

Her heartbeat thundered in her ears.

"Ye look bonny."

Pleasure warmed her cheeks despite her best efforts to squelch her reaction. His hand came up and gently, tenderly, stroked her cheek.

"You don't have to pretend to like me so well," she teased.

He gave a carefree shrug. "It's the truth. Ye look lovely. Touching yer cheek was the bit extra to convince the masses, but I canna say I minded it." He gave her a wink, and an excited energy fired through her.

No.

She couldn't let him ease his way past her defenses like this.

"It's yer turn." He gave her an urging nod.

"My turn?" She looked up at him. The light from all the candles flickered golden across his face and reminded her of the previous few times they'd spoken in the solar at Kindrochit.

Those nights seemed so very long ago.

Suddenly their charade was too intimate, too tempting.

"Aye. It's yer turn to tell me I look lovely too." He held his free hand toward her in invitation and she laughed in spite of herself.

She also had to grudgingly admit he did look handsome. He'd dressed like a laird again in a pale linen léine and a new plaid kilted over his narrow hips in pleats.

They stopped behind another couple to patiently await their entry.

His face grew serious, his gaze intent. "I've missed the sound of yer laughter, Ariana."

This was no jest to casually brush off, and no witty, diffusing remark swam up in her frantic thoughts. She'd been disarmed.

And like any good warrior, he took advantage of her lowered defenses. His fingertips grazed the edge of her jaw and he lowered his head to hers.

He brushed his lips across hers in that delicate, not-a-kiss way of his. She drew in a gasp of cool air and he straightened.

But there was nothing more to say before they were permitted entry into the castle with the low bow of a large, red-haired man wearing a kilt.

The room was lit in gilded light, revealing a blend of the dances she'd known in London and the rustic revelry the Highlands afforded. Lively music curled through the air and left almost every foot tapping. A cleared area of the great hall formed a dance floor where more elegantly dressed Englishmen twirled beside the Scottish couples in their beautiful plaids.

Ariana wanted to close her eyes and let herself drown in the dream of it all. This was the life she'd once been so accustomed to, the only life she'd ever known, before hunger and uncertainty had become her constant companions.

Was she truly ready to embrace such a precarious existence once more?

Connor's arm stiffened slightly beneath her fingers. He was staring across the room, at a man with long black hair. The man was dressed in similar attire to what Connor wore, only the plaid was a slightly different color and his shirt was a golden yellow color.

"It's Kenneth," Connor said, without pulling his gaze from the man.

Ariana left her own attention fixed on him as well, assessing the man who had taken everything from Connor, who had so horribly betrayed a friend.

"He hasna seen us yet." Connor slid his arm from Ariana's grasp. "I'd like to approach him alone."

Ariana had expected as much and allowed Connor to extricate himself. "I will not leave before saying goodbye."

Connor's gaze jerked from Gordon to her. "I dinna want ye to leave at all."

There was nothing to say to that. No placating lie of an intent to stay, no consoling croon of how she would miss him. To do any of those things would betray herself and expose unhealed wounds best left concealed.

He cradled her face in his hands like a lover. Her knees softened and she worried at their ability to keep her standing upright.

Those beautiful hazel eyes of his stared into hers, deep into her soul, until she feared the secrets of her reaction might be bared.

Was it possible for him to see how her poor heart raced, or the way her frantic lungs scarce drew air?

Then his mouth came down on hers. Not the soft, butterfly wing of a kiss he'd whispered over her lips only moments before, but the gentle caress of one's lips against another's, further warmed by the promising sweep of his tongue against the seal of her mouth.

"I trust ye to no' leave without saying goodbye." He gave her one last, heart-squeezing look and melted into the crush of English and Scottish nobles like a ghost.

Ariana, finally able to draw breath, pulled in a deep chestful of air. Not that doing so eased the dryness of her mouth. She did a cursory sweep of the room, seeking out the source of refreshment, and went still.

On the opposite wall was a row of tables, each framed by an eager crowd.

Card tables.

Then she heard it, like the distant pull of a siren's call: the subtle clinking of coins, the cheer of a winner's cry, the rapid-fire ticking of cards being shuffled against one another.

She strolled toward the tables before she'd made up her mind to do so, her body feeding off the bounty they offered. Everything in her went giddy with anticipation.

To feel the smooth caress of cards against her fingertips, to casually toss a coin or two into the pile as if they did not dictate whether or not she ate.

To win.

Her breath quickened.

An English gentleman turned toward her and smiled before shifting further right, clearing a place for her. "My lady, will you play?"

She drew two coins from her purse, two of the six she'd brought with her, and let them rain from her fingertips toward the small collection amassed on the table already. "Indeed, I will."

It was all she would need to sacrifice to gather the cards she'd need. And soon, oh soon, she would once again be winning.

• • •

After three long years, Connor was finally prepared to meet Kenneth Gordon again.

Connor passed through the crowd, careful to keep himself partially hidden by those around him. His gaze remained fixed on the man who had betrayed him, despite the numerous people who slipped into his line of vision.

The memory of Ariana's mouth still warmed his lips, a sweetness lingering from their kiss. Even if it had been he who'd kissed her.

Thoughts of Ariana could come later.

Now was for Kenneth, who had turned toward a narrow hallway and was quickly becoming little more than a retreating back. Had he seen Connor?

Was Kenneth running?

Connor made his way through the masses of people and

stopped when he saw Kenneth reappear in an alcove overlooking the party.

Silent as only the Shadow's son could be, Connor made his way to the alcove, creeping down the same hall and spiraling up the narrow staircase.

Kenneth turned abruptly and froze, his legs set in a wide stance of authority, his hand braced on the stone rail of the balcony with an ease too casual to be earnest.

Both men regarded one another for a long moment, a chance to assess three years and everything else in a fraction of a second.

In that time, Connor noted the white hair feathered through the dark at Kenneth's temples, and how the lines of his forehead had become deeply creased. Kenneth had also gotten larger, if such a thing were possible. His shoulders squared with a power he'd always worn with such admirable ease.

He swallowed once and the prominent lump in the center of his throat bobbed. "Ye always were stealthily quiet."

To see Kenneth again almost left Connor overwhelmed. So many emotions…all immediate, all intense.

The love, the hatred. The brother, the enemy.

Kenneth spoke in a voice softer than Connor had ever heard. "I thought ye were dead."

He rushed forward and Connor tensed to lift his blade free.

But it was not a shot to the gut or a fist to the face that came to him. Kenneth's arms wrapped around Connor in an embrace so fierce it robbed him of breath.

Not that he'd ever admit as much.

Kenneth gripped Connor's shoulders and pushed as far as his arm's length would allow. "I thought ye were dead." He repeated it in a louder voice, his excitement evident.

But Connor did not give in to the current of elation tugging at him. He didn't have the luxury to do so.

The last time he'd spoken to Kenneth was the day Connor had lost everything.

He pulled back in a hard jerk of anger. Emotion washed over

him in an unexpected surge and dragged him below the surface of his own rage. "Yer father took Urquhart."

Pain etched harder lines on Kenneth's face. "Connor—"

"He took Urquhart and he killed my da." The words came out through clenched teeth, but that did not make them silent.

Several people below looked up at them, but Connor paid them little mind.

Kenneth reached for Connor, as if he meant to embrace him once more. Connor stepped back, hands up to prevent the man he'd once called his brother from touching him.

"Connor, I couldna stop him. I tried. When that dinna work, I knew I had to save ye and Cora." Kenneth raked a hand through his hair. A spiky black strand of it jutted up from his temple, like the feathers of an odd little bird. The memory of his hair standing in tufts when not smoothed down tickled at Connor's memory. It'd been funny when they were lads. Connor found himself decidedly not in the mood to laugh at present.

"I know I can never make it up to ye." Kenneth's eyes searched Connor's, almost pleading. "I've cared for yer people, I've kept Urquhart from being taken by townsfolk."

Words meant to soothe only incensed. Sorrow went molten in Connor's veins, transforming into something he could more readily accept—anger.

"There's no' anything ye can do to make it right," Connor hissed. "Ye canna' ever bring back my da."

Kenneth shook his head, not even attempting to argue with what Connor had stated.

They both knew it was pointless.

Connor's deep, slow inhale trembled slightly under the weight of his rage.

He should kill Kenneth now.

End it while possible, while rage controlled all thought and action.

Connor closed his hand around the hilt of his dirk, but Kenneth did not move. Connor slid the blade from its sheath, but still Kenneth did not budge.

"Will ye hide behind yer guards?" Connor snarled.

"I'll hide behind no one and I'll no' defend myself against actions for which there is no forgiveness." Resignation dropped Kenneth's head lower and Connor knew his words to be true.

He'd confessed to having been wrong.

The rush of anger went still within Connor and left him drifting through what remained.

He stared at his friend for a long moment before letting the blade slip back into its sheath. Kenneth's shoulders did not slump in relief as most men's might. It was then Connor realized Kenneth had truly anticipated death.

And he had readily accepted his fate.

He raised his eyes without lifting his head. "There is much I would like to discuss with ye, Connor. Much I never thought I'd have a chance to say."

A flurry of activity below caught Connor's attention. The flash of a green dress. His stomach sank when he realized the location from which the disturbance had arisen.

The side of the room.

The card tables.

A small cluster of people had stopped and turned toward the table, observing it as one might a London play. His gaze settled on the brilliant green dress. Ariana was standing with several well-groomed Englishmen already before her and another behind her.

Connor muttered a curse under his breath. Five minutes he'd left her alone, and she'd made her way to the card tables. His irritation at her decision to leave grated through him. If she didn't last five minutes here, how the hell did she plan to survive on her own?

"Do ye know them?" Kenneth asked.

"I know her." It was all Connor had gotten out when one of the men reached out and grabbed Ariana's wrist.

All thought fled his mind and his body launched into action, propelling him through the crowd, away from Kenneth, and toward the men who sought to harm Ariana.

Chapter Thirty-Three

Ariana's wrist was caught in a viselike grip. The man's face was familiar. She'd seen him once at court, but her memory was little more than fractured thoughts and unfulfilled plans to escape.

"I asked if you were cheating, girl," the man snarled. His wig was set too far back and made his forehead seem to stop halfway over the top of his skull.

She could attack him. She could grab the wig and then rush at him when he was surprised at her assault.

The man's front teeth clamped flush together and his lips pulled back. "Answer me."

It would be an ideal way to escape were there not so many people watching.

The attack would be anything but discreet. And if she recognized one man, there would be others. Her name had remained untarnished thus far. She could not afford to—

His hand was ripped from her arm.

And Connor was there. At her side.

"Who is this?" the Englishman demanded.

"The man who isna going to let ye touch her once more." Connor's tone was low and threatening.

The Englishman smirked. "And if I do?"

Connor shifted from Ariana's side toward the front of her. "I dinna think ye want to." His shoulders squared. He was bracing himself for a fight.

The stubborn part of her balked at the idea that he thought her incapable of protecting herself, but the more logical part realized he was solving the socially complex situation she'd created.

A man could far more easily deliver a blow at a ball than a lady.

"Is there a problem here?" An unfamiliar male voice asked, his Scottish burr smooth and unfettered.

A quick glance confirmed it was Kenneth Gordon. He was taller than Connor and thick with muscle. Despite his bulk, he walked with the ease of a man half his size.

Relief at his arrival fluttered through Ariana for the briefest of moments.

When Connor first left, she had truly feared he intended to kill Kenneth—something she knew deep down he did not want.

"This girl cheated." The Englishman pointed an accusing finger toward her and Connor's body visibly flexed.

Kenneth lifted a hand in the air. "I'm sure ye're mistaken—"

"I'm sure I'm not." The Englishman's face had gone from a soft pink to a deep red and the skin on his cheeks shone in the candlelight.

"These are friends of mine." Kenneth's voice did not rise, but the man did not interrupt again. "Surely ye wouldna want to insult friends of the host. We greatly appreciate hospitality in the Highlands—as ye well know."

Now every person in the room appeared to be staring. The chatter had faded to almost nothing, and Kenneth's calm voice carried throughout.

"I'll ensure all funds are replaced," Kenneth continued.

"They're all still there." Ariana nodded toward the pile she left on the table.

The Englishman shot a dark look at Ariana, but allowed himself to be drawn away by one of his companions.

The crowd, deprived of their entertainment, turned from the scene and went back to their conversations and revelry.

Kenneth turned toward Connor. "Meet me tomorrow. Give me a chance to explain."

A pause ensued for a long moment before Connor finally nodded. "Aye, at noon then. By the church."

Kenneth nodded. The men embraced like friends and Kenneth gave Connor one last lingering look before disappearing into the crowd.

Finally, Connor turned and looked at Ariana. He didn't say a word, but the disappointment was evident in his gaze.

She hated how his reaction cut into her more than angry words possibly would have. She wanted to offer a justification for her actions, to find something else to blame other than what her gambling had been in the first place—spite.

She'd felt the need to prove to herself she could still slip cards and win—to prove she could still take care of herself.

And she'd failed.

Now it was not only Connor's disappointment she had to suffer, but her own.

He led her from the hall under the gaze of more than one English and Scottish noble, but he did not speak to her—not through the long walk back toward the inn where they stayed, nor when he helped her into her room.

Then he closed the door behind him, securing them both within. Alone.

And then he finally spoke.

"Ye're really terrible at cards, Ariana."

Resentment flared hot in her cheeks. "I'm better than you give me credit for."

He put up a single finger. She bit back her sharp reply, which was probably for the best, and crossed her arms, as if doing so might protect her from what he had to say.

"I saw the pile of yer winnings. It isna any wonder ye were caught." His jaw tightened and a line of sinewy muscle appeared on either side of his face. "First ye poison me, and then ye risk yer own freedom in an attempt to get a noticeable sum with which to escape."

His searching gaze sought to strip away her defenses, but she held fast to them. She tightened her arms over her chest, though it provided no more of a barrier.

"Ye're so desperate to leave." The edge in his gaze softened. "Why?"

Her cheeks blazed. There was more to her wanting to leave than simple rejection.

She knew he desired her. It was evidenced in his suggestion to continue to see one another in private at Kindrochit. And in the kiss he'd pressed to her lips at the ball.

The issue was love.

Or rather, its absence.

It was the lack of reciprocation of her affection and how truly painful a burden it was to bear.

The answer stuck in her throat and made her heart ache.

She shook her head rather than reply.

He backed away and leaned against the narrow wall near the door. But he did not leave.

His finger tapped on his arm, not in agitation, but in more of a pensive manner—or so it seemed.

Regardless, Ariana should not care. She went to her meager belongings to pack what she would need.

It would have been a larger set of provisions had she possessed more than the four meager coins in her pocket.

"Prove yerself to me," Connor said suddenly.

Ariana turned back toward him. "What?"

"Ye said ye're a good card player. Prove it and play with me. I want to see if ye win." He tilted his head as if daring her to accept his challenge.

Ariana felt the corner of her lip slide upward. He knew her well enough to understand her refusal of such a challenge would be almost impossible. "You'll let me take all your coin?"

He smirked. "It isna money I want."

"Then what is it you want?" Her breath quickened.

"If ye win, then ye can leave and I willna do a thing to stop ye."

And so his motive was suddenly clear. She eyed him warily. "And if you win? I have to stay?"

"Then ye explain to me the full reason why ye're leaving. I know ye're upset with me for asking ye to keep us a secret when we got to Kindrochit. But there is more to it than that. I can see it on yer face and I can feel it between us. Ye used to talk to me about everything. I want ye to talk to me about this." He sighed. "It's the only way I feel like I can get ye to speak with me."

He wanted her to confess her heart. She'd rather play for coin. But then if she won, she would be able to leave without worry he or the other girls would try to find her.

Her heart squeezed at the idea of one of the girls coming for her. She cared for them all so much more than she had realized she'd allowed herself to.

"And I get to kiss ye goodbye." He dipped his head to the side as if he didn't care one way or the other. Obviously he did, if he had made it part of the bet.

It was too easy.

"What else?" she asked.

Connor shook his head with a smile tucked poorly behind an indifferent facade.

She raised her eyebrow, and he grinned. "Ye canna cheat."

● ● ●

Connor knew Ariana wouldn't like his stipulation.

She wrinkled her nose. "You know I can't play well if I don't cheat." She put her hands on her hips, which only served to accentuate the narrowness of her slender waist in the fine green gown she still wore.

"Aye, if ye dinna get caught," he added playfully.

Ariana's mouth fell open in mock offense and he grinned before he could stop it.

He'd once cherished their banter, the comfort of their conversation. Having it back, even this one brief flash, made him understand how very much he'd missed it.

"Fine," Ariana conceded with a wry twist of her mouth. "But what will we use for chips? I haven't even coin to hold an entire game." She tossed four coins onto the bed where they landed soundless on the soft surface.

He smirked. She had more than that, but she obviously did not want him to know.

Clothing.

The idea rose in his mind without hesitation. Nothing would make her decide to finally at least be honest with him about the coin she carried like using clothing instead. Not that he needed to see her coin, but damn it, he just wanted some kind of truth from her.

Ariana regarded him with a dubious expression. "What?"

He shook his head, refusing to answer.

"Then why are you staring at me like that?" She gave his chest an accusatory poke.

Was he making a face?

"Like what?" he asked.

"Like a boy with a frog in his hands."

He let his gaze slide to the other side of the room where her two small packs lay ready for her departure.

"Clothing." His voice had a slightly choked sound to it. He cleared his throat and tried again. "We could use our clothing as chips."

She raised one highly arched brow sardonically. "Are you sure you want only a kiss if you win?"

He held up his hands in silent surrender. "I'll only take what ye willingly give."

She approached the small table on the opposite wall and withdrew a card deck from her bag. She stared at her bag for a long moment before finally standing. With her back settled against the wall, she sifted through the cards with careful consideration.

"Very well, I'm in." Her cheeks went pink. "Clothing as chips."

So she would not trust him with even the coin she carried. It was a blow to his ego. Connor took a place at the opposite side of the table, his own back pressed against the same solid wall as hers. She dealt with nimble fingers and cast a glance up at him before she took her stack of cards from the table.

"I'll be watching ye," he said.

She fanned out her cards in front of her face, so only her eyes were visible. "Oh, I know."

He held his own cards close to him and fought to keep his face impassive when she showed her first hand. A pair of kings.

A good hand, except he had three queens. Ariana gave him a calculating look from over the rickety table before she suddenly dropped about two inches lower.

From the base of her voluminous skirt came the tip of a plain looking brown shoe.

The foot nudging it forward was slender and clad in a white silk stocking he'd love to glide his hands up.

Never had a scuffed brown shoe held such appeal.

He wanted to see the next.

And he did. Hand by hand, he stripped away her other shoe and the clip in her hair, which made her tresses swirl free like a silken curtain twisted and released.

She really was truly horrible at cards when she didn't cheat.

Finally she gave a broad smile when he laid down a pair of threes he'd been bluffing on. Her hands fanned the cards over the stained table, revealing five cards of the same suit.

She held out her hand. "I'll be taking your shoe now."

"That isna fair when ye've lost so much already." He grasped the bottom of his léine and tugged it upward over his head.

When he freed his face from the length of linen, he found her mouth partially open and her cheeks a bonny flushed red. He handed her the wadded up fabric.

He gathered the cards and placed those in her hand as well. "Yer deal."

She licked her lips and let his shirt fall to the floor before shuffling the cards once more. Though he knew she would never admit to it, her gaze continually wandered toward his naked chest.

He had to concede, he felt a bit foolish in his plaid and boots. But with the way she kept staring at him, he wasn't about to change one damn thing.

In the two rounds of cards he had swapped out, she had only traded her cards once. Showing her hand later had proved what a mistake that had been on her part. She had absolutely nothing and hadn't even tried to pretend otherwise.

"Distracted?" he teased.

"Don't flatter yourself," she countered.

He laid out his two pairs. "Looks like I won."

Her mouth curled up. "It would appear you have."

She turned her back toward him where a complex series of ribbons secured the bodice of her gown. "If you'd be so kind."

"By all means." He came around the small table and grasped a silky bit of ribbon between his thumb and forefinger. The bow slipped free silently.

Row after criss-crossed row, he slid the ribbon free from the bodice until it sagged forward and Ariana was able to easily step out of the pool of green silk.

Her sark hung off her shoulders, leaving them bare, and her corset pushed her breasts up high and round on her chest.

She had lovely shoulders.

Perhaps it was an odd thing to note when her breasts and arse were so finely made as well, but her bare shoulders had the most delicate curve where they met her neck. He wanted to press his lips there, to where the skin would be warm and soft.

"Don't forget your cards." She nodded toward the table where a neatly dealt stack of cards rested in front of him.

When had she done that?

She put a hand on her hip and tilted her head. "Distracted?"

He nodded in consent. "Aye. Consider yerself flattered."

Distracted though he might have been, he played with the determination of a man about to lose everything.

And to him, he was.

Ariana brought a part of him alive he'd long since thought dead. She saw in him a goodness he never allowed himself to dare hope he possessed. He thought he was long since past meaning anything, having anything—but she'd seen through his fractured exterior and found the man beneath.

He'd be damned if he let her slip through his fingers.

And if he could convince her to open up about being angry at him, if he could just have a chance to get her to show any kind of emotion, perhaps he might be able to convince her to stay. He wouldn't give up until she was gone, damn it.

Aye, she'd been teasing and playful at their card game, but it was a facade he saw through. There was other emotion underneath, the kind that made her hard and apathetic.

He needed her to rage at him, to tell him what she'd locked up so deeply.

And if he failed at the endeavor, he'd at least get one last kiss.

Win after careful win, Connor found himself having to concentrate more with each article of clothing she removed.

The loss of her overskirts revealed the shadow of her slender, shapely legs beneath her sark when the firelight hit her just right. The loss of her corset and how it revealed the tips of her hardened nipples pointed against the thin white fabric.

Each piece revealed more and stirred deep memories of the night he'd finally had her.

Thus far he'd still only lost his léine.

Ariana took the stack of cards in her hand in preparation to shuffle them once more. But Connor couldn't let her go further. It was one thing to reduce a lass to her sark, and though he longed for the hem to slip upward and reveal her body one tantalizing inch at a time to him, it was quite another to reduce a lass to nudity.

"I think we've gone far enough," he said.

Ariana quirked a brow. "But you haven't fully won."

Connor lifted a plaid from where it laid over her bags and wrapped it around her shoulders. She pinched the fabric over her breasts and gave him a questioning look. "No' that the idea of ye naked isna a tempting one, because it verra much is, ye know what I want."

Ariana's playful gaze faded to something altogether more serious. "I do." She nodded.

"Then tell me." He tried to speak softly, as if doing so could offer further encouragement to her. "Tell me why ye want to leave."

Her jaw set with defiance.

"We had a deal," he reminded her.

All pretense of flirtation slipped away into an iced-over countenance. The Ariana he was beginning to grow used to.

And that wasn't what he wanted.

"Ye have to tell me." He was goading, and it was entirely intentional. "Ye promised ye would and I did beat ye."

Irritation sparked in her eyes and the cold look flamed into one of anger.

Victory flickered to life inside him.

This.

This was what he wanted.

Whether it came in the form of rage or sadness, he wanted something more than her acquiescent indifference, a break from her maddening apathy.

And judging from the flush creeping over her cheeks, he was finally about to get it.

Chapter Thirty-Four

That Connor wanted Ariana to give voice to what he should have guessed was almost more than she could stand. The hurt and anger in Ariana swelled hot in the back of her throat and burned at her eyes.

"You know why I want to leave." She threw the words at Connor like a dagger.

He folded his arms over his chest. Ever the stubborn one. "I'm almost certain I do, but I want to hear ye say it."

She clutched the plaid he'd given her more tightly over her shoulders. The fabric hugged her skin. While she had been almost offended when he'd first given her the plaid, she was grateful for it now.

Even if he was being a cur.

"You're cruel to make me say it." Emotion welled in her, approaching with the certainty of a thunderstorm, roiling and darkening.

"Ye're angry with me." It wasn't a question.

"I am." She spoke through clenched teeth. "Why would you make me do this?"

The patient calm of his face bled into one of pain. "Because I want to see some emotion from ye. I canna stand this indifferent front ye've been offering. This isna the Ariana I know."

The tether on all things civil and polite in her snapped. "This is the Ariana my life has made me. Am I mad at you? Yes." She stabbed a finger into his chest. "You're just like everyone else in my life. Like my parents who never cared for me beyond what my marriage could bring them, like my brother who tucked me away like a toy he no longer played with."

The words were flying from her mouth with an edge of vehemence. Not only could she not stop them, she also didn't want to.

"All my life, I've done what I'm supposed to. I've followed the rules and I've tried so..." The rage quivered through her muscles and she balled her fists to keep it from exploding out of her. "I've tried so damn hard. I wanted nothing more than to make them happy, to make you happy. To..."

The words died on her lips, melted by the hurt of what she'd almost said.

"To what?" Connor pressed.

The ache in her throat was unbearable and the warmth in her eyes spilled down her cheeks. She looked away, unable to meet his gaze when she finally answered. "To be loved. By them. By you."

The confession shattered her heart and suddenly it hurt to even breathe.

Connor stepped forward and his arms came around her, warm and strong and secure. She fell against his chest and gave in to the fiery pain of her heart breaking.

"I'm sorry." He spoke softly against her ear.

But his words brought no comfort. Sorry was not love, and the apology only made the pain scrape that much deeper.

Where a moment prior the release of her tears had been a much-needed reprieve, it now was unbearably intimate. She straightened and swiped at her eyes.

Her face felt hot and sticky and her head throbbed from having cried. She wanted to duck beneath the veil of her hair and hide from him.

No woman ever looked beautiful after crying—she was no exception. Looking thus in front of Connor only rubbed salt into her raw wound.

He nudged the underside of her chin up with his forefinger and tilted her face so she was looking at him. She tried to look away, but he guided her back with his thumb. "It's my turn to confess to ye."

She shook her head. She couldn't hear his reasons again. Not when she knew too well why he couldn't be with her. Hearing them again would not assuage her pain. It would only serve as a reminder. A prodding of an unhealed wound.

"That wasn't part of the deal," she whispered.

He smoothed the hair from her face with his large hand. His palms were cool against her temple. She wanted to close her eyes and let his calming hands soothe away the heat and the ache of her head.

But she needed to keep her resolve strong if she intended to leave.

And she *did* intend to leave.

"Ariana, I—"

She gave him a sharp look and shook her head. "You were promised a final kiss only."

"Aye, ye're right." He took her face in his hands and stared down at her for a long moment, as if he meant to trace every line into his memory.

Or perhaps she was romanticizing the moment and wishing that was what he did.

His warm lips came down on hers, so softly she almost did not feel the touch. It was too delicate a kiss. Too tender.

She wanted something final and fast.

The spicy scent of him spun around her like a spell, teasing out memories best left forgotten and coaxing her body to respond.

She lifted her face without meaning to do so.

She didn't want this sweetness. She wanted to feel the kind of hard kiss that would scrape her teeth against her lips and flare into a blind passion in which she could lose herself.

But his kiss remained tender, loving.

Dangerous.

His tongue brushed her bottom lip and finally, finally, he pulled away. He looked so deeply into her eyes, she felt as if he were brushing her soul. There was something deep in the way he gazed at her, something powerful enough to squeeze her heart. "Ariana, I love ye."

His words plunged her from a languid state into the cold shock of awareness. "What?"

He stroked her cheek. "I love the way ye laugh and how it makes me feel." His lips pressed against her cheek, warm and firm.

She stayed silent, wanting to believe and yet fearful to do so.

"I love yer determination and how ye accomplish things most others canna." He kissed her forehead.

"I love that ye're able to love others, despite yer own hurt. Despite yer determination not to." His mouth brushed the tip of her nose.

A ridiculous kiss.

Ariana leaned her head away from him and gave what felt like an awkward smile. "I believe I told you one kiss."

He held her face in her hands and didn't let her turn away from him. "And I love how damn stubborn ye are."

His mouth came down on hers, once more tender and sweet.

And while no less dangerous, this time she did not fight it.

His tongue swept across her bottom lip and she let her mouth part open. Connor groaned and deepened their kiss. His hands slid over her body, underneath the plaid to her waist.

The coolness of his palms seeped through the thin fabric of her sark and was like heaven against the heat of her skin.

Connor administered kisses down her jaw to the place just below her ear, where his lips made prickles of pleasure dance down her spine. "I dinna think I deserved ye." He kissed her there once more before letting his mouth slide lower.

"And do you think you do now?" She pushed him back slightly and stared up at him. His mouth was pink from their kisses and his hair was slightly mussed.

"No." His gaze was dark with tortured honesty. "But I canna stand the thought of no' having ye in my life."

His mouth came down on hers with the fierceness she'd wanted earlier, though for an entirely different reason.

Then she'd wanted it to erase the tenderness of his touch. Now she wanted it to sate the desire raging through her, the one wanting to touch all of him, the one wanting to claim and be claimed.

"I love ye, Ariana." His declaration was growled between their lips. He pulled back and stroked her face with a trembling finger. "I've no' anything to offer ye but my love and a dark past. I promise ye, everything I am, everything I have, is yers."

His words fell on her ears like a sweet melody and poured golden hope into her heart, sealing off the sting of pain.

He searched her gaze with his hazel eyes and once more she found herself studying the flecks of green and black in them. "Say ye'll stay."

Everything in her arched toward him the way flowers bend toward the sun. "Yes," she said with finality. "Yes, I'll stay."

• • •

After all this time, after all the torment he'd inflicted upon them both, Connor had Ariana.

The skin beneath her sark was warm against his hands, her words a soft breathy note in his ears, the touch of her lips sweet honey on his mouth—and yet he almost did not believe any of it for wanting it so badly.

She would stay.

She would be his.

The desperation pumping in his chest shifted then, from the desire to persuade to the desire to possess—to claim what was his.

Ariana must have felt it too, for her kisses became greedier, bolder—a flick of the tongue, a tug of her teeth across his lower lip, the tease of her fingers along his lower stomach.

Connor gave a low, hungry growl and pulled her against him.

He remembered his painful desire for her at Urquhart—it was nothing compared to the desire to reclaim what he'd once had and too quickly lost. It thundered in his veins with a force he could not, and would not, deny.

Her body was all firm curves beneath the crumpled fabric of her sark. The plaid she'd clung so tightly around her fell away in a wisp of tartan—a barrier willingly dropped.

Only one more stood in his way.

He tugged on the voluminous undergarment. Up, up, up, until her shapely legs appeared, the curve of her hips, the dip of her waist and swell of her breasts, and then her beautiful face. Her eyes were full of the quiet adoration they'd once held when regarding him.

His body ached for release, but he refused to succumb to the blatant desire as he had last time.

This time would be different.

Connor let his gaze wash over her, claiming her first with his eyes. He wanted to touch every part of her with every part of him, his hands and mouth and tongue, until he was so overwhelmed he fell to his knees before her. His fingertips drifted over her smooth shoulders and down to the swell of her breasts, where the pink nipples stood tight and eager.

He glanced up at her face to see her watching him in quiet study beneath heavy-lidded eyes, and let his fingertip drag across her nipple. She drew in a soft breath and drew her tongue over her lips.

Taste.

He wanted to taste her.

Slowly and purposefully, he leaned forward and ran the tip of his tongue along the underside of her breast before moving upward toward her nipple. A graze, a tease.

Her whimper told him she'd enjoyed it, and his cock lurched in greedy reflex.

He wrapped his right arm around her bottom and tugged her closer, so the flat of her belly lay against his chest.

And her breast was directly in front of his mouth. He opened his lips and drew in one pert little bud.

Ariana gave a soft moan. Her hips rolled forward against him, her body acting on instinct.

With flick after deliberate flick, he coaxed several more moans from her before switching to her other breast. Her hands found his shoulders and her fingers clung to him.

"Please, Connor…" She spoke in a breathless voice, and he knew she would be slick and ready were he to graze a finger between her legs.

Only it wouldn't be his finger.

He released his hold on her until her back touched the wall and he could see she was supported.

His breath came deep and ragged with his low level of control. Everything in him wanted to rip off his kilt and shove himself inside her like some rutting brute.

He felt near to exploding and she had yet to even touch him.

Not yet.

Not yet.

The words became a chant in his head, repeated over and over as a reminder.

He released her nipple and kissed lower down her stomach, past her navel to the slight thatch of hair between her narrow thighs.

Her legs parted instinctively, and before she could offer a modest protest, he closed his mouth over the sweet mound, parting her with his tongue.

She gave a shocked gasp and her body flinched. But she did not pull away.

Connor curled his tongue inside her where she was wet with wanting. The heady scent of her arousal filled him with a lust so powerful, it threatened all reason from his mind.

She was sweet under his tongue, an intoxicating fruit he could not cease savoring. He eased his tongue forward until he found the swollen bud of her pleasure.

Her cries turned husky.

He wanted to hear those cries become screams. The slow, delicate strokes of his tongue flicked faster against the core of her desire.

Ariana's hands on his shoulders turned into iron clamps, her fingers digging into the skin there. Her thighs tightened and a whimper came out of her.

Suddenly she gasped and gave a surprised cry. She clutched him with her hands, pulling him more tightly against her. Lust pounded in his temples and throbbed at his cock, leaving him blind to all else but the woman he pleased.

And how badly he wanted her.

He rose in front of her and pulled the heavy belt from his plaid. It landed on the ground with a metallic *clunk*. The plaid easily fell away, leaving him as naked as she.

He braced a hand on either side of her head.

Her eyes sparkled bright with the glow of her release and her cheeks and lips were red. His body pressed to the soft heat of hers and her hips immediately arched toward him in mutual longing.

"Yes," she whispered.

It was all he needed.

He grasped her thighs with his hands and lifted her against the wall with her legs spread before sheathing himself inside of her wet heat.

A cry of pleasure rasped in his throat. She was even tighter than he remembered, hot and slick—so, so slick.

Her strong legs wrapped around him and her arms curled about his neck.

He drew out and flexed forward, deeper inside her. She gave a long, low moan. In the back of his mind, he registered how the rough wall behind her bit into his palms.

He cupped her buttocks and lifted her away from the scraping wall. The slight shift caused her to glide and tighten against his cock. He turned with her in his arms, still inside her, and took the three steps to the bed before lowering them both onto it.

Ariana rolled her hips against his and a wave of pleasure tingled through him.

He braced himself on either side of her, the heels of his hands sinking into the bedding, and thrust into her. She threw her head back with a moan and moved her hips in time with his own desperate pumps.

He arched his back, leaning above her as he took her, watching the pleasure play on her face and how her firm breasts gave a little bounce with each thrust.

The pleasure coiled inside him, tight and hot and so damn close.

He lay atop her and buried his face in the perfume of her hair right as the world around him exploded in his release.

Everything swam white for a second with each pulsing throb of pure ecstasy. Her own cries sounded in his ears and the telltale squeeze of her around his cock told him she'd reached her own climax again.

They lay together, quiet and still, with only their rapidly beating hearts and strained breath to fill the silence, but the quiet did not carry with it the awkward discomfort it had of late. It was familiar. Comfortable.

Intimate.

Connor threaded his fingers through Ariana's small ones. Her skin was soft beneath his touch, exquisite. He loved their closeness. He loved being able to touch her again, kiss her again.

She smiled up at him the way she had once before, glowing with affection, and it left him near breathless with its impact.

"Ye're beautiful, Ariana," he said. And truly she was. Powerful yet feminine, strong yet kind, stubborn yet forgiving.

"I love ye." Last time he had said it out of desperation for her to remain. This time he said it with the whole of his heart.

The coolness of her blue-green eyes had melted to something warm and tender. She looked up at him now with all those lovely qualities shining like the most exquisite of gems. "I love you too, Connor Grant."

To hear the admission of her own heartfelt affection, to know he was loved by so wonderful a woman as Ariana Fitzroy, eased some of his burden.

Later, when they'd lain on the small mattress, twisted in the warmth of one another, there was a peace in his mind he had not known in some time. His people were alive and well, he would be meeting with Kenneth the following day to finally uncover a truth too long left untold, and he had Ariana.

But before sleep could cradle him, a realization crept into his mind the way a sliver of cold air seeps down the back of a jacket on a particularly bitter night.

Ariana had overlooked a lot of his sins to love him, and while he knew she was able to fend for herself, he couldn't stop thinking of all those he'd wronged—of all the faces of those he'd killed and their families, who would be vengeful.

Connor had enemies—rival clans, families of those he'd killed in battle. He'd have many more if it ever came out who he'd killed in his service to the king. Ariana would now have those same enemies.

In allowing himself to love her, he made her vulnerable.

She'd asked if he deserved her now. And he knew with all certainty, he did not.

He only hoped it would not be Ariana who would pay the price of his sins.

Chapter Thirty-Five

After three long years, Connor would finally have answers.

He had arrived early at the fountain near the small stone church where he'd promised to meet Kenneth. He'd not told Ariana of the fears keeping sleep at bay. Instead he'd let her sweetness ease the concern from his mind and he'd left her in their rented room.

"Connor." The rich note of male authority in the voice identified its owner before Connor even turned.

In the daylight, Kenneth did not appear as worn-out by the hardships of power. Aside from the white sifting through his temples, the lines of his face seemed to have softened in the soft gray light of a coming storm.

Silence settled between them, not awkward, yet not quite comfortable either.

Connor searched his mind for something to say, but it was Kenneth who finally spoke. "I know ye're angry with me and I dinna blame ye for that. But ye have to know I tried to stop him."

Him. The former laird of the Gordons—the man who had taken everything from Connor.

"He dinna listen, of course," Kenneth said. His voice went flat. "And I knew I couldna stop him. But I knew I could at least protect ye and Cora."

Anger flashed through Connor. "Ye saved us, did ye?"

Kenneth met the force of Connor's glare without flinching. "Did ye think it was a coincidence I was in the area, but had Cora away from the castle? Or that someone told ye where to find us?"

The idea jarred in Connor's brain and stunned him into silence for a brief moment.

No.

He'd never considered either of those instances a coincidence.

"Ye never told us about the attack." Connor couldn't keep the accusation from his tone. "Why?"

"They were still my clan, Connor. And it wouldna have stopped either of ye from going back to Urquhart. The best I could do was delay ye, keep ye from being surprised and killed before ye could fight."

Connor wanted to argue, but the protest died in his chest. Kenneth spoke true. Knowing about the attack would have only spurred Connor to get there faster. And even Cora would not have remained behind at the thought of their father, their people, in trouble.

Kenneth's jaw squared. "I couldna do anything to stop it. I couldna do anything more to save ye or Cora. I'd spent all these years assuming ye were both dead. I'm glad that is not the case for either of ye."

Connor's head snapped up. "Ye know Cora is alive?"

Rain flecked the cobblestones around them and together they moved beneath the eaves of the church.

Kenneth sank down onto the stone bench there and gave a deep sigh. "Were it no' for someone telling me she was alive, I might never have known."

"MacAlister," Connor surmised.

Kenneth looked up at where Connor still stood and narrowed his eyes. "How did ye know?"

"I found out about what ye were planning to do," Connor said in a lowered voice. "I know we havena seen each other in so many years, but I dinna understand it. Why would ye do something so foolish? Why would ye conspire with him to commit treason?" The weight of those questions had plagued Connor since he'd learned of the plot from Isabel.

A nun walked swiftly past with her head ducked against the rain. They watched her pass before Kenneth answered.

"It was foolish. I knew as much when I first agreed to play a part." He studied the distant fountain as if it somehow might contain the answer. Fat drops of rain splashed into the pooled water at its large basin. "I did it for her."

"Her?"

"For Cora. I've always loved her. When I found out she was alive…" Kenneth stopped talking and his brows flinched together. He cleared his throat before resuming speaking. "When I found out she was alive, I would have done anything to have her back again."

Connor lowered his head and gave a sardonic smile. "Even commit treason."

"That's done now that MacAlister is dead."

Connor stared down at Kenneth's profile and let everything he'd been told sink in. His heart grew heavy with contemplation.

After all this time, it was finally apparent that it was not Kenneth who had changed.

It was Connor.

The realization was a blow to the gut and he allowed himself to sink down onto the bench beside Kenneth.

Connor had allowed himself to be so blinded by the need for vengeance, he had turned his back on the survivors who had needed him.

It had been Kenneth who had cared and provided for them.

Connor had protected Cora the best way he knew by locking her in a place where no one outside could touch her.

It had been Kenneth who risked all to bring her love.

Connor had spent the years simmering in a stagnant pool of bitterness.

It was Kenneth he had to thank for having not only saved Connor, but Cora as well.

Had Kenneth not kissed Cora that day, had he not ensured Connor knew of the clandestine meeting, both Connor and Cora would have suffered the same fate as their father.

The understanding sat in Connor's gut with all the comfort of a sharp-edged rock. Not only had Kenneth done so much for them, Connor had repaid him by killing his father.

The act had been so easy to justify then. When Connor had been so damn angry, so blinded by bloodlust, wanting only to slake his insatiable need for revenge.

He stared down at his hands. Those hands had killed many. Some for the king, some in vengeance, some on the battlefield. How many had been hurt since the onset of his hatred?

Were it not for the need for retribution, Connor would never have been locked in servitude as the king's personal assassin.

He'd done it all wrong.

His heart slid heavy in his chest.

"Connor." Kenneth's hand settled on his shoulder, the same as he'd done when they were boys. A motion Connor had inadvertently adopted over the years.

The burden he had carried for so long was suddenly too heavy to bear. Everything in him buckled under the weight and his head bowed in defeat.

Kenneth didn't say his name again, but Connor knew he was awaiting a response.

"I was so angry." Connor's voice was strained with the admission. It wasn't the true confession he knew he needed to make, but it was the most he could stand to offer in the moment.

"Ye dinna know. I'd have been angry too." Kenneth squeezed his shoulder and let his hand drop away. "Connor, where have ye been these last three years?"

Connor's mouth was dry as straw and swallowing did nothing to assuage the discomfort. "I thought everyone was dead." He turned to his friend and looked him in the eye.

"I've been living in an abandoned castle, acting as the king's personal assassin."

The skin around Kenneth's eyes tightened and showed the lines there once more.

Connor's head swam, blurring warning with the need for

honesty. There'd been too many lies through the years, too many barriers between their friendship. "I went to the king for help and asked to be allowed to kill yer da."

Kenneth's brows flinched and his body tightened. "He fell down the stairs."

Connor dropped his gaze to his hands once more. His stained, murderous hands. "With a broken neck, aye?"

Kenneth pulled in a breath beside him.

"He'd killed my da!" The shout exploded from Connor's throat and echoed back to them, peppered with the pattering of rain. He shot Kenneth a hard look and found his friend staring back at him in horror.

"He killed yer da," Kenneth said quietly. "And I did everything I could to make it right, because the sins of the father are no' the sins of the son. Ye made the decision on yer own. It was yer sin which led to murder."

His words slipped into Connor's heart like the cold, unforgiving blade of a dagger.

Kenneth stood and backed away. "I dinna know the man ye've become, but I will always mourn the loss of Connor Grant. For truly he did die that day."

Then he turned on his heel and left Connor sitting on the bench, staring after him with a hollow gap where his heart had once been lodged.

As soon as Kenneth disappeared from sight, another thought wormed its way into Connor's mind and slithered into his thoughts.

Cora.

If Kenneth was willing to commit treason for her, what else would he be willing to do?

Did he even know where Cora was?

It wasn't a risk Connor was willing to take.

He shot off the bench and ran out into the rain toward the small rented room. He and Ariana would need to leave immediately to reclaim Cora.

Before Kenneth got to her first.

• • •

Packing their travel items gave Ariana a different feeling of relief than what she'd anticipated the day prior.

This one was warmer, ensconced in all the humming joy of love.

Ariana had just finished with the last bag when Connor came through the door.

Or rather burst through, as was the case.

"We need to go. Now." His usually calm demeanor held a frantic note of urgency. He glanced around the room in a wild sweep. "Do ye have everything?"

Fear scraped up Ariana's spine. In all the time she'd known Connor, she'd never seen him in such a state. As if…as if he were afraid.

"Connor, what is it?" she asked.

He hefted their heavy bag in both his hands. "Cora. I think Kenneth is going to take her."

She rushed to grab the bag containing the remainder of their food and followed him out the door. "Why?"

He didn't answer until they were in the inn's crude stable. The stalls were empty save the two with their horses.

"I told him," Connor said. "I told him what I've been doing for the king. No' about ye and the other girls, but about—" He glanced at the empty stalls and said in a quiet voice. "About what I've done for the king."

He swung the bags on the horses and secured them. "I told him about his da too."

Ariana's heart flinched for the pain his admission must have afforded both men. She wanted to ask more, but the hard set of Connor's face told her to let him be. For now.

Once the horses were saddled and readied with their gear, they led them into the grayness of the outside. Rain pelted down upon them in fat, splatting drops.

"Isabel was right. Kenneth was convinced to join MacAlister by an offer of marriage." Connor swung onto his horse and Ariana did likewise. "A marriage to Cora."

A chill spread through Ariana's veins. "You think he's going to try to take her now?"

Connor gave a sharp nod. "And he may keep her from ever seeing me again." He dragged a hand through his hair in an uncommonly nervous gesture. "I canna lose her."

They waited until their horses were outside the town before encouraging them to run. And run they did. Their steeds raced with such fervor, the rain slapped at Ariana's face in stinging lashes.

She held on to her reins despite how slippery they'd become in the rain, despite how she could not feel the thick leather straps due to the numbing cold in her fingers.

They rode like their lives depended on it, for surely someone's life might. How far did Kenneth's love for Cora go?

Would he use her to get even with Connor?

Time seemed to pass in a long, cruel stretch, and their pace was torturous.

By the time the crude structure of the abbey came into view, Ariana's body ached from staying atop the horse. Even her jaw hurt from having clenched it to keep her teeth from clacking.

Connor's command to his horse rose high over the wind and his horse shot ahead. But Ariana could not match his speed. No matter how much she wanted to, her horse and even her body would not comply.

She saw him stop at the gate and swing down from his horse. He'd already disappeared inside by the time she arrived. His horse was unbound in front of the large wooden door.

Ariana knocked so hard on its wet surface, pain lanced up her arm.

The gate did not open.

She tried again and this time it groaned slowly inward. But it was not a nun who stood on the other side.

It was Connor, his face dark.

Ariana's heart caught in her throat. "Cora..."

"She's gone. They tried, but couldn't stop her from being taken." He swept up onto his horse. "All they'll tell me was that a finely dressed man took her."

His jaw clenched in frustration. "I knew I should have moved her. Damn Kenneth. When we meet again—"

"No." Ariana swung up on her own horse and met Connor's hard look. "Let's not go to Kenneth just yet. He'll be expecting it. Let's go to Kindrochit." She surveyed the surrounding land. It was the same scenery they'd seen for the last fortnight they'd been traveling—golden green grass spattering the swells of hills. Similar, but the area itself was foreign.

"We're close enough, aren't we?" she asked.

"About two hours away." He nodded toward a pair of hills to the right.

"Perfect." She swung onto her horse and settled into the saddle. Her steed gave a soft whinny. "Sylvi and Delilah will have no doubt returned and Murdoch will be healing. We can devise a plan to save her. One Kenneth will not expect."

Connor's forefinger tapped absently against the reins while he thought. "Fine," he agreed. "To Kindrochit."

Their pace was faster than when they'd traveled to and from Urquhart, but it was by no means the same jarring speed that had threatened to tear her to pieces earlier.

She hoped she was right in stopping Connor from going straight to Kenneth. If the others were at Kindrochit as she hoped, they could coordinate a unified attack. Had Connor gone on his own, and had Kenneth been expecting him, there was a high possibility he would not make it out alive.

She chanced a sideways glance at Connor, discreetly studying the proud set of his jaw, the ease with which he rode his horse. He loved her.

No one had ever loved her.

And she wouldn't let him come to harm so long as she could help it. The churning rush of River Clunie met her ears before the peak of Kindrochit came into view. The roof, then the stone face with its dark windows. Then the castle appeared, with dozens of riderless horses bent over the lush grass.

Ariana slowed her horse on instinct and did a quick count. There were at least forty horses with empty saddles upon their backs.

Connor slowed beside her as well. "It's the king." There was something quiet and dark in his tone.

"Why do you think he is here?"

Connor smirked. "I'm going to guess it has something to do with my inability to kill Kenneth. A mercy I now find myself regretting."

As they descended the hill, a force of soldiers came into view. The telltale red and yellow uniforms of the Gentlemen Pensioners, the king's personal guard.

King James.

As Connor had correctly guessed.

They welcomed her and Connor with stern faces. "The king wishes to see you," said a man with dark hair.

Two guards came to stand beside them.

"I'd assumed as much," Connor said wryly.

Ariana's pulse quickened. This was no welcome.

They were being treated like criminals.

They strode in through the castle gates and through the courtyard to the great hall, inside which the king stood at the head of the room on the small, raised dais that usually sat empty. The king stood wearing the heavy mantle of authority, the typical scowl of disinterest on his face now a deeper shade of pink than Ariana remembered.

A woman with thick brown hair stood at his side, her nose and eyes reddened as if she'd been crying.

Connor surged forward, but was caught at the shoulders by the guards and held in position. "Cora." He bellowed her name with such volume, it echoed around them and caught at Ariana's heart.

"Connor, what have ye done?" Cora's voice was thin with emotion. "Why dinna ye tell me of all this?"

Connor's shoulders sagged and he looked more defeated than Ariana had ever seen him.

"Connor Grant." The king's voice rang sharp on the bare stone walls. "I hereby arrest you for the act of treason."

Chapter Thirty-Six

Treason meant death.

Ariana blinked in shock and turned to Connor to find him staring blankly at the king, as if he too could not believe the words.

The guard at Connor's side yanked his arms back and another came forward with manacles in his hands. They were large, clunky metal rings, stained dark from previous victims.

The idea of those slipping on Connor's wrists was more than she could bear.

She grabbed the hands holding Connor and jerked them free. "Don't touch him."

Before the man could react, she spun around and kicked the manacles from the other guard. They landed with a heavy metallic crash on the floor.

"I wouldn't resist if I were you." The king's voice broke through her frenzied desire to fight.

"Ariana, stop." Connor's warning made her cease.

She turned and looked toward the dais, where a guard had secured a blade against Cora's throat. Defiance flashed in Cora's brown eyes and Ariana knew if she kept fighting, Cora might too.

And Cora would likely die.

Doubtless Connor knew as much.

Ariana let her arms drop to her sides and did not move to stop the man who bent to reclaim the manacles from the ground before securing them on Connor's wrists.

"That's better." The king waved off the man threatening Cora.

Although the man moved back, he stood close enough to secure her in his grasp again at a moment's notice.

Ariana glanced around the room, seeking faces she'd come to know well. Percy, Liv, Sylvi, Delilah, Murdoch—even Isabel.

None were to be found.

Poor Murdoch had been lying abed with an injury when she'd left. And he was the kind of man who would not have given up the castle without a fight.

Her stomach twisted.

Sylvi and Delilah would have fought as well.

To the death.

Was everyone dead? Captured? The weight of loss crushed her heart.

"What is this treason ye accuse me of?" The rage simmering under the surface of Connor's composure rippled through his demand.

The king's lip curled with disgust. "You knew of a treasonous plot against me and yet you sought to let it come to fruition."

Ariana remembered the assassination Delilah and Sylvi had been investigating.

Perhaps this was not about Kenneth after all.

The plot Sylvi and Delilah were working so hard to uncover had held no real urgency. The House of Lords was months away from meeting.

Connor's hands curled into fists behind his back and Ariana could almost feel the frustration pounding through him. "We dinna have all the names yet."

The king narrowed his eyes. "You had the most important one and you didn't do anything with it. Kenneth Gordon is still alive." The king lifted his head in authoritative insistence. "And my cousin is dead."

Isabel.

Ariana's stomach dropped.

They thought her dead.

Connor tried to step forward again, but the king held up his hand and several pairs of arms pulled Connor back.

"You needn't explain why," King James said. "I already know. You want so badly to be free of your role with me."

A small sob hiccuped out of Cora and Connor's head turned in her direction.

"Why?" she mouthed.

Realization splintered through Ariana. Cora knew what Connor had done, and judging from the sick expression on his face, he had just realized as much.

"You lied to me." The king's voice pitched. "I trusted you to see those men dead in four months. You had your orders. You disobeyed and you killed a member of my own blood. My dear cousin, Isabel."

Cora was weeping softly now and Connor let his head fall forward.

Ariana's breathing came harder. Connor would have no explanation for the king. Lying would do little more than buy him time.

Movement occurred at the side window and snagged her attention. Several soldiers spoke to a man she recognized all too well.

The blond hair, the overly large frame, the chipped-toothed smile.

Murdoch.

"I dinna know she was yer cousin, your grace," Connor said. "And Laird Gordon was harder to get to than anticipated." His voice lacked the conviction it needed.

This would not go well.

Ariana turned her attention back to Murdoch. One of the soldiers clapped him on the shoulder like a brother and let him stroll away.

No arrest.

No manacles.

A dizzying rush of triumph tingled through her. It all clicked perfectly in her head, like a lockpick blindly stabbing through the darkness before catching.

It all made sense now.

The length of time Murdoch had been gone when initially searching for MacAlister when she'd first arrived. The way he'd led Connor to believe the people of Urquhart were all dead—it had been no mere coincidence or misunderstanding.

And the injury he'd sustained, the way he'd appeared to have slept for so long when he'd arrived and how her horse had been in the wrong stall.

He had killed Renny, and he'd taken a knife in the gut for his crime. The wound had looked fresh despite his claim it was several days old. She'd seen the confusion on Percy's face when she'd cared for it. But gentle Percy did not question his lie.

"I know you've lied to me, Connor." The king motioned to his guards with a sweep of his finger, and they inched closer to Connor. "After years of trusted friendship, I was going to give you an opportunity to tell me the truth. It appears even now you are unable to do so."

Ariana's mind swam.

Murdoch. All this time it was Murdoch.

But her newfound knowledge would do nothing stop the king.

There had to be something else. Some other way.

She scoured her brain for something to get them out, a way to free Connor, and sucked in a hard breath at what unraveled before her.

Isabel had once told her in confidence of the king's fear of witches. It was a dangerous gamble considering what was done to witches, but Connor would be safe.

Ariana's heart slammed harder in her chest.

This could be her death.

But it would save Connor.

"Connor Grant," the king said in a booming voice. "I hereby arrest—"

"It was me," Ariana said. She didn't let it scream from her as the clawing desperation inside her longed to do. No, she said it with the careful calm of one who had long since weighed her words.

The king stopped. "What did you say?"

Everyone turned to stare at her and the impact of what she was about to do slammed into her as though she'd run headlong into a stone wall.

Her pulse was jagged and wild.

Connor stared at her, confusion evident in the amber warmth of his eyes. She would never forget those eyes. And she would not regret this.

Love was a far greater reward than death was a punishment.

"I said…" Ariana stepped forward. Fear nipped at her waning bravery, but she swept it aside. "It was me."

• • •

What the hell was Ariana doing?

Connor stared in horror as she came forward to stand at his side in the fire of the king's accusation. She strode with a confident gait.

"Killing Laird Gordon and MacAlister were tasked to me." She spoke without looking at Connor.

He'd once told her the king didn't know the girls didn't kill. He regretted that now. "That isna—"

"I didn't tell Connor about Lady MacAlister—she was merely caught in the middle by accident. And I told him I did kill Laird Gordon." Ariana tilted her head in an arrogant manner. "But I did not."

The king cast an incredulous look at Connor. "And you believed this?"

"She's lying," Connor growled the words through his teeth, as if he could somehow convince the king with the force of his vehemence.

"I compelled him," Ariana said in a cool tone.

Everything inside Connor chilled to brittle ice.

No.

She was not going to do this.

The king went still and the color faded from his cheeks.

"I lied to him and compelled him to believe me," she said.

"Compelled." The king repeated the words with wide eyes. "Ye witch. Why?"

"Because I know a lot about you." She sneered. "Like all these years you've left Urquhart unguarded. And how Laird Gordon kept Connor's people safe when you failed."

Frantic fear clawed its way deep into Connor's heart. "Stop this, Ariana."

She turned to him and gave a gentle smile. "My hold on you is so deep, you cannot help but defend me."

Connor fought the manacles behind his back. They rattled with his effort and cut into the heels of his palms, all to no avail. "Dinna do this." He looked up at the king, whose face had gone completely white. "Dinna listen to her. She's lying."

But King James was not listening to him. He stared at Ariana with bulging eyes, his arms protectively crossed over his heart like a child who'd been frightened.

Ariana regarded the king once more. "I know it's you who betrayed Connor."

King James flicked an anxious glance toward Connor. He swallowed—a soft *thunk* in the great silence.

"I know many, many things, James." She said the king's Christian name as if it were a curse. "More than how you've dangled Connor's lands over him and how you've let his people go without a leader. Like how you worked behind his back."

"Stop this," the king hissed.

"No. I know how you've worked against him." She looked at Connor when she finished the sentence. "With Murdoch."

Connor ceased struggling and his body tingled as if he'd just been doused with water from the loch in winter.

Murdoch.

Connor looked to King James, but the monarch would not meet his eye.

King James shifted backward, almost cowering behind Cora, and shot an accusing finger toward Ariana. "Arrest her. Arrest the *witch*."

Soldiers shoved past Connor to do their master's bidding. Connor tried to lurch to the side, to do what he could to protect Ariana.

But it was no use. They surrounded her and she did not bother to fight.

Damn it, why didn't she even fight?

But he knew the answer.

It wasn't just Cora. It was him.

She knew that by accepting the blame herself, he would be free.

He watched her face through the bustle of activity. The manacles were unclasped from his wrists and snapped onto hers.

I'm sorry, she mouthed. *I love you.*

The words embedded themselves in his heart like a wickedly thorned burr. His body tightened with the need to fight.

As if sensing his intent, several guards grabbed him and held him back.

They took Ariana from him then. She walked calmly, with the authority of a queen.

And she did not look at him again.

Connor stared at her until she disappeared from view. "What will happen to her?" He unleashed his rage in a roar of words.

The king gave Connor a shrewd look. "Her hooks are in deep with you. She has truly bewitched you."

No mirth showed on his face. Connor had known of the king's paranoia against witches—there were many in Scotland who shared his fears—but never had he witnessed such a powerful man with such a dangerous fear.

"What will happen to her?" Connor asked again, more calmly this time.

"The same as what happens to all witches, and all other traitors against the crown—she'll be put to death." The king glanced out the window, where the day's sunlight was beginning to fade. "In the morning."

Connor had expected the answer, but it was still a gut punch. Ariana was slated to die.

For having saved him.

He wanted to bolt from the room and race after the soldiers who took her. A quick sword thrust to both their necks and she'd be free.

But he knew it wasn't that easy. After those two guards there would be dozens more. No amount of training could make those odds work in his favor.

He would need time to form a plan, and he'd have until morning.

"Forgive the barbarous nature of my threat earlier. It was wrong to obtain your sister, though I imagine you understand such things better than most." The king motioned to Cora to step down.

She cast a hesitant look at him before running off the dais and into Connor's embrace. He curled her trembling body in his arms. Her eyes and cheeks were wet with tears and she stared into his face with a wide, frightened gaze.

"And forgive me for what I've confessed on your behalf," the king added without emotion.

The understanding of Cora's words earlier, of her reaction now, crashed through Connor.

Cora knew the horrors of what he'd done, the men he'd murdered by order of the king.

Nausea clenched at his stomach. Not her.

Not Cora.

Connor's thoughts mired in his frustration.

All the years Connor had worked for him, had sacrificed his moral integrity and stained his soul the color of blood, and this, *this*, was how the king repaid his loyalty?

Stealing his sister and killing the woman he loved.

Connor shook his head. "After all I've done for ye, ye work with Murdoch to bring my demise."

"I couldn't have a powerful force such as you without a leash, could I?" the king asked. "Surely you don't blame me. After all, I have already extended my apology. And I'll be speaking with Murdoch later about his inability to provide me with correct information."

Cora was weeping softly now. Each shuddering breath she drew, no matter how discreet, was a blow to his heart. He held her to him and laid her head on his chest. He couldn't look down at her and see her pain, or even what might lie beyond.

Accusation.

Disgust.

Cora knew.

"And here is your retinue." The king indicated the far door where Sylvi led the other women toward him. Her gait was stiff and her face a storm cloud of fury.

"I must commend you for what you've been able to do with these women," the king said. "Who knew such softness could be turned to steel?"

Sylvi slid him a steely look from the corner of her eye. Respectful from a distance, but he knew what was grinding in her head.

Delilah followed behind Sylvi, then Percy and Liv.

Isabel was nowhere in sight.

Connor's world was spinning out of control. All the carefully woven lies were unraveling like a loose thread subjected to a hard pull, and he felt it all laid around him in a messy, ugly pile.

"Were you truly arrested for treason?" Sylvi demanded. Her gaze settled on where Connor held Cora in his arms for a moment, but she cut her stare back to him.

She gave the king a hard look. "This man's life has revolved around keeping you safe for the last three years. Our lives are spent ensuring all threats against you are dispelled. He is honorable and he is just."

The king smiled at her with the condescending patience one gives a petulant child. "I take it ye're the lass five men had to bring down. Impressive."

Sylvi's eyes narrowed to dangerous slits, an indication his praise had not pleased her. "There are a lot of people who want to kill you," she said in reply.

Connor knew she wanted to say more, but she wisely held her tongue.

If only Ariana had done the same. His gut clenched at the thought of her.

At least with the other girls now released, they could somehow band together—a unified force against the king's army.

If ever a small group stood a chance, it was them.

But it would still be dangerous.

The smile on the king's face faded. "Who wishes to kill me?"

Sylvi turned and regarded Connor with a look inviting him to speak. He released Cora with a gentle pat. "Delilah and I have been tracking a plot to assassinate you. Thomas Percy and several other men are responsible."

The sooner he told the king the information they had on the gunpowder gathering plot, the sooner they would be free to devise a plan to rescue Ariana.

And God help Murdoch if Connor saw him any time soon.

Chapter Thirty-Seven

The walls had ears and eyes.

It made speaking openly to the other women difficult, but certainly not impossible.

Connor had gathered them all in Percy's large room, including Cora. His sister regarded him with questions in her eyes, and he knew she wanted to talk with him. But not here. Not now. Not around everyone.

The familiar clean scent of herbs in Percy's workroom was a comfort, however small, in such perilous times.

"Where is Ariana?" Percy's pupils narrowed to small dots of black in her large blue eyes.

"One of the guards said she was under arrest." Sylvi spoke in a somber tone. Her gaze was sharp and Connor knew everything in her was on guard.

He understood all too well. His own body was tight with the threat of an impending attack, his senses on high alert and his nerves strung taut.

"They took her to the prison," Cora added.

The very thought of Ariana in prison coiled around his heart like a chain, heavy and tight and cold.

Delilah turned a horrified look on Connor. "Is that true?"

He nodded, unable to say the words aloud. "Where's Isabel?"

"Right here," came a feminine voice.

Connor glanced over his shoulder to find Isabel emerging from a false door in the wall. She wore a low cut gown garishly adorned with paste gems. Her eyes were lined with kohl and her lips smeared with carmine, as they had been the last time he'd seen her.

And truly he was grateful to see her now. After having been accused of killing her, it would not do well for the king to now find her alive and in Connor's care.

"I knew of Isabel's predicament." Percy sifted through a cabinet while she spoke. "I knew she couldn't be caught and so I hid her in the false wall here." She handed a neat stack of black clothing to Isabel and nodded toward the back wall, where Connor had built several false walls with hidden stairs around the castle. They all connected and had an exit from the castle to allow for escape should the need arise. With the crumbling deterioration of Kindrochit, he hadn't needed much skill, and the construction was almost easy. It had taken over two years to accomplish. Initially, he'd felt as though he'd wasted his time in constructing it. Now he was glad he had.

Isabel disappeared behind a screen.

"Connor." Liv stepped forward, the small gray kitten clutched to her chest. "Tell us what happened to Ariana. What are they going to do to her?" Desperation sharpened her voice and it made Connor wish he didn't have to recount the painful tale.

They all needed to know what fate would befall their friend, and then they could decide if they were willing to risk everything to save her.

• • •

The manacles cut into Ariana's wrists. They'd been drawn too tight across her skin. She'd tried rolling her wrists and wriggling them in an attempt to find a more comfortable position, but all her effort was in vain.

They'd forced her to walk through the courtyard under the encouragement of an army's glare, and they were now stopped in front of the prison. The smaller building was set apart from the main part of the castle and housed not only the prison but the larder as well.

She'd only ever seen the inside of the larder, where the weapons they used for practice were typically kept in a neat row along the walls.

"What will you do with me?" Ariana asked. "How long am I to stay your prisoner?"

The guards opened the door to the prison and an aggressive shove sent her sprawling inside. She staggered into the darkened room, momentarily blinded by the sudden absence of light.

The scrape of stones under her feet echoed around her, mimicking her unsure footing. A distinct mustiness inside mingled with the wet scent of earth and stone. A very thin crack of light showed from a bit of broken stone in one far corner, though it was meager enough to be nonexistent.

"Dinna worry." Murdoch's familiar voice sounded beside her ear. "Ye willna be here long."

She sensed more than felt him lean over her.

Her instincts lurched into action and she managed to jerk away from his face, but he caught the chain tethering her hands together before she could escape.

The darkness of the room became less impenetrable as her vision adjusted, and Murdoch's wild blond braids and hard face came into view.

His eyes narrowed with hatred. "How did ye know I was working with the king?"

She glanced around the room, confirming several other guards were in there with them. Were it just the two of them, she would have already managed to flee.

"No' feeling much like answering?" He snorted. "Ye'll be spending some time with me tonight and can answer then."

His hands gripped her shoulders and spun her around so her back faced him. "I'm verra proud of how it all worked out." The sour odor of liquor bathed over her neck and cheek. "But first I need to check ye. The lot of ye think ye're so clever, hiding yer weapons everywhere." His hands slid over her arms and down her waist. "I'm sure I'll find at least one."

Ariana closed her eyes against the assault of his greedy hands, but it only made her concentrate on his touch more. His fingers glided down her legs and slid across her thigh, where it was obvious no blade had been strapped.

He paused a little too long at her waist and pulled her back against him, where his enjoyment of his search was evident.

Ariana gritted her teeth and couldn't stop wondering at her own odds of defeating four people.

Murdoch's hands slid over her chest and danced over the top of her bodice.

The hidden dagger there.

Damn.

She straightened before he could notice it. "That is about enough. A woman can only endure so much offense upon her person."

Murdoch grabbed her by the throat in a painful squeeze and shoved his hand in to the confines between her breasts. His fingers were cold and rough.

He'd clumsily bumped the dagger several times and yet he allowed his probing fingers to prod within her bodice.

The cur.

With all the strength Ariana could muster, she exploded forward and used her head as a battering ram against his face. Pain blossomed over the front of her forehead and Murdoch jerked back from her with a curse.

His hand had clung to her dagger and tugged it free from her bodice with a savage rending that echoed around them.

Blood coursed down his mouth and chin. He held his free hand to the bridge of his nose. "Ye broke by dose, ye bitch." His *m*s came out like *b*s and his *n*s like *d*s, evidence that he was most likely correct.

Ariana glared at him and let all the hatred and anger within her radiate in his direction. "I'd have broken more had you not bound my arms behind me, you coward."

Murdoch looked behind Ariana to where the guards stood.

"Get the hell out." His gaze shifted to her and a chill moved down her spine. "I've got her from here."

The men's echoing footsteps thunked out of the narrow cell and left the prison disconcertingly quiet.

Ariana bent her knees slightly and braced herself for a blow. She wasn't disappointed.

Murdoch rushed upon her with such speed, even her preparation for the impact was not enough to keep her upright. His body slammed into her and she fell back against the hard floor.

She twisted herself when she landed so the solid part of her upper arm slapped against the stone rather than the back of her head.

The way Connor had taught her.

Murdoch grabbed her other arm and dragged her backward. She tried to drop her weight to the ground and make herself heavy, but he lifted her with ease regardless. Her feet kicked helplessly beneath her until she was shoved back against the wall.

"Ye found a way to save him today." Murdoch's broken nose made his speech difficult to discern. "Ye'll no' be here to save him next time."

Ariana twisted and fought against his hold. To no avail. If only her arms hadn't been bound. If only she were free. "Why? Why are you doing this to him? You both survived the attack at Urquhart. You stayed with him all these years, and now this?"

His lack of a reply scraped over her ragged nerves. "What does it matter?" she demanded. "If I'm going to die anyway, why not tell me?"

"Because they were always better than everyone else." Murdoch practically shouted the words, as if they'd been so long repressed, he had no choice but to let them explode from him. He turned his head and spit onto the ground. "Because that sister of his dinna even know I existed. But she thought the sun shone outta that Gordon lad's arse."

He pulled out the key and undid one of her manacles. Before

she could let a fist fly toward his face, he trapped her wrist in his large hand.

"So when I was offered a chance to get a higher lot in life than a constable's son could ever hope for, I took it." He threaded the manacle and chain through an iron loop bolted to the wall and clasped the cold cuff around her wrist once more.

"What chance?" she pressed. "Murdoch, what did you do?"

He grinned a broken-toothed, bloody smile at her. "What do ye think?"

Her world spun as if she'd been slapped. "It was you?" she asked, incredulous. "It was you who let Gordon in?"

"Aye. Killed my own da, who was trying to keep me from getting to the portcullis lever." His admission came with a sick sense of pride. "But before I could get my due, Connor swept in and killed Laird Gordon. When Connor found me, I had no choice but to go with him." His lips curled in disgust. "He had nothing to offer me, nothing but living in this shite place and being his hunting dog."

Her shoulder throbbed where she'd broken her fall, and she let her body relax slightly, not bothering to fight the metal bonds.

Contempt twisted his features, his appearance made all the more vicious by the glistening blood. "I even approached the king in London once for recompense for my part, to get the due owed to me from Laird Gordon. After all, it was the king who'd suggested the attack to Laird Gordon in the first place. And all he gave me was another shite position, this time playing watchdog."

Murdoch spit again and grimaced in pain at the obvious discomfort caused by his broken nose.

She was glad it hurt him, and that he suffered.

He'd made Connor grieve all these years.

"I knew somehow I'd get him then, when I had the ear of the king. I just dinna know it'd be through ye." Murdoch turned with a smirk. He locked her cell and jerked open the prison door.

The fading light of day flooded the room with such brilliance she was momentarily blinded before the door slammed shut and she was plunged in darkness once more.

Alone.

Fated to die.

With Murdoch's confession, which she would never be able to share with Connor.

. . .

The large area of Percy's workspace was beginning to feel like a cage. Connor paced its length again and again and again.

"If we all try to save her, we'll die." He kept his words quiet enough that the guards wouldn't hear, but firm enough that the women knew the severity of what he said.

Cora looked between him and the other girls with large eyes.

"Is it possible you underestimate us?" Sylvi tilted her head in challenging defiance and lifted a pale eyebrow.

He sighed. "Ye know I dinna underestimate ye."

Sylvi shrugged and walked off to examine a bottle on Percy's workspace. "We'd risk it for her, the same as she'd risk it for us."

Isabel left the entrance to the false wall and approached their clustered group. "What if we convince them she's a witch?" she offered. She wore full black clothing now and had covered the brilliant red of her hair with spare black cloth.

Liv folded her arms over her chest. "I think they're already pretty convinced."

"No, I mean we really convince them." Isabel grinned and the light of the room glinted off her sharp white teeth. "If they already think she's a witch, we can use her as a weapon. All we have to do is rescue her from the prison, then when she's in the courtyard, we'll make it appear as if she has incredible powers."

Isabel laughed, a stark sound in the otherwise quiet atmosphere. "They'll be so frightened of her, they won't even try to stop her."

After having seen how readily the king had fallen for Ariana's ruse, Connor had no doubt King James could be further tricked into believing her to have otherworldly powers.

But if the plan didn't work, they could all end up dead.

Then again, if they fought hand-to-hand against the guards, they could still end up dead.

"It just might work." Connor nodded to himself as a plan began to form in his mind. "Percy, see what ye have in yer stores to make Ariana look like she has powers. If anything needs to be detonated or thrown, have Isabel do it from the safety of the shadows."

Both women nodded.

"We'll need to let Ariana know somehow," Liv said. "The more she can act like a witch, the better this shall go." She scratched the kitten's chin. "Leave that part to me and Fianna." The gray cat lifted her chin and gave in to the stroking affection with a squinting look of exquisite happiness.

Percy studied Fianna. "Are you sure she's ready?"

Liv shrugged. "Now is as good a time as ever to try."

"Sylvi and Delilah." Both women turned to look at Connor. "I want ye to act as guards against the king's soldiers. Ensure nothing goes wrong."

"I can take on the guards myself and distract the king," Sylvi said with a slight frown.

Delilah regarded her with a long look. "Yes, the king will need to be distracted. I'd like to—"

"Delilah." Sylvi stared at her. "You don't have to do this. I know what he did to you."

"There are questions I should have asked him a long time ago." Delilah's face appeared pale despite the bravado of her words. "Now seems the right time. And the perfect distraction."

Something uneasy settled in the pit of Connor's gut.

Then there was just Cora.

Connor glanced around her room to find his sister.

"Where did Cora get off to?" he asked.

The other women searched the room as well and confirmed Connor's sudden fear.

Cora was missing.

Chapter Thirty-Eight

Connor was a visitor in his own chamber.

He sat in a large chair in front of the fire, awaiting the king, who had quickly commandeered the room as his own.

Cora still had not been found despite their search effort.

All the remaining possibilities of where she might be left Connor with more anxious energy than his body could stand. His foot bounced against the floor.

Perhaps she had hid in the walls like Isabel, preparing her own attack on the king.

Or maybe she was among the soldiers, playing hostess, though he did not consider the idea any more likely than that Ariana was a real witch.

Or mayhap Cora was meeting with the king herself, to further vouch for Connor's innocence—which could also explain why he had been summoned.

The door opened and the king walked in.

Alone.

Connor hadn't been alone with the king since he'd first been offered the opportunity to become the king's assassin.

The realization did not bring fond memories.

"It would appear I owe you more than a great apology. I owe you my thanks as well." The king settled into the opposite seat in front of the fire.

Darkness had fallen outside and the firelight glinted and winked off the king's gilded clothing.

"I asked around about what you've told me of Thomas Percy."

King James's words were drawn and slow, calculated, and it ate at Connor's patience like acid. He needed to find Cora.

The king flicked a finger at where the hem of his jacket had flipped up, revealing the silken underside. It fell into place unceremoniously. "You were right. My men are already investigating what they can while in Scotland and will return to London posthaste to gather the remainder of the information we need."

King James leaned forward in the seat. The chair groaned beneath him. "You saved my life."

Connor did not reply. He hadn't done it because it was expected of him, nor for a great love of the king himself. He'd done it in the hope one day the king would finally grant him the home he'd sought to reclaim all these long years.

"I know you're unhappy in your position and would like to get your land back." The king's eyebrows rose. "Urquhart."

Connor's heartbeat quickened, but he kept his face impassive.

"You've been a loyal servant," the king said magnanimously. "I'd like to give you Urquhart, but under two conditions."

The hope was crushed from Connor's chest. He knew too well how conditional favors with the king worked.

"First, I'd like you to be available for the occasional…task."

He still wanted Connor as his personal assassin. More people to die at Connor's hand, more faces to haunt his dreams.

"And second?" Connor asked in a wary tone.

"I'd like the woman, Sylvi, to stay in touch with me on any potential treasonous plots."

Connor wanted to slam the offer back in the king's face. But his people rose forefront to his mind.

Anise.

Tavin.

Tavish.

Renny.

Had he been the laird he was supposed to have been, Renny would still be alive.

However, Connor had not known they'd survived before. Now he knew. Now he would ensure they were never without his aid.

He could have Urquhart back.

Or he could ask for something more.

The king's offer was everything Connor had spent the last three years trying to obtain, but there was something far more pressing on his heart.

Ariana.

He could not let her die.

Even if it meant suffering another seven years of service to the king to reclaim his rightful home.

Connor had once tasted the idea of life without Ariana. It was a bitter reality. She'd brought joy to his somber life and eased away the burden of his sins with her optimism.

To see her light snuffed out and the world robbed of her beautiful soul was more than Connor could bear.

"It's a fine offer ye've extended, Your Majesty, but I'd like to ask something else of ye."

The king lifted his eyebrow with quiet interest.

Connor met the king's gaze. "Release Ariana."

King James pushed out of his chair and thrust himself upward onto his feet. "Absolutely not. She is a witch and will die. Your enchanted infatuation will die with her." He strode toward the door but paused before opening it. "I'd recommend you consider my offer before you find it retracted."

Without another word, the king stepped from the room and let the door close behind him.

She is a witch and will die.

Connor's gut twisted around those words. He hadn't truly expected the king to grant him his request, but at least he'd tried to save Ariana the safest way he knew how.

And he would not let her die.

With the king's rejection came, too, the necessity for battle.

Before going to Percy's room, where the women gathered, he did one last search through the false walls of the castle for Cora.

And once more did not find her.

She had left while they were locked in Percy's room. Not been taken—left.

She'd said nothing to him before her departure, but he'd seen the hurt in her eyes when he'd first been arrested. He knew what the king had told her.

More determined now than ever before, he made his way to where the women were preparing for battle. Dawn would come soon and he intended for them to attack before the king's Gentlemen Pensioners ever had a chance to touch Ariana.

He opened the door and looked at the solemn faces of the women.

"Are ye ready?" he asked. Liv was already gone. A good sign, as her task of loosing Fianna near the prison had to be completed before anything could truly begin.

Isabel slipped like a shadow into hiding, where there would be more false walls and staircases connecting throughout the castle.

Percy waited until the false door closed before giving a nod. "It's time."

. . .

The banging of mallets on wood had finally ceased. Ariana knew what it was they built just outside the prison doors. They'd spoken loudly enough for her to hear, no doubt intentionally.

A scaffold.

For her.

With the rising of the sun would come the hour of her death. Already a gray light seeped from under the crack beneath the prison door.

The idea of it welled inside her like a sob, helpless and hot.

To have lived her whole life without love, only to die when she finally found it—it was cruel.

She wanted more time to bask in the warmth of Connor's affection, to revel in the happiness of love. But none of it would be. All the dreams her heart had summoned melted like snowflakes floating too near an open flame.

A ball of anguish knotted in the back of her throat.

Her heart broke with a sob that echoed around her. Her muscles tensed with unspent rage. She did not seek to quell it, not when it didn't matter. It wouldn't save her.

Nothing would.

She gripped her manacles as tightly as she could and wrenched them down hard, wanting to feel the bite of the metal against her wrists. At least physical pain might dull her inner torment.

The unyielding bonds tugged at her palms and left her hands tingling. But that was not all.

A fine sifting of mortar floated from the rusted metal in the wall. Her heart went still and then renewed its beating with vigor. She gripped the heavy chains between her hands and shook them.

The metal loop wiggled where it was embedded in the wall. Kindrochit's deteriorating state might very well be the thing to save her.

Ariana sucked in a hard breath of air. The chains were cold against her already icy hands, but she paid that no mind and tightened her grip.

She widened her stance and jerked the chain toward her with everything she had. The metal bolt shot upward and then sagged an inch lower in a crumbling of mortar.

Her fingers ached with the effort and she flexed them to get feeling back in them before she tried again. The stink of rusted metal hung in the air from where it had warmed against her palms.

She grit her teeth and tugged at the chain once more.

The bolt shot free of the wall and the momentum of her effort sent her staggering backward. She fell hard to the ground and her head slammed back against the iron bars. The room flared with bright spots that didn't go away, even when she closed her eyes.

Ariana brought a trembling hand to her hair and the chains still binding her wrists together clinked. Her fingers found a nasty lump upon her scalp, but came away dry.

At least she was not bleeding.

Something warm and covered in fur brushed against her hand. Ariana lurched away from it, squelching a scream.

But the creature wasn't a rat.

Fianna nuzzled closer to her and rubbed her face against Ariana's exposed shin. The pink of Fianna's nose was cold and wet in contrast to the downy warmth of her head.

In a small cell of ugliness and impending death, the very sight of the small cat brought such lightness to Ariana's heavy heart, tears sprang to her eyes.

She glanced toward a narrow hole near the corner of the prison, where a slit of gray light showed through. Just large enough for a determined cat.

"We must do what we can to escape," she whispered to her companion.

Fianna rubbed against her shin once more in reply. Ariana bent to pet her and noticed something cool and stiff set on Fianna's back. Like leather.

Curious, she followed the leathery texture. It seemed to be the same gray color as Fianna and wrapped around the small gray body like a harness.

No, it *was* a harness.

A flap caught at Ariana's fingertip when she touched the leather over Fianna's chest. Ariana flipped it upward and let her finger probe inside the small pocket.

The crinkle of paper met Ariana's ears and her heart leaped. She pulled it free of the pouch, unfolded it and angled it toward the door where light was beginning to filter in.

Percy's graceful writing curled across the page, legible even in the dim light.

If you can escape, wait for us. Then be prepared to play the role of a vengeful witch—we will ensure your powers are true.

Ariana tucked the note into her stays to ensure no one would see it.

Her powers? What did Percy possibly mean by that?

"We must be ready," she said to Fianna in a quiet whisper. The cat stared up at her quizzically and licked at her front paw several times before rubbing it over her face.

Ariana pulled herself off the floor with a rattle of chains. The metal loop she'd pulled free from the wall hung from between the manacles like a heavy amulet. It would make things difficult, but not impossible.

She pushed her weight onto her right heel and twisted her foot. The base of the brown shoe Percy had given her swung open. Ariana worked her fingers into the open heel and pulled the dagger free from the underside of her foot.

It was not long, perhaps three inches, but the blade was sturdy and as thick as two thumbs set beside one another.

Enough to at least threaten, if nothing else.

She slid the sole of her shoe back into place and straightened, her fingers searching through the mess of her hair for the bit of silver.

Her fingertips met a cool line of metal.

Success.

She pulled the lockpick from her hair and settled before the locked gate. After having been locked in the room near Urquhart by Anise, Ariana had vowed to never forget the hairpin again. Footsteps crunched on the loose stones in front of the prison door.

She sucked in a deep breath and held it to keep her hands from trembling. She slid the pick blindly into the lock and searched...

The footsteps stopped.

Searched...

A key sounded in the heavy prison door.

Searched.

Click.

The pick gave under her fingertips and the cell door creaked open. Only a fraction of a second passed before the main door to the prison flew open and Murdoch stepped in.

He locked the door behind him, obviously assuming she was safely bolted to the wall.

Ariana had the advantage of his blindness on her side and could have attacked, but she held back and pulled the bars of her cell door into place.

Perhaps he might leave and his life would be spared.

Vile though he may be, she did not wish to kill again.

"I see ye got away from the wall," Murdoch muttered. "Maybe ye're a witch like ye claimed to be."

"Maybe this place is falling apart faster than anyone realizes," Ariana replied in a dry tone. Her heart roared so loudly in her ears, it was a wonder she could even hear her own voice.

Mudroch's eyes fixed on something. "Or maybe ye had help."

He strode across the room and Ariana saw but a flash of gray fur before Murdoch's foot came down hard.

"No!" The word ripped uselessly from her mouth.

Fianna darted away from him in the scantest breadth of time.

Murdoch did not give up so easily. He chased the kitten across the room in great stomping footsteps.

Nearer to her cell.

He gave a roar of impatience and edged the terrified kitten into a corner. Poor Fianna balled up and issued forth a useless hiss. Murdoch lifted his foot with a sneer of malice.

Ariana exploded from her cell with all her pent-up anger seething inside her and unleashed it upon Murdoch. Her body crashed into him so violently, he slammed back against the wall and his head knocked back against the stone.

A low groan came from his mouth and he looked down between them to where her dagger jutted from his chest amid a wash of blood.

Horror at her own actions trickled through Ariana like drips of melting snow.

She hadn't done it intentionally.

Had she?

It'd all happened so fast.

More footsteps sounded nearby. Not in front of the door, but close enough to set her heart on edge.

Ariana lowered Murdoch to the floor and pulled the key ring off his belt. Three iron keys jingled together.

Murdoch's breathing was labored and thick and bright red blood was smeared over his teeth.

She wanted to close her eyes and block out the sight of the life she was taking, to blot out the odor of his blood staining the air, but already there was too little time.

The footsteps outside were louder now.

In front of the prison door.

Ariana tried to slide the key into the manacles, but her hands shook too badly. Fianna nuzzled close to her feet, as if attempting to calm her.

Focus.

Ariana gritted her teeth and forced herself to focus on the dark keyhole. Quickly, she unlocked both manacles from her wrists.

Murdoch's glittering, narrowed gaze fixed on her while she worked in the semidark. He gave a long, low sigh, and finally his eyes slid closed.

"Forgive me," Ariana whispered. She grasped the handle of the dagger and pulled. It came free with a sucking sound, but the blade was still stained with Murdoch's blood.

The footsteps outside had stopped and the hairs on the back of Ariana's neck rose. She scooped Fianna into her arms and deposited the little cat near the hole in the corner of the room.

The door rattled and Ariana's heart lurched.

"Go," she whispered, and nudged the little cat forward.

Regardless of who stood on the other side of the door, she would not put the kitten in jeopardy.

Much to Ariana's great relief, Fianna darted through the hole and disappeared into the early gray of dawn.

The door swung open and Ariana spun to face her enemy, bloody dagger held at the ready.

Chapter Thirty-Nine

Ariana's would-be attacker entered, silent as a shadow. He was clad in all black with a hood drawn over his face.

She couldn't see who her opponent was, not that it would keep her from killing them if it meant her freedom.

"Ariana."

Her heart skittered in her chest.

She knew the man's voice, the honeyed burr with which he spoke her name.

Connor.

Relief crashed through her, washing away all the fear and stress and leaving behind a bone-deep exhaustion. As if all the tension from the last day and night had finally ceased and her body no longer had the strength to even stand.

Her legs didn't even have the chance to go soft before Connor's arms were around her. Strong and warm and smelling so wonderfully of him. Tears prickled in her eyes.

He pushed the hood from his head and his mouth came down on hers, deliciously sweet and familiar. Her body flared to life with the heat of desire, with the joy of being reunited.

He pulled back and cupped her face in his hands. "Why did ye tell the king ye were a witch? They meant to kill ye."

She stared deep into the hazel eyes she'd thought never to see again. "Because I love you."

"Then ye know the pain ye caused me by taking my place. It was too risky." His arms were around her once more. He stroked her face and she found herself wanting to close her eyes and surrender to his embrace. "We hoped ye'd free yerself and wait for me. It's why we sent the note. We dinna want ye escaping on yer own."

He went quiet then and stared at her for a long moment.

"I love ye, Ariana." His hand smoothed over her hair, as if he couldn't still his hands from touching her. "More than the sky above or the ground below or even the stone upon it which I gladly relinquish to save ye."

She pulled back this time and looked up at him. "What are you talking about?"

"I'll explain later." He pulled a tube of clear liquid from his jacket pocket as well as a candle in a small sconce and some flint. All of which he set gently on the ground. "For now, we must go."

He struck the flint, lighting the candle. The warm golden glow fell upon Murdoch's slumped body.

Connor glanced toward the dead man, then his attention snapped back to Ariana, his gaze immediately falling on her ripped bodice. "Did he hurt ye?"

She shook her head, and the lump where she'd smacked herself on the prison grating throbbed. "No, but he was trying to hurt Fianna."

"I'd have liked to have killed him myself." Connor took one last look at Murdoch and set the candle on the ground. "Then ye got Percy's note."

"Yes, but I—"

Connor grasped the sleeves of her dress and pushed them up to her elbows.

"What are you doing?" she asked.

"I'm going to set ye on fire, but dinna want yer clothes to catch." He spoke the odd statement as simply as he might have explained they'd be having haddock for supper rather than lamb.

"Dinna worry, Percy made this. Hold out yer hands," he instructed. "And dinna let this get on yer shoes or dress, aye?"

She bent forward at the waist to protect her shoes and the hem of her skirt and thrust her naked hands forward. "You should know about Murdoch," she said. "Connor, he's been trying to ruin you since the beginning."

A clear liquid poured from the large vial and splashed against her fingers. It was greasy between her fingertips, but she did not complain. Not when she knew how many things were so much worse.

Connor nodded. "Aye, I figured as much. He was the constable's son. A trusted man of our clan. He and his da both were."

"He killed his own father, Connor." She said it softly, hating to remind Connor of that awful day.

His jaw went hard. "Aye."

"But, Connor, that wasn't it. The king—"

"Enough." He nudged her forward. "The liquid will burn yer skin if we let it set too long. I'll set yer hands on fire, they'll stay lit for but a moment. The girls are ready to make ye a true witch in the eyes of the Crown."

He lifted the candle to her hands and pulled a glass globe from his pocket. "Go and dinna look back. I'll be at yer side after this." He pressed his lips in a hard kiss before resting his forehead against hers. "I love ye, Ariana."

"But Connor, the king—"

The single flame of the candle licked across the heel of her palm, and both hands erupted into flame.

"Now!" He spun her around toward the open door.

She strode outside, where the dawn made the sky softer than the stubborn night. Her hands glowed orange in the half light and several men stopped to stare in her direction.

She could sense the blistering heat from the fire dancing over her skin, but whatever oil Percy had fashioned left her flesh untouched.

"How dare you put me in a prison?" she shouted into the thin morning air. "Do you have any idea what I can do?"

Hesitation stalled her into place for a moment, accentuated by the fear of having said the wrong thing or acted the wrong way.

She stretched her arms over her head, where the flames sputtered around her fingers and went out.

An explosion sounded behind her and smoke billowed out on either side of her. It filled her vision with a gray white fog and bloomed around the courtyard.

A strong hand grabbed her arm. "This way," Connor said. "Percy and the others will ensure there is smoke everywhere."

Several more blasts sounded in the distance. Ariana fought her instinct to duck and remained confidently upright, as if she'd truly been the one to set the world aflame.

"We need to find the king," Connor said in her ear. "We need him to fear you so greatly, he'll never seek you out again after this."

She nodded, but wasn't certain if he saw or sensed the action. She continued to press forward, through the ubiquitous cloud.

Several men sputtered and called out to one another in the milky blindness. Yet no one stopped them or even approached them as Connor led her into the castle.

The air cleared immediately, and her eyes widened in relief to finally see the distinct outline of everything familiar once more.

Connor's hand was warm on her arm, his grip firm.

There, on the other side of the great hall, was exactly the man she knew she was supposed to trick. King James.

He stood about forty feet away with an arrogant tilt to his head, his shoulders artfully squared. Delilah stood at his side with a hand in the crook of his arm.

The king stopped when his gaze landed on Ariana. His face colored. "It's you."

Ariana strode forward with all the confidence she would need to pull off the ruse. "Don't you know witches are not easily killed?"

His face went pale, and she let herself smile to see it.

"I know a lot about you, James." His Christian name sounded odd on her tongue, as it had before, and speaking to him with such disrespect felt wrong in the giddiest of ways.

"More than just how you have your top nobles killed one at a time." She sauntered forward again, and a chair shoved back from its place when she passed.

The king stared at the chair then turned to Delilah, who slipped her hand from his arm and turned to go.

"Don't leave me." All his pretenses had fled and he sounded like a child having a tantrum. "You know how to fight. Protect me."

Delilah looked over her shoulder at him. "Perhaps I don't remember you well enough to help." Her voice was cool and held an unnatural edge to it, suggesting there was more to her discussion with the king than there appeared.

Delilah left the room without once turning around.

King James let his gaze move back to Ariana. "Please, I'm a monarch. I have all of England and Scot—"

"Enough!" Ariana shouted the word and threw her arms out in front of her.

Every piece of furniture in the room—the chairs and small card tables, even the clock—all jerked back against the far walls in a unified shriek of wood on stone.

King James's eyes went large in his white face.

"I know it's because of you that Connor is an assassin." She tilted her head. "Care to find out what else I know? It's something I'm sure Connor would love to hear."

The king shook his head with such vigor that the black felt hat he wore shifted from its position and lay slightly cocked atop his brow.

No false magic was needed for the impact of a truthful declaration, for no amount of explosions or moving furniture could have had the force of what she was about to say.

Ariana strode forward again. "The reason Connor's father is dead, the reason so many of his people died, the reason you have possession of Urquhart and Connor at all, is because it was your order which let Urquhart fall. It was you who gave permission for Laird Gordon to attack."

* * *

All this time, the hell of Connor's world had been caused by the king.

Everything seemed to shrink around him until the only thing

left in his vision was King James and the fearful look he cast down the hall.

"Is this true?" Connor asked.

But he didn't need to. Ariana would never say it if it weren't, and certainly the king would not be looking at him with such pathetic fear.

"It was ye. All this time. It was ye and ye dinna tell me." Connor stepped forward and the king stepped backward.

The last three years came crashing down around Connor and dragged him under the current of his emotions. The hurt, the anger, the fear, the loss. So much loss.

Connor balled his hands into fists, but could still feel the tremor in them. "Ye took everything from me."

He took another step forward. "My da." Another step. "Cora's youth."

And another step.

"The lives of good people."

He stopped.

"My freedom."

The king looked to both sides and saw there was no way out. He was cornered.

Rather than cower, he straightened his back with his chest puffed out in what was most likely his idea of a regal look. An impossible achievement, given the way his hat had settled crookedly on his head.

"It was necessary," King James said. "Yer father had a great amount of wealth, but while he was a respectful servant, he did not offer to fund the Crown. Laird Gordon proposed the attack and said he'd generously support the building of several new ships. I couldn't refuse."

Connor stalked closer now, past Ariana. "And why dinna ye tell me?"

The king sniffed. "Don't be a fool. Why would I possibly allow myself to lose someone so valuable as you?"

Connor had been nothing more than the king's tool. He'd

known this those last few years, but he hadn't known of the king's role in his father's death. Now the knowledge, both old and new, crashed together in a whirl of madness in his soul.

Without thinking, he swept his blade from the scabbard.

"I wouldn't do that if I were you." An arrogant smile jerked the corners of King James's mouth upward. He nodded toward the back of the room.

Connor glanced behind him and found the room filling with the king's soldiers.

"Get back," Ariana cried out in a confident voice. She lifted her arms over her head, but nothing happened.

There was a moment's pause, in which Ariana remained as she was, obviously waiting for her "power" to lash out.

"You don't want my wrath." She didn't look at him when she gave the warning. He knew she wouldn't. It would betray them all.

Out of the corner of Connor's eye he saw a splash of red and yellow along an alcove at the side. A soldier had his arm locked around Isabel with a blade pressed to her throat. Then, like a nightmare, Sylvi materialized from the shadows.

Without hesitation, she pulled a pistol from her waist, took aim, and fired at the soldier holding Isabel.

A cloud of smoke exploded in the small area between the three of them and Connor's heart stopped for a brief moment.

Pistols were notoriously inaccurate. It was why he never bothered with them. He didn't know where the hell she'd gotten it or even had learned to shoot it, but he hoped to God she'd hit the soldier.

And not Isabel.

Shouts rang out at the front of the great hall and tugged Connor's attention from the scene with Sylvi to the great group of soldiers rushing toward him and Ariana.

Their eyes were wide with fear and they ran with the force of a startled herd.

Connor raced in front of Ariana to take the brunt of their attack. All she had was the meager dagger. He pulled the dirk from his boot and gave it to her. At least two small blades were better than one. And Ariana had always been good with the small weapons.

Red swelled around them in a rising tide of soldiers, interrupted only by the slender blades of their swords. Several lunged at him, but he was able to easily deflect their blows. Metal rang against metal behind him and he knew Ariana was doing the same.

His body operated in smooth, calculated motions, falling back on the lessons he'd honed since his youth, when he fought with his father.

Energy fired through him.

His da.

The Shadow of the Highlands.

This fight was for him, to avenge his wrongful death.

Connor knocked a soldier aside and thrust his blade into another behind him. He pulled it free only to face yet another.

Suddenly Liv was beside him, and Sylvi, and even Percy. The women had fought their way to the center of the men and now Connor stood back to back with the women of Kindrochit.

Sunlight streamed in through the windows and bathed the room in a golden glow, and the blood glinted around them like rubies.

Duck.

Lunge.

Attack.

Everything reactive and automatic.

But for every soldier in a red coat and yellow feathers who fell, there was another to take his place.

There were so many of them.

So damn many.

Something on the hill outside the window pulled Connor's attention momentarily from battle. Horses. Scores of horses riding over the hill like they were being chased by the very devil himself.

Connor's heart tumbled into his stomach.

No matter how valiantly he and his girls fought, they could not survive another round of soldiers.

If they even survived the first.

Connor turned his gaze from the window and resolved not to look back again. The idea of more soldiers was too crushing.

He shoved the thought from his head and lost himself to the steady rhythm of battle instead.

Duck.

Lunge.

Attack.

The doorway became crowded with men and a riotous shouting roared above the sound of battle.

English soldiers did not roar.

Connor allowed himself to look up at the curtain of men sweeping through the room and almost cried out in relief.

Not a single man wore red.

No, they all wore either kilts or trews.

Scotsmen.

They descended upon the soldiers with a ferocity the men could not fend off, and the battle, which surely would have dragged on painfully long, was over in minutes.

When all the men had gone still, Connor let his arm fall in limp exhaustion, as did the women around him. He turned to them and found each one still standing—with a few scratches and cuts, but standing nonetheless.

"I'm so verra proud of the lot of ye." He grinned at them and stared at each one in turn before finally letting his gaze fall on Ariana.

There was a cut on her cheek, where a couple drops of blood had chased one another down to her jaw, and a red circle of blood showed on the upper arm of her sleeve. But she was alive.

And she was safe.

"Connor." A male voice boomed through the great hall before Connor could speak to Ariana, before he could even pull her into his arms.

He surveyed the crush of those standing and those fallen until he saw who had spoken. A tall man with dark hair and a far too familiar face.

Kenneth Gordon.

It was Kenneth who had come to his rescue.

"I believe ye might want to see this," Kenneth said, nodding to where Connor had built a false wall in the large, open room.

Connor approached, and found Delilah with King James's neck locked in the crook of her elbow. A blade glinted at his neck.

"Now's yer chance," Kenneth said, nodding toward the king. "For freedom."

Chapter Forty

"I dinna want to kill him." Connor didn't take his eyes off where Delilah held the king trapped with her elbow and her blade. "But I do want my freedom."

"Granted," the king said readily. His hat had disappeared and a tuft of his auburn hair jutted up on the side. "I'll give you Urquhart back and release you of your debt to me."

"My debt to ye?" Connor spit. "The debt ye led me to believe I owed." He pulled in a long, slow breath for patience. "I can still kill ye."

"It'd cause a war," King James said with a snide grin.

"Aye," Connor conceded. "One many Highlanders would want and one ye wouldna care about because ye'd be dead."

The king shrank back against Delilah, who removed her blade and pushed him away from her. But it wasn't Connor's words which frightened the king. It was Ariana.

She had appeared beside Connor, as if she could not stay away. And truly he was grateful, for he wanted her by his side, not just in this moment of victory, but for the rest of his life.

"If you ever try to hurt Connor," Ariana said in a threatening tone, "I'll find you, and I will kill you."

"And if ye ever try to accuse her of witchcraft, I'll kill ye myself." Connor stared hard at the king. "It doesna matter what shadow ye hide under, how many guards ye have protecting ye or how safe ye think ye are. I'll always find ye."

The king's face paled and the line of his mouth almost disappeared from view.

"And if ye try to harm either one of them," Kenneth said, "ye'll have a war on yer hands between the Highlands and England. And I dinna think yer men would stand a chance against Highlanders." He glanced over his shoulder toward the fallen English soldiers. "The Grants have the protection of the Gordons and all our allies as well."

Connor turned to Kenneth and gave him a grateful nod. "Thank ye."

Kenneth lifted his shoulders in a shrug. "Our clans are united now." He raised his brows at Connor. "Through marriage."

Cora.

A brotherly kick of protection slammed into Connor.

Kenneth must have expected Connor's reaction, because he put up his hand and spoke in a calm voice. "She came to me." He turned toward the entrance of the great hall and nodded. Cora strode out from around the corner. She wore a fine arisaid with a kerchief atop her brown hair.

His sister, a wife.

Connor drew in a breath at the sight. He beckoned her closer and she obeyed, marching forward with her back straight and proud.

Smudges of exhaustion showed dark under her eyes, and the closer she got, the more uncertain her steps grew, until she was directly in front of him.

"Are ye verra upset with me, brother?" she asked solemnly.

There was much Connor wanted to say—how dangerous her decision had been, how she shouldn't marry a man she didn't know, how people change over time.

But then Kenneth slipped his hand into Cora's where it hung at her side. Their fingers entwined. She glanced back at him and he smiled in a way Connor had only seen when they were lads.

Connor gazed down at Ariana and she tilted her head in understanding. He wanted to cradle her beautiful face in his hands and kiss her senseless.

He turned back to Cora. "Are ye verra happy with him, sister?"

Her eyes twinkled, and it carried away all signs of exhaustion from her face. "I wouldna have ridden like the devil to him otherwise. And I wouldna have ridden back just as hard to explain it to ye." She shook her head. "I know how ye are. Ye'd assume he kidnapped me and work out some way to rescue me when I dinna need rescuing."

Arguing was useless and so Connor merely chuckled. "Then I'm happy for ye, Cora." He glanced behind his sister, at Kenneth. "And ye too. But I'll warn ye, ye've got yer work cut out for ye with this one."

Connor regarded the king where he'd stood watching the exchange with a look of frightened self-interest. "Take yer men, go back to England, and leave me be, or ye know what will happen."

The king nodded.

"Go on then." Connor jerked his head toward the door and the king all but slithered away, his battered men crawling behind him.

And, finally, Connor was free.

• • •

Ariana opened the door to the study to find Connor in his usual place before the large fire. The sun had long since set and the chaos of the day was finally going quiet.

"You asked to see me?" she said.

Connor turned and looked at her. It was the first time they'd been alone since the attack and the moment hung between them like the final note of a dance.

"Ariana." He closed the distance between them and caught her in his arms. His mouth was on hers in an instant, insistent and ravenous and filled with all the love she had longed for. "I thought I'd lost ye."

"You know I'm too stubborn to die that easily," she said between kisses.

He lifted her and spun her around with a warm laugh.

"Oh, Connor," she breathed. "You have everything you've ever wanted. I'm so happy for you."

He shook his head. "I dinna have everything I want."

"What do you not have?"

"My wife to give me a wee babe to whom I can pass on my da's legacy."

A sudden moment of fear gripped her heart. "Your wife?"

"Aye." Connor took her hand in his and gently caressed her knuckles with his thumb. "I dinna have one of those either. I'd like her to be ye."

Her relief came out of her in a laugh.

"Are you asking me to marry you, Connor Grant?" Her tone was light and teasing.

"Aye, I am." He stroked a hand down her uninjured cheek. "I canna imagine bringing joy back to Urquhart without the verra person who makes me the happiest."

Her heart welled with such love as she had never known to the point it felt near bursting. "I can't say yes if you don't ask me."

Connor sank reverently to his knees in front of her and clasped both her hands in his. "Ye always saw so much more of me than the man mired down by the weight of his own sins and ye brought happiness to a life I thought I could no' ever enjoy. I love ye, Ariana, and I'd be humbly honored if ye'd agree to become no' just my wife, but also the lady of Urquhart Castle."

"Then I'd be humbly honored to say yes." She pulled at his hands, urging him to his feet.

He pulled her to him and stared down at her. "I've been longing to hold ye in my arms all day."

A tingle pulsed between her thighs. She knew exactly what he meant. The heart-pounding battle, the fear of loss, the indescribable desire—it all shot into her blood.

Before she could reply in kind, his mouth came down on hers and he pulled her body against his. Together they had fought the battle. Together they had won. Together they would celebrate their love.

For they belonged together—mind, body, heart, and soul.

Epilogue

MAY 1606

The sun rose near Urquhart Castle, emerging from the water in a golden globe of light. Its warmth settled against the hills and bobbed atop the water like floating bits of cut gemstone.

Ariana rested a hand atop the large crenellation of the castle wall and closed her eyes to the subtle breeze stirring her hair and gown.

The weather had been soft lately, almost as if gently welcoming the changes to her life.

"There's my beautiful wife." Connor's voice broke through her thoughts. She opened her eyes and found him standing beside her, tall and breathtakingly handsome in his saffron-colored léine and the fine plaid belted around his waist.

A gold pin shone at his shoulder, where the length of plaid had been pinned into place.

He looked every bit the laird of the castle.

"I'm glad ye're awake, lass. I've got a surprise for ye." He put his arms around her waist and pressed a kiss to her lips. His mouth was cold from having just recently shaved.

"I've one for you too." She couldn't help the smile of sheer joy on her lips and gave in to the temptation to stroke her fingertips over his smooth jaw.

He caught her hand and pressed a sweet kiss to her palm. "Mine first. Come downstairs."

Their fingers twined together, pleasantly warm where their skin touched, and together they made their way down the stone staircase along the curtain wall.

A lot had changed at Urquhart since Connor had resumed his

role as laird. Not just the castle, but the land itself. All memories of what had gone wrong were swept away by what was right. The people had come back, slowly at first, and then so quickly they'd almost run out of bedding.

Only one year and already the scar on Urquhart had faded, as all great scars do, from flesh to heart—never forgotten, but not so painfully obvious either. They were all stronger for having suffered and survived.

The Grant clan lived their lives fully and with the appreciation of people who knew how easily it could all be lost.

Near the stable stood three travelers with cloaks thrown about their shoulders and a pile of sacks at their feet. One with white-blonde hair strewn back in braids, one with loose curls the color of summer wheat, and another with tresses of gleaming copper.

Ariana's breath caught in her throat. "Is it—?"

Connor grinned. "Here she is, girls."

The trio turned around and confirmed what Ariana thought she'd seen. Delilah, Sylvi, and Liv.

At Urquhart.

Ariana embraced each woman with great affection. Delilah in her pretty velvet riding habit, Sylvi in the men's clothing she often preferred when traveling, the collar raised high to cover her neck, and Liv.

Ariana's eyes tingled with tears when she saw Liv. She was beautifully vibrant with her red-gold hair and eyes the same gray of a gentle summer storm. Her cheeks were rosy with good health and a smile shone on her lips like the sun.

While Ariana had wanted to see Percy and Isabel as well, she knew they would most likely not leave Kindrochit.

A sleek gray cat snaked between Ariana's ankles. She looked down and gasped. "Surely this isn't Fianna."

"It is." Liv grinned and lifted the cat into her arms. Fianna contently allowed herself to be cradled like an infant, the hum of her purr evident even from where Ariana stood.

"We're heading back to Kindrochit," Sylvi said. "And happened to be in the area."

Her voice had taken on a level of authority and reminded Ariana very much of Connor.

Not long ago, he'd told her Sylvi had begun her own private spy ring for nobles who could afford their fee.

Where once they had all been trapped, they now knew freedom.

"Are your endeavors going as planned?" Ariana asked benignly. Truth be told, what Connor had told her left her terribly curious. She'd wanted to press them for information, but knew doing so would be dangerous in the open.

"Very well." Sylvi gave a cocky, lopsided grin. "Maybe while we're here, we can get in a sparring session? No one can beat me anymore."

"Aye, I think I may take ye up that." Connor put an arm around Ariana's shoulder and squeezed gently. "How about ye, Lady Grant?"

Ariana ducked her head to hide her smile. "I don't think that would be a good idea."

Connor studied her a moment, his brow furrowed. She let the silence hang for a delicate moment before adding, "It might hurt the baby."

His eyes went wide, and then a large grin spread over his lips. "Are ye—do ye mean—is that—"

"Yes," Ariana said with a laugh. Never had she seen her confident husband trip over his tongue before.

He stared in awe at her flat stomach.

Liv's arms wrapped around Ariana in a sweet embrace. "I know you'll care for that child for both of us," she whispered. A quiet note only for Ariana to hear, for only Ariana would understand.

Delilah gave an excited little clap and Sylvi gave a nod of approval.

Connor, however, was still staring at her.

"Are you happy, husband?" she asked.

"I'm going to be a da," he said in a soft, wondrous tone.

"Yes," Ariana said. "A wonderful one."

He placed a hand on her stomach and she could not help but note how his fingers trembled.

Theirs would be a child who would know love from the day of its birth and whose legacy would be forever protected by the power its parents built. And it would not be the only child in their beautiful happy world, not when there was so much more for Connor and Ariana to share with one another.

Not when there was a life of love to be lived.

Acknowledgements

Thank you first and foremost to all of my readers out there—it means so much to me that you've taken the time to read my books. Without you, none of this would be possible.

Thank you so much to my wonderful agent, Laura Bradford, for her constant guidance and support. And thank you to the wonderful staff at Diversion Books. Jaime Levine, it's been such an honor to work with you. Thank you also to Sarah Masterson Hally, Nita Basu, and Taylor Ness for all your hard work in making *Highland Spy* come into being.

Thank you to the fabulous women who are part of my Marvelous Ladies for your support and encouragement with this book and all my other ones as well. Thank you to my amazing beta readers who help keep me in line and challenge me to always write the best book I can put out there: Liette Bougie, Kacy Stanfield, Carin Farrenholtz, Karen Archer, and Ashley Collins.

Thank you to Janet Kazmirski, who is not only the best, most supportive mom ever, but also my eagle-eye spot checker for anything I miss.

And always, thank you to Mr. Awesome and my darling minions for their unending love and support and encouragement. They are always there to cheer me on.

MADELINE MARTIN is a *USA Today* bestselling author of Scottish-set historical romance novels. She lives in Jacksonville, Florida with her two daughters (AKA OldestMinion and YoungestMinion) along with a man so wonderful, he can only be called Mr. Awesome. All shenanigans are detailed regularly on Twitter and on Facebook.

Her hobbies include rock climbing, running, doing crazy races (like Mud Runs and Color Runs), and just about anything exciting she can do without getting nauseous. She's also a history fan after having lived in Europe for over a decade, and enjoys traveling overseas whenever she can.

Madeline loves to hear from her readers. You may find various ways to connect with her and find more information on her at: **www.MadelineMartin.com**

WANT TO SEE ANOTHER MERCENARY MAIDEN
FIND LOVE IN THE HIGHLANDS OF SCOTLAND?

DON'T MISS

HIGHLAND
Ruse

THE NEXT INSTALLMENT BY *USA TODAY*
BESTSELLING AUTHOR MADELINE MARTIN.

MORE SIZZLING HIGHLAND ROMANCE BY
MADELINE MARTIN

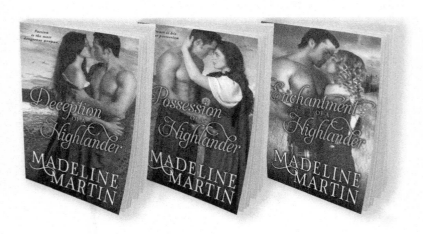

CPSIA information can be obtained
at www.ICGtesting.com
Printed in the USA
BVOW04s2328051216
469891BV00001B/1/P

9 781682 302958